GEORGE SAND was born as Amantine-Aurore-Lucile Dupin on 1 July 1804. From her father's death in 1808, she was raised at Nohant in Berry, France, which was her grandmother's home and where she herself would spend the greater part of her life, although she travelled widely and frequently stayed in Paris. A prolific writer of plays, short stories, novels, and journal articles, she published her first novel, *Indiana*, in 1832. Closely allied with major socialist thinkers in the years leading up to the revolution of 1848, she was distressed by the violence and brutality of the uprisings and sought in subsequent novels to reconcile socialist theory with the harsh teachings of experience. Her interest in music, which is a dominant feature of *The Master Pipers*, is also reflected in her earlier novel, *Consuelo*, published in 1842, while her love of the countryside in the Berry and Bourbonnais regions of France, together with her desire to give permanence to local customs and beliefs, can be seen in her pastoral novels *Little Fadette*, *The Devil's Pool*, and *François the Foundling*. She continued writing until her death in 1876.

ROSEMARY LLOYD's books include *The Land of Lost Content: Children and Childhood in Nineteenth-Century France* (1992). She has translated Baudelaire's *Short Prose Poems* (1991).

THE WORLD'S CLASSICS

GEORGE SAND

The Master Pipers

*Translated with an Introduction
and Notes by*

ROSEMARY LLOYD

Oxford New York

OXFORD UNIVERSITY PRESS

Oxford University Press, Great Clarendon Street, Oxford OX2 6DP

Oxford New York
Athens Auckland Bangkok Bogota Bombay
Buenos Aires Calcutta Cape Town Dar es Salaam
Delhi Florence Hong Kong Istanbul Karachi
Kuala Lumpur Madras Madrid Melbourne
Mexico City Nairobi Paris Singapore
Taipei Tokyo Toronto Warsaw

and associated companies in
Berlin Ibadan

Oxford is a trade mark of Oxford University Press

British Library Cataloguing in Publication Data
Data available

Library of Congress Cataloging in Publication Data
Sand, George, 1804–1876.
[Maîtres sonneurs. English]
The master pipers/George Sand; translated, with an introduction
and notes by Rosemary Lloyd.
p. cm.—(The world's classics)
1. Man-woman relationships—France—Fiction. 2. France—Social
life and customs—19th century—Fiction. 3. Country life—France—
Fiction. I. Lloyd, Rosemary. II. Title. III. Series.
843'.7—dc20 PQ2407.M6E5 1994 93-31046
ISBN 0-19-283097-X

3 5 7 9 10 8 6 4 2

Printed in Great Britain by
Caledonian International Book Manufacturing Ltd
Glasgow

CONTENTS

CONTENTS

INTRODUCTION

A laconic mention, dated 31 December 1852, in the diary her friend Alexandre Manceau used for recording George Sand's myriad activities, indicates that she began work that day on a *paysannerie* (peasant study) provisionally entitled *La Mère et l'Enfant* (*Mother and Child*). On 3 February Manceau noted that the work would probably be called *Les Maîtres Sonneurs*, and on Saturday 26 February we find that 'Madame', despite a mild migraine, had completed the novel. Published in serial form in the Parisian daily, *Le Constitutionnel*, between June and July 1853, it appeared in volume form later that year. A tribute to her extraordinary energy and a monument to her unceasing desire to use literature to find solutions to pressing social and human problems, George Sand's *The Master Pipers* offers a triumphant and symphonic union of many of her central concerns.

In the bleak aftermath of the 1848 revolution, with many of her utopian-socialist hopes quashed, in all the bitterness of her deeply troubled relationship with her daughter Solange, and in the sorrow of losing her long-time lover Chopin, first through the break-up of their relationship and then through his death in 1849, she revealed her strength of character and appetite for work in her exploration, within this novel, of the themes of violence, equality, love, both erotic and maternal, and the nature of the gifted individual. Like many intellectuals of her day, she realized that the rapid changes in social and industrial conditions would bring with them an inevitable and possibly unrecoverable loss of traditional customs and speech patterns, and she seizes on the novel, as she used her journalistic writing, to capture in more permanent form the songs, the superstitions, and the sayings that permeated the imaginations and convictions of the French peasantry. And through it all shines her deep love of the countryside in which she grew up, the rolling pastures around Nohant, and the woods and mountains of the Bourbonnais district to the south and east.

Like many writers and thinkers in the 1830s and 1840s,

George Sand enthusiastically, but not uncritically, embraced at least some of the ideals of such socialist thinkers as Saint-Simon, in whom she applauded the rejection of personal property but whose cult of the individual she detested,[1] Louis Blanc, whose history of the revolution she ardently admired,[2] Lamennais, whom she evoked as a great thinker and whose portrait she lovingly inscribes in her *Histoire de ma vie* (*Story of My Life*),[3] and especially Pierre Leroux, with whom she founded two reviews, the Parisian based *Revue indépendante* and the provincial *L'Eclaireur de l'Indre*. In a letter to Marie-Sophie Leroyer de Chantepie, George Sand affirmed:

I believe in the life eternal, in humanity everlasting, in endless progress; and, as I have embraced the beliefs of Pierre Leroux in this regard, I refer you to his philosophical arguments. I do not know whether they will satisfy you, but I cannot give you any that are better. For my part, I found they completely resolved all my doubts and established the foundation of my religious faith.[4]

What she rejected in all these thinkers was their call for violent revolution. She herself yearned for peaceful and gradual change, and her fears of the destructive nature of their revolutionary violence not only proved well founded in the uprisings of 1848, but also informs much of *The Master Pipers*. The novel's exploration of a slow evolution towards tolerance and equality should not be seen as mere idealistic utopianism, but the result of an ardent desire to find an alternative to the catastrophic and ultimately self-defeating belligerence of most of the social theorists of her day. The marriage of the placid self-satisfaction of the Berry peasants and the free but rootless spirits of the Bourbonnais woodcutters paves the way for the combination of adventure and stability, energy and tranquillity, that represented for George Sand the ideal French type. The creation of these types through a fusion of realism and

[1] Letters of 12 Apr. 1835 and 20 Oct. 1835 (*Correspondance*, ii. 854 and iii. 10). George Sand's correspondence has been published by Classiques Garnier in some 20 volumes, between 1964 and 1991, edited by the doyen of Sand studies, Georges Lubin.

[2] See her letters of Oct. and Nov. 1847 (*Correspondance*, viii. 107, 122).

[3] *Histoire de ma vie*, ii (Paris: Pléiade, 1971), 349.

[4] Letter of 28 Aug. 1842 (*Correspondance*, v. 757).

idealism is typical of Sand's aesthetics. In her preface to *La Mare au diable* (*The Devil's Pool*) she characteristically draws antithetical inspiration from a Holbein engraving of death as a ploughman, which she links to the powerful satires of Dürer, Michelangelo, Callot, and Goya, concluding that such images of what Coleridge terms 'the nightmare life-in-death' merely created fear, and fear, she insists, 'does not cure selfishness, but increases it'. Her vision of the mission of art, on the contrary, is one of 'sentiment and love', with the novel replacing the parables as a means of teaching understanding and tolerance: art, she adds, is 'not a study of positive reality but a search for an ideal truth'.[5] In this, she is, of course, following in a long tradition of pastoral idylls, but infusing into that tradition both the energy of a strong socialist message, and an urgency stemming from the conviction that a way of life would soon cease to exist. The poet and critic Théodore de Banville, writing before the publication of *The Master Pipers* but drawing on his knowledge of her earlier pastoral novels, brilliantly recreates the atmosphere of these works, and suggests their artistic and literary parallels:

Who but George Sand could have found the secret of this elegant, harmonious and cunning style, with its simultaneously naive and mannered nature, the style she so intelligently gave to her imaginary peasants, thus making them more true than truth itself? She rediscovered in Virgil and Theocritus the great art of the idylls of antiquity and like them she shows us gentle Arcadia with all its greenery, and brings it alive with laughing groups, the harvester sleeping the sleep of the weary under the midday sun, the washerwoman up to her thighs in the river, and at evening, to the sound of delicate pipes, on grass strewn with flowers and where full goat-skin bottles lie carelessly scattered, the races, the wild games, the light dances! She brings back to life that happy world we have so deeply loved, and if at times, in imitation of Ronsard, she obeys a whim and calls her Galathea Margot and her Daphnis Toison, we have no cause for fear, that does not mean we are in Berry or Nivernais, but truly in the very heart of the valley of Tempe! [...] But, you ask me, does this mean that George Sand's countryside is not the real countryside, that her peasants are not real peasants? On the contrary, they are just as real as

[5] *La Mare au diable* (Paris: Garnier-Flammarion, 1964), 30.

those shepherds whom Watteau has allowed to wander in his vast landscapes with their abundant fountains, as true as those architraves in which Boucher or Lancret have allowed the luminous caprices of their fantasy to blossom. The countryside truly is the real country-side, since it's full of air and sun, and those characters are indeed alive, since they have the animation and the smile of life itself. And since when has a genius been asked to do anything other than confer human movement on the ideal figures he or she has seen in dreams?[6]

The soft washes of Boucher and Watteau, and the sentimen-tality of Lancret, certainly offer a visual parallel to George Sand's world in *The Master Pipers*, but the luminous quality Banville so characteristically evokes is shown to have a darker side, one without which the ideal would not have that sense of truth on which her theoretical writing invariably insists.

While her anthropological and proselytizing aspirations make of the main protagonists somewhat idealized figures, George Sand nevertheless creates minor characters who are far less admirable, showing the selfish, grasping, gossip-mon-gering side of the peasants, as well as their nobility and selflessness. In accordance with her aesthetic goals, she also blends idealism and realism by anchoring her utopian vision in the deep soil of tradition, customs, and everyday experi-ence. Woven into the story are allusions to superstitions such as the Great Beast, in fear of which Tiennet's father keeps above the mantelpiece a gun loaded with bullets blessed by the priest, the Rake Elm, allegedly haunted by a giant carrying a rake, and the cockatrice, said to announce the onset of plagues and wars. Oral tradition as a source of knowledge about the past plays an important role in associating Tiennet's disquiet in the cemetery, not merely with the village's own dead, but with the whole sweep of history dating back to the wars with the English. People George Sand encountered in the area around Nohant provided the basis for some of the characters: Joey the star-gazer draws some of his characteristics from a local child she was trying to educate, while the innkeeper from Saint Chartier steps directly into the text from an encounter George Sand relates in a letter written in April 1851:

[6] *Critiques* (Paris: Charpentier, 1917), 115. The review is dated 15 Jan. 1851.

M. Benoit, innkeeper and road-surveyor from Saint Chartier has just
left. 'I say, My Lady, I've come to ask you to put me in one of your
works.' 'But why, M. Benoit?' 'So that people will talk about me.
You've made people talk about Denis Ronciat. That imbecile is really
furious. Now I said to him: "You're a bloody ass. If it cost me no
more than 50 francs of my own money, I'd ask that woman to put
me in one of her works, just so people would talk about me in 3 or
4 thousand years from now, whereas otherwise I'll die like a dog
without anyone knowing that Jean Benoit ever existed."' Verbatim.[7]

Such minor figures are brought vividly to life by the narrator's
sharply observant eye, forging a world whose existence swiftly
becomes totally convincing: Thérence's little black mark at the
side of her mouth, Huriel's piratical ear-ring, plump little
Charley bounding out almost naked to embrace his 'dearie',
Brulette, and above all, perhaps, the wonderfully comically
depicted aunt:

She had the funniest face you could ever wish to see, very white and
very fresh, although she was fifty and had given birth to fourteen
children. I've never seen such a long nose, with such small eyes, set
deep on each side of her face as if with a drill, but so bright and so
cunning that you couldn't look at them without wanting to chatter
and laugh.

Equally economical and amusing is the description of the
aunt's physical reaction to a little wine: 'the tip of her nose
turned as red as a berry and her large mouth, where there were
enough white, close-packed teeth for three people rather than
one, was grinning all the way to her ears.'
 In addition to such figures, elements of the familiar countryside, villages, rivers, forests, and the ancient oak near which
Tiennet first encounters the mule-driver and his train, fuse to
create an intensely believable world, all the more so in that
journeys between the two regions, Berry and Bourbonnais,
cause in the various protagonists a sense of displacement, a
need to learn to appreciate the beauty of regions with which
they are not familiar, and to convince others of a beauty that
hitherto they had simply taken for granted. The idealization of

[7] *Correspondance*, x. 183. Denis Ronciat lived at Saint Chartier. His name
appears in an announcement of a sale in 1842.

the home territory, in other words, has to confront the doubts and criticisms of the strangers, and becomes as a result not merely deeper and more tolerant, but also more clearly understood and formulated. Huriel, revealing the beauty of his Bourbonnais countryside to a reluctant but not unresponsive Tiennet, draws on lyrical gifts more indicative of the musician than the muleteer in him, even though his metaphors all stem from a reality with which his hearers would have been perfectly familiar:

Aren't these rocks just perfect for acting as our chimney, our dressers, and our chairs? And isn't this your third meal today? Doesn't that silvery moon shed a better light than your old tin lamp? Has our food, which I carefully covered with my tarpaulins, suffered at all from the rain? Doesn't this great fire dry the air around us? Don't these damp branches and grasses smell better than your provisions of cheese and rancid butter? Don't you breathe better under the great vaults of those branches? Look at them, lit by our fire light! Wouldn't you say that there are hundreds of branches criss-crossing just to protect us? If, from time to time, a little breeze shakes the damp leaves over our heads, don't you see diamonds falling down to crown us?

The discovery of this beauty, and the acceptance of different ways of life, are an essential part of the maturation process for both Tiennet and Brulette, but such descriptions also reveal George Sand's own characteristic desire to teach her readers to appreciate landscapes with which they may not have been familiar but which were, for all that, still French.

The need to learn is not, moreover, restricted to the appreciation of landscape or custom. The whole work clearly functions, at one of its many levels, as a novel of education, a *Bildungsroman*. This, too, is characteristic of George Sand, who shows in all her writing a strong didactic purpose. In her *Nouvelles Lettres d'un voyageur* (*Further Letters from a Traveller*), she gives what is perhaps her most forthright statement on the pedagogical role of the writer:

I considered I was perfectly correct to persuade myself that one ought to instruct one's fellows, and that the duty of anyone who possessed a particular gift, large or small, was imperiously traced out: to communicate one's beliefs in spite of all insults, to reveal oneself, to give oneself, to immolate oneself, to expose oneself to all the abuse, all the calumnies, all the rebuffs that notoriety brings, provided one says, well or poorly, something deeply felt, something experienced or judged in the very depths of one's being. Had my nature and my education allowed me to acquire knowledge, I would have liked to explore the whole world as an erudite and as an artist, two intellectual functions for which I felt within myself, I will not say the potential, but at least an intense attraction and an ardent desire. Mine was a more humble destiny, and I studied, more or less at random and because no better subject presented itself, the feelings and struggles of the human being, and little by little I learnt to love this career performed by those who have no career, a career purely practical people despise deeply and cannot understand at all.[8]

The desire to learn is encapsulated in two of the novel's central figures: Brulette, whose sharpness and good memory are apparent as early as her days at catechism school, and who is determined to learn to read and write, rare skills in those days for a peasant woman; and Joseph, who also learns to write and who, despite his inability to retain anything at the catechism school, shows himself remarkably quick and perceptive in learning to play musical instruments. The love of teaching is also very much in evidence in the novel. Both Brulette, overcoming natural tendencies in herself, and Thérence, drawing on natural abilities, learn to take pleasure in teaching the little boy, Charley, while Bastien, the great woodcutter, delights in conveying to Joseph the practice and theory of bagpipe playing, and Tiennet, as narrator, frequently seizes on the slightest opportunity to educate his listener about forgotten traditions, unknown regions, words no longer in current usage, the history of the castle at Le Chassin, or the horseplay indulged in at weddings.

Learning, in a more general sense, is also central to the psychological development of the main characters. Brulette's frivolous and flirtatious nature has to be subdued, and her energies harnessed in other directions, if she is to become a fitting wife for Huriel; but it is typical of George Sand that she makes that maturation the result, not of ideas imposed from

[8] *Nouvelles Lettres d'un voyageur*, 28 Apr. 1868; quoted in Pierre Vermeylen, *Les Idées politiques et sociales de George Sand* (Brussels: Editions de l'université de Bruxelles, 1984), 98.

the outside, but of a determined and conscious stand by the individual herself. Brulette realizes that the kind of power she enjoys over the boys who court her depends merely on transient things—her beauty and her youth—and accepts what are clearly a series of trials in order to make herself worthy of the man she loves. Separation from him, and willingness to submit to his will in the knowledge that he also is willing at times to submit to hers, are only part of this series of trials: more important, perhaps, is the fact that she agrees to care for the unknown little boy, Charley, whom the monk brings to her. The habit of teaching adolescents how to bring up children by letting them practise on foundlings and bastards was well established in the French aristocracy, and is recorded in other classes as well—Mme de Genlis drew on the practice when she was preceptress to the royal children; when she was nine years old, the working-class Suzanne Voilquin's mother put her in charge of her baby sister; and the middle-class Athénaïs Michelet reports being reared by her little brother when she was a baby—but what is perhaps strikingly different in George Sand is her straightforward acceptance of the fact that not all women have natural maternal gifts. Her own fraught relationship with her daughter Solange must have made her aware that the saccharine image of mother–child relationships consecrated by male Romantics was not always applicable to real life.

If Brulette has to put aside a life of pleasure and sociability in order to achieve adulthood, Huriel, too, has to undergo a form of sentimental education. His trade as a roving mule-driver, and particularly the sense of freedom and camaraderie it gives him, are shown to be flawed in that the customs and practices of the brotherhood promote violence and lawlessness. Abandoning that career for the steadier yet still relatively mobile existence of a woodcutter is a decision he takes not merely to win Brulette, but in recognition that submission to the customs of the brotherhood has forced him into a situation in which he unwillingly murders a colleague. Huriel's acceptance of his own guilt in this affair is also what enables him to contemplate marriage with Brulette even if, as he initially fears, Charley is her own illegitimate child. Here, in the stress placed on the difference between taking life and giving life, even outside the law, George Sand is clearly drawing on personal experience, examining her own conscience as the mother of a daughter conceived in adultery.

Marriage, indeed, is presented in the novel as a form of reward for an emotional education successfully completed by both male and female characters. The acceptance of the partner as equal, the willingness to seek out a way of life that will bring most happiness to both members of the couple, the rejection of the injustices explicitly embodied in the Napoleonic code of laws, are all central tenets of George Sand's image of the ideal union of male and female. While many of her male contemporaries regarded her, since the publication of her novel *Indiana* in 1832, as a virulent and dangerous opponent of marriage, she herself constantly argued that her opposition was not to the institution as such but to the inequity of its conception in the code. Eighteen months before writing *The Master Pipers*, she asserted in a preface to her novel *Mauprat*:

what marriage lacks are elements of happiness and fairness, of an order too lofty for contemporary society to bother about them. Our society attempts, on the contrary, to diminish that sacred institution by making it no more than a contract based on material concerns. Society attacks marriage from all sides simultaneously, for such is the nature of its morals, such its prejudices, such its hypocritical incredulity.[9]

The Master Pipers presents itself, at one level, as a study in tenderness, rather than passion, in which love is anchored firmly in the acceptance of the independence and individuality of the beloved. Joseph's passion for Brulette, the violence of his sense of betrayal when he believes her to be the mother of Charley, and his refusal to accept that she may not return his love, are punished in the novel as images of an emotion which is profoundly destructive, just as Thérence's jealous and unrequited love of Joseph is depicted in a strongly negative light.

Nevertheless, Joseph's destiny draws not merely on the elements of the *Bildungsroman* and the love story that offer

---

[9] *Mauprat* (Paris: Folio, 1981), 33.

clearly delineated underlying codes in this novel, but also on the traditions of the *Kunstlerroman*, the story of the artist. In this, George Sand interweaves numerous, richly evocative threads: the conviction, best illustrated in the novels and short stories of the German Romantic writer, E. T. A. Hoffmann, that muse and mistress must remain forever separated, that marriage to the muse meant the destruction of the artist's gifts; the exploration of the envy aroused in the merely skilful by the exceptionally talented; the analysis of the gifted child, whose intelligence remains hidden until he discovers the instrument or the vehicle that will set it free. The novel is both analytical and symbolic in its portrayal of the extraordinary metamorphosis of Joey star-gazer into Joseph the brilliant bagpipe player, whose skilful blending of the minor and major modes offers a musical equivalent for the marriage of plain and mountain that alone will produce the ideal French type. Moreover, despite the speed with which she wrote, Sand attempts to use the novel not merely to teach about music and to capture the threatened art of the bagpipe player, but also to establish a complex network of connections linking landscape, music, memory, and language, in her descriptions of Joseph's playing. While the artistic transposition of painting into poetry, or novel into canvas, was widespread at the time, and while much music drew its inspiration from literature, relatively few novels attempted to find a stylistic equivalent for a form of music. Hoffmann's own novels, for all their nervy brilliance, are more concerned with analysis than transposition, and when Marie d'Agoult transposes her love affair with Liszt into a confessional novel, she makes the central male character a great painter rather than a great musician. Sand's ambitious representation of the bagpipe playing of Huriel, his father, and Joseph himself is, therefore, a rare achievement, even if it remains, undeniably and unsurprisingly, steeped in Romanticism. Two elements are emphasized above all else. First, music's power to abolish time, allowing Brulette direct access to her childhood memories, for instance, when she listens to Joseph playing the flute. Second, its ability to create harmony from the disparity of nature: the dreamy melancholy of the mountains, reflected in the minor mode,

blends with and enriches the tranquillity, joy, and self-satisfaction of the plain, represented by the major mode, while
Joseph's compositions recreate in the mind of the receptive
listener memories of water, bird song, wind, and stars.

In this vision of the temper and potency of music, George
Sand is drawing not only on her conversations with Chopin,
but also on the convictions of many of her contemporaries: Madame de Staël, in her highly influential work *De
l'Allemagne* (*On Germany*), insists that 'the delicious reverie
into which music plunges us annihilates all thoughts that
words might express';[10] the Saint Simonians considered it the
greatest of the arts; Lamennais and Delacroix valued it highly,
the latter capturing in two magnificent portraits the intensity
of Chopin and the energy of Paganini; Nerval, in *Les Filles du
feu*, and Mérimée in such stories as *Lokis*, both incorporated
folk-songs in their writings as a means not merely of conveying the richness of the natural heritage but also of expressing
the universality and timelessness of human emotions.

In the chilling, Gothic conclusion to Joseph's quest to become a master piper, Sand also draws on Romantic images of
the doomed artist, crushed by an uncomprehending and hostile audience. But in doing so, she also both intensifies the
allusions to Orpheus that her presentation of his music had
already lightly suggested, and expands the hints of a pact
made with the devil in exchange for outstanding musical gifts.
Here, too, while there is a sound realistic explanation for
Joseph's death, there remain overtones of the fantastic that
transform her general aesthetics of realism and idealism into a
far bleaker mode.

Despite the speed at which she wrote the novel, and despite,
too, an evident pleasure in spinning her tale of adventure,
George Sand has forged for it a supple but firm structure. Far
from being 'picaresque' as has been claimed, the plot is strikingly economical and harmoniously unified: no episode is
included merely for the sake of padding or for the pleasure of
including a particular aspect of peasant life. Every scene plays
an indispensable role in leading up to the dénouement, and

[10] *De l'Allemagne* (Paris: Charpentier, 1852), 406.

each is further exploited to build up a complex picture of the psychology of her characters. Even so apparently peripheral a scene as the woodcutter's explanation of the major and minor modes, or his performance of the song he has composed about the three lovers and their lass, offers a rich and subtle emblem of the tale itself, with the fluctuating importance of the Berry characters and the Bourbonnais characters corresponding to a piece of music moving between the major and the minor mode, and the woodcutter's verses serving to comment on the different natures of Huriel, Joseph, and Tiennet.

Just as music provides a stylistic and structural framework for the novel, so also, if at a more superficial level, does the traditional dance, the *bourrée*. Based on the stylistic representation of a young woman at first repulsing and then pursuing a young man, the *bourrée* symbolizes the two central love affairs in the novel, and in the way in which it transforms apparently lethargic and heavy peasants into light-footed creatures of youth and beauty, it also stands for the transforming power of folk art in the life of rural France. Its narrative and symbolic importance to the novel is, however, never overstated, but treated with considerable subtlety and lightness of touch.

The desire to preserve threatened art forms and customs within the novel finds a further parallel in George Sand's determination to allow the central character to tell his own story, despite the linguistic and stylistic obstacles this inevitably raises. In George Sand's prefatory letter she touches on these problems, but insists that Tiennet's story would lose much of its power and beauty were it to be transcribed into a purely literary mode. While there are few deliberate archaisms, she does use local terms such as *ébervigé* (stargazer), *bouaron* (cowherd), *blaudes* (smocks) and *imbriaque* (mad), and certain dialectal turns of phrase that give a freshness and charm to her style. In general, Tiennet's voice draws on local customs, superstitions, syntax, rhythms, and terms, but his language is forged into a writerly style that successfully negotiates the twin pitfalls of, on the one hand, appearing to condescend by simplifying the peasant's expression of experience, and, on the other hand, of imposing on him a mastery of style and perception that belong purely to the studied and literary.

Above all, perhaps, this is a novel of discovery—discovery of music, of love, of the self, of language, and of nature. The vibrant descriptions of the areas through which the characters travel, their own defence of the landscapes and life styles they most love, their growing awareness of the richness other traditions and other places can offer them, make of it an archetypal novel of quest and fulfilment, enriched by its multiple and apparently effortless interweaving of tradition, superstition, and custom. The exploration of childhood and old age, of sexual love, maternal love, and sibling affection, as well as the analysis of friendship, adds a particular warmth to the tale of adventure. The extraordinary resonance provided by the musical theme is given further intensity and urgency by the utopian solution, in which major and minor, the wild energy the Berry lacks, the reliability and good sense the mule-drivers need, and the stability wanting in the Bourbonnais woodcutters, all fuse through the marriages of Brulette and Huriel, Tiennet and Thérence. It is, perhaps, one of the most purely enjoyable and certainly one of the richest novels George Sand ever wrote.

A NOTE ON THE TEXT
AND TRANSLATION

For this translation I have consulted the following editions of *Les Maîtres Sonneurs*, all published in Paris: Alexandre Cadot, 1853 (4 volumes); Calmann-Lévy, 1899; Garnier Frères, 1958; Gallimard, 1979; Garnier, 1980. In preparing the edition, I have drawn extensively on the notes and chronologies in Georges Lubin's masterly edition of George Sand's correspondence, on Marie-Claire Bancquart's fine introduction and notes to her edition (Gallimard, Folio, 1979), and on Pierre Vermeylen's *Les Idées politiques et sociales de George Sand* (1984). My translation attempts to give the flavour of the original but without offering equivalents of the dialectal terms, since any such venture risks, at best, being misleading, and at worst making the characters appear ridiculous. My thanks are due to the many students at the University of Cambridge with whom I read and discussed this novel, and to Patrick Meadows and Jeff Holt at Indiana University, who tried out various terms on French relatives to see if they were still in current usage. I owe a particular debt of gratitude to the staff of the Indiana University Main Library and, in particular, to its delivery service, as well as to the friends and colleagues in Bloomington who have been unstinting in their friendship and support.

SELECT BIBLIOGRAPHY

There is an edited English translation of George Sand's autobiography: *My Life*, trans. D. Hofstadter (London: Gollancz, 1979). The complete text is also available in a group translation ed. Thelma Jurgrau, *Story of My Life* (Albany: State University Press of New York, 1991). A translation of selected writings is available under the title *In Her Own Words*, trans. J. A. Barry (Garden City, NY: Anchor Books, 1979).

There are numerous biographies of George Sand. The following is a brief list of the best of these:

Barry, J. A., *Infamous Woman: The Life of George Sand* (Garden City, NY: Doubleday, 1977)

Cate, Curtis, *George Sand: A Biography* (Boston: Houghton Mifflin, 1975)

Dickenson, Donna, *George Sand: A Brave Man, The Most Womanly Woman* (Oxford: Berg, 1988)

Maurois, André, *Lélia: The Life of George Sand*, trans. G. Hopkins (London: Jonathan Cape, 1953)

Toesca, Maurice, *The Other George Sand*, trans. Irene Beeson (London: Dennis Dobson, 1947)

Two biographies of Chopin might prove useful for a further understanding of *The Master Pipers*:

Atwood, W. G., *Fryderyck Chopin: Pianist from Warsaw* (New York: Columbia University Press, 1987)

Zamoyski, Adam, *Chopin: A New Biography* (Garden City, NY: Doubleday, 1980)

This is a very brief sample of the secondary works available in English:

Crecelius, Katherine, *Family Romances* (Bloomington, IN: Indiana University Press, 1987)

Evans, David Owen, *Social Romanticism in France* (Oxford: Oxford University Press, 1951)

James, Henry, *French Poets and Novelists* (London, 1878)

Naginski, Isabelle, *George Sand: Writing for Her Life* (New Brunswick: Rutgers University Press, 1991)

Select Bibliography

Powell, David, *George Sand* (Boston: Twaynes World Authors Series, 1990)

Thomson, Patricia, *George Sand and the Victorians* (London: Macmillan, 1977)

A CHRONOLOGY OF
GEORGE SAND

1773   Birth of GS's mother, Antoinette-Sophie-Victoire Delaborde.

1778   Birth of GS's father, Maurice Dupin de Francueil.

1799   20 May, birth of Honoré Balzac (later, Honoré de Balzac).

1802   26 February, birth of Victor Hugo. Birth of Alexandre Dumas *père*.

1803   28 September, birth of Prosper Mérimée.

1804   5 June, marriage of Maurice Dupin and Antoinette-Sophie-Victoire Delaborde. 1 July, birth of Amantine-Aurore-Lucile Dupin (GS). December, Napoleon proclaims himself Emperor.

1808   17 September, GS's father thrown from horse and dies instantly. Henceforth GS will be raised at Nohant, the home of her paternal grandmother who becomes her legal guardian in 1809.

1810   1 March, birth of Frédéric Chopin near Warsaw. 11 December, birth of Alfred de Musset.

1811   19 February, birth of Jules Sandeau. Birth of Théophile Gautier.

1815   18 June, Battle of Waterloo. Defeat of Napoleon. Restoration of Bourbon Monarchy.

1817   3 May, birth of Alexandre Manceau.

1818   GS sent to a convent in Paris to complete her education. Although she sees this as an abrupt dismissal from childhood, she also realizes its importance in forming her mind.

1820   Return to Nohant, where GS takes over most of the responsibility for running the estate. Birth of Fromentin.

1821   9 April, birth of Charles Baudelaire. 12 December, birth of Gustave Flaubert. 26 December, GS's grandmother dies.

1822   17 September, GS marries Casimir Dudevant. The marriage is to prove deeply unhappy, due to the violence and infidelity of Dudevant.

1823   30 June, birth of Maurice Dudevant.

1824   Death of Louis XVIII and accession of his brother Charles X.

1828   13 September, birth of GS's daughter Solange, probably fathered by one of GS's lovers.

1830   July, revolution in Paris; abdication of Charles X. 7 August, Louis-Philippe, the Duc d'Orléans, proclaimed King. November, GS discovers her husband's 'will' which she considers an insult. Quarrel leads to the establishment of a *modus vivendi* in which Dudevant will give GS an allowance and permit her to spend half of every year in Paris.

1831   4 January, GS leaves Nohant for Paris with her lover Jules Sandeau. Meets several writers including Balzac. Begins writing for daily paper, *Figaro*. 24 December, publishes *Rose et Blanche* jointly with Sandeau.

1832   19 May, *Indiana*, under her own signature, is published to considerable popular acclaim. Signs contract with François Buloz to contribute regularly to prestigious periodical *La Revue des deux mondes* (RDM). *Valentine* published in November.

1833   Liaison with Sandeau ends. Abortive affair with Mérimée. 31 July, publication of *Lélia*, which preaches revolt against the hypocrisy and tyranny of marriage. During the summer GS begins love affair with the poet Alfred de Musset. In December leaves for Venice with Musset.

1834   GS and Musset fall ill in Venice. GS has affair with Pagello, the doctor who had provided medical attention. Return to France. End of liaison with Musset. Publication of *Jacques*. Between 1834 and 1836 she publishes her *Lettres d'un voyageur* in *RDM*. Meets Liszt. In November sits for painter Eugène Delacroix who will be a frequent visitor to Nohant.

1835   Publishes *André* and *Leone Leoni*. Liaison with lawyer Michel de Bourges, an ardent republican. While at Nohant suffers violent attacks by Dudevant.

1836   February, Musset publishes his semi-autobiographical

Confession d'un enfant du siècle. Legal separation from Dudevant. She is granted sole custody of Solange, shared custody of Maurice, and is acknowledged as the owner of Nohant. Friendships with many leading writers, artists and thinkers, including Pierre Leroux, who inspires her with his brand of socialism. Publishes short novel *Simon*. November, first meeting with Chopin.

1837   *Mauprat* and *Les Maîtres-Mosaïstes* are published. Liszt and Marie d'Agoult visit Nohant. 19 August, death of GS's mother.

1838   Liaison with Chopin. Publication of *Spiridion*. Balzac visits GS at Nohant. Trip to Majorca.

1839   Publishes *Les Sept Cordes de la lyre*.

1840   Chopin and GS's close friend, the great singer Pauline Viardot, begin collecting songs and music of Berry. In the years leading up to the revolution of 1848, GS reveals her optimism and trust in the possibility of social change. Publication of *Cosima*, *Gabriel*, and *Le Compagnon du tour de France*.

1841   GS provides financial support for Pierre Leroux's socialist review, *La Revue indépendante*, to which she also contributes many articles. Ends contract with Buloz. Publishes *Horace* in which she reveals her faith in the mission of the people.

1842   *Un Hiver à Majorque*. Publication of her long novel *Consuelo*, which sets a story of adventure against the background of eighteenth-century musical life.

1843   Begins publishing sequel to *Consuelo*, *La Comtesse de Rudolstadt*.

1844   Launches a republican paper with the help of friends from the Berry region, *L'Eclaireur de l'Indre et du Cher*. Publishes short novel *Jeanne*.

1845   Publication of *Le Meunier d'Angibault*, which further explores republican ideals and is set, like *The Master Pipers*, in the area around Nohant. Publishes *Le Péché de M. Antoine* and writes *La Mare au diable* in four days.

1846   *La Mare au diable*, pastoral novel exploring peasant society and superstitions of the Berry region. July, English writer Matthew Arnold visits Nohant.

1847   February, GS and Solange visit the studio of the sculptor
            Auguste Clésinger, who makes busts of each of them.
            Marriage of Solange and Auguste Clésinger, against the
            wishes of GS. Chopin sides with Solange and his liaison
            with GS comes to an end. Begins writing autobiographi-
            cal *Histoire de ma vie*. Begins publication of *François le
            champi*.

1848   23–24 February, barricades and fighting in the street lead
            to abdication of Louis-Philippe. 29 April, Constituent
            Assembly elected by universal male suffrage. 23–25 June,
            serious uprisings in Paris. 4 July, death of Chateaubriand,
            whose *Génie du christianisme* had so affected GS in her
            adolescence. 10 December, Louis-Philippe elected Presi-
            dent of the Republic. 23 December, death of GS's half
            brother. Despite involvement in the revolution, and sub-
            sequent threats against her at Nohant, writes *La Petite
            Fadette*, a study of adolescence and twinship.

1849   Publication of *La Petite Fadette*. 10 May, birth of
            Solange's daughter Jeanne. October, death of Chopin.

1850   18 February, important article by Sainte-Beuve on GS's
            pastoral novels. April, beginning of GS's longest-lasting
            liaison, with Alexandre Manceau. 19 June, *La Presse*
            publishes chapter of Chateaubriand's *Mémoires d'outre-
            tombe* devoted to GS. 20 August, death of Balzac. Univer-
            sal male suffrage abolished.

1851   Writes the plays *Claudie* and *Le Mariage de Victorine*.
            Publishes various articles about customs and superstitions
            of Berry. Beginning of marionette theatre productions at
            Nohant. 2 December, Louis Napoleon's *coup d'état*.

1852   21 November, plebiscite ratifies Napoleon III as emperor.

1853   Publication of *Les Maîtres Sonneurs*.

1854   27 February, death of Lamennais. June, publication of
            Jacques. *Histoire de ma vie* begins to appear in the pres-
            tigious daily paper *La Presse*.

1854–6   Crimean War. England and France allied against Russia.

1855   14 January, death of Solange's daughter Jeanne triggers
            correspondence with Victor Hugo whose daughter
            Léopoldine had died in 1843. GS's play, *Maître Favilla*,
            has a successful run at L'Odéon in Paris.

1856   Three of GS's plays performed in Paris, but without much success. Publication of Hugo's *Les Contemplations*.

1857   2 May, death of Musset. Publication in serial form in *La Presse* of *La Daniella*, a pro-republican novel. Difficulties with censor. Publications in volume form of Flaubert's *Madame Bovary* and Baudelaire's *Les Fleurs du mal*. Manceau buys a house at Gargilesse where GS is often to stay. Publication in *La Presse* of *Les Beaux Messieurs du Bois doré*.

1858   GS reconciled with Buloz, the editor of the influential periodical *La Revue des deux mondes* which prints her *L'Homme de neige* from June to September.

1859   Publication in *RDM* of *Elle et Lui*, written at Gargilesse. This publication, which was thought to evoke the affair between GS and Musset, sparks off responses by Musset's brother Paul (*Lui et Elle*) and by the poet Louise Colet (*Lui*). GS in contact with the critic Sainte-Beuve and the artist and writer Fromentin. Publication of *Les Légendes rustiques*.

1860   July–September, publication in *RDM* of *Le Marquis de Villemer*, *Jean de la roche*, and *Constance Verrier*. October–December, GS suffers serious illness.

1861   February–June, convalescence at Tamaris in the Var. This inspires her book, *Tamaris*, published in 1862. May, publishes *La Ville noire* and *La Famille de Germandre*. GS refuses a subsidy offered her by Napoleon III.

1862   17 May, marriage of GS's son Maurice and Lina Calamatta.

1863   3 January, publication of Fromentin's *Dominique* dedicated to GS. Beginning of GS's correspondence with Flaubert. The anti-clerical novel *Mademoiselle la Quintinie* published in *RDM*, arousing both enthusiasm and scandal. July, birth of son of Maurice and Lina. 13 August, death of Delacroix. Gautier and Dumas *fils* stay at Nohant.

1864   Difficult relationships between Manceau and Maurice force GS and Manceau to settle in Palaiseau, near Paris. July, death of Maurice's son.

1865   19 January, death of Proudhon. 21 August, death of Manceau at Palaiseau.

1866   10 January, birth of Aurore, daughter of Maurice and Lina. GS stays twice at Croisset, Flaubert's home.

1867   March, publication of *Le Dernier Amour*. 31 August, death of Baudelaire.

1868   Birth of Gabrielle, daughter of Maurice and Lina. GS spends more and more time at Nohant, where she receives Flaubert, Turgenev, and Juliette Adam. Publication in *RDM* of *Mademoiselle Merquem*.

1869   Publication of *Pierre qui roule* in *RDM*. 28 February, death of Lamartine. 9 March, death of Berlioz. Death of Sainte-Beuve. 13 October, publication of Flaubert's *L'Education sentimentale* which he had read to GS earlier in the year.

1870   Deaths of Mérimée and Dumas *père*. 14 July, beginning of Franco-Prussian war. 4 September, Third Republic proclaimed. 15 September, Siege of Paris begins.

1871   8 March, death of Casimir Dudevant. 28 March, Proclamation of the Paris Commune. 22–28 May, violent and brutal crushing of Paris Commune. GS publishes *Le Journal d'un voyageur pendant la guerre*.

1872   23 October, death of Gautier. Publication in *Le Temps* of *Nanon*, and of children's stories in *RDM*.

1873   9 January, death in England of Napoleon III.

1874   Publication in *RDM* of *Ma Soeur Jeanne*. GS's health deteriorates.

1875   Publication in *RDM* of *Flamarandes* and *Le Tour de Percemont*.

1876   Publication of *Les Contes d'une grand-mère*. 8 June, GS dies of an inoperable intestinal blockage at the age of 72. She is buried at Nohant.

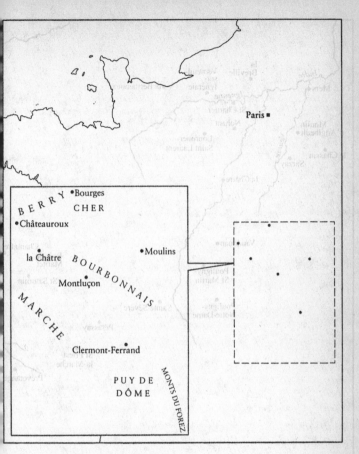

MAP OF WESTERN FRANCE

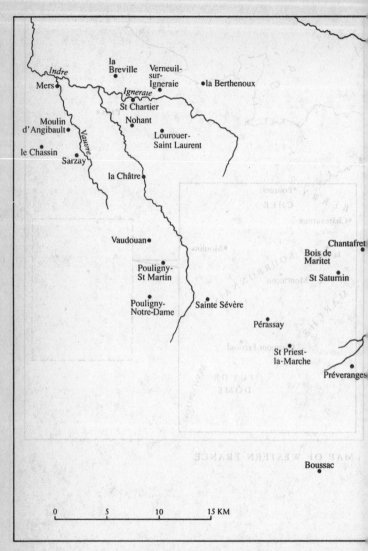

MAP OF THE AREA SURROUNDING NOHANT

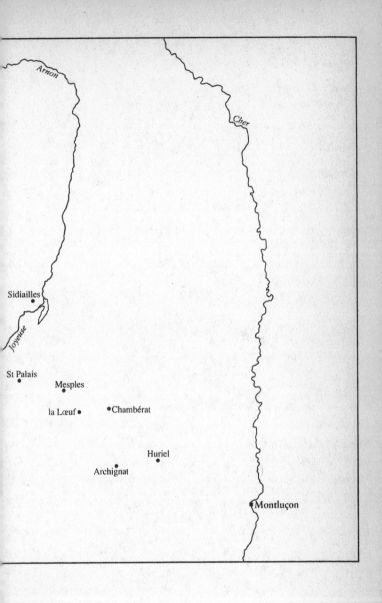

THE MASTER PIPERS

THE MASTER PIPERS

To M. Eugène Lambert*

My dear child, since you love listening to me tell the tales that were told by peasants in the evenings, during my youth, when I had time to listen to them, I shall try to remember the story of Etienne Depardieu, and to reunite the fragments of it that are scattered in my memory. He told it to me himself, over several evenings when the *breyage* was taking place: as you know, that's the term given to the late hours of the night when the hemp was being crushed and when, by tradition, everyone brought their own tale. Old Depardieu has long been sleeping the sleep of the just, and he was already rather old when he told me the story of the innocent adventures of his youth. That's why I'll put the words into his mouth, and imitate his manner as far as I can do so. You won't accuse me of being stubborn about this, for you know, through the experience of your own ears, that the thoughts and emotions of a peasant can't be translated into our style without becoming completely altered and without sounding disagreeably affected. You know, too, from what your own soul has experienced, that peasants guess or understand much more than one thinks they can, and you have often been struck by their sudden insights which, even where questions of art are concerned, resemble revelations. If I had come to tell you, in my language and in your own, certain things that you've heard and understood in their language, you would have found them so unlikely that you would have accused me of adding to them without realizing I was doing so, and of attributing to the peasants thoughts and emotions they could not have. Indeed, you only need to introduce, into the way you express their ideas, one word which is not part of their vocabulary, to feel inclined to throw into doubt the very idea they expressed. But, if you listen to them speak, you realize that if they do not possess, as we do, a choice of suitable words for all the shades of our thoughts, they do at least have enough words to express what they think and to describe what has struck their senses. So it's not, as critics have said, for the childish pleasure of seeking out an expression that is not used in literature, and even less to resurrect old idioms and dated terms, which, moreover, everyone understands and recognizes, that I'm going to subject myself to the small task of preserving Etienne Depardieu's tale in the colours which naturally belong to it. I do it because I cannot make him speak as we do, without altering beyond recognition the workings of his thoughts, in discussing points which would not have been familiar to him, but which he clearly had a great longing to understand and about which he wanted to be understood.

If, despite the care and attention I'll give it, you still find from time to time that my narrator sees too clearly or too darkly into the subjects he raises, blame only the weakness of my translation. Forced to choose, among the terms that we use, those that everyone will understand, I knowingly deprive myself of the most original and expressive of terms, but I'll try at least not to introduce into them those that the peasant in whose mouth I put them would not have known. Such a peasant, far superior to those of today, took no pride in using words that his audience and he himself did not know.

I dedicate this book to you, not to give you a proof of maternal love, for you have no need of that to feel part of my family, but to leave you something apart from myself by which to remember this Berry which has become almost your adopted homeland. You will remember that at the time when I was writing it you used to say: 'By the way, I came here, almost ten years ago, to stay for a month. I really must start thinking of leaving.' As I could see no reason why you should leave, you pointed out to me that you were a painter, that you had been working for ten years to represent what you saw and felt in the countryside, and that the time had come to seek out in Paris the guidance that comes from the thoughts and experience of others. I let you go, but on condition that you would come back and spend your summers here. From now on, don't forget that promise. I'm sending you this novel, like a far-away sound of our bagpipes, to remind you that the leaves are opening, that the nightingales have arrived, and that in the fields the great spring festival of nature is about to begin.

George Sand
Nohant, 17 April 1853

opening, that the nightingales have arrived, and that in the fields the great spring festival of nature is about to begin.

she'd have liked to find another partner, but having nothing
apart from her bright eyes and her clear voice, she thought
herself lucky not to be turned away for her rent, and to
have as proprietor and neighbour an old man who was hon-

FIRST EVENING

I didn't come down with the last rain, père Etienne remarked,
in 1828. I came into this world, as far as I can make out, in the
year '54 or '55 of last century. But, since I don't have any clear
memories of my first years, I won't tell you anything about
myself before the time of my first communion, which took
place in '70, at the parish of Saint Chartier,* which in those
days was served by abbot Montpérou, who today is profoundly deaf and badly crippled.

It's not that our parish at Nohant was closed down in those
days, but, because our curé had died, the two churches were
combined for a while under the Saint Chartier priest, and we
used to go to his catechism school every day, myself, a little
girl who was a cousin of mine, a lad called Joseph, who lived
in the same house as my uncle, and a dozen other children
from our village.

I call him my uncle to simplify things, for he was my great-
uncle, the brother of my grandmother, and his name was
Brulet, so his granddaughter, being the only heir to the line-
age, was called Brulette, and no one ever mentioned her
Christian name, which was Catherine.

I'll tell you straight away how the land lay there. I already
felt I loved Brulette more than it was my duty to love a cousin,
and I envied Joseph for living with her in a little house a
gunshot away from the last houses in the town, and a quarter
of a league away from my house. So he saw her constantly,
and before the time that brought us together for catechism, I
didn't even manage to see her every day.

Here's how it came about that Brulette's grandfather and
Joseph's mother lived under the same thatch. The house belonged to the old man, and he'd rented the smaller half of it to
her, a widow who had no other children. Her name was Marie
Picot, and she was still of marriageable age, for she was not
much over thirty, and her face and figure still showed she'd
been a very pretty woman. Here and there, people still called
her fair Mariton, which pleased her more than a little, for

she'd have liked to find another partner, but having nothing apart from her bright eyes and her clear voice, she thought herself lucky not to have to pay too much for her rent, and to have as proprietor and neighbour an old man who was honourable and helpful, who hardly troubled her at all, and who often gave her a helping hand.

Old Brulet and the widow Picot, called Mariton, had been living in this way in perfect harmony for a dozen years or so, from the day when, Brulette's mother having died in giving her birth, Mariton had begun looking after the baby and had brought her up with just as much love and respect as if the little girl had been her own child.

Joseph, who was three years older than Brulette, had been rocked in the same cradle, and the little doll had been the first burden entrusted to his arms. Later, old Brulet, realizing that his neighbour found it hard to keep an eye on two sturdy children, had taken the boy into his rooms, so that the lass slept with the widow and the lad with the old man.

The four of them, moreover, used to eat together, Mariton preparing the meals, doing the housework, and repairing the clothes, while the old man who was still a good worker, hired himself out as a journeyman and provided the bulk of their funds.

It's not that he was very rich and that their lifestyle was at all superior; but the widow was likeable and kindly, and kept him good company, and Brulette looked on her so completely as her own mother that my uncle was used to considering Mariton as his daughter or at the very least his daughter-in-law.

There was nothing in the world as pretty and lovable as the little girl Mariton brought up in this way. Since Mariton loved cleanliness and dressed herself as elegantly as she could afford to, she'd trained Brulette from an early age to do the same, and at the stage when children crawl about and love rolling around like little animals, she was so well behaved, so attractive, and so adorable in everything she did, that everyone wanted to kiss her: but even then she was sparing in her caresses and was affectionate only to those who deserved it.

When she turned twelve, she could, at times, be just like a

little woman; and, if she forgot herself so far as to caper around at catechism, carried away by her youth, she would quickly pull herself together again, as if she were driven even more by self-respect than by piety.

I don't know if we could have said why it was, but all of us boys at the catechism school, despite our differences, noticed how different she was from the other little girls.

As for the boys, I'd have to confess that some of us were already quite old: for instance, Joseph was fifteen and I was sixteen, which was shameful for both of us, or so the curé and our parents told us. This delay arose from the fact that Joseph was too lazy to get any learning into his head, and I was too much of a bandit to pay attention; and the result was that for three years we'd been expelled from the class, and if it hadn't been for abbot Montpérou, who was less of a stickler than our old curé, I think we'd be there still.

Besides, it's only right to confess that boys are always less mature mentally than girls are: so, in every band of apprentice Christians, there has always been a visible difference between the two types, the males being already fully grown and strong, the females still quite small and only just beginning to wear bonnets.

Moreover, we all went there as ignorant as each other, unable to read, even less able to write,* and capable of memorizing things only in the same way that little birds learn to sing, without knowing plainsong, or Latin, and doing it entirely by listening. All the same, the curé knew perfectly well who in our group was capable of a deeper understanding, and who best remembered his words. Of all these sharp minds, the sharpest was little Brulette's, among the girls, and the dullest was Joseph's, among the boys.

It's not that he reasoned any more foolishly than anyone else, but he was so incapable of listening and of accepting ideas he barely understood, he showed so little taste for the information provided, that I was amazed, for I developed a pretty good liking for it, once I'd managed to keep my body still and to control my wandering imagination.

Sometimes Brulette would scold him about it, but that led only to tears of vexation.

'I'm no more of an unbeliever than anyone else,' he used to

say, 'and I don't mean any offence to God. But the words just won't go into my memory in the right order. There's nothing I can do about it.'

'There is so,' the little girl would reply, for already she had got into the way of ordering him about. 'If you really wanted to you could! You can do whatever you want! But you let your mind wander on all sorts of other things, and the abbot is quite right to call you Joseph the dreamer.'

'He can call me whatever he likes,' Joseph would answer, 'that's a word I don't understand.'

But the rest of us understood it perfectly well, and we explained it in our childish language by calling him Joey star-gazer, and the name stuck, to his great annoyance.

Joseph was a sad child, physically weedy and naturally introverted. He never left Brulette's side and was very much under her thumb. Nevertheless, she used to tell him he was as headstrong as a sheep, and she would chide him at every turn. But even though she didn't reproach me much for my laziness, I wished she'd spend as much time thinking about me as she did about him.

Although he made me feel jealous, I was more friendly towards him than towards my other class-mates, because he was one of the weakest among us, and I was one of the strongest. Moreover, if I hadn't stood up for him, Brulette would have held me very much to blame, and when I used to say to her that she liked him better than she liked me, even though we were related, she'd reply: 'It's not for his sake, but for his mother's, whom I love more than either of you. If anything were to happen to him, I'd never dare go back home. And since he never thinks about what he's doing, she's charged me time and again to think for the two of us, and I always try to do so.'

I often hear middle-class people say: 'I went to school with so and so; he's a friend from college days.' We peasants, who didn't even go to school when I was a boy, what we say is: 'I went to catechism with so and so; he's my friend from first communion days.' That's the starting point of great friend-ships between young people, and also sometimes of great feuds that last your entire life. In the fields, at work, on feast days, you see each other, you talk, you meet and part again, but at catechism school, which lasts a year and often two, you have to put up with each other, or help each other out, for five or six hours a day. We used to set out in a group, each morning, walking across the meadows and pastures, along little paths, over stiles, following cart routes, and we'd return in the evening wherever our fancy led us, for we'd take advantage of our freedom to run in all directions, like frolicsome birds. Those who enjoyed each other's company barely left each other's sides, those who weren't nice went off on their own, or banded together to play tricks on the others and frighten them.

Joseph had his own little ways, which were neither terrible nor sneaky, but which weren't particularly pleasant either. I don't remember ever having seen him really happy, or really frightened, neither very pleased nor very cross about anything that happened to us. In battles, he never got out of the way, and he received blows he didn't know how to return, but he didn't complain about them. It almost seemed as if he didn't feel them.

Whenever we stopped to lark about, he used to go off on his own, and sit or lie down about three or four yards from the rest of us, not saying a word, giving answers that had nothing to do with the questions he was asked. He appeared to be listening to something or looking at something others were unaware of, and that's why he was taken to be one of those who are *lost in the clouds*. Brulette, who knew his whims and didn't want to talk about them, often used to call him without getting any reply. Then she'd start singing, which was a sure way of bringing him back to earth, as you whistle to stop someone snoring.

I've no idea how to explain why I'd become attached to a comrade who was such a poor sport, for I was the complete opposite. I couldn't bare being alone, and was always listening to others or watching them, enjoying talking and asking questions, bored when I was on my own, and seeking out merriment and friendship. That may perhaps be the reason why I pitied him for being so serious and introverted, and why I got into the habit of imitating Brulette, who always helped him, giving him more aid than she got back, and putting up with his moods rather than controlling them. In what she said, she certainly bossed_him around, but as he was incapable of obeying any command, it was she, and therefore I myself, who followed in his train and waited patiently for him.

At last the day of our first communion came, and, as we came back from mass, I'd made so firm a promise not to fool around, that I followed Brulette to her grandfather's house, since she was the best example I could set myself.

While she did as Mariton asked and went to milk the goat, Joseph and I stayed in the room where my old uncle was chatting with his neighbour.

We were looking at some devotional pictures the curé had given us as a memento of the sacrament, or to put it more accurately, I was looking at them on my own, for Joseph was dreaming of something else, and was leafing through them without seeing them. No one was paying any attention to us and Mariton was talking about the service with her old neighbour.

'I'll tell you one thing, neighbour,' she said. 'My Joey isn't too bright. Well, it's a sad thing, but I know it's true. He gets it from his dear dead father, who never had more than two ideas a week, but who was a good man for all that, who knew right from wrong. But it's still a weakness if you have so little ability to put ideas together, and if, to make matters worse, you get yourself married off to a madcap, everything goes wrong in the shortest possible time. So I've come to see, as my lad's legs grow long, that it's not his brain that's going to feed him, and if I could leave him a bit of money, I'd die more easy. You know how much good a little nest-egg can do. In our poor households, that can be a real godsend. I've never been able to save anything at all, and it must be true that I'm no longer young enough to be attractive, since I can't find a new husband. Well, if that's how it is, then God's will be done! I'm still young enough to work, and since we're on the subject, I thought I'd tell you, neighbour, that the innkeeper at Saint Chartier is looking for a barmaid; he pays good wages, thirty crowns a year! And then there are the tips which add on half as much again. With that, especially seeing I feel so strong and alert, in ten years I'll have made a fortune, and ensured myself a comfortable old age, as well as being able to leave something for my poor child. What do you think about that?'

Père Brulet thought for a while and then answered: 'You're making a mistake, neighbour; truly, you're making a mistake!'

Mariton thought a bit, too, and understanding what the old man meant, she answered: 'You're probably right, indeed you are. A woman in a country inn leaves herself open to criticism. And even if she behaves perfectly, no one is going to believe she does. Isn't that what you have in mind? Well, what else can I do? It'll deprive me of any chance of remarrying, but we don't regret what we suffer on our children's behalf, and we even take a kind of pleasure, more or less, in what we suffer.'

'The point is that there are worse things than suffering,' my uncle said. 'There's shame, and shame rebounds on the children.'

Mariton sighed. 'Yes,' she said. 'You're exposed to insults every day in places like that. You always have to be on the defensive and protect yourself . . . If you get too angry, and that drives the customers away, your boss is hardly going to be pleased.'

'Besides,' said the old man, 'there are innkeepers who seek out women with pretty faces and good temperaments like yours to fill their bars, and sometimes all that's needed, for one innkeeper to do better than the next one, is a barmaid who's a bit forward.'

'Well, who can tell,' said Mariton. 'You can be cheerful and pleasant and serve people swiftly, without allowing yourself to be offended . . .'

'Bad language is always offensive,' said old Brulet. 'And it must cost an honest woman dear to grow accustomed to such behaviour. Just think how mortified your son would be, if he happened to hear the tone in which the carters and tinkers bantered with his mother!'

'Praise be he's so simple!' replied Mariton, looking at Joseph.

I looked at him, too, and was astonished he hadn't heard any of the words his mother had been saying, for she hadn't been talking quietly enough to prevent me hearing everything.

And I gathered from this that he was *hard of hearing*, as we used to say, in those days, about people who were deaf.

Soon after that, he got up and went to join Brulette in her little milking shed, which was merely a humble lean-to made of planks stuffed with straw, in which she kept a flock of a dozen or so animals.

He threw himself onto the bundles of firewood and, since I'd followed him, fearing to appear nosy if I stayed in the house without him, I saw he was crying inside, even though there were no tears in his eyes.

'Are you sleeping, Joey?' Brulette asked him. 'You're lying there like a sick sheep. Come on, give me the firewood you're lying on, so I can let my sheep eat the leaves.'

So saying, she began to sing, but very softly, for it's not fitting to shout on the day of your first communion.

It seemed to me that her song had its usual effect on Joseph in waking him from his day-dreams. He got up and went away, and Brulette said to me: 'What ever's the matter with him? He's even sillier than usual.'

'I think,' I said to her, 'that he really did hear that he's going to start work and will have to leave his mother.'

'But he expected that,' Brulette replied. 'Isn't that normal, that he should start earning his living, as soon as he's received the sacrament? If I weren't lucky enough to be my grandfather's only child, I'd have to leave home, too, and earn my living among others.'

Brulette didn't seem to me to be very sad at the thought of being separated from Joseph, but when I told her that Mariton was going to hire herself out, too, and live far away from her, she began to sob, and running off in search of her, she said to her as she flung her arms around her neck: 'Is it true, my dear, that you want to leave me?'

'Who told you that?' said Mariton. 'It isn't decided yet.'

'It is so,' Brulette exclaimed. 'You said it, and now you want to keep it hidden from me.'

'Since there are nosy boys who can't hold their tongues,' Mariton said, looking at me, 'I'll have to confess. Yes, daughter, you'll have to take it like a brave and reasonable child who today has given her soul to the good Lord.'

'But, grandpa,' Brulette said to her grandfather, 'are you going to let her leave? Who's going to look after you?'

'You will, daughter,' replied Mariton. 'You're big enough to follow your duty. Listen to me, and you, too, neighbour, for this is something I haven't told you yet . . .'

And, taking the girl on her lap, while I leant back against my uncle's legs (since he looked so unhappy that I was drawn to him), Mariton went on trying to convince both of them.

'It's been a long time now,' she said, 'that only your friendship has kept me here, for I'd have gained much more if I'd paid you for keeping my Joseph, while I earned enough to cover those expenses and to put some aside, by working for others. But I felt I owed it to you to bring you up, my Brulette, because you were the younger, and because a girl needs a mother longer than a boy does. I wouldn't have had the heart to leave you before the time came when you were able to do without me. But now that time has come, and if anything can console you for my loss, it's the fact that you'll feel you're being useful to your grandfather. I've taught you how to care for a family, and everything a good girl needs to know to look after her kin and her house. You'll put that knowledge to good use, because you love me, and to bring me honour for the way I've taught you. It'll be a source of consolation and pride for me to hear everyone say that my Brulette cares devotedly for her grandfather, and husbands her resources like a little woman. Come now, take heart, and don't make me lose the little courage I have left, for if you're sad to see me go, I'm even more unhappy about it than you are. Remember, I'm leaving M. Brulet, who's been the best of friends to me, and my poor Joey, who's going to miss his mother and your house very much indeed. But since it's my duty to go, you really wouldn't want to dissuade me.'

Brulette went on crying over it until evening fell and was in no state to help Mariton do anything at all. But when she saw Mariton hiding her tears as she prepared our supper, she threw her arms around her neck, promised to do as she was told, and set about working with a brave face.

I was sent to find Joseph who, not for the first time, nor the last, had forgotten that it was time to come home and behave like ordinary folk.

I found him in a corner, thinking on his own and staring at the ground, as if his eyes wanted to take root there. Unusually for him, he let fall a few words which showed me he felt more discontent than regret. He wasn't surprised to be starting work, for he knew he was of the age to do so, and had no other choice; but, although he gave no hint that he'd heard his mother's plans, he complained that no one loved him and no one thought him capable of doing any good work.

I was unable to make him explain himself any more than that, and throughout that evening, during which I was invited to say my prayers with Brulette and him, he seemed to sulk, whereas Brulette paid everyone twice as much attention as usual.

Joseph was hired by père Michel, at the Aulnières estate, as a cowherd. Mariton became a barmaid at the Crowned Ox in Saint Chartier, a tavern owned by M. Benoît.* Brulette stayed with her grandfather, and I remained with my family, who, since they owned a little property, found that I came in more than handy to help them work it.

The day of my first communion had shaken me considerably. I'd made a great effort to behave in the rational way befitting someone of my age, and my time at the catechism school with Brulette had changed me, too. The thought of her was always connected for me in some way with my thinking about the good Lord, and, while I became more mature and sensible in my behaviour, I felt my imagination drifting away in foolish thoughts of love. These thoughts were not only unsuitable in connection with someone my cousin's age, but were, even for me, rather ahead of their due time.

Around this time, my father took me to the Orval fair, near Saint Amand, to sell a brood mare, and, for the first time in my life, I was away from home for three whole days. My mother* had noticed I wasn't sleeping long enough or eating heartily enough to sustain my growth, which was more rapid than is usual in our area, and my father thought a little amusement would do me good. But I didn't enjoy seeing new people and places as much as I would have six months before.

I suffered from a silly yearning that made me look at all the girls without daring to say a word to them; besides, I was thinking of Brulette, whom I fancied I could marry, for the sole reason that she was the only girl who didn't frighten me, and I thought about how old she was and how old I was, which didn't make the time pass any more quickly than the good Lord had ordained that it should.

Returning from the fair along a hollow lane, with me sitting behind my father on another mare we'd bought there, we chanced upon a middle-aged man with a small cart, which was heavily laden with furniture. Since the cart was drawn only by a donkey, it had become bogged and couldn't move at all. The man was in the process of lightening the load, putting some of it on the path, and when my father saw this, he told me to get down and lend a hand to someone in need. The man thanked us for this offer, and said, as if he were talking to his cart: 'Come on, my dear, wake up. I wouldn't want you to be overturned.'

Then I saw a pretty girl get up from a mattress in the cart. She seemed, on first sight, to be about fifteen or sixteen, and, rubbing her eyes, she asked what the matter was.

'The road is bad, daughter,' said the man, taking her in his arms. 'There you are, don't put your feet in the water. I should tell you,' he added to my father, 'that she has a fever from growing too quickly. What a great sprig of ivy she is, for a child who's only eleven and a half.'

'Good Lord!' said my father. 'That's a fine lass you have, and pretty as the day is long, although her fever has made her pale. But it will pass, and if you feed her up a bit, she won't suffer in the long run.'

When he spoke like that, my father's head was still full of the language used by the horse traders at the fair. But when he saw that the girl had left her clogs in the cart, and that it wouldn't be easy to retrieve them, he called me, saying: 'Come lad! You're strong enough to carry her for a moment or two.'

And, putting her in my arms, he replaced the exhausted donkey with our mare and pulled the cart out of the mire. But there was another boggy spot that my father knew about because he'd made the journey several times, and telling me to follow, he led the way with the other peasant, who was pulling the donkey along by its ears.

I carried that tall girl and looked at her in astonishment, for although she was head and shoulders taller than Brulette, you could see by looking at her face that she wasn't any older.

She was pale and thin, like the flame that burns from pure wax, and her black hair, under a curious little bonnet, which had been pushed askew while she slept, fell onto my chest and hung down almost to my knees. I'd never seen anything so perfectly formed as that pale face, her light blue eyes, lined with very thick lashes, her sweet, weary air, and a little, pitch black mark at the corner of her mouth which gave her a strange kind of beauty that was hard to forget.

She seemed so young that my heart said nothing close to hers, and it may have been less her lack of years than the langour caused by her illness that made her seem so much of a child to me. I didn't speak to her, and walked on, without finding her too heavy, but enjoying looking at her, as one feels about any lovely thing, girl or woman, flower or fruit.

As we drew closer to the second muddy ditch, where her father and mine set to work again, the one pulling his horse, the other putting his shoulder to the wheel, the girl spoke to me in a language that made me laugh, for I understood not one single word. She was astonished at my astonishment, and speaking to me this time in the language we use, she said: 'Don't hurt yourself by carrying me. I can walk without my clogs, I'm as used to that as anyone else.'

'Of course you are. But you're sick,' I answered, 'and I could easily carry four your size. But where are you from? Why did you speak so strangely a moment ago?'

'Where am I from?' she exclaimed. 'I'm not from anywhere. I'm from the woods, that's all. And you, where are you from?'

'Well, my clever one, if you're from the woods, I'm from the wheat!' I replied, laughing.

I was going to ask her more about herself, when her father came to take her back from me.

'Come,' he said, after shaking my father's hand. 'Many thanks, good people. And you, my dear, give a kiss to this fine lad who's carried you as if you were a reliquary in a shrine.'

The girl wasn't the least bit reluctant, for she wasn't old enough to be embarrassed, and not seeing anything wrong in it, she obeyed without any more ado. She kissed me on both cheeks, saying: 'Many thanks, my fine servant.' Her father took her back and returned her to her mattress, where she seemed eager to go back to sleep, unconcerned about the jolts and mishaps of the route.

'Farewell once more!' said her father, taking my knee to lift me back onto the mare's rump. 'A fine boy!' he said to my father, looking at me, 'and as advanced for the age you tell me he is, as my girl is for her age.'

'He also suffers from growing pains,' my father replied. 'But, with the good Lord's help, work can cure all ills. Forgive us, if we go ahead, but we're far from home and want to arrive before nightfall.'

On that, my father spurred our mare on, and as she started to trot, I turned round and saw that the man with the cart had taken the right-hand fork and was heading in the opposite direction from us. I was soon thinking of other things, but when my thoughts turned to Brulette, I mused on those unabashed kisses and wondered why Brulette responded by patting my cheek whenever I wanted to kiss her. And, as the road was long, and I had risen before daybreak, I fell asleep behind my father with the two girls' faces strangely mingled together in my sleepy head.

My father pinched me to wake me up, for he felt me weighing heavy on his shoulders and was afraid I'd fall off. I asked him who those people were we'd met.

'Who?' he asked, teasing my slow mind. 'We've met more than five hundred folk since this morning.'

'The donkey and the cart?'

'I see!' he answered. 'On my oath, I don't know. It didn't occur to me to ask. They must be from the area around Boussac, or between Châteauroux and Vatan, for they spoke with a strange accent.* But I was so busy making sure the mare could pull well that I didn't take much notice of anything else. She really does pull well, and isn't shy of hard work. I think she'll do a fine job so I really didn't pay too much for her.'

No doubt the journey did me good, because from then on my health began to mend and I started enjoying work. My father had put me in charge of the mare, and then of the garden, and finally of the meadow, and little by little I discovered how pleasant it was to dig and plant and harvest.

My father had long been a widower, and now he was eager to let me reap the benefits of the inheritance my mother had left me. So he gave me my share of all our little profits, and wanted nothing more than to see me become a good farmer.

It didn't take him long to notice that I had a real appetite for such work, for if young people need a good deal of courage to deprive themselves of pleasure when others are drawing the benefit of it, they hardly need any to knuckle under when it's in their own interest to do so, particularly when they share with a good family, who are truly honest in dividing things among themselves and all working in harmony.

It's true that I still liked talking and playing about on Sundays, but no one blamed me for that at home because I was a good worker for the rest of the week. My work gave me good health and a cheerful disposition, and I got a bit more reason in my head than I'd had at the start. I forgot the fumes of love, for nothing calms you down as much as sweating away with a pickaxe from sunrise to sunset. And when night comes, if you've been working with the fertile, heavy soil of our district, and that's the harshest mistress you could find, you take less pleasure in thinking than in sleeping to prepare yourself for the next day.

That's how I gradually reached the age when it was permissible for me to think, not about little girls any more, but about grown-up girls. And just as when I first took pleasure in thinking of them, I still found my cousin Brulette firmly established at the top of my preferences, ahead of all the rest.

She'd stayed on alone with her grandfather, and had done her best to grow up swiftly in good sense and bravery. But there are children who are born with the gift or the destiny of always being spoiled.

Mariton's rooms had been rented to mère Lamouche, from Vieilleville, who wasn't well off and who quickly set about serving the Brulets as if she'd been their servant, hoping she could thus earn their good will when she confessed she couldn't pay her ten crowns rent. That is indeed what happened, and when Brulette saw how much she was helped and flattered, and how swiftly the old woman anticipated her every need, she took the time to grow up at her leisure, letting her beauty and her mind flower without over-exerting either her soul or her body.

SECOND EVENING

Thus little Brulette became lovely Brulette, who was much talked about in the region, since, in living memory, no more beautiful girl had been seen, none with a more attractive figure, none whose hair was more softly golden, none whose cheek was pinker; her hand was like satin and her foot was as small and delicate as a lady's.

That description will tell you my cousin didn't do much work, rarely went out in bad weather, was careful to shade herself in the sun, hardly ever did the washing, and never worked her four limbs to the point of weariness.

Does that make you think she was lazy? She certainly wasn't that at all. She did everything she couldn't avoid doing, and did it perfectly swiftly and well. She was too intelligent to abandon good order and cleanliness in her lodgings, and too reasonable not to care for her grandfather and anticipate his wishes exactly as it behoved her to do. Moreover, she was too fond of finery not to have some handiwork always in train. But exhausting work was not something anyone had ever mentioned to her. There wasn't any need for it, and it would be wrong to lay the blame for it at her feet.

There are families in which suffering comes of its own accord to warn the young that we're not in this world to amuse ourselves, and that it's our task to earn our bread in the company of those who are dear to us. But, in père Brulet's little house, there was little to do to make ends meet. The old man was only in his seventies, and he was a good worker, skilled at stoneworking, which, as you know, is a valued craft in our region. He was a reliable worker and in constant demand, and thus made a good living. Moreover, since he was a widower and had no other dependents, apart from his granddaughter, he could put a little money aside for the days when illness or an accident made it impossible for him to work. By good fortune he was able to continue in good health, so that, while he knew nothing of riches, he knew nothing of need either.

My father, however, used to say that our cousin Brulette was too fond of easy living, by which he meant that she would have to set her sights lower when the time came for her to settle down. He agreed with me that she was as amiable and pleasant as anyone in the way she spoke, but he didn't give me the slightest encouragement to connive about marrying her. He considered her too poor to be such a fine lady, and he often repeated that where marriage is concerned you need either a very rich girl or one who is very courageous. 'At first sight, they're equally desirable,' he used to say, 'but perhaps, on second thoughts, I'd go for courage even more than money. But Brulette doesn't have enough of either to tempt a wise man.'

I could see perfectly well that my father was right, but Brulette's beauty and her gentle words weighed even more heavily with me and with the other young men who sought her out. As you can well imagine, I wasn't the only one attracted to her. Ever since she'd turned fifteen, she'd been surrounded by beaux as crazy as I was, whom she controlled and kept in check, using the good sense she'd developed in childhood. You might say she'd been born with a clear sense of her own worth, even before compliments made her fully aware of it. So she enjoyed receiving praise and obedience from all around her. She never let anyone be forward with her, but she let them be timid, and like many others I was attracted to her by a strong desire to please her, although, at the same time, I was annoyed to find myself with so many others.

But there were two of us who were allowed to talk to her rather less publicly, to address her informally, and to accompany her home when she was on her way back from mass or a dance. Those two were Joseph Picot and myself, but it wasn't of much use to us, and it could well be that, although we didn't talk about it, we each blamed the other.

Joseph was still at the Aulnières farm, half a league from Brulet's house and about a quarter league from my place.

He'd progressed to being a ploughman, and although he wasn't handsome, he could appear so to those who aren't repelled by a face that looks unhappy. His face was thin and sallow, and the way his brown hair hung lankily down his brow and along his cheeks made him seem weaker than he was. Nevertheless, he wasn't misshapen and his body didn't lack grace. I observed in the hard line of his jaw something that I'd always noticed was the very opposite of weakness. People thought he was ill because he moved slowly and had none of the gaiety of youth; but since I saw him very frequently, I knew that he was like that by nature and that it wasn't caused by any illness.

For all that, he was a very poor worker of the soil, he wasn't very good at caring for the animals, and there wasn't a shred of lovableness in his nature.

His wage was the lowest you could pay a ploughman, and even so, people were amazed that his boss was willing to keep him so long, for he was incapable of making things prosper either in the fields or in the stables. And if you criticized him for this, he put on such an angry, resentful expression that you didn't know what to think. But old Michel insisted that Joseph had never answered back, and that he preferred those who obey without arguing, even if they do scowl, to those who flatter and deceive with caresses.

His great reliability, and his invariable scorn for injustice of all sorts, thus made his master value him, although he still used to say it was a great shame to see so honest and sensible a lad with such weak arms and so little stomach for his work. But such as he was, he retained him out of force of habit, and also out of consideration for old Brulet, who was one of his oldest friends.

In what I've just told you about him, you can hardly think

it likely that he appealed to girls. They merely looked at him in surprise that he so rarely raised his eyes, which were large and bright, like those of an owl, and didn't seem to be of much use to him.

All the same, I was always jealous of him, because Brulette constantly paid attention to him in ways she never did to anyone else, and forced me to pay attention to him too. She never scolded him now, and seemed willing to accept his moods as God had made them, without letting anything annoy or irritate her. So she put up with his lack of gallantry and even his lack of politeness, although she demanded so much from others. He could do thousands of stupid things, like sitting down on the chair she'd just got up from and letting her find another; or not picking up her balls of wool or thread when she dropped them; or interrupting her, or breaking some tool or utensil she used: and she never said an impatient word, whereas she scolded me and teased me if I did even a quarter of the boorish things he did.

What's more, she took as much care of him as if he'd been her brother. She always had a piece of meat in reserve when he came to see her, and whether he was hungry or not, she made him eat it, telling him he needed to build up his blood and strengthen his stomach. She kept an eye on his clothes just as sharply as Mariton had done, and repaired them herself, saying that his mother didn't have time to cut and sew. And, finally, she would often take her animals to pasture in the area in which he was working, and chatted with him, even though he himself had little to say and when he did say anything, he said it badly.

What's more, she wouldn't let anyone despise or mock him for his melancholy air and his vacant expression. She would reply to any criticism one might make by saying that his health wasn't good, that he was no more stupid than the rest of us, that if he hardly said a word, that didn't mean he wasn't thinking, and that, all in all, it was better to say nothing than to talk when you had nothing to say.

I often itched to contradict her, but she would quickly stop me by saying: 'Tiennet, you must have a really nasty nature to want to let others mock that poor boy instead of standing up for him when they hurt him. I'd have thought a relation of mine would be better than that.'

So I did what she wanted me to do and defended Joseph, although I couldn't see what sort of illness or affliction he could be suffering from, unless distrust and laziness are natural infirmities, as could be the case, although it seemed to me within the power of a man to cure himself of them.

For his part, Joseph, although he wasn't hostile towards me, treated me just as coldly as he treated all the others, and didn't seem to acknowledge in the slightest the way I helped him whenever we met. Either he was in love with Brulette like all the others, or he loved only himself, but in any case he used to smile at me in a strange way, and behaved almost scornfully towards me whenever she gave me the slightest mark of friendship.

One day when he went so far as to screw up his nose at me, I decided to have things out with him, as gently as possible, so as not to anger my cousin, but openly enough for him to feel that since I tolerated his presence in her company, he should do the same by me. But as there were other beaux of Brulette's around us, I put off my plan until such time as I could find him alone, and, with that in mind, the next day I went to meet him in the field where he was working.

I was amazed to find that Brulette herself was with him, sitting on the roots of a large tree on the bank of the ditch where he was meant to be cutting thorns to make plugs. But he wasn't cutting a thing, and the only work he was doing was honing something he thrust into his pocket the minute he saw me, closing his knife and falling silent, as if I were his master who had caught him out, or as if he'd been telling my cousin deep secrets and I'd interrupted them.

I was so disturbed by this that I was going to go away without saying a word, when Brulette stopped me, and, continuing with her spinning, for she'd put aside her work to talk with Joseph, she invited me to sit down beside her.

I took it as a trick to calm my resentment and I refused, saying that it was hardly inviting weather for sitting in ditches. It's true that it was, if not cold, at least very damp; the thaw had made the water muddy and the grass dirty. There was still snow in the furrows, and the wind was keen. To my mind, Brulette and Joseph must have found something very interesting to have made her bring her flock outdoors on that day, given that, so often, she was more than willing to let the neighbour guard them.

'Joey,' said Brulette, 'your friend Tiennet is cross because he thinks the two of us have a secret. Don't you want me to tell him about it? His advice won't hurt anything and he can tell you what he thinks of your plan.'

'Him?' said Joseph, beginning to screw up his nose as he'd done the day before.

'Does your nose get out of joint everytime you see me?' I asked him, pretty cross. 'I could really straighten it out for you in a way that would cure you once and for all.'

He gave me a furtive glance as if he were ready to bite, but Brulette touched his shoulder gently with the tip of her distaff, and calling him to her, whispered in his ear.

'No,' he answered, without troubling to hide from me what he was saying. 'No. Tiennet's not the slightest use in advising me. He knows no more about it than your nanny goat. And if you say the slightest thing to him, I won't say anything more to you.' And on that note he picked up his spade and billhook, and went to work further off.

'Oh dear,' said Brulette, as she got up to gather her flock together, 'now he's cross again. But really, Tiennet, it's not serious, I know his moods, I know there's nothing we can do, and the best thing is for us not to bother him any further. He's a boy who's had a bee in his bonnet ever since he came on this earth. He doesn't know how to explain it, and the best thing we can do is let him alone; because if we tease him with questions, he'll start crying, and we'll have hurt him for nothing.'

'But it seems to me, Brulette, that you know how to wheedle things out of him.'

'I was wrong,' she said. 'I thought he was really unhappy. What he's upset about would make you laugh if you heard it, but since he doesn't want to tell anyone but me, let's not give it a second thought.'

'If it's so small a matter, perhaps you won't be so concerned about it in future.'

'So you think I worry about it too much, do you? But don't

I owe that to the woman who brought him into the world, and who raised me with more care and caresses than she gave her own child?'

'Well, that's a good reason, Brulette. If it's Mariton you love in her son, well and good. But in that case, I'd love to have Mariton for my mother. I'd be better off then than in being your cousin.'

'Now just you leave such silly sayings to my other beaux,' answered Brulette, blushing a little, for compliments had never made her cross, even if she did pretend to laugh at them.

As we left the field opposite my house, she came in with me to say hello to my sister. But my sister had gone out, and because her sheep were across the path, Brulette didn't want to wait for her to come back. To keep her there a little longer, I dreamt up the idea of taking off her clogs so that she could remove her snow galoshes and warm them up. And since that obliged her to sit down and wait for me, I tried to tell her more clearly than I'd dared to before how unhappy my love for her was making me.

But the devil take it! I just couldn't find the right words for such a speech. I would willingly have said the second and third but the first word just wouldn't come out. My forehead was beaded with sweat. Brulette could easily have helped me out, if she'd wanted to, for she knew what tune I was singing from having heard others hum it to her. But with her, you needed patience and care, and although I wasn't a complete beginner in the art of love-making, what I'd said to others who were more approachable than Brulette (and I flirted with them only in order to be bolder with her) had taught me nothing I could say to a girl of such high merit as my cousin.

All I could do was resort to criticizing her pet, Joseph. At first she laughed it off, and then, little by little, when she saw I wanted to make something serious of it, she looked even more serious.

'Let's leave that poor unfortunate lad alone,' she said. 'He's got enough problems.'

'But what problems, and why should we pity him? Has he got a weak chest, or is he mad, that you're so eager for no one to touch him?'

'It's worse than that,' Brulette answered. 'He's an egotist.'

'Egotist' was one of the curé's words, and Brulette had remembered it, although it wasn't in use among us at that time. Since Brulette had a good memory, she did, from time to time, use words that I, too, might have learnt but that I hadn't retained, and therefore didn't understand.

I was so ashamed that I didn't dare ask her what the word meant, and pretended to accept her explanation. Moreover, I imagined that Joseph was suffering from some deadly disease, and that such great misfortune made all my injustice towards him despicable. I begged Brulette's pardon for having teased him, and added: 'If I'd only known earlier what you've just told me, I wouldn't have felt either resentful or sulky at the poor chap.'

'How is it you never noticed?' she answered. 'Can't you see how he lets people do things for him and look after him without ever thinking of saying thank you; or how the slightest moment of forgetfulness on your part offends him and the slightest teasing affronts him, how he sulks and suffers about things others wouldn't notice, and how we always have to make the running in being friends with him, while he doesn't understand that such behaviour isn't simply his due but rather what one does for God, through loving our neighbour?'

'And that's caused by his illness?' I asked, rather intrigued by Brulette's explanations.

'Isn't that the worst thing you can have in your heart?' she answered.

'Does his mother know he has in his heart an incurable illness?'

'She suspects it, but you can understand that I don't discuss it with her, because I don't want to hurt her.'

'And nothing's been tried as a cure?'

'I've done what I can, and will go on doing so,' she replied, continuing a conversation in which we were completely at cross purposes, 'but I fear that by being gentle with him I'm only making him worse.'

'It's certainly true,' I said after chewing the matter over, 'that that boy has always been rather strange in his appearance. My late grandmother who, as you know, boasted she could read the future, used to say of him that he had misfortune written on his face, and that he was doomed to live in suffering or to die in the flower of his age, because of some line or other he had on his brow. And since the day when she said that, I'd have to confess to you that whenever Joey is unhappy I imagine I can see that ill-starred line, although I really don't know exactly where my grandmother saw it. Then I feel a bit frightened of him, or rather it's his fate that I'm frightened of, and I feel I want to spare him all criticism and all unhappiness, as if he were someone who didn't have much longer to enjoy life.'

'Bah!' said Brulette, laughing. 'Those really are my great-aunt's dreams, I can remember them very clearly. Didn't she also tell you that light-coloured eyes, like Joseph's, see spirits and all sorts of things others don't see? I don't believe a word of all that, and I don't believe he's in any mortal danger either. You can live for ages with the sort of mind he has. You relieve your feelings by tormenting others, and he may indeed end up by burying all of us, while every hour he's threatening to let himself die.'

I no longer understood anything, and I was going to ask more questions, when Brulette asked me for her socks back, and quickly put her feet in them, although her clogs were so small that I wasn't even able to put my hand in them. Then, remembering her dog, and lifting up her skirts, she left me. I was deeply concerned and astonished at what she'd just told me, and was no further forward with her than I'd been on the first day I set eyes on her.

The following Sunday, as she was setting out for the mass at Saint Chartier, which she preferred to that of our own parish, because there was dancing in the square between mass and vespers, I asked if I could go with her.

'No,' she said to me, 'I'm going with my grandfather and he doesn't like to see me followed on my way by a pack of beaux.'

'I'm not a pack of beaux,' I said. 'I'm your cousin, and my uncle has never told me to get out of his path.'

'Well,' she answered, 'get out of it by yourself, just today. My grandfather and I are going to chat with Joey, who's in the house, and is coming to mass with us.'

'Does that mean he's going to ask for your hand in marriage and you're only too happy to accept him?'

'Have you taken leave of your senses, Tiennet? After what I told you about Joey?'

'You told me he had an illness which would make him live longer than other people, and I don't see anything in that to calm me.'

'What do you mean, calm you?' asked Brulette in astonishment. 'What illness? Wherever have you left your wits? Goodness me, I think all men must be mad!'

And taking her grandfather's arm as he came towards her with Joseph, she went off as light as a feather and as gay as a lark, while my good old uncle, who considered she was a cut above everyone else, smiled at the passers by and looked for all the world as if he were saying: '_You_ can't boast of having a girl like this to show off!'

I followed them from a distance to see if Joseph would flirt with her on the way, if he would take her arm, if the old man would leave the two of them together. He did nothing of the sort. Joseph always walked on the left of my uncle, while Brulette was on his right, and they seemed to be deep in serious conversation.

On the way out of mass, I asked Brulette to dance with me. 'Oh, you've left it very late,' she said. 'I've promised at least fifteen bourrées.* You'll have to come back around the time for vespers.'

This time it wasn't Joseph who made me feel jealous, since he never danced, but the sight of Brulette surrounded by all her beaux, so I followed Joseph to the Crowned Ox, where he went to see his mother, and where I was going to kill time with some friends.

I was a bit of a frequenter of taverns, as I've told you: not because of the bottle, which has never sent me out of my wits, but because I love company, conversation, and singing. There I found several girls and boys I knew, and sat down with them, while Joseph sat down in a corner, drinking nothing, saying nothing, sitting there only to please his mother, who, as she came and went, was very glad to see him and to say a word to him now and again. I don't know if it had occurred to Joseph to help her in her work when she had so many people to serve, but Benoît wouldn't have tolerated so absent-minded a boy among his bowls and bottles.

You can't have failed to hear tell of the late Benoît. He was a large man, with a lofty bearing, rather rough in his manner of speaking, but a lover of life, and on occasion a good conversationalist. He was fair-minded enough to treat Mariton with the esteem she deserved, for, to tell the truth, she was the very queen of barmaids, and his hotel had never had so much custom as had appeared since she'd started working there.

The fate old Brulet had foretold for this woman had not, however, befallen her. The dangers of her situation had cured her of all flirtatiousness, and she was able to command respect as much on her own account as because of her employer's riches. To tell the truth, it was above all for her son's sake that she'd harnessed her spirit to her task and to a degree of prudence stricter than her own nature would have accepted on its own behalf. She was such a good mother that, instead of losing esteem, she'd gained even more since she'd begun working in the tavern; and that's something rarely seen in our area, or elsewhere, from what I hear tell.

Seeing Joseph paler and more careworn than ever, I remembered what my grandmother had said of him, and the strange illness that Brulette had discerned in him, and my heart was touched. No doubt he still bore me ill will for the harsh words I'd uttered in talking to him. I wanted to make him forget them, so I forced him to come and sit at our table, where I thought I'd make him a little tipsy without his realizing what was happening, for, like all young men of my age, I considered the fumes of white wine a sovereign remedy for sadness.

Joseph, who paid little attention to what went on around him, let us fill his glass, and raised his elbow so often that anyone else would have felt the effects of it. Those who were urging him to drink, and setting him an example without thinking about it too deeply, soon succumbed. As for me, I wanted to keep my legs for the dance with Brulette, so I stopped as soon as I felt I'd had enough. Joseph fell into deep contemplation, leaning on his elbows, and seeming neither duller nor brighter than before.

No one payed him any attention anymore. Everyone was laughing and chattering, unaware of him, and they began to sing, as you sing when you've drunk a few glasses, everyone singing in their own key and their own measure, one table saying their refrain beside another table saying their own different refrain, and all that going on at the same time, creating a madman's sabbath noisy enough to split your head, and all done to make people laugh and shout all the more loudly, because you can't hear yourself think anymore.

Joseph stayed there without moving, looking at us in amazement, for quite a while. Then he got up and left without saying a word.

I thought he might be ill, and followed him. But he walked straight and quickly, like a man unaffected by wine, and he went off so far away, climbing the hill above the town of Saint Chartier, that I lost sight of him and retraced my steps so I wouldn't miss my dance with Brulette.

My Brulette danced so prettily that everyone watching her devoured her with their eyes. She adored dancing, clothes, and compliments, but she didn't encourage anyone to pay her serious compliments, and when vespers had sounded, she went away to church, sensible and proud, and she certainly prayed a while there, but remained conscious that all eyes were focused on her.

As for me, I remembered that I hadn't paid my bill at the Crowned Ox, and returned to settle it with Mariton, who seized the opportunity of asking me where her boy had gone.

'You made him drink,' she said, 'and he isn't used to it. The least you could do is not let him go off on his own. An accident can happen so quickly!'

THIRD EVENING

I climbed back up the hill and took the path I'd seen Joseph choose. I asked about him all along the route and had no word of him, except that he'd been seen heading in that direction but no one had seen him come back. That took me just to the right of the forest, where I went to question the forester, whose ancient house overlooks a great section of sloping forest. It's a very gloomy place, although you can see so far, and the only things that grow there, along with the oak thicket, are bracken and furze.

The forester in those days was my godfather Jarvois, a native of Verneuil.* Now I didn't often come walking so far, so as soon as he saw me, he celebrated my arrival in such a friendly way that I couldn't just go on without celebrating too.

'Your friend Joseph came this way about an hour ago,' he said to me, 'to ask if the charcoal burners were in the forest. Probably his boss asked him to make enquiries. His speech wasn't slurred, and he was pretty sure on his legs. He went up as far as the big oak. There's no reason for you to worry about him. Since you're here, you must drink a bottle with me, and wait until my wife gets back from rounding up the cows, for she'd be cross if you left without seeing her.'

Since there was no longer any reason to worry, I stayed with my godfather until almost sunset. It was around the middle of February and, when I saw night coming on, I bade farewell and took the path downhill, so as to reach Verneuil and return directly home by Englishmen's track,* without going back by Saint Chartier where I had no further business.

My godfather gave me directions, for I'd only crossed the forest a couple of times before. As you know, in this region we don't travel much, especially those of us who work on the land, and who live around our dwelling places like chickens around their coop.

So, despite warnings, I headed too far to my left, and instead of meeting the Great Oak path, I found myself among the birches, a good half a league from the point I should have reached.

Night had completely fallen, and I couldn't see my hand in front of my face, for in those days the forest of Saint Chartier was still a fine forest, not so much because of its extent, which has never amounted to much, but because its trees are so old, and barely let any light filter through between sky and earth.

What that added in terms of greenness and splendour, you were made to pay for. There was nothing but thorns and scrub, rough paths, and ravines covered with a black, light mud, which didn't cling too much to your shoes, but in which you sunk up to your knees if you left the path at all. The result was that, when I realized I was lost in the forest, and torn and mired in the clearings, I began to curse my bad luck and the inhospitable country.

Having floundered around long enough to have warmed myself up, although the evening was pretty cold, I found myself among dry bracken, so tall that it came up to my chin, and when I lifted up my eyes I could see, against the grey of the night sky, a kind of vast black mass in the middle of a clearing.

I realized it must be the oak,* and that I'd arrived at the very edge of the forest. I'd never seen the tree, but I'd heard people talk of it, for it was renowned as one of the oldest of the region, and, from what others had said, I recognized its shape. You'll have seen it too. It's a misshapen oak, and since its top was broken off in its youth by some accident or other, it's grown out rather than up. Its leaves, dried out through the cold of winter, still clung on, and it seemed to rise up towards the sky like a great rock.

I was heading in that direction, thinking I'd find the path which cut directly through the wood, when I heard the sound of music, which resembled that of bagpipes, but which was so loud it was more like thunder.

Don't ask me how something that ought to have reassured me, by indicating the presence of a human being, scared me out of my wits, as if I were a small child. I have to confess that despite being nineteen years old and having a good pair of fists, from the moment I knew I was lost in the forest I'd felt ill at ease. It wasn't the fear of the few wolves that come down from time to time into the forest from the great woods of Saint Aoust* that made me lose heart, nor was it the fear of meeting some malevolent human. I was chilled to the bone by the sort of fear you can't explain to yourself, because you've no real idea what's caused it. The darkness, the winter fog, all the noises that you hear in the woods, and that are different from the noises of the plains, endless stupid tales you've heard told and that come back to you, and the thought that you're on your own far from home—that's quite enough to disturb you when you're young, and even when you're no longer young.

Mock me if you will. That music, in a place where so few people went, seemed to me the work of the devil. It was too loud to be natural, and above all it was a sad and strange song, that resembled no air known in Christendom. I walked more quickly but then I stopped, amazed at another noise. While the music brayed away on one side, a little bell rang out on the other, and these two sounds came towards me, as if to stop me going either back or forward.

I threw myself to the side, doubling up in the bracken, but the movement this caused brought something bounding at me on all fours, and I saw a great black animal come leaping towards me. I couldn't keep my eyes on it, for it kept running and then disappearing.

At the same moment, all through the bracken, a number of identical animals came leaping, running and stamping, all, so it seemed, heading towards the bell and the music, which at that moment sounded as if they were near each other. There may well have been some two hundred of these animals, but I saw at least thirty thousand of them, for fear was making my heart pound, and I was beginning to see sparks and white spots before my eyes, the sort that fear brings to those who give in to it.

I don't know how I came to make it to the oak; I certainly wasn't aware I was moving. I found myself there, amazed at having covered that distance with the speed of a whirlwind, and when I regained my breath, I could no longer hear anything, nearby or far away. I couldn't see a thing anymore, underneath the tree, or in the bracken, and I wasn't sure I hadn't dreamt the whole thing up, together with the wild music and the malevolent animals.

I began to pull myself together and look at what sort of a place I'd come to. The limbs of the oak covered a large, grassy area, and it was so dark there that I couldn't even see my own feet; the result was that I tripped over a large root and fell, hands first, on the body of a man who was lying there as if dead or asleep. I've no idea what fear made me say or shout out, but my voice was recognized, and immediately Joey's voice answered: 'So it's you, is it, Tiennet? And what are you doing here so late?'

'What about yourself, what are you doing here?' I asked, only too happy and relieved to find him there. 'I've been looking for you all afternoon. Your mother was worried about you, and I thought you must have gone back to her place ages ago.'

'I had things to do here,' he answered, 'and before returning, I was resting, that's all there is to it.'

'Aren't you afraid to be here at night like this in so ugly and gloomy a spot?'

'Afraid of what, and why? I don't understand you, Tiennet.'

I was ashamed to admit to him how stupid I'd been. Nevertheless, I took the risk of asking him whether he hadn't seen people and animals in the clearing.

'Yes, I did,' he answered. 'I saw a lot of animals and people, too, but none of them is the slightest bit evil, and the two of us can go away without any fear of misfortune.'

I imagined from the sound of his voice that he was somewhat amused at my fear, and I left the oak with him. But when we'd gone out of its shadow, it seemed to me that Joey had neither the dimensions nor the appearance he used to have in the past. He appeared to me to be taller, carrying his head higher, walking with a more lively step, and speaking more boldly. That didn't reassure me in the least, for all manner of wild surmises went through my mind. It wasn't just from my grandmother that I'd heard that people whose faces are pale, whose eyes are green, who are habitually sad, and who speak in a way that's hard to follow are likely to form pacts with evil spirits, and, in all countries, old trees are infamous for being haunted by wizards and *others*.

I didn't dare breathe while we were in the bracken, for at every moment I expected to see again those figures that had appeared before me, either in dream or in reality. Everything remained still, and no noise could be heard, except that of the dry branches snapping beneath our feet or some lingering fragments of ice crackling as we walked.

Joseph, who was leading the way, didn't choose the broad path, but cut across the thicket. He reminded me of a hare who knew all the twists and turns, and he led me so quickly to the Igneraie ford,* bypassing the potters' settlement, that I felt I'd got there through some form of enchantment. There he left me without having opened his mouth, except to tell me he wanted his mother to see he was safe and well, since she was worried about him. Then he took the path back to Saint Chartier, while I went straight home through the broad commons.

No sooner had I found myself back in an area I knew, than my anxiety left me and I was very deeply ashamed at not having overcome it. Joey would probably have told me what I wanted to know, if I'd asked him, since, for the first time, he no longer looked half asleep and, just for a moment, I'd caught him out with a laugh in his voice and an air that showed he wanted to be helpful.

Nevertheless, after I'd slept on all this, and my senses had calmed right down again, I felt certain I hadn't dreamt what had taken place in the bracken, and I felt there was really something rather sinister about Joseph's composure. The animals I'd seen there, in such large numbers, weren't any ordinary presence. In our area the only flocks we have are flocks of sheep, and what I'd seen were animals of a quite different size and colour. They were neither horses, nor cattle, nor sheep, nor goats, and in any case, no animals were permitted to feed in the forest.

Today, looking back at myself, I think I was pretty stupid. But all the same, man does interfere in matters where there are unknown elements, especially those matters to which the good Lord alone has the secret.

The fact remains, I didn't have the courage to question Joseph, for if it's a good thing to appear curious where noble ideas are concerned, evil thoughts shouldn't attract your curiosity, and, what's more, you're always put off at the thought of sticking your nose into matters where you might find more than you'd bargained for.

FOURTH EVENING

Something else gave me even more food for thought in the ensuing days. People at the Aulnières farm realized that Joey was occasionally spending the night away from home.

People teased him about it, since they assumed he had some little sweetheart, but however carefully they followed him and spied on him, they never saw him head towards any habitation, or meet any living soul. He would go off across the fields, and melt away so quickly and so cunningly that there was no way anyone was going to discover his secret. He would return at daybreak, and set to work like the others, and instead of appearing weary, he seemed nimbler and happier than usual.

This was observed three times in the course of the winter, which that year was hard and long. There was no snow or wind capable of stopping Joey wandering at night, when the time had come for his whim to be fulfilled. People began to think he was one of those who walk and talk in their sleep, but that had nothing to do with it, as you shall see.

What's more, on Christmas night, as Véret the clogmaker was off to celebrate with his family at Lourouer,* he saw beneath the Rake Elm,* not the giant who is said to walk there often with his rake on his shoulder, but a tall dark man with the air of a rogue, who was murmuring softly with another man, shorter than he was and looking slightly more of a Christian. Véret was not exactly frightened, and walked by them close enough to be able to hear what they were saying. But as soon as the other two had caught sight of him, they separated; the dark man strode off somewhere, and his comrade, going up to Véret, said to him in a voice that struck Véret as strange: 'Where are you off to, Denis Véret?'

The clogmaker began to feel surprised, and knowing that one ought not to reply to things at night, especially when they're near evil trees, he went his way, turning his head in the other direction, but the person he'd considered a spirit followed him, walking behind him, and treading in his footsteps.

When they were at the top of the plain, the pursuer turned off to the left, saying: 'Good evening, Denis Véret.'

And it was only then that Véret recognized Joseph and laughed at himself, but still couldn't imagine for what reason and in what company he had been at the elm between one and two in the morning.

When this story reached my ears, it caused me some distress, and I reproached myself for not having led Joey away from the path of evil it seemed he wanted to take. But I'd let so much time go by that I didn't have the courage to go back. I discussed it with Brulette, whose only response was to laugh it off, which led me to believe that they were secretly in love with each other, and that I'd been taken for a ride, like folk who want to see magic tricks and see only smoke.

I was more upset than angry; Joseph was so crazy and so poor a worker that he seemed to me a really sorry companion, and a weak support for Brulette. I would have felt quite justified in telling her that, even leaving myself out of it, she could have made a better choice, but I didn't have the courage to do so, because I was afraid she'd be angry and I'd lose her friendship, which I still delighted in even if that was all she'd give me.

One evening as I came home, I found Joseph sitting beside a spring called the Spring of Springs.* My house was known in those days as the Par-Dieu Cross, because it was built at a crossing of paths, half of which have since been destroyed. It overlooked that great and splendid grassland which you've recently seen sold and subdivided, but which used to be common land or no man's land. It's a great pity for the poor folk who used to feed their animals there, and who weren't able to buy any of it for themselves. It was a thoroughfare and a broad pasture, bright green, and well irrigated, as it happened, by the beautiful water of the spring, which was not controlled, but wandered hither and yon over a vast sweep of short grass, which was constantly grazed by the flocks, and which delighted all those who looked at it.

I would simply have greeted Joseph and passed on, but he rose and began to walk beside me, trying to chat to me, and appearing so nervous that it made me anxious too.

'Whatever is the matter with you?' I asked him at last, seeing that he spoke in a rambling way, and sighed and twisted his body around as if he'd sat on an ants' nest.

'How can you ask such a question?' he said impatiently. 'Doesn't that have any effect on you? Are you deaf?'

'What do you mean? What is it?' I cried, thinking he was seeing things, and not wanting to have anything to do with it myself.

Then, as I listened, I could just make out in the distance the sound of bagpipes, which didn't strike me as being at all out of the ordinary.

'Well,' I said to him, 'it's just some piper or other returning from a wedding over towards Berthenoux.* What's it to do with you?'

Joseph replied with a self-assured air: 'It's Carnat's bagpipes, but he's not the one who's playing them . . . It's someone who's an even clumsier player than he is!'

'Clumsy! You consider Carnat clumsy when he plays the bagpipes?'

'It's not his hands that are clumsy, but the ideas he expresses, Tiennet! What a wretch! He doesn't deserve to be able to afford the bagpipes! And the person who's trying them out just now would be well served if God drew the breath from his breast.'

'Well, all that's very odd. I don't see what you've got in mind. How can you be sure that's Carnat's bagpipes? It seems to me, personally, that bagpipes are all much of a muchness and they all blare out the same sound. I can certainly hear that whoever is playing there doesn't have the puff he needs, and that the tune is a bit crippled, but that doesn't worry me, since I couldn't even play as well as that. Do you think you could do any better?'

'I don't know! But one thing's sure, there are players who do better than that piper, and better than his teacher, Carnat, too. There are some who know what they're about.'

'Where did you find them? Where are they, these people you're talking about?'

'I don't know, but somewhere or other the truth can be found. The only problem is to stumble upon it, when you don't have the time or the means to seek it out.'

'Can it be, Joey, that you're dreaming of making music? That would really surprise me. All the time I've known you,

you've been as dumb as a fish, never remembering or thinking about any song, and when you tried to play the straw pipes, as a lot of shepherds do, you changed all the tunes you'd heard, so that no one recognized them anymore. Where music's concerned, people thought you even more innocent than all the innocent children who think they're playing bagpipes with a set of reed pipes. Well, if you say Carnat isn't to your taste, although he plays such well-measured dance music for us, and moves his fingers so cleverly, then all I can think is that you don't have a good ear.'

'Yes, yes,' replied Joseph, 'you're right to criticize me, for what I say is stupid, and I'm talking about things I know nothing about. Well and good, sleep well, Tiennet. Forget what I said, because it isn't what I meant to say, but I'll think about it, and try to express it better another time.'

And he was on the point of leaving abruptly, as if sorry he'd spoken, when Brulette, who came out of our house with my sister, stopped him and brought him back to me, saying: 'It's time this matter was cleared up. Here's my cousin, who's listened to so many tales she thinks of Joey as some kind of werewolf, and the time has really come to sort it all out.'

'Have it your own way, then,' Joseph answered. 'I'm sick of being taken for some kind of sorcerer, and I'd much rather be taken for an idiot.'

'No, you're neither an idiot nor a madman,' answered Brulette, 'but you're certainly obstinate, my poor Joey! Let me tell you then, Tiennet, that this boy has nothing bad in mind. It's just that he has a fantasy about music, which is not so much unreasonable as dangerous.'

'Well,' I answered, 'now I understand what he was saying just a minute ago. But where on earth did he stumble across such an idea?'

'Just a moment!' said Brulette. 'Don't let's irritate him unjustly. Don't be so quick to say he's incapable of playing music. Perhaps you think, like his mother and my grandfather, that his mind is closed where music's concerned, as it was in the past at catechism school. If you ask me, it's you and my grandfather and dear Mariton who know nothing about it. Joseph can't sing, and it's not because he's short-winded, but because the sounds don't come out of his throat as he'd like them to. And because he's not happy with himself he prefers not to use his voice at all, seeing that it's so uncontrollable. So, as is only natural, he wants to make music on an instrument whose voice can replace his own, an instrument that'll sing everything that comes into his head. It's because he's always lacked that borrowed voice that our Joey has always been sad or dreamy or somehow lost in a world of his own.'

'It's exactly as she says!' said Joseph, who seemed relieved to hear this lovely young girl free him of his thoughts in making them understandable for me. 'But what she hasn't told you is that she has a voice that can replace mine, a voice so soft, so clear, a voice that repeats so precisely what she hears, that even when I was a small child I used to find my greatest delight in listening to her.'

'But,' Brulette went on, 'we've still got a bone to pick on this subject. I used to like imitating all the little country girls, who, when they watch their flocks, have a tradition of singing their songs at the top of their voices, so they can be heard from a distance. And since by shouting like that I exceeded my strength, I spoilt everything, and hurt Joey's ears. And then, when I settled down to singing in a reasonable way, it turned out that I had such a good memory for all things that can be sung, things that please our Joey, as well as things that drive him into a fury, that more than once I've seen him suddenly give me the slip and go off without saying a word, even though he'd asked me to sing. As far as that goes, he's not always polite and courteous, but, since it's him, I laugh it off instead of getting angry. I know perfectly well that he'll come back, for his memory isn't perfect, and when he hears some song or other that he doesn't consider too ugly, he runs to ask me to sing it, and he's certain to find it in my head.'

I pointed out to Brulette that Joey's lack of memory didn't seem to indicate that he was born to play the bagpipes.

'Heavens above! Now there you're really going to have to turn your judgement inside out. You see, my poor Tiennet, neither you nor I know *what's really what*, as he says. But, by living with his dreams, I've finally understood what he can't or daren't say. *What's really what* is that Joey wants to invent his music himself, and he really does invent it too. He's been able to make a flute out of reeds and he sings on it, I've no idea how, for he's never been willing to let me or anyone else from our house hear him play. When he wants to play his flute, he goes off on a Sunday, and even at night, in places where no one goes, and he plays away to his heart's content. And when I ask him to play for me, he tells me he doesn't yet know what he wants to know, and that he'll entertain me when it's worth my trouble. That's why, ever since he dreamt up this flute-playing, he goes away on Sundays, and sometimes during the week, at night, when the desire to play is too strong. So you see, Tiennet, it's all pretty innocent, but now the three of us really ought to have things out. The thing is that Joey's set his heart on using his first wages (for up to now he's given all his earnings to his mother to keep) to buy a pair of bagpipes, and since he says he's not much good as a worker, and because he'd dearly like to save Mariton from working so hard, he plans to become a professional bagpiper, and it's true that they earn good wages.'

'It would be a good idea,' said my sister, who'd been listening to us, 'if it were really true that Joseph had talent, but before he buys his bagpipes I think he ought to make sure he knows how to use them.'

'Well, all that's just a question of time and patience,' said Brulette. 'But that's not what's holding him up. Don't you know that for quite a while Carnat's boy has also been trying to play the pipes, just so that he can keep his father's place as local piper?'

'Of course,' I answered. 'And I can see what will come of it. Carnat is old, and there would have been the possibility of taking over from him, but his son, who wants the position, will keep it, because he's rich and has a lot of support in the region, whereas you, Joey, you don't yet have enough money to buy bagpipes, you don't have a teacher, and you don't have people who like your music enough to support you.'

'That's what's really what,' said Joey sadly. 'All I have so far is my idea, my reed pipe and *her*.'

So saying, he pointed at Brulette who took his hand in a very friendly fashion and answered: 'Joey, I truly believe in your dream, but I can't tell how that dream is to become a reality. Wanting to do something isn't the same as being able to do it; dreaming and playing the flute are two very different matters. I know you have in your ears, or in your brain, or in your heart, a true form of the good Lord's music, because I saw it in your eyes when I was little, and more than once, sitting me on your knees, you said to me as if you were under a spell: "Listen, don't make a sound and try to remember." Well, then I would listen very carefully, and all I heard was the wind talking in the leaves, or the water shimmering over the pebbles; but you heard something else, and you were so sure you did that I believed it too.

'Well, Joey, keep in your secret heart those pretty songs that you find good and sweet; but don't try to become a minstrel, because if you do one of two things will happen: either you'll never succeed in making your bagpipes say what the wind and water murmur in your ears; or if you do become a great musician, the other little music-makers of our area will quarrel with you and prevent you from playing. They'll wish you ill, and they'll put difficulties in your path, as is their custom, when they want to prevent someone participating in their profits and their prestige. For them it's a question both of money and renown. There's a dozen of them here and in the neighbourhood who don't get on at all well with each other, and who help each other and work together only when it's a question of preventing any new seeds growing in their hay-fields. Your mother, who listens to the pipers chatting on Sundays, for they're all thirsty folk and used to drinking deep into the night after the dances, is very unhappy at the thought that you're considering entering into such a league. They're rough and evil, and they're always the first to throw themselves into quarrels and fist fights. Because they're always either celebrating or unemployed, they're drunkards and spendthrifts. Besides, they're people quite unlike you, and with them you'd go downhill, or so she thinks. I think they're jealous and malevolent, and that they'd crush you underfoot, intellectually and perhaps also physically. And that's why I beg you, Joey, at least to put off your plans and postpone your ambition, perhaps even renounce it altogether, if that's not asking too much of your friendship for me, for your mother and for Tiennet.'

I supported Brulette's argument, for it seemed good to me, much to Joey's despair, but he summoned up his courage and said to us: 'I'm very grateful for your advice, dear friends, because I know you're thinking of my own good, but I would beg you to give me the right to think for myself for just a little while longer. When I've reached the stage I think I can attain, I'll invite you to hear me play the flute or the bagpipes, if it pleases the good Lord to let me buy a pair of bagpipes. Then, if you think I'm worth something, my playing will be good enough for me to make use of it, and for me to wage war for the love of music. If not, I'll go on digging the earth, and I'll amuse myself with my flute-playing on Sundays, without profiting from it or offending anyone by it. Promise me that, and I'll be patient.'

We promised him we would, just to calm him down; for he seemed more offended by our fears than touched by our interest. I looked at him against the night sky, which was studded with stars, and could see him all the better because the spring's fine water lay before us like a mirror that reflected back onto our faces the whiteness of the sky. I could see his eyes, which were of the same colour as the water, and which always seemed to be watching things others couldn't see.

About a month later, Joseph called on me at home. 'The time has come,' he said, looking at me with a clear gaze and speaking in a firm voice, 'when I want the only two people I trust to hear how I can play the flute. So I'd like Brulette to come here tomorrow evening, because then the three of us won't be disturbed. I know your people are setting out tomorrow morning on a pilgrimage, connected with your younger brother's fever; that means you'll be alone in your house, which is so deep in the countryside that we run no risk of being overheard. I've told Brulette, and she's agreed to leave the town after dark; I'll wait for her along the little path, and we'll come here and join you, without anyone being any the wiser. Brulette is relying on you never to breathe a word about it, and her grandfather, who treats her every wish as his command, is also willing, providing you pledge your word of honour, which I've already given for you.'

At the time we'd agreed on, I was standing in the gateway, having closed all the door-casings so that if any peasants should happen to pass, they'd think I was either out or in bed, and I waited for Brulette and Joseph to arrive. It was spring-time, and, as there had been thunderstorms during the day, the sky was still laden with heavy clouds. Warm gusts of wind carried all the lovely fragrances of the month of May. I listened to the nightingales calling to each other in the countryside as far as the ear could hear, and thought that Joseph would have a hard time making music as fine as that. I watched all the little points of light in the houses of the distant town go out one by one; and about ten minutes after the last light had been blown out, I saw the young couple right in front of me. Their footsteps had been so quiet on the fresh grass, and they had so carefully avoided the large bushes growing along the path, that I had neither heard nor seen them coming. I invited them inside, where I'd lit the lamp, and when I saw the two of them, she with her head-dress always so attractively displayed, and with her air of quiet pride, he always so cold, and so lost in thought, I found it hard to think of them as two lovers afire with passion.

While I chatted a little with Brulette to show off the finer points of my house, which was quite attractive, and which I would have liked her to want to live in, Joseph, without saying a word to me, had set about preparing his flute. He found that the damp weather had made it a bit hoarse, and he threw a handful of dried hemp stalks in the fire to warm it up again. When the stalks burst into flame, they sent a great flood of light over his face as he leant towards the hearth, and I felt he looked so strange that I mentioned it in a whisper to Brulette.

'It's all very well for you to think that he hides during the day, and only goes out at night to play his flute to his heart's content, but I myself know that there is within him and about him a secret he's not telling us.'

'Oh!' she laughed, 'you only say that because Véret the clogmaker imagines that he saw him with a great black man at the Rake Elm.'

'Well, it's possible he dreamt it,' I answered, 'but I, for my part, know perfectly well what I heard and saw in the forest.'

'What did you see, Tiennet?' Joey asked suddenly, having heard every word of our conversation, although we were talking so softly. 'What did you hear? What you saw was my friend, and I can't show him to you, but what you heard, you're going to hear again, if you like.'

On that he blew into his flute, his eyes aflame and his face glowing as if in fever.

Don't ask me what he played on his flute. Maybe the devil could have recognized the tune, but as for me I couldn't place it at all, except that it did seem to me that it was the same tune I'd heard played on the bagpipes in the bracken. But when I'd heard it then I was so terrified that I didn't bother much about listening to it all. Now, either because the piece was long or because Joseph improvised, he didn't stop playing for at least a quarter of an hour, his fingers moving so delicately, never getting short of breath and making such a full sound on his wretched reed that at certain moments you'd have thought there were three bagpipes playing all together. At other times, the music was so quiet you could hear the cricket in the house and the nightingale outside; and when Joey played softly I admit it gave me great pleasure, although the piece as a whole was so unlike what we're used to hearing that it made me think of a witches' sabbath for madmen.

'Hey there!' I said to him when he'd finished. 'That's certainly mad music! Where the devil did you get that? What's the point of it, and what's it supposed to mean?'

He didn't give me any sort of answer, and didn't even seem to hear me at all. He was watching Brulette, who was leaning back against a chair with her face turned towards the wall.

As she didn't say a word, Joey suddenly blazed with anger, perhaps with her, perhaps with himself, and I saw that he was about to snap his flute between his hands, but at that moment the beautiful girl looked in his direction, and I was astounded to see tears pouring down her cheeks.

Then Joey ran to her, and, seizing her hands in his own, asked: 'Tell me what this means, sweetheart. Tell me if you're crying because you pity me or if it's because you're happy.'

'I don't know,' she answered, 'whether enjoying something like that can make you cry. So don't ask me if it's because I'm pleased or sad; all I know is that I can't help it.'

'But what did you think about while I was playing?' asked Joey, watching her closely.

'I thought of so many things that I couldn't describe them all to you.'

'Just tell me about one of them then,' he insisted, in a tone of voice that hesitated between impatience and command.

'I didn't think about anything,' said Brulette, 'but I remembered hundreds of moments from my past. I didn't seem to see you playing, although I could hear you quite clearly; but I thought I saw you at the age when we lived together, and I felt I was carried towards you by a high wind that floated us over ripe corn or over wild grass or running water, and I could see meadows and woods and springs, fields full of flowers, and skies full of birds swooping through the clouds. In my dream I also saw your mother and my grandfather sitting in front of the fire and chatting about things I couldn't hear, while you were kneeling in a corner saying your prayers, and I felt I was asleep in my little bed. And I saw the earth covered with snow, and traps filled with skylarks, and nights bright with shooting stars, and we were watching them, the two of us sitting on a little mound while the animals made the small munching sounds they make when browsing on grass. Indeed, I saw so many dreams that they're all confused in my mind, and if that made me want to cry, it's not because I'm unhappy, but because it shook me in a way I don't want to explain to you at all.'

'That's wonderful,' said Joey. 'That's what I was thinking about and what I saw when I was playing my flute, and you saw it too! Thank you Brulette! Thanks to you I know I'm not mad, and that there is a measure of truth in what you hear as well as in what you see. Yes, yes,' he went on, striding around the room and holding his flute above his head, 'this wretched bit of reed does speak; it does say what you're thinking; it shows you things as if you saw them with your eyes; it tells stories with words; it loves as we love with our hearts; it lives and exists! And now Joey the madman, Joey the innocent,

Joey the dullard, you can come out of your imbecility; you are as strong, as knowledgeable, as happy as anyone else!'

So saying, he sat down without paying the slightest attention to anything else that happened around him.

FIFTH EVENING

We stared at him, Brulette and I, for this was no longer the Joey we'd known. My own feeling was that it was all rather like the stories told in our region about the master pipers who, so it's rumoured, can make the wildest beasts fall asleep and lead packs of wolves by night along the pathways, as you or I might lead our flocks to the fields. Joey didn't seem to me at all his normal self as he sat before me. Formerly puny and pale, he now appeared taller and better-looking, just as he'd looked when I'd seen him in the forest. He'd become good-looking, his eyes gleamed like rays from a star, and if anyone had judged him the most attractive lad in the world they wouldn't have been wrong at that moment.

It also struck me that Brulette was charmed and bewitched by him, because she had seen so many things in that flute music when I'd seen nothing at all, and I was wasting my breath telling her that Joey's music would never make anyone dance, apart from the devil, she didn't listen to a word I said, but begged him to begin all over again.

He set about it willingly, starting out with an air that resembled the first one, but that nevertheless was not exactly the same. That showed me he hadn't yet had any change of heart, and was quite unwilling to conform to the style of our region. Seeing how intently Brulette listened and seemed to delight in it, I made a real mental effort to enjoy it too, and it seemed to me that I grew so used to that sort of music that my heart, too, was moved by it, for I too had a kind of dream and I thought I saw Brulette dancing all alone in the light of a fine moon under flowering bushes of white mayflower, and shaking her pink apron as if she were about to fly away. But suddenly I heard nearby the sound of a little bell, just like the one I'd heard in the bracken, and Joey's flute playing stopped as if cut off right in the middle.

Then I awoke from my dreaming and realized that the little bell was no dream. I saw Joey had stopped playing, had leaped to his feet, and looked utterly taken aback, and that Brulette was staring at him, just as astonished as I was myself.

Then all my fears came flooding back. 'Joey,' I said to him reproachfully, 'there's more to this than you're admitting! You didn't learn what you know all on your own. Outside you have a companion who answers you whether you will or no. Now look, send him on his way quickly, because I don't want him in my house. I invited you, but I didn't invite him, or any of his band. Tell him to be off, or I'll sing him a refrain that will really make him angry.'

So saying, I took down from the chimney piece an old rifle belonging to my father. I knew it was loaded with three bullets blessed by the priest, for the Great Beast has always been in the habit of frolicking around the Spring of Springs, and although I'd never seen it, I was always ready to receive it, knowing that my family stood in great fear of it and that it had frequently molested them.

Instead of answering me, Joey burst out laughing and, calling his dog, went to open the door. My own dog had followed my people on their pilgrimage, so I couldn't check whether it was the real world or the spirit world that was making the bell sounds outside, for you know that animals, and dogs in particular, are well versed in this question, and bark in a way that conveys their knowledge to humans.

It's certainly true that Parpluche, Joey's dog, instead of flying into a fury, had rushed ahead to the door, and that he leapt out joyously when he saw it opened; but it was possible that the dog had also been bewitched, and as far as I was concerned none of this bode any good at all.

Joey went out, and the wind, which had risen again, immediately blew the door shut between him and us. Brulette, who had also jumped up, seemed about to open it again to see what was going on; but I quickly stopped her, remonstrating with her that there was some evil secret in all this, a statement that frightened her, and made her wish she'd never come.

'Don't be scared, Brulette,' I said to her. 'I believe in evil spirits, but I'm not afraid of them. They harm only those who seek them out, and the most they can do to true Christians is to give them a fright. But that fear is something one can and should resist. Listen, you say a prayer and I'll guard the door, and you can be sure nothing harmful will come in here.'

'But the poor lad,' Brulette answered. 'If he's got into bad ways, shouldn't we try to bring him back?'

I motioned to her to be quiet, and standing behind the door with my rifle loaded, I listened as hard as I could. The wind was blowing hard, and the little bell could be heard only intermittently, and seemed to be going away. Brulette stayed at the back of the house, half laughing, half trembling, for she was a girl without many worries who frequently mocked the devil, but who, for all that, had no wish to meet him.

Suddenly, not far from the door, I heard Joey's voice as he returned, saying: 'Yes, yes! As soon as Midsummer's Day* comes! My thanks to you, and to the good Lord! I'll do as you ask, I promise you that.'

As he spoke of the good Lord, my courage returned to me and opening the door a little, I looked outside, and by the light coming from the house I recognized Joey beside a man who looked really ugly, for he was black from head to toe, including his face and his hands, and behind him he had two great dogs as black as himself, who were prancing about with Joey's dog. And then he answered with so loud a voice that Brulette heard him and trembled: 'Farewell, my boy, until we see each other again. Here, Clairin.'

No sooner had he said that than the bell jingled and jangled, and I saw a skinny little horse come bounding up to him, its coat rough and hairy, and its eyes like glowing coals, and on its neck a bell gleaming like gold. 'Bring in your herd!' said the tall black man. The little horse galloped off, followed by the dogs, and their master, shaking Joey's hand, set off too. Joey came back in and shut the door, saying to me with a mocking air: 'Now just what are you doing, Tiennet?'

'And you, Joey, what have you got there?' I replied, for I could see that he had under his arm a package wrapped up in a black cloth.

'That? The good Lord has sent it to me at the promised time! Come here, Tiennet! Come here, Brulette! Look, look at the fine present the Lord has given me!'

'The good Lord doesn't have angels as black as that, and He doesn't give anything to evil doers.'

'Be quiet,' said Brulette. 'Let him tell us what's happened.'

But barely had she finished speaking when, from the great grassy path of the Spring of Springs, no more than twenty paces from the house, and separated from it only by the garden and the hemp field, there came the noise of a mad witches' sabbath, as if two hundred demented animals were all galloping about at the same time. And the bell jangled, the dogs barked, and the loud voice of the black man was shouting: 'Quickly, quickly, here, here, to me, Clairin, closer, closer. There are still three missing! Your turn Wolfcub, your turn Satan! Quickly, quickly, let's go!'

Now this really gave Brulette such a fright that she stepped back from Joey and came to stand beside me, which put great heart in me, so that I took up my rifle again, and said to Joseph: 'I've no intention of letting your friends celebrate at night around here. Brulette has had enough of it, and she'd very much like to be safely back home. Now, you bring an end to this spell, or I'll send your witches packing.'

Joey stopped me as I was on the point of leaving. 'Stay there,' he said to me, 'and don't go interfering with things that don't concern you. You could come to regret it later on. Keep quiet and look at what I've brought you, then you'll know what's going on.'

As the din was fading into the distance, I agreed to look, all the more so as Brulette was wild to know what the package was, and when Joseph had unwrapped it, he revealed bagpipes so large, so plump, so beautiful that they truly were something wonderful, quite unlike anything I'd ever seen.

The pipes had a double drone, one of which, when completely assembled, measured five feet in length, and all the wood used in the instrument, which was of black cherry, dazzled your eyes with all its lead embellishments, which gleamed as if they were made of fine silver, and were encrusted over all the joins. The wind bag was made of fine leather, clad with a cover in blue-and-white-striped calico. And all the work that had gone into it had been done in so craftsmanlike a fashion that all you had to do was puff lightly to fill the whole instrument and create a sound like a clap of thunder.

'So the die has been cast, then?' asked Brulette, to whom Joseph barely listened, he was so happy undoing and reassembling all the sections of his bagpipes. 'You're going to become a piper, Joey, with no care for the difficulties in your way and for the worry it'll cause your mother.'

'I'll be a piper,' he said, 'when I know how to pipe. Until then, a lot of wheat will grow in the fields and a lot of leaves will fall in the woods. Don't let's worry about what will happen, but just bear in mind what the facts are now, and don't let me hear you accusing me of being in league with the devil any more.

'The man who brought me this is neither a wizard nor a demon. He's a bit rough at times, his work obliges him to be so, and, as he's going to spend the night not far from here, I'd advise and beg you, Tiennet, not to go in his direction. Forgive me for not telling you his name and what work he does; what's more, you must promise me not to say you've seen him or that he went this way. That could bring trouble not just to him, but to us as well. All you need to know is that he's a man of good counsel and good judgement. He's the one you heard in the bracken of the Saint Chartier forest, playing a set of bagpipes like this. Although he's not a piper by trade, he knows a great deal about them, and played tunes for me that are much more beautiful than any of ours. He's the one who realized that, because I didn't have enough money, I was prevented from buying such an instrument, and he was willing to accept a small deposit and trust me for the rest. He promised to bring me the instrument about this time, and he's willing to wait for the rest of his money until I can afford to pay him. For these pipes cost a good eight pistoles, you see, and that's almost a year's salary for me. Well, I had only a third of that sum, and he said to me: "If you trust me, hand it over, and I'll trust you in just the same way." That's how it came about; I didn't know him at all, and we had no witnesses, so he could have swindled me if he'd wanted to do so.

And if I'd asked you for your advice, you've got to agree you'd have tried to dissuade me. But you can see that he really is a man of his word, for he said to me: "I'll be going past your village around next Christmas, and I'll give you your answer then." At Christmas time, I waited for him at the Rake Elm, and he went by and said to me: "They aren't finished yet, they're working on them. Between the first and the tenth of May, I'll pass this way again and I'll bring them to you." And here we are on the eighth of May. He was in our area, and, just as he was going a little out of his way to seek me out in the village, he heard the music I was playing on the flute as he went past us, and knew that I alone in this region knew that melody. And I for my part heard and recognized his clairin. And that's how it came about, without the devil playing any role in it, that we greeted each other, promising to see each other again on Midsummer's Day.'

'If that's the way of it,' I answered, 'why didn't you ask him to come in here, where he could have rested and re-freshed himself with a good glass of wine? I'd have given him a warm welcome for having carried out his promise to you so honourably.'

'Oh! as for that,' said Joey, 'he's a man who doesn't always behave like others. He has his little ways, his ideas and his reasons. Don't ask me for more than I can tell you.'

'So he hides from honest folk, does he?' asked Brulette. 'That strikes me as being worse than a wizard. He's someone who does evil deeds, since he travels at night and you can't introduce him to your friends.'

'I'll tell you all that tomorrow,' said Joseph, smiling at her fears. 'As far as this evening is concerned, you can think what you like, but I won't tell you any more. Come on Brulette, you can see the cuckoo says it's midnight. I'm going to take you home, and I'll leave my bagpipes with you, where they'll be safely hidden. You know I can't try them out anywhere around here, and it isn't yet time to make myself known as a piper.'

Brulette bid me goodnight very warmly, putting her hand in mine. But when I saw that she put her whole arm in Joseph's to walk off with him, jealousy once more rushed through my veins. I let them set off on the path, and taking a direct short cut beside the hemp field, I crossed the little meadow and hid behind the hedge to see them pass by together. The weather had cleared a little, and, as rain had fallen, I saw Brulette let go of Joseph's arm to lift up her dress more easily, saying to him: 'It's not easy to walk side by side along here. You go first.'

In Joey's place, I'd have offered to carry her along such a bad path, or, if I hadn't dared take her in my arms, at the very least I'd have gone behind to feed my eyes to my heart's content on her pretty legs. But Joey did nothing of the sort. The only thing in the world he was concerned about was his bagpipes, and, watching him fold them up carefully and gaze on them lovingly, I could see perfectly well that for the moment they were his heart's sole desire.

I went back home much more reassured, and went to bed, a little weary both in body and in mind.

But I'd hardly been there more than ten minutes when I was woken up by Monsieur Parpluche, who, having frolicked about with the stranger's dogs, came back in search of his master, and scratched on my door. I got up to let him in, and, as I did so, I realized there were sounds coming from my oats, which were growing green and tall behind the house. It sounded to me as if the oats were being grazed by the strong teeth and cultivated by the four hooves of some animal to which I hadn't sold my crop before I'd even harvested it, as one might sell one's chickens before they were hatched.

I ran over, armed with the first stick that came to hand and whistling to Parpluche, who took not the slightest notice and went off in search of his master, after he'd sniffed around in the house.

As I came into my little oat field, I could see something rolling on its back, legs in the air, crushing the crop this side and that, getting up, leaping, grazing, and simply taking whatever it wanted. For a moment I didn't dare run towards it, not knowing what sort of an animal it might be. I couldn't see anything clearly apart from the ears, which were too long to belong to a horse, while the body was too black and too fat to be that of a donkey. I went softly up to it. The animal didn't appear to be either bad tempered or wild, and I then realized that it was a mule, even though I'd rarely seen one before, since in our region we don't breed mules, and the mule-drivers rarely pass our way. I was about to seize it and already held it by a few hairs when, lifting its rump and striking out with its hind legs, it gave me a dozen or so kicks from which I didn't have time to protect myself. Then it leapt over the ditch like a hare and disappeared so fast that in a second I'd lost sight of it.

I didn't take kindly to the thought of having my crop spoiled if the animal returned, so I put aside all thoughts of sleep until I'd sorted the matter out. I went back to the house to get my coat and shoes, and, closing the doors, I went through the fields in the direction the mule had taken. I had a certain suspicion that it was one of the mule train that belonged to the dark man, Joseph's friend. Moreover, Joseph had advised me to keep my eyes closed. But since I'd set hands on a living animal I no longer felt the slightest fear. No one loves ghosts; but once you're sure you're dealing with something solid, it's a different matter. Given that the dark man was a man, however strong he might be and however much it might suit him to cover his features with dirt, he didn't scare me any more than a weasel.

I'm sure you've heard tell that in my youth I was one of the strongest men in the region, and even now I'm not afraid of anyone.

In addition, I could run like a hare, and I knew that if I got into dangers beyond my power to deal with on my own, you'd have to be a winged bird to catch me in a race. Having taken the precaution of fetching a rope and loading my own rifle, which didn't have any bullets blessed by the priest, but which had a surer aim than my father's, I set out in search of the mule.

I hadn't gone two hundred yards when I saw three other animals just like the first in my brother-in-law's silage field, carrying on in the most dishonest way imaginable. Like the first one, they let me go up to them, but then they immediately took off and disappeared into another property, which was part of the Aulnières farm, where a group of other mules were gambolling about, all in fine fettle, as wide awake as mice, and frolicking in the light of the rising moon in a real *chasse à baudet*, which, as you know, is danced by the devil's donkeys when the sprites and goblins gallop through the clouds above.

Here there was no question of magic. It was a matter of fraudulent use of pasture, and the ravages were abominable. It wasn't my harvest, and I could have said to myself that it was no business of mine; but I felt enraged at having run for nothing after these wicked animals, and you can't watch the good Lord's fine grain being wasted without feeling some regret.

So I went into that great field of wheat in which I could see not one Christian soul, but a great uproar of mules, hoping I could catch one that would serve as proof when I complained about the damage caused to my fields.

I picked out one that seemed more sensible than the others, and when I got close to it, I saw that it wasn't the same kind of beast at all, but the little thin horse that wore a bell around its neck, this bell, as I learnt later, being called the clairin in the Bourbonnais lands, and giving its name to the animal that wears it. Knowing nothing of the customs of the world in which I found myself, it was by the greatest of chances that I happened to choose the best device, which was to get hold of the clairin and lead it away, by which method I might succeed in attracting a mule or two as well.

The little animal, which struck me as affectionate and tame, let me pat it and lead it off without the slightest difficulty; but as soon as it began to walk its bell began ringing, and to my great surprise I saw all the mules gallop up from where they had scattered through the corn, and they flew behind me like bees following their queen. I saw by this that they were trained to follow the clairin, and that they recognized the sound of the bell, just as good monks recognize the matins bell.

SIXTH EVENING

I didn't have long to wonder about what I would do with this band of criminals. I headed straight for the Aulnières farm, thinking, correctly, that I would have no trouble opening the gate into the farmyard, take all my tribe in there, and then I'd be able to wake up the farmers who, told about the damage, could do as they saw fit.

I was approaching the farm when, by chance, I thought I saw on the road a man running behind me. I loaded my rifle, thinking that if it were the mules' owner, I'd have a bone to pick with him.

But it was Joseph, returning to Aulnières from having taken Brulette home.

'Whatever are you doing, Tiennet?' he asked as soon as he caught up with me, running as fast as he could. 'Didn't I warn you not to leave home? You're putting yourself in mortal danger: leave that horse and don't worry about the animals. When something can't be prevented, it's better to put up with it than to go in search of something worse.'

'Thanks, my fine friend,' I replied. 'You've got some pretty nice pals, who come and let all their cavalry feed on my pastures, and I'm supposed not to open my mouth? Well and good! Go your ways if you're afraid, but as for me, I'm going right to the end and I'll get my rights either by justice or by force.'

As I was saying this, having stopped with the animals to answer him, we heard a barking in the distance and Joey, violently seizing the rope I'd been using to lead the horse, said to me: 'Watch out, Tiennet! Here come the mule-driver's dogs. If you don't want to be eaten, let the clairin go. And here he is, too, for he's recognized his watchdogs' voices and you're really in trouble now.'

He was telling the truth; the clairin had pricked his ears to listen, then, laying them flat back, which is a sign of deep scorn, he began neighing, leaping, and bucking, making all the mules around us start dancing about, so that we only just had time to withdraw, letting the whole lot go off at top speed in the direction of the dogs.

I wasn't at all happy about giving up and as the dogs, having assembled their maddened herd, looked as if they were coming to us to bring us to book, I prepared to put a bullet into the first of the two that approached me.

But Joey went towards him and the dog recognized him. 'Well, Satan,' he said, 'you've been a bad dog. You were amusing yourselves chasing some hare in the wheat instead of guarding your animals, and when your master wakes up, you'll be in real trouble if you're not at your post, with Wolfcub and the clairin.'

Satan understood that his behaviour was being criticized, and obeyed Joey, who called him over towards a large fallow field where the mules could feed without causing any damage, and where Joey told me he'd stay and watch them until their master returned.

'That's all very well, Joey,' I answered. 'It's not going to pass over as simply as you think, and if you won't tell me where these mules' master is hiding, I'll stay here and wait for him too, to let him know what's what, and to insist he repay me for the damage he's caused.'

'I can see you know nothing about mule-drivers' lives, since you think it's so easy to push them about. And I think it's true that this is the first time a mule-driver has come this way. This isn't their normal route, for they usually go down from the Bourbonnais woods through those of Meillant and L'Epinasse to reach the woods of Cheurre.* It's just by sheer chance that I happened to meet some mule-drivers in the Saint Chartier forest where they were resting en route to Saint Août, and among them was this one, whose name is Huriel,* and who's now going to the Ardentes* ironworks bringing coal and minerals. He was quite willing to add a couple of hours to his route to help me out. The result is that having left his companions and the heath lands which lie along the route such mule-drivers usually take, and where the mules can graze without harming anyone, he may well have thought he could do the same in our grain-growing country. And even though it's very wrong of him, it won't be easy to make him understand that he hasn't the right to do so.'

'Oh yes it will,' I replied. 'He's just going to have to hear it from me, since now I know what it's all about. Oh! Mule-

drivers! We know what they are, and you remind me of
what I've heard my godfather Gervais the forester say. Those
are wild people, evil and uncouth, who'd kill a man in a
wood with as little conscience as they'd kill a rabbit. They
think they've the right to feed their animals scot-free, at the
peasants' expense, and if you don't like it and they're not
numerous enough to resist, they come back later with their
companions to kill off your cattle, burn your buildings or
worse still, since they're as thick as thieves.'

'Since you've heard tell of such things,' said Joseph, 'you
can see that with so small an amount of damage we'd be
wrong to make the farmers run a bigger risk, not to mention
your family. I certainly don't approve of what's happened,
and when master Huriel told me he was going to pasture his
animals here, and sleep under the stars as they do in all
weathers and all places, I showed him that stubble, and advised him not to let his mules wander in the sown fields. He
promised me he wouldn't, for he isn't ill-intentioned; but he's
hot-blooded and he wouldn't run away from a band of men
who attacked him. Of course he could remain here, but I ask
you, Tiennet, whether the loss of ten or twelve bushels of
grain (and I'm estimating it on the high side) is worth a man's
life and all that ensues for those responsible. So go back to
your property, drive off the wicked animals, but don't go
picking quarrels with anyone. If anyone asks you anything
tomorrow, say you saw nothing, for bearing witness against a
mule-driver in the courts is almost as bad as bearing witness
against a lord.'

Joseph was right. I had to yield to the inevitable, and I
took the path back to our house. But I wasn't happy about
it for all that, since withdrawing in the face of a threat is a
wise course for the old, but a source of chagrin for the
young.

I was nearing our house, fully determined not to go back to
bed, when I thought I could see a light in it. I redoubled my
steps, and finding the door wide open, although I'd left it
latched, I went forward without hesitating and saw a man in
my chimney place, lighting his pipe from a blaze he had lit. He
turned to look at me as calmly as if it was I who was entering

his house, and I recognized the coal-covered man whom Joseph had called Huriel.

Then I was seized with anger again and closing the door behind me: 'Good!' I said striding over to him. 'I'm glad you've come into the wolf's den. We've got a word or two to say to each other now.'

'Three, if you like,' he said, squatting on his heels and drawing the fire into his pipe, for the tobacco was damp and wouldn't catch. 'In your house there isn't even a handful of coal to catch fire!'

'No, but there is a good stick to warm your shoulders.'

'Whatever for, if I can ask?' he said without losing an ounce of his self-assurance. 'You're angry about my coming in without asking your permission? Why weren't you here? I knocked on the door to ask for fire, no one refuses that. Silence implies consent, so I pushed the latch. Why don't you have a lock if you're afraid of thieves? I looked towards the beds, I found the house empty. I lit my pipe and here I am. Whatever can you complain about in that?'

In saying these words, he picked up his rifle as if to examine the breech, but it was to let me know that if I was armed, so was he, and that two could play at that game.

It crossed my mind to take aim at him, just to make him behave respectfully, but as I looked at his blackened face, I found in it so open an air, and an eye so lively and so good-natured, that I felt less anger than pride. He was a young man of about twenty-five at the very most, tall and strong, and, had he been washed and shaven, he could have been rather attractive. I put my rifle against the wall, and went up to him without any feeling of fear.

'Let's have a talk,' I said, sitting down beside him.

'As you like,' he answered, also putting his rifle against the wall.

'You're the man they call Huriel?'

'And you're Etienne Depardieu?'

'How do you know my name?'

'In the same way you know mine, through our young friend, Joseph Picot.'

'So it's your mules I've just caught?'

'You've just caught my mules?' he said, half standing up in surprise. Then he began to laugh and said: 'You're joking. You don't catch my mules as easily as that.'

'Yes you do,' I said. 'You catch them by leading off the clairin.'

'So you know how to do it, then?' he asked suspiciously. 'And the dogs?'

'There's no need to fear dogs when you have a good rifle in your hands.'

'You're not saying you killed my dogs?' he said, leaping to his feet. And his face blazed with anger, which showed me that if he was jovial by nature, he could, when necessary, be quite terrifying.

'I could have killed your dogs,' I replied. 'I could have taken your animals into a pound on a farm where you'd have found a dozen stout lads to argue with. I didn't do so, because Joseph pointed out to me that you were alone, and that it was cowardly to put a man in a position where he might be killed, just because there had been some damage. I accepted that argument, but now we're one to one. Your animals spoiled my field and my sister's; moreover, you've just come in here in my absence, which is dishonest and insolent. You'll apologize to me for your behaviour, and offer me recompense for the damage to my grain, or else . . .'

'Or else what?' he asked, with a contemptuous laugh.

'Or else we'll plead our case according to the rights and customs of Berry, which I think are the same as those of Bourbonnais, when you take fists for lawyers.'

'So might is right?' he asked, rolling up his sleeves. 'That suits me better than going before the judges, and provided you're alone, and don't act treacherously . . .'

'Let's go outside,' I said to him. 'You'll see that I'm alone. You're wrong to insult me, for when I came in here I had you in my rifle sights. But guns are made for killing wolves and mad dogs. I didn't want to treat you like an animal, and although you're now in a position to shoot me down too, I think it's cowardly for men to resort to bullets, since the good Lord gave us strength instead. You don't seem to me to be any more one-armed than I am myself, and if you've any courage . . .'

'My lad,' he said, drawing me up to the fire to look at me, 'you could be making a mistake. You're younger than me, and although you look lean and solid, I won't guarantee you'll come out of it whole. I'd rather you asked me politely to pay you what I owe you and trust to my justice.'

'That's enough of that,' I answered, knocking his hat into the ashes to make him angry. 'It'll be the one who's most beaten who'll be the most polite in a few minutes.'

He picked his hat up calmly, put it on the table and said: 'What are your customs here?'

'Between young men,' I answered, 'there's no cheating and no treachery. We wrestle, and we strike each other wherever we can, except in the face. Anyone who takes a stick or a stone is considered a scoundrel and an assassin.'

'That's how we do it, too. Come on then. I intend to spare you, but if I go at it more intently than I mean to, give up, because there comes a moment, as you know, when you can't really answer for yourself any more.'

When we were outside, on the short grass, we took off our coats, so as not to cause any useless damage, and began to fight, grasping each other's sides and lifting each other up. I had the upper hand because he was a head taller than I, and his great length gave me a better target. Moreover, he wasn't angry, and because he thought he'd best me too quickly, he didn't use all his strength. The result was that I knocked him down at the third attempt, and stretched him out under me, but he mustered his strength, and, before I had the time to hit him, he rolled over like a snake, and grasped me so tightly I couldn't breathe.

Somehow I managed to get up before he did and to attack him again. When he saw he was dealing with someone serious, and was receiving heavy blows to the stomach and shoulders, he also dealt me some violent blows, and I have to admit his fist weighed as much as a smithy's hammer. But I'd have died rather than let anything show, and each time he shouted 'Give in!', I found the heart and strength to repay him in his own coin.

The result was that for a good quarter-hour the fight seemed equal. At last I felt I was tiring, while he was only just getting into the swing of things, for even if his reflexes were no better than mine, he had age and temperament on his side. Eventually, through sheer strength, I found myself underneath and firmly beaten without a chance of getting out. Nevertheless, I wouldn't plead for mercy, and when he saw I'd let myself be killed first, he behaved with real generosity. 'That's enough,' he said, letting go of my throat. 'Your head's harder than your bones, I can see. And I'd break them for you before I could get you to give in. All the better! Since you're a man, let's be friends. I apologize for going into your house. Now let's see the damage my mules caused. I'm ready to pay you as sincerely as I beat you. Afterwards, you'll give me a glass of wine so we can leave each other on friendly terms.'

Once the transaction had been concluded and I'd put in my pocket three fine crowns he gave me for myself and my brother-in-law, I went to draw some wine and we sat down at the table. Three two-pint pitchers disappeared in the time it takes to say Jack Robinson, for we'd got pretty thirsty playing that particular game, and master Huriel had a coffer that held as much as you wanted. He struck me as a good companion, a good talker and easygoing. As for me, because I didn't want to drag my feet either in actions or words, I filled his glass every minute, and made him oaths of friendship by the armful.

He didn't seem to feel any after-effects from our struggle, but I certainly did. Not wanting to show it, however, I offered to sing him a song, and even, with some effort, managed to extract one from my throat, which was still warm from the pressure of his hands. All he did was laugh at it.

'My friend, neither you nor your people know anything about singing. Your melodies are insipid, and you're all short of breath, just like your thoughts and your pleasures. You're a race of snails, always breathing the same wind and sucking the same sap. You think the world ends at those blue hills that encircle your sky, the blue hills that are my country's forests. But let me tell you, Tiennet, that's where the world begins, and you could stride along as fast as your legs would take you for many days and nights before you'd leave those great woods, in comparison with which yours are just beds of staked peas. And when you've reached the end of those forests, you'll find mountains, and yet more woods such as you've never seen, for that's where the fine tall firs of the Auvergne grow, which you don't find in these fertile plains. But what's the point of telling you about lands you'll never see? The man from Berry, as I know, is a stone that rolls from one furrow to another, always returning to the right-hand furrow when the plough has pushed it for one season to the left-hand one. He breathes a heavy air, he likes his comfort, he has no curiosity, he cherishes his money and never spends it, but he doesn't know how to increase it, and lacks both invention and courage. I don't mean you, Tiennet, when I say this; you know how to fight, but only to defend your property, and you couldn't acquire any wealth by the sweat of your brow as we do, we wandering spirits who live everywhere as if in our own backyard, and who seize by ruse or strength what people aren't willing to give us.'

'Yes. You're right,' I answered. 'But aren't you leading the life of a brigand? Look, my dear Huriel, wouldn't it be better to be less well off, and have nothing on your conscience? For after all, when you enjoy your ill-gotten gains in your old age, will you have a clear conscience?'

'Ill-gotten? Look, Tiennet my friend,' he said with a laugh, 'I imagine you have, like all the little land-holders of this area, twenty sheep or thereabouts, two or three goats, and perhaps a donkey to feed on the common lands. When you inadvertently let them strip trees and eat the green wheat of a neighbour's field, do you run to offer compensation? Don't you take them away as quickly as possible and say nothing when you see the guards appear? And if they take you to court, don't you swear at them and at the law? And if you could get them in some tight spot, without risk to yourself, wouldn't you pay them what you owe in good cudgel blows? Look! What makes you respect the law is either cowardice or necessity, and if you criticize us, it's because we escape, because you're envious of the freedom we're able to seize!'

'I can't accept a morality so alien to my own, Huriel; but we've got a long way from music. Why did you mock my song? Are you claiming you know better ones?'

'I'm not claiming anything, Tiennet; but I'm telling you that songs, freedom, beautiful wild lands, lively minds, and no offence meant, the art of getting rich without becoming stupid, all that is as closely linked as the fingers on your hand; I tell you that shouting isn't singing, and that you can bellow like the deaf in your fields and your taverns, but all the same that isn't music. Music dwells with us, and not with you. Your friend Joey felt that perfectly well, for his senses are keener than yours; as for you, my poor Tiennet, I can see I'd be wasting my time trying to show you the difference. You're a true Berry man, just as a sparrow is a sparrow, and what you are now is what you'll be fifty years hence; your mane will have gone white, but your brain won't have changed a jot.'

'Why do you take me for such a fool?' I asked, somewhat mortified.

'Fool? Not at all,' he said. 'Open-hearted and clear-sighted in your own interest, that's what you are, and what you'll continue to be. But lively of body and light of soul, you could never be that. Here's why,' he added, pointing to the furniture in the house. 'Here you have fine, well-stuffed beds, where you sleep in down up to your eyebrows. You are men of the spade and the mattock, you perform great tasks in the light of the sun, but then you need an eiderdown of fine feathers to make you sleep. We men of the forest, we'd be ill if we had to bury ourselves alive in sheets and blankets. A hut of branches, a bed of bracken, that's our furniture, and what's more, those of us who travel all the time, and don't care to pay for inns, can't bear a roof over our heads. In the depths of winter, they sleep in the open on the mule packs, and use the snow as their linen. Now here you have dressers and tables, chairs, fine plates and dishes, stoneware cups, fine wine, a pot hanger, soup bowls, and goodness knows what else. You need all that just to be happy. At every meal you spend a good hour loading yourselves up, your jaws work as if you were cows chewing the cud. The result is that when you have to get back on your hindlegs and go back to work, you're depressed, and that depression returns two or three times every day. You're ponderous, and no more light-hearted than your beasts of burden. On Sundays, leaning on your tables, you eat more than you need, and drink more than you want, thinking that you're entertaining yourselves and refreshing yourselves by getting

indigestion. You sigh over girls who think you're lack-lustre
without knowing why, dancing your slow bourrée in rooms or
barns where you're stifled, you turn a day meant for lightness
and rest into yet another weight on your stomachs and spirits;
and as a result the whole week seems to you sadder, longer,
and harder. Yes, Tiennet, that's the sort of life you lead.
Because you're too fond of your creature comforts, you give
yourself too much work, and in order to live well, you don't
live at all.'

'Well then, how do you live, you mule-drivers?' I asked,
rather shaken by his disapproval. 'Look, I can't talk about
your part of the country, Bourbonnais, because I don't know
it at all, but let's talk about you, the mule-driver I've got
sitting opposite me, drinking hard, putting your elbows on the
table, not exactly plunged in gloom at finding a fire somewhere or other to light your pipe and a Christian soul to chat
with. Are you really made any differently from other men?
And when you've led that hard life you're so proud of for
twenty-odd years, and you've got all that money saved from
having deprived yourself of everything, aren't you going to
spend it by getting yourself a wife, a house, a table, a good
bed, some fine wine, and a bit of rest?'

'Now that's a lot of questions all at once, Tiennet. For
someone from Berry, you're not too bad at thinking things
out. I'll try and answer. You can see I'm drinking and chatting, because I like wine and I'm a man. I'm even more fond
of good meals and good company than you are, for the reason
that I don't need them, and they haven't become a habit for
me. Because I'm always on my feet, eating lightly, drinking at
springs I happen across, and sleeping in the shelter of the first
oak I meet, when it does transpire that I find a good table and
plenty of wine, it's a real feast for me, but it's not a need.
Often I live alone for weeks on end, so that the company of a
friend turns any day into a holiday, and in an hour's conversation I can tell him more than in a whole day spent in a
tavern. So I enjoy everything more than you folk do, because
I don't over-indulge in anything. If a nice young girl or a
determined woman comes to seek me out in my copse, she
does so because she wants to tell me that she loves me or

desires me. She knows perfectly well that I don't have the time to go and hang around her for hours, like a fool, waiting until she can give me some of her time, and I confess that where love is concerned, I love what can be chanced upon, and not what you have to seek out and wait for. As for the future, Tiennet, I don't know if I'll have a house and family, but if that happens, I'll be more grateful than you to the good Lord, and I'll appreciate my good fortune better than you would. But I swear that my housekeeper won't be one of your fat, red-cheeked girls even if she has 20,000 crowns for her dowry. Anyone who loves freedom, and true happiness, doesn't marry for money. I'll never love any girl who isn't as pale and slim as our birch trees, one of those sweet, alert lasses that grow in the shade of our woods, and sing better than your nightingales.'

A girl like Brulette, I thought. Fortunately she's not here, because it would be just like her, who despises all the men she knows, to fall head over heels in love with this mud-daubed man just on a whim.

The mule-driver went on: 'So, Tiennet, I'm not criticizing you for following the path in front of you, but my path goes further and pleases me more. I'm glad to know you, and if ever you need me, just call me. I don't ask you to do the same for me, because I know that when a plain dweller has to travel a dozen leagues to visit a relative or friend, he makes his confession to the priest and draws up his will. For us, it's different. We fly like the swallows, and you can find us almost anywhere. Until we meet again, then, give me your hand, and if ever you tire of your life on the land, call the black crow of Bourbonnais to your aid. He'll remember that he piped a tune on your back without anger, and that he gave in to you because he valued your fine courage.'

SEVENTH EVENING

At that, Huriel went off in search of Joseph and I sought my bed, despite the mule-driver's derision, for if, until then, a desire to save face had made me hide, and curiosity had made me forget, the pain I felt in my bones, I was none the less dead beat, from head to toe. It seems that master Huriel set off again quite cheerfully, without any after-effects, but for my part I was obliged to spend about a week in bed, for I was spitting blood and my stomach felt as though it had been torn from its roots. Joseph came to pay a visit and was amazed to see me in such a state; but through a sense of shame I had no wish to tell him what had happened, since Huriel, in talking about me, hadn't mentioned quite how we'd reached our understanding.

In the farms around us there was great amazement at the damage to the Aulnières wheat, and the tracks of the mules along our paths set imaginations afire.

When I gave my brother-in-law the money I'd won for him at such cost, I told him everything, but I swore him to secrecy, and as he was a good and prudent lad, the story went no further.

Meanwhile, Joseph had hidden his bagpipes in Brulette's house and couldn't use them, because, first, haymaking left him no time to do so, and, secondly, Brulette was afraid of Carnat's spitefulness, and was still trying to make him give up the whole idea.

Joseph pretended to accept her arguments, but it was soon apparent to us that he was working out a new plan, and was hoping to be hired in another parish where he'd have more elbow room.

As Midsummer's Day drew closer, he no longer made a secret of this plan, and advised his master to find another ploughman, but he refused to tell us where he wanted to go, and since he habitually answered 'I don't know' to everything he wanted kept secret, we really assumed he was going to hire himself out like all the others, without having any fixed plan in mind.

As the hiring fair is the occasion of great merrymaking in our town, Brulette went along for the dancing, and so did I. We thought we might well find Joseph and discover by the end of the day who his new master would be, and what place he'd decided on, but neither in the morning nor in the evening did he appear in the town square. No one saw him anywhere in the town. He'd left his bagpipes with Brulette, but on the previous day he'd taken away all the belongings he normally left in père Brulet's house.

As we were returning home that evening, Brulette and I, with the full throng of her beaux and with other girls from our parish, she took my arm and, walking with me on the grassy border of the road, she said: 'Tiennet, I'm really worried about Joey. I saw his mother just now in the town, and she's very upset and can't imagine where he can have gone. For a long time now he's been hinting that he's going further away, but there's been no way of finding out where, and today the poor woman is terribly upset.'

'What about you, Brulette,' I asked. 'It strikes me you're far from happy and you didn't seem to dance with the same light-heartedness as on other holidays.'

'You're right there,' she answered. 'I really like that poor lunatic. Partly out of a sense of duty, for his mother's sake, but also because I admire his flute playing.'

'Do you really mean his flute playing had such an effect on you?'

'There's nothing wrong with that, cousin. What criticism can you make of me if I do admire it?'

'Nothing, but . . .'

'Come on, make a clean breast of it,' she said, laughing. 'You've been harping on that string for ages and I'd really like to strike the final chord on the topic, so it'd be over and done with.'

'Well then, Brulette,' I said, 'let's stop talking about Joey and talk about us instead. Can't you get it into your head that I really love you? Can't you tell me whether one day you'll love me too?'

'Oh come on! Are you really serious this time?'

'This time and all other times. It's always been very serious on my part, even if I was so embarrassed I put it in playful terms.'

'Well then,' said Brulette, walking more quickly so the others wouldn't hear. 'Tell me how and why you love me, and then I'll answer you.'

I saw she wanted praise and pretty words, and I wasn't the

greatest player of that particular game. I did my best, and told her that ever since I'd been on this earth, I'd thought only of her, because she was the most lovable and beautiful of girls; even when she was only twelve she'd already bewitched me.

I wasn't telling her anything she didn't know, and she admitted she'd realized it perfectly well in the days of the catechism school. But, teasingly, she said: 'So tell me how come you're not dead from grief, given that I put you so firmly in your place? And how did you manage to grow so strong and healthy, when, so you tell me, love made you wither on the vine?'

'That's hardly the serious explanation you promised me,' I answered.

'Yes indeed it is, because it's meant seriously. For the only man I'll ever choose is the one who could swear that he's looked at me alone, loved me alone, desired me alone in his entire life.'

'Well, if that's the case, Brulette, well and good! I needn't fear anyone, apart from your Joey, who I agree has never looked at any girl, but whose eyes never see anything, not even you, since he's leaving you.'

'Let's leave Joey out of this. I'll agree with you there,' replied Brulette, rather sharply. 'Since you boast you can see so clearly, confess that, despite your liking for me, you've already ogled more than one girl. Look, don't lie, I can't bear lies. What tales were you telling so joyfully to Sylvaine, last year? And not more than a month or two ago, to Bonnin's oldest daughter? You danced with her, under my very nose, two Sundays running. Do you think I'm blind, and that you can pull the wool over my eyes?'

I was rather mortified at first, and then, encouraged by the thought that there was a measure of jealousy in all this, I answered her frankly: 'The tales I told those girls, cousin, weren't pretty enough to be repeated to anyone who respects herself. A boy can fool around to amuse himself, and the regrets he feels about it afterwards prove all the more clearly that his heart and mind weren't involved.'

Brulette turned red. But she answered immediately: 'Well, Tiennet, can you swear to me that my nature and my beauty were never lowered in your esteem by the beauty and sweetness of any other girl, and that that has been the case ever since you came into this world?'

'I'd take my oath on it,' I answered.

'Well, do so. But put your mind and faith into what you're going to say. Swear to me by your mother and father, by the good Lord and your conscience, that no girl has ever seemed to you as lovely as I am.'

I was on the point of swearing, when somehow or other a memory made my tongue tremble. I may have been very simple in paying it any attention, since it wouldn't have been worth worrying about for a livelier mind than mine, but I was incapable of lying, at the instant when the image appeared so strongly before my eyes. And yet, I'd forgotten it until that moment, and would never perhaps have thought of it again, had Brulette not asked her questions and made her demands.

'You're in no hurry about it,' she said. 'But I prefer that, since I'd respect you if you said the truth and despise you if you lied.'

'Very well, Brulette!' I answered. 'Since you insist on my being just, you be just, too. In my entire life, I've seen two girls, two children, you might say, and I'd have hummed and hawed about preferring one over the other if anyone had said to me in those days, when I was only a child myself: "Here are the two lasses who'll listen to you later on. Choose the one you'd rather have for wife." No doubt I would have said "My cousin", because I knew you were a friend, and I knew nothing about the other one, having seen her for only ten minutes in all. And yet, now I come to think about it, it's possible I'd have felt some regret, not because she was a more perfect beauty than you are, I don't think that's possible, but because she gave me a warm, good kiss on each cheek, something I hadn't then, and still haven't, ever received from you. Which might have led me to believe that she was the sort of girl who'd give me her heart one day quite openly, whereas the prudent nature of your own heart held me then, and still holds me, in pain and fear.'

'And where's that girl now?' asked Brulette, who seemed struck by what I was saying. 'What's her name?'

She was much amazed to learn that I knew neither her name nor her country, and that in my memory I could call her only 'the maid of the woods'. I told her in all simplicity the little adventure with the bogged cart, and she seized the opportunity to ask me more questions than I could answer, for my memories were already somewhat confused, and I didn't consider such a little matter as important as Brulette wanted to believe it was. Her mind worried away at every word she extracted from me, and she seemed to be asking herself questions, rather regretfully, to see if she was pretty enough to be so demanding, and if the way for a girl to please a man was by being frank or by hiding her feelings.

Perhaps she was tempted, just for a moment, to flirt with me so I'd forget the little phantom I had in my mind, who made her feel more jealousy than she need have. But after a few jesting words, she answered my reproaches by saying: 'No, Tiennet, I won't blame you for having had eyes for a pretty girl, when it's all as innocent and natural as you say it was; but that piece of folly we were playing with has turned my thoughts somehow or other to serious matters concerning you and me. I'm a flirt, cousin, I feel the need to flirt right to the ends of my finger tips, and I don't know how I'll get over it. But, given my nature, I can think of love and marriage only as bringing all comfort and fun to an end. I'm eighteen, and that's already the age when you should start being thoughtful, but being thoughtful still comes to me like a punch in the stomach, whereas you, ever since you turned fifteen or sixteen, were already asking questions about how to be happy in love and marriage. And on that score, your straightforward heart gave you a correct answer: what you needed was a good friend, as candid and just as you are yourself, someone who wasn't malicious or proud or silly. Well, I'd be deceiving you wickedly if I told you I was just right for you. Whether it's capriciousness or distrust on my part, I don't feel drawn to any of the boys I could choose, and I wouldn't want to give my word that I'll change in the near future. The older I get, the more I like my freedom and gaiety. So be my friend, my comrade, my cousin. I'll love you in the same way I love Joey, and even more, if you're a more faithful friend to me than he is. But don't think of marrying me. I know your family would be against it, and I'd be against it in spite of myself, and would be disappointed that I'd let you down. Look, people are staring at us. Here they come running after us to interrupt a conversation that's gone on too long. Will you promise not to hold it against me, resign yourself to the inevitable, and go on being a brother to me? If you say yes, we'll leap over the midsummer fire together, and you and I will gaily open the dance.'

'Very well, Brulette!' I said with a sigh. 'It'll be as you want it. I'll do all in my power not to love you any more, just as you command, and, whatever happens, I'll be a good relative and a good friend to you, as it's my duty to be.'

She took my hand and, delighting in making her beaux run after her, she ran with me to the town square, where already the old people of the area had piled up the logs and straw for the midsummer fire. Since she was the first to arrive, Brulette was asked to light the fire, and soon the flames rose up higher than the church door.

But we had no music to dance by, until Carnat's son, whose name was François, arrived with his bagpipes. He didn't have to be asked twice to help us out, for he, too, had a soft spot for Brulette, just like the rest of us.

We began dancing joyfully, but after a few minutes, everyone complained that the music was no good. François Carnat was still too much of a beginner, and we couldn't get into the rhythm. He didn't mind being teased, and kept going, happy to have a chance to practise, for I think it was the first time he played in public.

But that didn't suit anyone, and when we saw that the dance, instead of refreshing legs that were already weary, merely made them exhausted, there was talk of either going home or of the men going to finish off the evening in a tavern. Brulette and the other girls protested, calling us tipplers and louts; and we were in the middle of debating all this when suddenly a tall, good-looking chap appeared among us, before we'd even seen what direction he came from.

'Well then, boys and girls!' he called out, in a voice so loud it covered all the din we were making and was heard by every single one of us. 'Do you still want to dance? Well, cheer up. Here's a piper who's happened by, and who'll give you as much music as you like. What's more, he'll not even take any money from you for his services. Give me that,' he said to François Carnat, 'and listen to me. You may find it useful, for even if I'm not a musician by trade, I know a little more about it than you do.'

And without waiting for François's agreement, he blew into the bagpipes and began to play, to the cries of the girls and the great gratitude of the boys.

As soon as he'd started speaking I'd recognized the voice and Bourbonnais accent of the mule-driver. But I couldn't believe my eyes, so greatly changed was he, and so much improved by it.

Instead of his coal-stained smock, his old leather gaiters, his dented hat, and his black face, he was wearing new clothes, all in fine white drugget, marbled with blue, his linen was of high quality, and he had a straw hat with ribbons of thirty-six colours. His beard had been trimmed, his face washed and as pink as a peach: in short, he was the most handsome man I'd ever set eyes on in my life: as tall as an oak, his body well formed, his legs taut and muscular, his teeth like a chaplet of ivory beads, his eyes like two knife blades, and all this with the attractive air of a kindly lord. He ogled all our girls, smiling at those who were pretty, laughing from ear to ear at those who lacked grace, but showing himself to be a joyful and good companion to everyone, encouraging and enlivening the dance with his eyes, his feet and his voice, for he blew only lightly into the pipes, so clever was he at controlling his wind, and between each blow he would tell us a thousand quips and jokes which made everyone madly happy.

Moreover, instead of counting the repetitions and pauses like the professional minstrels, who stop as soon as they've earned their two sous per couple, he piped for a good fifteen minutes, changing his tunes subtly, for he moved from one to the other seamlessly. And he gave us the finest dances in the world, all unknown to us, but so attractive and so easy to dance to that we seemed to fly through the air rather than jig on the grass.

I truly think he would have piped and we would have danced all night without either party growing weary, if he hadn't been interrupted by père Carnat, who was in the inn run by mère Biaude and heard his pipes played so well that he hastened over full of astonishment and pride at his boy's skill. But when he saw a stranger holding the instrument, and François taking his part in the dance without feeling anything was amiss, he was overwhelmed with rage and, shoving the mule-driver unexpectedly, made him stumble and fall from the rock he stood on, right into the middle of the dance.

Huriel was somewhat surprised at such treatment, and turning round, saw Carnat in a fury, ordering him to give the instrument back to him.

You never knew Carnat the piper; even in those days he was fairly elderly, but he was still solid and as spiteful as an old devil.

The mule-driver was on the point of showing him his fist, but held back by the sight of Carnat's white hair, he returned the bagpipes calmly and answered: 'You could have warned me in a more gentlemanly fashion, old chap; but if it annoys you to see me take your place I'll give it back with all my heart, and all the more so as I'd be delighted to have a turn at dancing, if the young people of this region will accept a stranger in their company.'

'Yes, yes, dance! You've earned it!' the whole parish shouted out. Everyone had gathered around his fine music and already they were wild about it, the old just as much as the young.

'Well, then,' he said, taking Brulette by the hand, whom he'd looked at more than any other girl, 'I request as payment to be allowed to dance with this pretty blonde girl, even if she's already promised the dance to another.'

'She's promised it to me, Huriel,' I answered, 'but as we're friends, I'll yield my right to this dance.'

'Thanks!' he replied, shaking my hand. And he added in my ear: 'I didn't want to give the impression I knew you, but if you see nothing wrong in it, then all the better!'

'Just don't tell people you're a mule-driver and all will be well.'

While everyone was asking me about the stranger, another question arose on the minstrel's stone: old Carnat was unwilling either to play himself or to let his boy play. What's more, he sharply scolded him for letting a stranger take his place, and the more people tried to smooth things over by telling him that Huriel wasn't taking any money for it, the more furious he became. He reached the point of going berserk when père Maurice Viaud told him he was envious, and that the stranger could give a lesson to all the pipers in the region.

Then he came and stood in the middle of our group and, addressing Huriel, asked him if he had a permit to play the pipes, which made everyone laugh, the mule-driver more than anyone else. Finally, when this old crosspatch insisted that he answer, Huriel told him: 'I don't know the customs of this region, old chap; but I've travelled enough to know what the law is, and I know that nowhere in France do artists need a permit.'

'Artists?' asked Carnat, astonished at this word that he, no more than the rest of us, had ever heard spoken. 'What do you mean by that? Are you just saying something stupid?'

'Not at all!' answered Huriel. 'I'll use the term "music players" if you like. I can tell you I'm free to play music without paying any duties to the King of France.'

'Well, I know all that, but what you don't know is that, in this region, the music players pay a sum to the fraternity of minstrels to earn a license allowing them to play, and they receive from the minstrels a permit, if they're accepted after a series of examinations.'

'Yes indeed! I know all that, and I know full well how much money changes hands in those examinations. I wouldn't advise you to put me to the test in that way, but fortunately for you, I'm not in your line of business, and I make no claims on you. I play free wherever it pleases me to do so, and that's something no one can prevent me from doing, for the good reason that I have been accepted as a master piper, whereas you who speak so loudly may well not have been.'

Carnat calmed down a little at this, and they each whispered some words that no one else could hear, by which they could tell that they belonged to the same order, if not the same

chapter. Having no more objections to make, given that
everyone bore witness to the fact that Huriel had played
without asking for any payment, the two Carnats withdrew,
grumbling furiously, and muttering rude remarks that no
one wanted to notice, just because we wanted to get it all over
and done with.

As soon as they'd left, we called on Marie Guillard, a little
girl with an excellent voice, and made her sing so that the
stranger could have the pleasure of dancing.

He didn't dance in the same way as the rest of us, but he
fitted in very well with our movements and our beat, although
he had a better way of doing it, and moved his body so freely
that he seemed even more handsome and taller than usual.
Brulette was struck by this, for at the moment when he kissed
her, as is our custom at the beginning of each dance, she went
bright red and looked embarrassed, quite unlike her usual self,
for normally she remained calm and indifferent to such kisses.

That made me believe she'd rather overstated her scorn for
love; but I didn't let my thoughts show, and I admit that, in
spite of everything, I for my part was quite bowled over by the
mule-driver's great abilities and his fine manners.

When the dance was over he came to me, holding Brulette's
hand, and saying to me: 'Your turn, comrade. I can't thank
you any more warmly than by returning your pretty dancer to
you. She's a true beauty of my own country, and because of
her I'll have to make amends to the Berry race. But why end
the festival so early? Doesn't your village contain another set
of pipes than those belonging to our old sourpuss?'

'It does indeed,' said Brulette, whose longing to go on
dancing made her reveal the very secret she'd wanted to keep.
But immediately she caught herself up, blushing, and added:
'At least, there are reed-pipes, and swineherds who can play
more or less presentably.'

'Fie on reed-pipes! If you happen to laugh you swallow
them and that makes you cough. My mouth's too big for that
sort of instrument, and yet I'm the one that wants to make you
dance, sweet Brulette. That is your name, I've heard it,' he
added, moving the two of us a little away from the rest. 'I
know you have in your home a fine and noble set of bagpipes,

that come from the Bourbonnais region, and belong to a certain Joseph Picot, your childhood friend and your companion in the catechism school.'

'Oh! How do you know that?' asked Brulette in astonishment. 'Do you know our Joseph then? Perhaps you could tell us where he's gone.'

'Are you worried about him?' asked Huriel, watching her closely.

'So worried that I'd be heartily grateful to you for telling me what news you have of him.'

'Well, I do have news for you, my sweet, but I won't tell you until you give me his bagpipes, which he's asked me to bring to him in the region where he's now living.'

'What?' asked Brulette. 'He's already far away then?'

'Far enough not to want to come back.'

'Is it true he won't return? Has he really gone away for good? That really makes me feel I don't want to laugh and dance.'

'Oh, my lovely child,' said Huriel. 'Are you that little Joseph's fiancée? He never told me that!'

'I'm no one's fiancée,' Brulette replied, pulling herself up.

'And yet, here's a pledge I've been asked to show you, should you doubt that I've been entrusted to return his bagpipes to him.'

'Where is it? What pledge?' I asked in my turn.

'Look at my ear,' said the mule-driver, lifting a handful of black, tightly curled hair, and showing us a little silver heart, threaded by its ring onto a large ring of fine gold that went through his ear in the fashion of middle-class men in those years.

I truly believe that those pierced ears began to bewitch Brulette, for she said to him: 'You're not what you seem, and I can see perfectly well you're not a man to want to deceive poor folk. Besides, it really is mine, that pledge you wear there; or rather it's Joey's, for it's a gift his mother gave me on the day of my first communion, and that I gave him in remembrance of me, the following day, when he left home to become a ploughman. Well, then, Tiennet, go to our house and find the bagpipes, and bring them here, under the church porch where it's dark. Make sure no one sees where you found them, for père Carnat is an evil man who could cause my grandfather problems, if he knew we'd all helped in such a thing.'

EIGHTH EVENING

I did as I'd been ordered, leaving Brulette alone with the muledriver, very much against my will, in a part of the square which nightfall had already made very dark. When I returned, carrying the bagpipes folded up and dismantled under my smock, I found them still in the same place, chatting very animatedly, and Brulette said to me: 'Tiennet, I call on you as a witness to the fact that I'm not willing to give that man the pledge that's hanging in his ear. He's insisting he won't give it back to me, because it really belongs to Joey, but he says Joey won't take it back from him. It's only a small matter, and isn't worth ten sous, but I don't like giving it to a stranger. I wasn't more than twelve years old when I gave it to Joey, and you'd have to be really finicky to see anything wrong in such a gift, but since it seems there was something wrong in making it, that's yet another reason why I should refuse to give it to someone else.'

It seemed to me that Brulette was trying too hard to convince the mule-driver that she wasn't in love with Joseph, and the mule-driver for his part struck me as being very pleased to find that she was heart whole and fancy free. In any case, he wasn't in the least embarrassed about paying court to her in my presence.

'My sweet,' he said to her, 'you're wrong to mistrust me. I don't want to show your gifts to anyone, although if they'd been given to me I'd have good reason to be proud of them. But I admit here, with Tiennet as witness, that you're not encouraging me to love you. Whether or not that will prevent me from doing so is another question. But at the very least you're forced to put up with the fact that I'll remember you, and that I value this ten sous pledge in my ear, more than anything I've ever desired. Joseph is my friend, and I know he loves you, but that lad's idea of friendship is so sedate it won't even cross his mind to ask me to return the pledge. Well then, if we see each other again in a year or in ten years, you'll find it still there, unless the ear itself is no longer in place.'

So saying, he seized Brulette's hand and kissed it, and then set about assembling and tuning the bagpipes.

'What are you doing?' she asked. 'For my part, as I've told you, given that Joey is leaving his mother and his friends for a long time, I'm too sad to want to amuse myself. As for you, you're running the risk of having a fight on your hands, if other local pipers happen by.'

'Bah! We'll just see about that. Don't you worry about me, and as for you, Brulette, you'll dance, or I'll think you're in love with that ingrate who's leaving you.'

Whether because Brulette was too proud to let him think that of her, or because the devil of the dance was stronger than she was, as soon as the bagpipes had been assembled and Huriel had blown into them, their sound was such that she couldn't keep still and let me lead her off into the bourrée.

Well, my friends, you wouldn't believe what cries of pleasure and wonder there were on the square at the thunderous noise of those Bourbonnais bagpipes and at the return of the mule-driver, whom everyone thought had left. People were only dancing half-heartedly and were about to stop, when Huriel reappeared on the minstrel's stone. Immediately it was as if everyone had gone mad, the little groups of four or eight were replaced by groups of sixteen or even thirty-two, holding hands, leaping, shouting, and laughing, with such an uproar that the good Lord Himself couldn't have got a word in edgeways.

Soon afterwards, old and young, little children who could barely keep their legs under control, grandfathers who could hardly stay upright on theirs, old women who jigged about in the old-fashioned way, clumsy lads who'd never been able to follow the beat, everyone got going, and it wouldn't have taken much more for the parish bell to start up as well! Just think: music which was the most beautiful ever heard in our region and which didn't cost a farthing! It even seemed to be helped along by the devil, since the piper never asked for a break, and exhausted all the dancers without growing weary himself. 'I want to have the last one!' he shouted, each time anyone advised him to have a rest. 'I want the whole parish to die dancing. I want everyone still to be here at sunrise, still on their feet and in good form, and everyone begging me to stop!' And he went on piping and we went on dancing like madmen.

Mère Biaud, seeing there was an opportunity for work and profit, had ordered that benches and tables be carried out, and food and drink, and because there wasn't enough food for all these stomachs hollowed out with dancing, everyone set about giving the friends and relatives that were present all the victuals they'd stocked up on for the coming week. Someone brought a cheese, someone else a bag of walnuts, a third provided goat meat, or a suckling pig, which was roasted or grilled at the hastily erected kitchen. It was like a wedding to which neighbours had all invited each other. Children didn't go to bed, and no one had time to give them a thought, so little groups of them fell asleep on the wood used for making tools, which was always piled up on the village green, to the wild noise of the dance and the pipes, which stopped only long enough for the piper to knock back a mug of the best wine.

The more he drank, the more vigorous he seemed and the more admirably he played. Finally, when even the sturdiest dancers began to feel hungry, Huriel was forced to stop, for want of dancers to please, and, having won his bet to dance us all into the grave, he agreed to dine. Everyone invited him, and argued over the pleasure and honour of feasting him, but seeing Brulette coming to my table, he accepted my invitation and sat down beside her, overflowing with wit and good humour. He ate well and quickly, but instead of being weighed down with digestion, he was the first to lift his glass to sing, and although he'd blown for six hours like a storm, his voice was as fresh and as accurate as if nothing had happened. We tried to outdo him, but the most famed singers soon gave up for the pleasure of hearing him, for all our songs were worth nothing in comparison with his, both for their melody and their words. We even found it hard to sing the refrains with him, for everything in his repertoire was new to us, and the quality of his songs surpassed all our learning.

Everyone left their tables to listen to him, and at the moment when the rising sun began to break through the leaves, we were surrounded by a crowd more charmed and more attentive than at the finest sermon.

Then he rose, climbed on his bench and raised his empty glass to the first ray of sunlight that passed over his head, saying, with an air that made us all tremble, without knowing how or why: 'Friends, here comes the good Lord's torch! Put out your little candles and greet what's brightest and most beautiful in the world!'

'And now,' he said, as he sat down again and put his up-turned glass on the table, 'we've chatted enough and sung enough for one night. What are you doing, sacristan? Go and ring the angelus and we'll see who makes the sign of the cross in good Christian fashion! That'll tell us who's enjoyed themselves honestly, and who's drunk themselves into a stupor. After we've all given thanks to God, I'll leave you, my friends, thanking you for having celebrated my arrival so well and shown such confidence in me. I owed you some reparation for damage I'd unwillingly caused some of you not long ago. Guess if you can what I'm talking about, but for my part I'm not going to make any confessions. Yet I believe I've done my best to amuse you, and since pleasure is worth more than gain in my eyes, I think we're even now.'

And as there were people who wanted to make him explain his meaning, he called out: 'Quiet, the angelus is ringing!'

And he went down on his knees, causing everyone else to do likewise, and what's more, they did so with exceptional thoughtfulness, for that man seemed to hold sway over the minds of men.

When the prayer was over, we looked for him, but he'd disappeared, so completely disappeared that there were people who rubbed their eyes, thinking that they'd dreamed that night of joy and madness.

NINTH EVENING

Brulette was trembling all over, and when I asked her what was the matter, and what she was thinking about, she told me as she lifted the back of her hand to her cheek: 'That man's likeable, Tiennet, but he's very bold.'

As I was a little more fired up than usual, I found the courage to say to her: 'If a stranger's mouth has offended your skin, that of a friend could take away the stain.' But she pushed me away, replying: 'He's gone, and there's wisdom in forgetting those that go away.'

'Even poor Joey?'

'Oh! He's a different case.'

'Why is he different? You don't answer. Oh Brulette, you've got a soft spot for . . .'

'For whom?' she asked sharply. 'What's his name? Tell me, since you know him.'

'Well,' I answered, laughing, 'he's the black man for whom Joey sold his soul to the devil, and who frightened you so much, one spring evening when you were at my place.'

'No, no, you're just teasing! Tell me his name, what he does, where he comes from.'

'Certainly not, Brulette! You say that out of sight is out of mind, and I'd prefer not to make you change your mind.'

The villagers were much amazed to see that the piper had left as if by a miracle before anyone had thought to ask who and what he was. Some had indeed asked him certain questions; but he'd told one that he came from the Marche* and was called such and such, while he'd said something quite different to a second, and no one knew the truth. I threw out yet another name to them, just to put them off the track, not that Huriel the spoiler of crops had any cause to fear anything from anyone, after Huriel the piper had so whipped up everyone's feelings in his favour, but I did it to amuse myself and also to enrage Brulette. Then, when people asked me how I came to know him, I answered, mockingly, that I didn't know him, that he'd just taken it into his head, when he arrived, to greet me as a friend, and I'd answered in the same strain as a joke.

Nevertheless, after Brulette had asked me some searching questions, I was forced to tell her what I knew about him, and although it didn't amount to very much, she was sorry to hear it, for, like many local people, she was deeply prejudiced against foreigners, and especially against mule-drivers.

I thought that such repulsion would make her forget Huriel pretty quickly, and, if she did think about him, she scarcely showed it, for she went on leading the happy life she liked, without showing anyone any preference, saying that, because she wanted to be as faithful as a wife as she was carefree as a girl, she had every right to take her time and study those around her; and as for me, she often repeated that all she wanted was my faithful and unruffled friendship, without any idea of marriage.

Since there was nothing melancholic in my nature, Brulette's behaviour didn't make me languish in any way. I really rather shared her feelings in regard to freedom. I used my own freedom as boys will, and took my pleasure where I found it, without accepting any chains. But, once my ardour had calmed, I would always return to my lovely cousin, and found in her a sweet, honest, and delightful companion, whom I would greatly have missed had I decided to sulk and not see her. She was wittier than all the other girls and women of that area. Moreover, her home was pleasant, always clean and well ordered, with no hint of any privation, and on winter evenings, as at all other leisure times throughout the year, it was always crowded with the finest young people of the parish. The girls took pleasure in going wherever she went, because there were always plenty of boys around her, and from time to time they landed a husband of their own. And Brulette used the high value placed on her sound mind and her pretty expressions to encourage young men to pay attention to the girls who desired them, and showed herself to be generous in this matter, just as the rich are generous when they know they themselves will never want for anything.

Grandfather Brulet loved these young folk, and delighted them with his old songs and the many fine stories he knew.

Sometimes Mariton would also come for a short while, with the sole aim of talking about her son, and she was a woman with a silver tongue, who was still youthful and offered the girls an excellent example of how to dress, for she chose elegant clothes in order to please her master Benoît, who wanted her warm smile and her openness to act as a good advertisement for his inn.

It wasn't rare for hurdy-gurdy* players of the area, seeing a group of young folk gathered around, to set about arranging a dance outside the door, so that Brulette, in her little house, although she owned nothing more valuable than her pleasantness and her warmth, became like a queen whom ugly or abandoned girls criticized under their breath, but whose company others found more of a help than a hindrance.

Almost a year had passed by in such entertainment without our having received any other news of Joey than two letters in which he let his mother know that he was in good health and earning a good living in the Bourbonnais. He didn't mention the place where he was staying, and the two letters carried different postmarks. What's more, the second wasn't particularly easy to understand, even though our new curé was very skilful at reading handwriting. But it seemed that Joseph was taking lessons, and that he had attempted, for the first time, to write himself. Finally, a third letter came, addressed to Brulette, and the curé read it very easily and said it was clearly expressed. That letter said that Joey was a little ill and had entrusted a friend to send news. It was merely a spring fever, and there was no cause for concern. Furthermore, the letter said that he was with friends who were habitual travellers and were setting out for the region around Chambérat,* from where they'd write again if his condition happened to grow any worse despite the great care they were taking of him.

'Oh, dear God!' said Brulette, when the curé had told her what was written on the paper, 'I'm so afraid he's become a mule-driver, too, and I wouldn't dare tell his mother either about his illness or about the career he's adopted. The poor soul has enough to worry about as it is.'

Then, looking at the letter, she asked what the signature said. The curé, who hadn't paid much attention to it, took his glasses and began to laugh, saying he'd never seen anything like it, and it didn't matter how many times he tried, all he could see, by way of a name, was a picture of an earlobe, with a ring and a kind of heart slipped on to the ring. 'It must be the symbol of some guild or other. All brotherhoods have their emblems, and no one knows a thing about them.'

But Brulette understood perfectly well, and was a little perturbed, seizing the letter and examining it often, as I can well believe, with an eye that was less indifferent than she claimed. For the idea sprouted in her mind that she should learn to read, and she set about it very secretively, with the help of a woman who had in the past been a noblewoman's chambermaid, and had retired to our town to run a haber-dasher's shop. This woman often came to chatter in my cousin's house where all the world gathered.

It didn't take much time for so clever a mind to learn a great deal about reading and writing, and one fine day, I was greatly astonished to find that she was writing songs and prayers that seemed cunningly wrought. I couldn't help wondering if it was in order to correspond with Joey, or with the handsome mule-driver, that she was learning pranks above her station.

'As if it had anything to do with that bumpkin and his pierced ears!' she answered, laughing. 'Do you think I'm so thoughtless a girl as to send letters to a strange boy? But if Joseph comes back to us as a scholar, he'll have acted wisely in putting his stupidity behind him, and as for me, I'm not exactly unhappy at being a little less stupid than I was before.'

'Brulette, Brulette,' I said to her, 'you're turning your thoughts away from your region and your friends! It'll end in tears! You ought to be careful. I'm just as worried about you here as about Joseph far away.'

'You've no need to worry about me, Tiennet. My head's screwed on properly, whatever people may say. As for our poor lad, I'm really concerned about him; for it's now nearly six months since we've had news of him, and that fine mule-driver, who gave us such promises to send word of him, hasn't given it a thought. Mariton is grieved that Joey is so forgetful of her, for I didn't let her know about his illness, and he may perhaps be dead without anyone suspecting it.'

I pointed out to her that in that case we'd certainly have been told, and that no news is good news.

'You can say what you like,' she answered. 'Two nights ago I dreamed I saw the mule-driver turn up, bringing back Joey's bagpipes and telling us he'd perished. Since that dream, my heart has been heavy and I keep blaming myself for having let so much time go by without thinking of my poor childhood friend and without attempting to write to him. But where would I have sent my letter, since I don't even know where he is?'

As she was saying this, Brulette, who, as it happened, had been standing by the window and looking out, gave a little cry and went quite white with fear. I looked out as well, and saw Huriel covered with coal dust, his face and clothes equally black, as I'd seen him the first time. He came towards us, and children ran away from him, crying, 'It's the devil! The devil!', while the dogs barked at him.

Startled by what Brulette had told me, and wanting to spare her from learning any bad news too quickly, I ran to meet the mule-driver, and my first words were to ask him just in case, for I was very worried: 'Is he dead, then?'

'Who? Joseph? No, praise be to God! But you know, then, that he's still unwell?'

'Is his life in danger?'

'Yes and no. But I want to tell you about him in Brulette's presence. Is this her house? Take me to her.'

'Yes, come this way!' and running ahead, I told my cousin not to be alarmed, and that the news was not as bad as she expected.

She quickly called her grandfather, who was doing some carpentry in the next room, and set about receiving the mule-driver in fitting style. Nevertheless, seeing him so different from her memory of him, so barely recognizable in his coal dust and his coarse clothing, she was put out of countenance and turned her eyes away in sadness and embarrassment.

Huriel realized this perfectly well, for he began to smile, and lifting up his wild black hair as if by chance, but in such a way as to show Brulette he was still wearing her pledge in his ear, he said: 'It is indeed me, and no one else. I've come from my region on purpose to tell you about a friend, who, thanks be to God, is neither dead nor dying, but about whom I must nevertheless talk to you for a bit at your leisure. Do you have time now?'

'We've plenty of time,' answered père Brulet. 'Sit down, friend. We'll get you something to eat and drink.'

'I don't need anything,' said Huriel, taking a seat. 'I'll wait until your usual dinner time. But before I say anything I need to let the people I'm talking to know who I am.'

'Go ahead,' said my uncle. 'We're all ears.'

TENTH EVENING

Then the mule-driver said: 'My name is Jean Huriel. I'm a mule-driver by trade, and the son of Sébastien Huriel, who is known as Bastien the great woodcutter, a highly-renowned master piper and a worker who is greatly valued in the Bourbonnais woods. Those are my names and my titles, and I can prove they are truly mine. I know that to inspire more trust in you I ought to have presented myself to you as it lies in my power to do, but those who follow my trade have a certain habit . . .'

'As for your habit, my lad,' said père Brulet, who was listening to him very closely, 'it's something I know well. A good habit or a bad one, according to whether you yourselves are good or bad. I haven't lived all these years without knowing what mule-drivers are, and as I've travelled outside this region in the past, I know your habits and customs. People say your fellow workers are guilty of many misdeeds: people have seen girls kidnapped, Christian folk beaten, why, even killed in evil disputes, and their money stolen.'

Huriel laughed and said: 'I think those stories have been greatly exaggerated in the telling. The things you're talking about are so much in the past that the perpetrators couldn't be found, and the fear that folk in your region felt has embroidered the stories so much that, for many a long year, the mule-drivers haven't dared leave the forests except in great bands, and even then in great peril. The proof that they've much improved and no one need fear them any longer is that they themselves no longer fear anything and that I'm here all alone among you.'

'Yes,' said père Brulet, who wasn't easy to convince. 'But you've put black all over your face for all that! You swore to your brotherhood you'd follow its orders, which are to go in this disguise in areas where you're still suspect, so that if one among you does something evil, no one can say, in looking at the others later on, "That's him" or "That's not him". Moreover, you're each responsible for the others. That has its good side, for it makes you faithful friends, and everyone is devoted to everyone else. But it leaves a great doubt over the rest of your religion, and I won't hide from you the fact that if a mule-driver, however good a lad he might be and however much money he might have, were to ask me if he could marry into my family, I would offer him my wine and my soup with all my heart, but I wouldn't countenance his marrying my granddaughter.'

'Well,' said Huriel, his eyes aflame and gazing boldly at Brulette, who was pretending her thoughts were elsewhere, 'it hadn't occurred to me to present myself for such a reason. You've no need to refuse me, père Brulet, for you don't know if I'm married or a bachelor, I said nothing about that.'

Brulette lowered her eyes right to the ground so that we couldn't see whether she was pleased or angry at the compliment. Then she regained her courage and said: 'You didn't come about that. You came about Joey, for you have news to give us about him and I'm deeply worried over his poor health. My grandfather here brought Joey up, and is interested in him. Couldn't you talk about him before you get onto any other matters?'

Huriel looked very closely at Brulette, and seemed to overcome a momentary disappointment and to pull himself together before he spoke. Then he said: 'Joseph is ill, ill enough for me to decide to come to the girl who caused his illness and ask: "Are you willing to cure him and is it in your power to do so?"'

'Whatever are you talking about?' asked my uncle, cupping his ear, for he was beginning to be a little hard of hearing. 'How can my granddaughter cure the lad we're talking about?'

'If I talked about myself before talking of him, it's because what I have to say about him is rather delicate, and you might not have accepted it from just anyone. Now, if you consider me an honest man, let me tell you all I think and all I know.'

'You needn't have any fears about telling us,' said Brulette sharply. 'I'm not worried about what anyone thinks of me.'

'I think only well of you, lovely Brulette,' replied the mule-driver. 'It's not your fault that Joey loves you. And if you return his love in the hidden depths of your heart, no one has the right to blame you for that. It would be possible to envy Joseph in that case, but not betray him or cause you any pain. Let me tell you how things have been between him and me since we first became friends, and I persuaded him to come to my country to learn about the kind of music he loves so much.'

'I don't know that you really did him a great service there,' said my uncle. 'It seems to me that he could have learnt it just as well here and without distressing and worrying his friends.'

'He told me, and since then I've experienced the truth of it myself, that he wouldn't have been tolerated by the other pipers. Moreover, I owed it to him to tell the truth since he'd trusted me pretty much at first sight. Music is a wild plant, which doesn't grow in your land. It's happier in our heathlands, I couldn't say why, but it's in our woods and ravines that it thrives and flourishes like the flowers in spring. It's there that music is invented and that ideas abound, enough for all those areas that have none of their own. That's the source of the best things you hear your pipers play, but as they're lazy or penny-pinching, and as you're always satisfied with having the same dish served up to you, they come to us only once in their lives, and dine on that for the rest of their time on earth. And now they even have pupils who play our

old tunes over and over again, corrupting them as they do
so, and who think they've no need to come and consult our
old experts. So a well-meaning young lad like you, I said
to Joseph, who's willing to go and drink at the source, will
return so fresh and so well fed that no one could withstand
him.

'That's why Joey agreed to leave on the following Midsummer's Day and go to Bourbonnais, where he'd find both work
to support him in our woods, and lessons from the best of
masters. For I must tell you that the most famous inventors of
music are in the high Bourbonnais, towards the pine woods,
near where the Sioule river* flows down among the Dôme
mountains,* and my father, a native of the village called
Huriel, from which he took his name, has spent his life in the
best places, and is still in good breath and knows many
examples of that beautiful art. He's a man who doesn't like to
work two years running in the same place, and the older he
gets, the livelier and more changeable he becomes. Last year
he was in the forest of Tronçay, then he went to the forest of
Epinasse, and right now he's in the forest of Alleu,* where
Joey, who never stops chopping, cutting, and piping with him,
has faithfully followed him, and he loves him as if he were his
son and is delighted to be loved in return.

'He's been as happy there as a lover can be, when he's
parted from his beloved. But life isn't as gentle and comfortable in our region as it is in yours, and although my father,
drawing on his experience, wanted to hold him back, Joseph,
in his eagerness to succeed, has rather overextended himself
with our instruments which, as you were able to see, are of
a different size from yours, and weary the heart until one
finds the correct way of blowing into them. The result is that
he's been racked by fevers and has begun to spit blood. My
father knows what the matter is, and because he also knows
how to control it, he's taken Joey's bagpipes away and advised
him to rest. But if his body has benefited in one area, it's
got worse in another. He's stopped coughing and spitting
blood, but he's fallen into despair, and has become so weak
that there have even been fears for his life. So a week ago,
when I returned from one of my travels, I found Joey so

pale I didn't recognize him, and so weak on his legs that he couldn't stand up.

'When I asked him about it, he said very sadly and in floods of tears: "It's all too clear, my dear Huriel, that I'm going to die in the depths of these woods, far from my country, my mother and my friends, and I'll never have been loved by the girl to whom I would so much have liked to reveal all I've learnt. Despair is eating my mind and impatience is drying up my heart. I'd have preferred it if your father had let me destroy myself playing the bagpipes. I would have faded away, sending the one I love all the sweet nothings my lips couldn't tell her, and dreaming I was at her side. Père Bastien probably had the best of intentions, for I felt perfectly well that I was killing myself in playing too ardently. But what will I gain in dying less quickly? I'll still have to renounce life, since, for one thing, I have nothing and am beholden to you because I can no longer work as a woodcutter, and for another thing my chest is clearly too frail for me to be a piper. So it's all up with me. I'll never be worth anything and I'm dying without even had the pleasure of being able to remember a single day of love and happiness."

'Don't cry, Brulette,' went on the mule-driver, seizing the hand with which she was wiping her face. 'All isn't lost yet. Listen to the end of my story.

'Seeing the distress the poor lad was suffering, I went in search of a good doctor, who examined him and told us there was in all this more melancholy than illness, and that he was sure he could cure him, if he could refrain from piping and if he could be dispensed from woodcutting for another month.

'There was no difficulty where the second point was concerned, for my father isn't hard up and nor am I, thanks be to God, and there's no great merit in our caring for a friend who can't work; but the sorrow of not piping and of being there, far from his kin, unable to see Brulette, and without being able to make any progress, made a liar of the doctor. Almost a month has passed by and Joey is no better. He didn't want to let you know, but I convinced him to do so. What's more, I wanted to bring him back with me. I'd even put him on one of my mules and was bringing him home when, after two leagues, he became very weak, and I was obliged to return him to my father, who said to me: "Go to the lad's region and bring his mother or his fiancée back. His only illness is sorrow, and when he sees one or the other he'll take heart again, and regain his health so that he'll be able to complete his apprenticeship here or else go back home."

'Joey was greatly shaken when he heard my father say this. "My mother," he kept crying like a child, "I want my poor mother to come as soon as she can!" But he very quickly pulled himself together and said: "No! No! I don't want her to see me die. Her unhappiness would make me die too unhappily myself." "And Brulette?" I whispered to him. "Oh, Brulette wouldn't come, Brulette's kind, but it's not possible that she hasn't already chosen a lover who won't allow her to come and console me."

'Then I made Joey swear that he'd at least be patient until my return, and off I went. Père Brulet, you decide what should be done, and you, Brulette, consult your own feelings.'

'Master Huriel,' she said, leaping to her feet, 'I'll go, although I am not Joey's fiancée as you claim, and I'm under no obligation to him, except that his mother nourished me with her milk and carried me in her arms. But what makes you think that this young man is in love with me, since, as true as my grandfather is sitting there, he's never said a single word about it to me?'

'So he did tell me the truth!' Huriel exclaimed, as if delighted with what he'd heard. But calming down immediately, he added: 'It's true all the same that he may well die of it, all the more so since he's lost all hope, and I must plead his case and speak of his feelings for him.'

'Has he asked you to do so?' said Brulette proudly, and also with some disappointment in the mule-driver.

'I'll have to accept the responsibility for it, asked or not. I want to have a clear conscience on this score . . . because he confided in me about his pain and asked me to help him. This is how he talked to me: "I wanted to devote myself to music, as much because I love it as out of love for my sweet Brulette. She thinks of me as her brother, she has always taken great care of me, and she's pitied me, too. But that didn't stop her paying attention to all and sundry, except for me. And I can't blame her for that. She's a girl who loves flirtation and everything that brings people glory. She has every right to be coquettish and to show herself off to good advantage. It makes my heart ache, but the fault lies with my own worthlessness, if she gives her friendship to men who are worth more than I am. Such as I am, unable to work hard, or speak sweetly, or dance, or joke, or even sing, feeling ashamed of myself and my lot, I certainly deserve her to consider me as the last among those who might aspire to her hand. Well, do you see, the pain of it will make me die if it continues, and I want to find a cure for it. Something inside me tells me that I can play better music than all those who are involved in musicmaking in our region; if I succeed in doing that, I'll no longer be worthless. I'll become something more than the others and, as that girl has taste and a skill in singing, she'll understand, all on her own, what I'm worth, and what's more, her pride will be flattered by the esteem with which I'm regarded." '

'To hear you speak,' said Brulette with a smile, 'it's as if I could hear him himself, although he's never told me that. He's always been prickly, and I can see that for him it's also a matter of pride to win me; but since such an illness brings him to death's door, I'll do everything that a friendship such as I feel for him can do to give him fresh heart. I'll go and see him with Mariton, if, of course, that's what my grandfather advises and wants me to do.'

'Going with Mariton,' père Brulet replied, 'doesn't seem possible, for reasons known to me and that you'll soon know, my dear. Take it from me, for now, that she can't leave her master, because of difficulties he's having with his business. Moreover, if it's possible that Joey's illness may clear up, there's no point in upsetting and worrying his mother. I'll go with you, because I'm sure, since you've always guided Joseph in the best way, that you'll still have enough power over him to restore him to courage and reason. I know what you think of him, and I'm of the same opinion; moreover, if we find his case is desperate, we'll write straight away to his mother to tell her to come and close his eyes for him.'

'If you'll allow me to accompany you on this voyage,' said

Huriel, 'I'll lead you directly, in the space of twenty-four hours, to the area where Joseph is living now. I could even do it in a single day, if you're not too afraid of poor roads.'

'Let's talk of that at dinner,' my uncle answered. 'As for your company, I would indeed like it, and I'll even demand it, for you've spoken very well and I'm not unaware of what an honest family you belong to.'

'So you know my father, do you?' asked Huriel. 'When he heard Joseph and me talking about Brulette, he told us that, as a young man, his father had had a friend called Brulet.'

'That was me. I was a woodcutter with your grandfather for a long time, thirty years or so ago, in the area around Saint Amand,* and I knew your father when he was very young. He used to work with us and even at that stage he played the bagpipes wonderfully well. He was a very likeable lad, who can't yet be much afflicted by old age. When you told us your name just now I didn't want to interrupt you, and if I scolded you a little on the customs of your trade, it was only by way of testing you. So, take a seat, and feel free to help yourself to whatever we can offer you.'

During supper, Huriel showed himself to be as reasonable a talker, and just as pleasant and serious as we had found him to be amusing and agreeable on Midsummer's Eve. Brulette listened closely and seemed to grow used to his coal-burner's face; but when the talk turned to the distance that had to be covered, and the way in which they would travel, she grew worried for her grandfather's sake, thinking he'd be tired and disorientated. And as Huriel couldn't dispute the fact that such a journey would be difficult for a man of his age, I offered to go with Brulette in my uncle's place.

'That's the best of ideas,' said Huriel. 'If there's only the three of us, we'll take the short cut, and by leaving tomorrow morning we can get there tomorrow evening. I have a sister, very sensible and kind-hearted, who'll share her own hut with Brulette, for I won't hide from you the fact that, where we are, you'll find no houses and no sleeping places like those you're used to.'

'It's true,' replied my uncle, 'that I'm pretty old for sleeping in the bracken, and although I don't coddle my body, if I were to fall ill out there, I'd put you in a real quandary, my dear children. Now if Tiennet goes, I know him well enough to entrust his cousin to him. I'm relying on him not to let her go an inch away from him should there be any danger for a young girl, and I'm relying on you, too, Huriel, not to expose her to any accident on the way.'

I was very happy at this decision and delighted at the idea of accompanying Brulette. I was also honoured at the thought of protecting her if need be. We parted at nightfall, and before daybreak we were back again at Brulette's door. Brulette was already prepared to leave, her little packet in her hand. Huriel led his clairin and three mules, on one of which there was a very soft and very clean saddle, on which he placed Brulette. Then he mounted the horse, and I leaped on the back of another mule, somewhat surprised to find myself there. The third mule, loaded with great new baskets, followed of its own accord, and Satan brought up the rear. No one in the village was awake yet, and that was a bit of a disappointment to me, for I'd have liked to inspire a bit of jealousy in so many of Brulette's gallants who had many a time filled me with fury. But Huriel seemed eager to leave the region without being closely examined and criticized, within Brulette's hearing, for his black face.

We hadn't gone far before he made it clear to me that he wasn't going to let me control things as I might have wished. We were at the Maritet woods* by midday and had covered about half the journey. Nearby was a little place called La Ronde, where I'd have liked to go and buy us a good lunch, but Huriel teased me for my taste for proper meals, and, since he saw Brulette was of his opinion, for she was in a mood to accept everything in good spirits, he made us go down a little gully through which flowed a narrow stream called the Leaf-Bearer, because, at least in those days, it was completely covered in great swathes of water-lilies, and also shaded by the forest foliage, for, on both sides, the trees grew right down to its banks. He left his animals in the reeds, chose us a good place cooled by wild grass, opened the baskets, unstoppered the barrel, and served us as fine a meal as we could have made at home, and very cleanly too, with so much attention to

Brulette that she couldn't help showing how much it pleased her.

And as she saw that before touching either the bread, or the white napkin wrapped around the provisions, he washed his hands very carefully in the stream, right up above his elbows, she said to him laughingly with her little air of gracious command: 'While you're at it, you might also wash your face, so we can really see that you are the handsome bagpiper who played on Midsummer's Eve.'

'No, my sweet. You'll have to get used to the other side of the coin. All I ask from your heart is a little friendship and esteem, for all I'm a pagan mule-driver. So I've no need to please you with my face, and it's not for your sake that I'd whiten it.'

She was mortified, but she didn't give up. 'It's not right to frighten one's friends. As you are now, there's a risk that fear might steal my appetite away.'

'In that case, I'll go and eat on my own, so as not to disgust you.'

He did as he said, sat down on a little rock that thrust into the water, behind the place where we were sitting, and began to eat on his own, while I seized on the opportunity to serve Brulette.

At first she laughed at this situation, because she thought she'd angered him and that pleased her, as such a situation pleases all flirts. But when she tired of the game and wanted to bring him back, she tried in vain to stir him up with words, for he held firm, and every time she turned her head in his direction, he turned his back on her, hiding from her, and replying to what she said with a thousand apt jokes without showing any hard feelings, which, for her, was perhaps the worst part of the whole business.

The result was that she regretted what she'd said and, when he said something a little sharp about prudes, she thought he meant it for her, and two tears rolled down her cheeks, although she would dearly have liked to prevent them falling in my presence. Huriel didn't see them, and I didn't let on that I'd seen them either.

When we had eaten enough for the moment, Huriel asked

me to pack the rest of the food and added: 'If you're tired, my dears, you can take a nap here, for our animals need us to let the heat of the day go by. This is the time when the flies are fiercest, and in this grove the animals can rub and shake themselves as they please. I'll rely on you, Tiennet, to keep good watch over our princess. As for me, I'm going into the forest a little way to see how the good Lord's work is going forward.'

And with a light step, feeling the heat no more than as if we were in the month of April, although we were well into July, he climbed up the hill and disappeared under the great trees.

ELEVENTH EVENING

Brulette did her best to hide from me her disappointment at seeing him depart, but as she didn't feel in the mood for chatting, she pretended to sleep on the fine sand of the bank, her head resting on the panniers that had been taken off the mule in order to let it rest a little, and her face protected from flies with her white handkerchief.

I don't know whether she slept, I spoke to her two or three times without getting any answer, and as she'd allowed me to put my face on the edge of her pinafore, I kept still, but at first without sleeping, for I felt myself a little disturbed by her presence.

Finally weariness overcame me, and I lost consciousness for a while. When I came back to myself, I heard people talking and recognized from the voices that the mule-driver had returned and was chatting with Brulette. I didn't want to disturb the pinafore in order to hear them talking more clearly, but I gripped it tightly in my hands, and the girl couldn't have taken a single step away, even if she'd wanted to do so.

'But I've at least the right,' Huriel was saying, 'to ask you how you've decided to behave towards that poor child. I'm a closer friend of his than I'm allowed to be of yours, and I'd rebuke myself for having brought you to him if your plan was to deceive him.'

'Who's said anything to you about deceiving him? Why do you criticize what I intend to do without knowing what it is?'

'I'm not criticizing it, Brulette. I'm just asking you as someone who's very fond of Joseph and who esteems you enough to believe you'll be open with him.'

'That concerns me alone, master Huriel. You're not the judge of my feelings and I don't have to confide them in anyone. I don't ask you if you're open and faithful with your wife.'

'My wife?' asked Huriel, as if astonished by her statement.

'Well, yes. Aren't you married?'

'Who told you that?'

'I thought you said so at our place last evening, when my grandfather, imagining you'd come to ask my hand in marriage, was quick to refuse you.'

'I didn't say anything about it, Brulette, except that I wasn't asking for your hand. Before you have the hand, you have to have the heart, and I've no right to yours.'

'At least I can see you're more reasonable and less bold with me than you were last year.'

'Oh! If, at your village feast, I put things a bit too strongly, it's because those words came into my head like that when I saw you; but since then time has gone by, and you ought to have forgotten any offence I caused.'

'Who says I remember? Did I reproach you in any way?'

'You reproach me in the way you're behaving, or at least you haven't forgotten, since you're not willing to talk to me openly about Joseph.'

'I thought,' said Brulette, with a hint of impatience in her voice, 'that I'd explained about that very clearly last night. But what connection can you possibly see between those two things? The more I'm supposed to have forgotten you, the less right you have to press me to tell you about my feelings for anyone.'

'Look, my sweet,' said the mule-driver, who didn't seem to share any of Brulette's little reservations, 'you spoke very well last night about the past, but you barely touched on the future, and I still don't know what you plan to say to help Joseph regain an appetite for life. Why do you refuse to let me know straightforwardly what you're going to do?'

'What is it to you? If you're married, or even if you've merely pledged your word, you've no right to look so deeply into girls' hearts.'

'Brulette, you're determined to make me say whether or not I'm free to pay court to you. But won't you tell me anything about your own position? Have I no right to know whether one day you'll favour Joseph, or whether you've given your word to someone else, even if it's only that great boy there asleep on your apron?'

'You're too inquisitive!' said Brulette, getting up and quickly pulling her apron away, so that I was forced to let go, pretending to have just woken up.

'Let's go,' Huriel said, apparently untouched by Brulette's bad mood, and still smiling with his white teeth and his large eyes, the only parts of his face not in mourning.

We returned to the Bourbonnais track. The sun was hidden behind a heavy cloud that was covering the sky, and it was beginning to thunder near the horizon.

'That storm's nothing,' said the mule-driver, 'it'll pass by on our left. If we don't meet another when we turn towards the tributaries of the Joyeuse,* we'll get there without any problems, but the weather is so heavy we should be ready for anything.'

Then he unfolded his coat, which he'd tied behind his back together with a beautiful, brand-new, woman's cloak that filled Brulette with wonder.

'You're not going to tell us you're not married,' she said with a blush, 'unless that's a wedding present that you've bought on your journey?'

'That may be,' said Huriel, in the same tone. 'But if it happens to rain, you'll be the first to wear it, and you won't find it any too warm, with a cape as light as yours.'

As he'd predicted, the sky cleared on one side and grew darker on the other and, as we were crossing a flat heath between Saint Saturnin and Sidiailles,* it suddenly got worse and a violent wind beat against us. The countryside was becoming wild, and despite myself I was filled with sadness. Brulette, too, found the spot barren, and pointed out that there wasn't a single tree to provide shelter. Huriel teased us.

'Anyone can see you're from the wheat-growing country! As soon as you step on heather, you think you're lost.'

As he was leading us in a straight line, knowing, like the back of his hand, all the little paths and tracks along which a mule could pass to make the journey shorter, he made us leave Sidiailles on our left and go down directly to the banks of the little Joyeuse river, a poor stream that didn't look particularly evil, and which he nevertheless seemed eager to cross. As soon as we'd crossed it, the rain began to fall and, to avoid getting wet, we were obliged to stop at a place called the Paulmes mill. Brulette wanted to go on, and that was also the mule-driver's advice, for he felt we shouldn't wait and let the tracks get muddy, but I pointed out that Brulette had been entrusted to me, and I shouldn't expose her to illness, so Huriel for once submitted to my will.

We stayed there two full hours and when it was possible to risk going outside, the sun started blazing down. The Joyeuse had swollen so much that it was now a real river that would have been difficult to ford; fortunately, it lay behind us, but the paths had become abominable, and we still had a small stream to cross before reaching Bourbonnais.

As long as it was light, we were able to proceed, but when night fell, it was so dark that Brulette was afraid, although she didn't dare say so. Huriel, who realized this by her silence, dismounted from his horse, and, driving the animal before him, since it knew the way as well as he himself did, he took the bridle of the mule that carried my cousin and led it very adroitly for more than a league, supporting it so it didn't stumble, and sinking into water or sand up to his knees, taking no care of himself, and laughing every time Brulette said she was worried about him or begged him not to kill himself for her sake. Such behaviour showed her he was certainly a more faithful and helpful friend than any simple lover, and that he knew how to be of great assistance to her without making a fuss about it.

The countryside struck me as increasingly unattractive. There was nothing but little green hills cut through by streams bordered by a lot of grasses and flowers that smelled good, but couldn't in the least improve the fodder. The trees were beautiful and the mule-driver claimed that this land was richer and prettier than ours because of its pastures and its fruit, but I couldn't see any great harvests and would have liked to be back in our own country, particularly when I saw I was no use at all to Brulette, and that it was all I could do to get myself out of the marshes and pot-holes along the path.

At last the weather lifted and the moon appeared. We found ourselves in the woods of La Roche, at the point where the Arnon and another tributary whose name I've forgotten flow together.

'Stay up here,' said Huriel. 'You can even get off and stretch your legs. It's sandy here and the rain has barely got through the oaks. But I'll go and see if we can cross the ford.'

He went down to the river and soon returned, saying: 'The ford is flooded and we may need to go back up as far as Saint Pallais to cross over to Bourbonnais. If we hadn't stopped at the mill on the Joyeuse we'd have been ahead of the flood and would have been home by now, but what's done is done. Let's see what we can do. The water level is dropping. If we stay here, we'll be able to cross in four or five hours and we'll reach our destination at dawn, without tiring ourselves and running any risks. For between the two branches of the Arnon, we have a dry plain, whereas if we go back up as far as Saint Pallais in Bourbonnais, we risk floundering around all night and still not arriving any earlier.'

'Well,' said Brulette, 'let's stay here. It's dry and the weather is clear, and even if we are in a rather wild wood, I won't be afraid if the two of you are here.'

'Now there's a brave traveller at last!' said Huriel. 'Well, let's have some supper since we've nothing better to do. Tiennet, tie up the clairin, for we've a lot of other woods bordering on this one, and I wouldn't guarantee that there are no treacherous wolves around. Unsaddle the mules, they won't wander away from the bell, and you, my sweet, help me light a fire, for the air is still damp and I don't want you to catch cold while you're eating your fill.'

I felt very down-at-heart and dejected, although I couldn't understand why. Either I was ashamed to find I was of no use

to Brulette on such a voyage, or the mule-driver was right to
tease me, it was as if I were homesick.

'But what have you got to complain about?' Huriel said to
me. He grew steadily happier as we became steadily sadder.
'Aren't you like a monk in a refectory here? Aren't these rocks
just perfect for acting as our chimney, our dressers, and our
chairs? And isn't this your third meal today? Doesn't that
silvery moon shed a better light than your old tin lamp? Has
our food, which I carefully covered with my tarpaulins, suffered at all from the rain? Doesn't this great fire dry the air
around us? Don't these damp branches and grasses smell
better than your provisions of cheese and rancid butter? Don't
you breathe better under the great vaults of those branches?
Look at them, lit by our fire light! Wouldn't you say that there
are hundreds of branches criss-crossing just to protect us? If,
from time to time, a little breeze shakes the damp leaves over
our heads, don't you see diamonds falling down to crown us?
What strikes you as so sad about the thought that we're alone
in a place you don't know? Doesn't it unite everything that's
most consoling in life? First God, who is everywhere, then a
charming girl, and two fine friends ready to help each other?

'And then, do you really think man was made to sit tight all
year round? It's my opinion, on the contrary, that it's our
destiny to travel, and that man would be a hundred times
stronger, gayer, healthier in body and mind, if he hadn't spent
so much time seeking comfort, which has made him soft,
fearful, and subject to illness. The more you flee from heat and
cold, the more they injure you when they do catch you. You'll
see my father, who, like me, may well have slept in a bed no
more than ten times in all his life. See if he has aches and
rheumatism even though he works in his shirt sleeves in the
depths of winter!

'And then, too, isn't it delightful to feel you're more solid
than the wind and thunder? When the storm howls, isn't that
the finest of music? And the rivulets that rush into ravines and
leap from root to root, carrying pebbles, and leaving their
foam on the fronds of bracken, don't they, too, sing wild
songs that bring pleasant dreams, when you fall asleep on the
islands they can cut around you in a single night? Animals

languish in poor weather, it's true, the birds fall silent, the foxes go underground, even my dog seeks out shelter under my horse's belly; but what separates man from animals is the ability to remain tranquil and light of heart in the midst of battles in the sky and the whims of the clouds. Man alone, since he can use his reason to safeguard himself against fear and danger, has the ability and the instinct to feel what's beautiful in such an uproar.'

Brulette was listening to the mule-driver in great astonishment. She followed his glance and his gestures, and took pleasure in everything he said, without explaining to herself how words and ideas with which she was so unfamiliar were stirring her up and setting her heart on fire. Indeed, I, too, felt rather moved by them, although I resisted them to some extent. For beneath his coal dust, Huriel had so friendly and resolute a face that you were won over despite yourself, as happens when you're beaten at a game by a player so fine that you admire him even though you lose your money.

We were in no hurry to finish our supper, for to tell the truth we were perfectly dry, and when our fire was merely a pile of warm ashes, the weather had become so mild and clear that we were in high spirits, and the mule-driver's joyous conversation and fair words had lifted our spirits and made us feel perfectly content. From time to time, he fell silent to listen to the river that still rumbled away fairly loudly, and as the water that had fallen on the highlands was spreading out in its bed in countless thousands of little rivers, there seemed no likelihood that we would be able to continue our journey before daybreak. After Huriel had gone off yet again to check up on things, he returned to advise us to sleep. He made a bed for Brulette with the animals' saddle packs, and wrapped her up well in all the extra clothing he had, always very gaily and without flirting with her anymore, but treating her with the same care and gentleness he'd have shown a little child.

Then he stretched out, with neither cloak nor cushions, on the earth that had dried out near the fire, inviting me to do likewise, and soon he was sleeping like a log, or near enough.

I was perfectly at ease, but I wasn't asleep, for I couldn't appreciate that sort of dormitory, when I heard in the distance the sound of a bell, as if the clairin had broken free and wandered into the forest. I got up and saw it still tranquilly standing in the spot where we'd placed it. It was, therefore, another clairin, warning us of the approach or nearness of other mule-drivers.

At that moment I saw Huriel sit up, too, listen, and then stand right up and come over to me. 'I sleep soundly,' he said to me, 'and when I've only my mules to protect I can sometimes forget myself completely: but as in this case I'm protecting a very precious princess, it's a different matter, and I was only half asleep. You were doing the same, Tiennet, and that's all to the good. Speak softly, and don't let's move, for I'd be just as happy not to be recognized by my work mates. But as I made a good choice of the place we're in, there's little likelihood of our being discovered.'

He'd barely finished speaking when a black face slid through the trees and passed so close to Brulette that it wouldn't have taken much for him to have tripped over her without seeing her. It was a mule-driver, who immediately gave a great shout and a kind of whistle, to which other identical shouts replied from various spots all around, and in a flash we were surrounded by half a dozen of these devils, each more horrible to look at than the preceding one. We'd been betrayed by Huriel's dog who, recognizing friends and acquaintances in the mule-drivers' dogs, had gone to meet them and guided their masters to our resting place.

However much Huriel tried to hide it, he showed how worried he was, and although I'd gently warned Brulette not to move, and had stood in front of her to hide her, it seemed impossible, now they'd surrounded us, to keep her hidden from them for long.

I had a vague idea of the danger we were in, and guessed it more than I could see it, for Huriel hadn't had time to explain to me the varying degrees of Christianity in the people among whom we now found ourselves. They were talking with him in the dialect of the high Bourbonnais region, which borders on the Auvergnat speech, and which our friend spoke as well as they did, although he was born in the lowlands. I only understood a word here and there, and could see they treated him in a friendly fashion, and were asking him what he was doing there and who I was. I could see he was eager to send them off, and he even said to me, in words they, too, could understand, for they could follow the Christian tongue: 'Come, friend, let's wish these friends good day and go our ways again.'

But instead of letting us get ready and go on our way, they found the place a good spot to warm up and rest, and set about unpacking their mules so they could feed until daybreak. 'I'm going to shout that I've seen a wolf to get them off for a moment,' Huriel whispered to me. 'Don't move from here, and make sure *she* doesn't either. I'll be back. Get the mules ready and we'll leave quickly, for staying here is the worst thing we can do.'

No sooner said than done, and the mule-drivers ran in the direction from which he shouted. Unfortunately, I wasn't patient enough, and thought I could profit from the confusion by escaping with Brulette. I was able to get her up without anyone seeing her, for until then the cloaks had covered her so well that she'd been taken for a pile of rags or equipment. She did indeed say to me that Huriel had told us to wait; but I was filled with rage, fear, and jealousy. All I had heard tell about the community of mule-drivers came back to me; I had suspicions about Huriel himself, and as a result I lost my head, and, seeing a thicket hard by, I seized my cousin resolutely by the hand and ran towards it with her.

But the moon shone so brightly and the mule-drivers were so near, that we were seen, and a shout went up: 'Hey! Hey! There's a woman!' And as all those rascals set out to pursue us, I saw there was no solution other than death. Then, turning around like a wild boar, and lifting up my stick, I was about to let fly at the jaw of my closest pursuer a blow that may well have sent him to a place other than paradise, when Huriel caught my arm, as he suddenly appeared at my side.

Then he spoke to them with much force and resolution, and this provoked a kind of quarrel, of which neither Brulette nor I understood a word, and which hardly seemed reassuring, for although they sometimes listened to Huriel, at other times they didn't pay him any attention, and two or three times one of those rogues, the one who seemed the most energetic, put his devilish claws on Brulette's arm as if to lead her away. Had I not sunk my nails into his skin, which was as tough as a billy goat's hide, to force him to let go, he would have torn her from my arms with the aid of his comrades, for there were eight of them at that stage, all armed with solid spears and apparently quite used to quarrels and injustice.

Huriel, who kept his head better than I did, placed himself between us and the enemy, and prevented me from striking the first blow, which, as I later realized, would have spelt the end for us. He set about speaking, sometimes in a tone of remonstrance, sometimes with an air of menace, and finally he turned to me and said in our tongue: 'Tiennet, tell them it's true that this is your sister, an honest girl, who's been promised to me and is visiting Bourbonnais to meet my family. These people, my work mates, who are good folk as regards right and justice, are only seeking a quarrel because they don't believe me. They've taken it into their heads that we were chatting here with a woman who just happened along, and they're insisting on keeping us company. But I'm telling them, and this I swear to God, that before they slight this girl, even in a single word, they will have to kill the pair of us, and have our blood on their heads and their souls before heaven and man.'

'Well, so what if that is the case?' replied one of these mad men, in the same French tongue. This was the man who was always thrusting up to me and whom I longed to stretch out on the ground with a blow in the stomach. 'If you make us kill you, too bad for you! There's no lack of ditches hereabouts to bury two asses! Let them come searching afterwards! We'll be far away, and the trees and stones have no tongues to tell of what they've seen!'

Fortunately this man was the only scoundrel in the band. He was rebuked by the others, and what's more a big redhead, who seemed to have the attention of the rest, seized him by the arm and pushed him far from us, reproaching him and cursing him in his dialect, in a voice that made the whole forest tremble.

From that moment on, the greatest danger had passed, the thought of spilt blood having roused, in a timely way, the consciences of these wild men. They turned the matter to laughter, and teased Huriel who replied in the same vein, putting a brave face on things. But they still didn't seem to have made up their minds to let us leave. They wanted to see Brulette's face, which she kept hidden in her cape and which, uncharacteristically, she would have liked to pass off as old and ugly.

But she suddenly changed her mind when she guessed that the harsh words spoken to Huriel in the Auvergne dialect concerned her and were pretty unsavoury. Filled with anger and pride, she broke away from my arm, and, throwing her cape away from her head, she said in a voice that was both angry and courageous: 'You heartless men, fortunately I don't understand what you're saying to me, but I can see only too well that your intention is to insult me in your thoughts. Well, look at me, and if you've ever set eyes on the face of a woman who deserves respect, recognize that mine has every right to it. You should be ashamed of your vile behaviour, and let me continue on my way without having to hear any more from you.'

Brulette's action might have been foolhardy, but it performed a kind of miracle. The big redhead shrugged his shoulders and whistled for a minute or two, while the others consulted each other in astonishment. Suddenly, he turned his back on us, saying in his loud voice: 'That's enough chat! Let's be off! You elected me chief of the band, I'll punish anyone who torments Jean Huriel any further, for he's a good mate, and all mule-drivers think highly of him.'

They went away, and Huriel, without making any comment or even saying a single word, harnessed up the mules double quick, made us mount them, and going ahead, but looking back at every step, led us rapidly to the river's edge. It was still very high and threatening, but he didn't dither about going in, and when he reached the middle he shouted to us: 'Don't be afraid! Come on!' And as I hesitated a little about getting Brulette wet, for her feet were already covered by the water, he came back to us as if in anger, and struck the mule to make it move into the deepest part, swearing and saying it was better to be dead than insulted.

'My thoughts exactly!' said Brulette in the same tone. And striking the mule, she threw herself boldly into the current, which foamed up as high as her mule's chest.

TWELFTH EVENING

There was a moment when the animal seemed to lose its footing, but Brulette at that moment was supported by both of us, and showed a great deal of courage. When we reached the far bank, Huriel, still whipping our mounts on, made us start galloping, and it was only when we reached the plain, under the sky and in sight of houses, that he let us draw breath.

'Now,' he said, walking between Brulette and me, 'both of you deserve some criticism from me. I'm not a child who'd put you in a dangerous position and just abandon you. Why did you run from the place where I advised you to wait for me?'

'Are *you* criticizing *us*?' said Brulette, rather sharply. 'I would have thought the boot was on the other foot.'

'Well, you start then!' said Huriel, in thoughtful tones. 'I'll speak afterwards. What do you blame me for?'

'I blame you for not having foreseen that dangerous encounter. I blame you above all for having made my grandfather and me trust you enough for me to leave my house and the region where I'm loved and respected, and for having led me into wild woods, where you had the greatest difficulty in saving me from being offended by your friends. I don't know what foul words they wanted to say to me, but I could see all too clearly that you were forced to vouch for me as a virtuous girl. Can it be then that my virtue comes into question when I travel with you? Oh, this has been an ill-starred voyage! This is the first time in my life that I've been insulted, and yet I thought I'd never see the day when such a thing would happen!'

At that, her heart burst with distress and unhappiness, and she began to shed great tears. At first Huriel didn't answer. He was deeply unhappy. Finally, he took heart and said to her:

'Brulette, it's true you were misjudged. You'll be avenged, I guarantee you that! But as I wasn't able to punish them straight away without exposing you to danger, the suffering I feel deep in my heart from reining in my rage defies all words, and you could never understand it!'

The tears he had been holding back made it impossible for him to continue.

'I don't need to be revenged,' said Brulette, 'and I beg you not to think of it any more. For my part, I'll just try to forget it.'

'But nevertheless you'll curse the day when you trusted yourself to me!' he said, clenching his fist as if he almost wanted to knock himself out.

'Come, come,' I said in my turn, 'you mustn't quarrel now that the danger and the evil are past. I accept that I was in the wrong. Huriel was leading the mule-drivers off in one direction and would have saved us in the other direction. I was the one who threw Brulette into the wolf's den in the belief that I could save her more quickly.'

'There would certainly have been no danger if it hadn't been for that,' said Huriel. 'It's true that there are rascals among the mule-drivers, as there are among all men who live in a wild way. There was such a one in that band, but you saw how the others reproached him. It's also true that many others among us are ill-bred, and their jokes are in bad taste, but I don't know what you mean when you speak of our community. We're linked to each other by money and pleasure, as we are by losses and dangers, we respect each other's women as all Christians do, and you saw perfectly well that honesty is also respected for its own sake, since all you had to do was speak proudly to bring those men back to a sense of their duty.'

'And yet,' said Brulette, who was still angry, 'you were very eager to make us leave, and we had to escape swiftly at the risk of drowning ourselves in the river. You can see quite clearly that you're not in control of those wicked minds and that you were very afraid that they might return to their evil plans.'

'All that's because you wanted to flee with Tiennet. They

thought you weren't meant to be there. If you hadn't shown fear and distrust you wouldn't even have been seen by my companions, but both of you thought ill of me, isn't that the case?'

'I didn't think ill of you,' said Brulette.

'Well, I did, at that moment,' I answered. 'I confess it, because I don't want to tell a lie.'

'Well at least that's better. I hope you'll have a change of heart where I'm concerned.'

'It's already happened,' I said. 'I saw how resolute you were, and how you controlled your anger at the same time, and I recognize that it's better to know how to speak well from the beginning than to end by doing so. Blows always come too soon. Had it not been for you, I'd be dead now and so would you, because you'd have stood up for me. And that would have been a great disaster for Brulette. So now we're out of it, thanks to you, and I think we should all three of us be better friends henceforth.'

'Well and good!' replied Huriel, shaking my hand. 'That's the good side of the Berry man, his good sense and his calm reasoning. Are you a Bourbonnais girl, then, Brulette, that you're so sharp and headstrong?'

Brulette agreed to put her hand in his, but she was still troubled. As I thought she was cold from having got so wet in the river, we made her go into one of the houses to change, and to restore herself with a finger of hot wine. Daylight had come, and the people of that area seemed helpful and friendly.

When we set out again on our journey, the sun was already warm, and the countryside, which was raised up between two rivers, delighted the eyes by its sweep which reminded me of our plains. Brulette's bad mood had past, for, as I'd talked to her by the Bourbonnais people's fireside, I pointed out to her that a virtuous girl isn't sullied by comments made by drunks, and that if such comments counted for anything no woman would be pure. The mule-driver had left us for a minute, and when he returned to lift Brulette into the saddle she couldn't help crying out in astonishment. He'd washed himself, shaved, and dressed in clean clothes, not as finely as she had seen him once, but his bearing was attractive enough and his clothes refined enough to do her honour.

Nevertheless, she neither complimented him on this nor joked with him, but just looked at him a lot, as if she were getting to know him again, although she did so only when his eyes were not on her. She seemed sorry to have been rather harsh with him, but she didn't know how to take back what she'd said, for he'd changed the conversation, telling us about the Bourbonnais country that we'd entered when we crossed the river, informing us about their livelihoods and their customs, and reasoning like a man who isn't a fool on any subject.

Two hours later, having suffered no more weariness nor difficulty, but having climbed constantly, we reached Mesples* which is the parish next to the forest in which we were to find Joseph. We merely passed through the village, where Huriel was greeted by many men who seemed to hold him in high esteem, and by girls whose eyes followed him, and seemed astonished at the company he was taking with him.

We still hadn't arrived at our destination. It was in the depths of the woods, or to put it better, at their highest point, for the Alleu wood, which joins that of Chambérat, covers a plateau from which descend the sources of five or six little rivers or streams, and in those days formed a wild region surrounded by heaths that were more or less deserted, from which the view extended far out in all directions, and in all those directions all you could see were other forests or heaths going on endlessly.

All the same, we were still only in the lower Bourbonnais, which borders on the highest part of Berry, and Huriel told me that the country went on going up right to the Auvergne. The woods were beautiful, full of thickets of white oak, which is the finest species. The streams which cut through these woods creating ravines in thousands of places, made damper areas where alders grew, and willows, and aspen, all of them tall, strong trees, far outstripping those of our country. That was also where I first saw a tree whose trunk was white and whose foliage is superb, a tree that doesn't grow in our region and which is called the beech. I truly believe it's the king of trees after the oak, and if it's less beautiful than the oak, you could almost say even so that it's the prettier of the two. They were still fairly rare in that forest, and Huriel told me they grew in great numbers only in the middle of the Bourbonnais country.

I looked at all these things with great wonder, constantly expecting to see more rare things than were actually there, and amazed that the trees didn't have their heads in the earth and their roots in the air, so greatly do we worry about things that are far away and that we've never seen. As for Brulette, either she had a natural inclination for wild places, or she wanted to console Huriel for the criticisms she'd levelled at him, for she admired everything more than was reasonable, and paid honour and reverence to the slightest little flowers along the path.

We'd been walking for a good while without meeting a living soul, when Huriel said to us, pointing to a clearing and a great pile of cut trees: 'We're at the place where they cut the trees, and in two minutes, you'll see our town and my father's castle.' He said that laughingly, and yet we were still looking for something like a hamlet or houses, when he added, pointing out to us two huts made of wattle and daub that looked more like animals' lairs than human dwelling places: 'These are our summer palaces, our pleasure domes. Wait here, I'll run and let Joseph know.'

He galloped off, looked into the entrances of all these shacks, and came back to tell us, rather worried but hiding his worry as best he could: 'No one's here, that's a good sign. That means Joseph's well. He must have accompanied my father to work. Wait for me a little longer. Have a rest in our cabin, which is the first one here, just in front of you. I'll go and see where our invalid is.'

'No, indeed,' said Brulette. 'We'll go with you.'

'You don't mean you're afraid here? You've no reason to be. Here you're in the domain of the woodcutters, and, unlike the mule-drivers, they're not the devil's sidekicks. They're good country folk, like the people of your own region, and where my father reigns you have nothing to fear.'

'I'm not afraid of your people,' said Brulette, 'but I am worried not to see Joey. For all we know he may be dead and buried. The thought came into my mind a minute ago, and my blood ran cold.'

Huriel turned pale, as if the same idea had seized hold of him, too. But he didn't want to pay any attention to it. 'The good Lord won't have allowed that to happen! Get off your mules and leave them here, for they wouldn't fit through the thicket, and come with me.'

He took a path that led to another cutting, but there, too, we saw neither Joseph nor anyone else.

'You must think these woods are deserted,' Huriel said to us. 'Nevertheless, I can see, from the marks of fresh cuts, that the woodcutters have been working on them all morning. But this is the hour when they take a brief siesta, and they may well be lying down in the heather where we won't see them, unless we step on them. But listen! That's a sound to delight the heart! That's my father playing the pipes, I recognize his way of playing, and that's a sure sign that Joey isn't any worse, for it's not a sad tune, and I know my father would be sad if any misfortune had befallen Joey.'

We followed him, and it really was such beautiful music that Brulette, although eager to arrive, couldn't help stopping from time to time as if charmed.

Although I was not as gifted as she was in understanding such a thing, I, too, felt shaken in all five senses nature had given me. As I approached, it seemed to me that I was seeing things differently, and that I was breathing and walking in a new way. The trees seemed more lovely, as did earth and sky, and my heart was filled with a contentment whose cause I couldn't have explained. And at last we saw, on some rocks, beside a gentle murmuring stream full of flowers, a sad-looking Joey, standing beside a seated man who was piping for the poor invalid's pleasure. The dog Parpluche was beside them and seemed to listen, too, as if he were a person gifted with intelligence.

As no one yet took any notice of us, Brulette stopped us going any closer, for she wanted to look carefully at Joseph and discover his condition by his appearance before she spoke to him.

Joseph was as white as a sheet and as thin as a dead stick, showing us only too clearly that the mule-driver had not lied about him. But what consoled us a little was the fact that he was almost a head taller than he had been, something people who saw him every day would not have noticed, and which revealed to the two of us that he was ill because he'd grown so quickly. Although his cheeks were hollow and his lips were white, he had become a really handsome man, for despite his languorous state, his eyes were clear, and even as lively as running water, his hair was fine and parted above his white face in a way that recalled the good Lord Jesus, and this made him look like an angel, as unlike a peasant as an almond flower differs from an almond in its husk.

What's more, his hands were as white as those of a woman, because it was some time since he'd worked, and the Bourbonnais clothing he'd become accustomed to wearing made him look more free and easy, and better built, than his former hemp smocks and his heavy clogs.

But after we'd given all our attention to Joseph, we were obliged to look, too, at Huriel's father, a man whose like I have rarely seen, believe you me, and who, without having studied very much, had a broad knowledge and a mind which would not have demeaned someone richer and better known. He was a tall, strong man, as fine a figure as Huriel himself was, but broader of girth and shoulders; his heavy head and short neck recalled those of a bull. His face was not at all pretty, since his nose was flat, his lips thick and his eyes round; but for all that you couldn't help wanting to look at it, and the more you looked, the more you were seized by his air of strength, authority, and kindness. His big black eyes shone like two lightning bolts and his large mouth, when he laughed, would have brought you back to life from the worst of deaths.

At that moment his head was covered with a blue handkerchief, tied at the back, and he wore hardly any other piece of clothing than his breeches and his shirt, with a great leather apron, exactly the same colour and just as hard as his travel-worn hands. His fingers, which had been crushed and cut by many accidents in which they hadn't been spared, resembled misshapen box-tree roots, with great knots along their length, and you'd have said the only use they could be put to was as hammers to break stones. Nevertheless, he manipulated them as subtly on the chanter of his bagpipes as if they'd been light spindles or the slim feet of little birds.

Beside him lay the carcasses of great oaks newly cut or split asunder, among which could be seen the instruments of his work, his axe gleaming like a razor, his saw, which was as flexible as a reed, and his earthen bottle, whose wine kept his strength up.

Suddenly Joey, who had been listening without seeming to breathe, so happy and relieved it made him feel, saw his dog Parpluche come towards us to caress us; he lifted his eyes and saw us standing ten paces from him. His pallor turned to a fiery red, but he didn't move because he thought at first that this was a vision of people that the music made him imagine.

Brulette ran to him, arms outstretched. Then he cried out, and fell down on his knees, as if choking for breath, which filled me with fear, for I had no idea that love could be so strange, and I thought the shock had dealt him a death blow.

But he returned to his senses very quickly, and began to thank Brulette, and me, as well as Huriel, in words that were so friendly and which came so easily to his lips that you could truly say that it wasn't the same Joseph as the boy who for so long had answered 'I don't know' to everything you might say to him.

Père Bastien, or rather the great woodcutter, for that was the name he was known by in his region, put down his bagpipes and while Brulette and Joey talked to each other, he shook my hand as if he had known me since the day I was born.

'So this is your friend Tiennet?' he said to his son. 'Well, his face inspires confidence, and so does his physique. I think I'd have a hard time wrestling with him, and I've always noticed that the strongest men were the gentlest. I've seen the truth of that in you, Huriel, and in myself, for I've always felt I'd rather love my neighbour than crush him. Well, then, Tiennet, let me bid you welcome to our wild woods. You won't find here fine, pure wheat bread and salad greens of all kinds such as you find in your garden. But we'll try to feast you with good conversation and open friendship. I see you've come with the lovely girl of Nohant, who is a kind of sister and little mother to our Joey. That's good of you, for he lacked the heart to get better, but now I won't worry about him any more, and she seems the right doctor for him.'

He said this as he watched Joey, who was sitting on his heels at Brulette's feet and holding her hand as he drank his fill of her, and asked her about his mother, about Brulette's grandfather, about the neighbours, and the entire parish.

Brulette, seeing that the great woodcutter was talking about her, went up to him and apologized for not having greeted him first, but he made no bones about picking her up bodily and setting her on a rock as if to see all of her, just as if she were a saint or some other precious thing. Putting her back on the ground, he kissed her forehead, saying to Joey, who blushed as much as Brulette: 'You told me the truth! She's pretty from head to toe, and she looks to me to be perfect and unspoiled. Soul and body, she's of the finest quality you can get; you can see that in her eyes. So tell me, Huriel, for I've no way of knowing, being blind where my own children are concerned, is she as lovely as your sister? It seems to me she's no less lovely and that if both of them were mine I'd be quite incapable of saying which one I was prouder of. Come, come Brulette, don't be ashamed at being pretty, but don't be vain either. The worker who makes such a fine job of the creatures of this world did not consult you, and you have no hand in his work. But what he does for us can be spoilt by folly or stupidity, and I can see by the way you carry yourself that, far from being foolish or silly, you respect his gifts in your own being. Yes, indeed, you're a lovely girl, with a healthy heart and a firm spirit. I know you well enough, through your decision to come here, and comfort this poor lad, who called for you as the thirsty land calls out for rain. Many another wouldn't have done as you have, and by doing it you've earned my respect. So I ask you to give me your friendship, and I promise you that while you're here, I'll be a father to you; just as I ask your friendship for my son and daughter, who'll be your brother and sister.'

Brulette, whose heart had been heavy because of the ill treatment she'd received from the mule-drivers in the woods of La Roche, was so touched by the esteem and compliments of the great woodcutter that tears leapt into her eyes, and throwing her arms around his neck, she could answer him only by kissing him as if he were her own father.

'That's the best of answers,' he said, 'and I'm happy with it.
Well then, my children, I've had my rest and now it's time I
was back at work. If you're hungry, here's my sack and my
few provisions. Huriel will leave shortly to tell his sister to
come and join us, and you others, my Berry friends, you'll
chat with Joseph, for I imagine you've a lot of things to talk
about. But unless you're with him don't go far from the hum
and noise of my axe, for you don't know the forest and you
could get lost.'

At that he set to work on the trees, having hung his bagpipes on one that was still standing. Huriel ate a little with us,
and when Brulette asked him about his sister, he said: 'My
sister Thérence is a good, kind girl about your age. I won't
say, like my father, that she could stand comparison with you,
but, such as she is, she's worth looking at, and she's not the
silliest of girls either. She's used to following my father wherever he goes in the forest, so that he lacks for nothing, for a
woodcutter's life, like that of a mule-driver, is very harsh and
very sad if he has no heart's companion.'

'And where is she now?' asked Brulette. 'Can't we go in
search of her?'

'I don't know where she is,' said Huriel. 'I'm surprised that
she didn't hear us coming, for she usually doesn't go far from
the huts. Have you seen her today, Joey?'

'Yes, but not since morning. She was a little down-hearted,
and complained of a headache.'

'It's not like her to complain of anything!' said Huriel. 'Well
then, excuse me, Brulette, I'll go and find her as quickly as
possible.'

THIRTEENTH EVENING

When Huriel had left us, we walked and talked with Joseph,
but, thinking he was pleased to have seen me, but would be
even more pleased to be alone with Brulette, I left them
together and went to join père Bastien and watch him at work.
You couldn't imagine a more delightful sight, for in my

entire life I've never seen a man carry out his work in so hearty
and cheerful a manner. I truly think he could easily have done
the work of four of the strongest Christians in a day, and that
he could do so without ever stopping laughing and talking
when he had company, or singing and whistling when he was
alone. He was so warm-blooded and energetic, that he made
me want to help him, and I was sorry not to have any work of
my own to do. He told me that in general the splitters and
cutters were people who lived near the woods in which they
worked, and that when their homes were hard by they would
come for the day. Others, who lived rather further away, came
by the week, returning home each Saturday. As for those who,
like him, came down from the high country, they signed on for
three months, and their cabins were larger, better built and
better stocked than those of the woodcutters who worked by
the week.

It was more or less the same situation with the charcoal
burners. That term doesn't refer to those who buy charcoal
to sell it again, but those who are employed by the owners
of the woods and forests to make it themselves. There were
also some who had bought the right to trade in it, just as
there were mule-drivers who traded on their own account,
but generally their trade consisted merely in transporting
goods.

These days, the mule-drivers' trade is diminishing, and will
die away. Now we have better tracks through the forests, and
there are fewer of those terrible spots which pose such problems for horses and carts, and where the mule train is the only
possibility. The number of smithies and factories that still use
charcoal has much diminished, and we don't see many of
those workers in our region nowadays. But there are still some
who travel through the great woods of Cheurre in Berry, just
as one still sees the cutters and splitters of Bourbonnais, but in
the days I'm talking about, when the woods still covered at
least half our provinces, all these trades were greatly sought
after and very profitable, so that when a forest was being
exploited, you'd find in it a whole population of these different tradespeople, some from the area itself and others from
places far away, and each had their own customs and guilds,

and as far as possible, they all lived on good terms with one another.

Père Bastien told me, and later I was to witness it myself, that all the men who worked in the woods grew so used to this hard, varied existence, that they suffered from a kind of homesickness when they had to live on the plains. As for himself, he loved the woods as deeply as if he'd been a fox or a wolf, even though he was the best Christian and the most entertaining companion you could find.

Nevertheless, he didn't mock me, as Huriel had done, for my preference for my own country. 'Every country is beautiful,' he said, 'just because it is our own. It's good that each of us should have a particular liking for the land that nourished us. It's a grace given by the good Lord so that the gloomy and poor lands won't be abandoned. I've heard tell from folk who have travelled far afield that there are lands under heaven that snow or ice covers pretty well the whole year through, and others where fire comes out of the mountains and ravages everything. But still they go on building fine houses on those devilish mountains, and still they go on digging holes to live in under that ice. People fall in love there, get married, dance, sing, sleep, raise children just as they do in our own country. So let's not despise anyone's family or house. The mole loves its dark cave as the bird loves its nest in the tree tops, and the ant would laugh in your face if you tried to convince her that there are kings whose palaces are finer than her little nest.'

The day moved on without bringing Huriel back with his sister Thérence. Père Bastien was a little surprised by this, but not worried. On several occasions I went over to Brulette and Joseph who were not far away; but when I saw that they were still talking and paying no attention to my approach, I went off again alone, finding the time hanging heavy on my hands. Before anything else, I, too, was a real friend of that dear girl. Ten times a day I'd believe myself in love with her, ten times a day I'd think I'd recovered, and most often I no longer convinced myself sufficiently to feel unhappy about it. I'd never been particularly jealous of Joseph before the moment when the mule-driver had told us of the great fire that was consuming young Joey, and since that moment, strangely enough, I hadn't felt any jealousy at all! The more compassionately Brulette treated him, the more it seemed to me that she was doing so through a sense of nothing more than friendship. And that saddened me instead of delighting me. Since I no longer held out any hope on my own account, I at least hoped to keep her nearby and have the company of someone who put all those around her at their ease, and I also felt that, if anyone deserved to be chosen by her, it was this young lad who had always loved her, and who no doubt would never earn the love of any other girl.

I was even surprised that this wasn't how Brulette herself secretly thought, especially when she saw that Joey, despite his illness, had become kind, knowledgeable and an amusing talker. There was no doubt this change was due to the company of the great woodcutter and his son, but he'd invested a lot of his own will-power, and she should have been grateful to him. Nevertheless, Brulette didn't seem aware of this change and it seemed to me that, on our way there, she had paid much more attention to the mule-driver Huriel than she had ever paid to anyone else. That was the thought that troubled me more and more as time went by, for if her fancy were dwelling on this stranger, two great sorrows lay in store for me: the first was that our poor Joey would die of grief as a result, and the second was that our lovely Brulette would leave our land and I would neither see her nor talk with her anymore.

I'd reached that point in my thinking when I saw Huriel return, bringing with him a girl who was so lovely that Brulette came nowhere near her. She was tall, slender, broad-shouldered and loose-limbed, like her brother, in all her movements. Her skin was by nature brown in tint, but living constantly in the shadows of the woods, she had grown pale rather than white, yet that sort of pallor charmed the viewer at the same time as it surprised him, and all the features of her face were perfect. I was certainly a little shocked by her straw hat, which turned up at the back like the poop of a boat, but it revealed a chignon of hair so black and abundant that one quickly grew used to looking at it. What I noticed in the first moment was that she was not as gracious and didn't smile as much as Brulette. She didn't try to make herself prettier than she was, and she appeared more determined, warmer in will, and colder in manners.

Because I was sitting down against a pile of cut wood, they didn't see me, and when they stopped near me at the fork of a path, they spoke to one another as people do when they are alone.

'I won't go,' fair Thérence was saying in a resolute tone. 'I'll go to the huts to prepare their supper and their beds; that's all I want to do just now.'

'And you won't speak to them? You're going to show them what a bad mood you're in?' asked Huriel who seemed surprised.

'I'm not in a bad mood,' the girl replied, 'and what's more, if I am in a bad mood, I'm not obliged to show it.'

'But you do show it, since you won't go and tell that girl you're here, although she must be getting tired of the company of men and would be very satisfied, I bet, to be with another young girl.'

'She can't be bored unless she has a hard heart. But it's not my job to amuse her. I'll serve her and help her, that's all my duty tells me to do.'

'But she's waiting for you. What am I going to say to her?'

'Tell her whatever you like. I don't have to account to her for my behaviour.' At that the woodcutter's daughter set off on the path, and Huriel stood for a moment in thought, like a man who is trying to guess something.

He was going on his way, but I remained where I was, as still as a stone. I had experienced something like a surprising dream when I first set eyes on Thérence. I said to myself: 'I know that face. Who does she look like?' And then, as I looked at her while she was speaking, I realized that she reminded me of the little girl in the bogged cart who had made me dream through a whole evening, and who could well be the reason why Brulette, finding me too simple in my tastes, had turned her thoughts away from me. And finally, when she passed close by me as she went away, even though her look of resentment was very different from the sweet, calm face I'd remembered, I saw the black mark she had at the corner of her mouth, proving that it was indeed the girl of the woods whom

I had carried in my arms and who had kissed me as willingly at that time as she now seemed ill-disposed to welcome me.

I ruminated for a long time over such a meeting, but finally the woodcutter's bagpipes, sounding a kind of fanfare, made me aware that the sun had just set.

I had no difficulty finding the path to the lodges, as they call the forest worker's huts. Huriel's was the biggest and the best constructed, and consisted of two bedrooms, including one for Thérence. In front of it was a kind of lean-to, tiled with green broom, which provided much protection from wind and rain. Hewn logs, set on tree trunks, formed a table which had been set for the occasion.

Normally, the Huriel family lived only on bread and cheese, with a little salt meat once a day. This diet was the result neither of avarice nor poverty, but of simple habits, for these woodland people consider as a pointless nuisance our need to eat something hot, and to make women work in the kitchens from morning to night.

Nevertheless, because she expected that either Joseph's mother or Brulette's grandfather would come, Thérence had wanted to make them comfortable and the day before she had stocked up on provisions at Mesples. She had just lit the fire in the clearing, and summoned her neighbours to help her. These were two woodcutters' wives, one old and the other ugly. These were the only women in the forest, for these people are neither accustomed, nor wealthy enough, to bring their families into the forest with them. The neighbouring lodges, which numbered six, housed a dozen men who were beginning to gather a heap of sticks to eat their supper in each other's company, dining on their poor morsel of bacon and their rye bread. But the great woodcutter went up to them before he put down his tools and took off his apron, and said with his open friendly air: 'Brothers, today I have strangers with me, and I don't want them to suffer our usual customs, but it'll never be said that a roast was eaten and Sancerre wine was drunk at the lodge of the woodcutter without all his friends taking part. Come, I want to introduce you to our guests. Now, don't refuse, if you don't want to disappoint me.'

No one refused, and there were about twenty of us gathered

there, I won't say around the table, since those folk don't care for comfort, but sitting on stones or the grass, or lying full length on wood chips, or stretched out on a twisted tree, and all looking less like a company of Christians—baptized though they may have been—than a herd of wild boars.

Meanwhile fair Thérence came and went, and still didn't seem willing to notice us in the slightest, when her father, who'd called her, but to whom she hadn't appeared to pay any attention, caught her as she passed by, and, bringing her along in spite of herself, introduced us to her: 'Forgive her, my friends. She's a wild child, born and raised in the heart of the forest. She's shy but she'll get over it, and I'd ask you, Brulette, to encourage her for she grows on you as you get to know her.'

At that Brulette, who was neither embarrassed nor ill-disposed, opened her arms and threw them around Thérence's neck, while Thérence, who didn't dare stave her off, but didn't know how to let herself go, stood stock-still watching her and did no more than lift her head and eyes which until then had been firmly fixed on the earth. In that position, seeing each other so close, with their eyes looking into each other's eyes, and their cheeks almost against each other's cheeks, they made me think of two young heifers, one of which thrusts its head forward to play while the other, suspicious and already cunning with her horns, waits in order to strike home a treacherous blow.

But Thérence seemed suddenly won over by Brulette's gentle gaze, and pulling her face back, she dropped it on the other's shoulder, to hide the tears which filled her eyes.

'Well, well,' said père Bastien, encouraging and caressing his daughter. 'That's what's called being unsociable. I would never have believed that a girl's shyness would go as far as tears. But, it takes a wise mind to understand children! Come, Brulette, you seem to me the more rational of the two of you, go with her and don't leave her until she's spoken to you. It's only the first word that's hard.'

'Of course I will. I'll help her and at the first command she gives me I'll obey her so well that she'll forgive me for having frightened her.'

And while the two of them went off together, the great
woodcutter said to me: 'Now that's women for you! The least
coquettish of them (and my Thérence is among their number)
can't come face to face with a rival in beauty without being
either inflamed with chagrin, or frozen with fear. The loveliest
stars in the heavens stay side by side harmoniously, but whenever there are two daughters of mother Eve, there's always at
least one who's hurt by the comparison made between herself
and the other.'

'I think, father,' said Huriel, 'that you're not being just to
Thérence right now. She's neither shy nor envious.' And he
added in a whisper: 'I think I know what she's unhappy about,
but it would be best to pay no attention to it.'

They brought roast meat, beautiful yellow mushrooms that
I couldn't find the courage to taste, although I saw everyone
around me eating them without any worries; fricasseed eggs
with various strong herbs, griddle cakes made of black wheat;
and cheeses from Chambérat,* famous throughout the land.
All those present made a feast of it, but in a very different way
from ours. Instead of taking their time and enjoying each
morsel, they bolted it down as if they were starving, which in
our part of the world would scarcely have been seemly, and
they didn't wait until they were well fed before they began
singing and dancing, right in the middle of the feast.

These people, whose blood is less staid than ours, seemed
incapable of staying still. They didn't wait patiently until they
were offered another dish. They would bring along their bread
to have some stew put on it, refused plates, and would go back
to where they'd been sitting or lying. Some also ate standing
up, while others chatted and gesticulated, each telling a tale or
singing a song. It was as if there were bees buzzing around a
hive: it made me feel giddy and didn't put me in the mood for
feasting.

Although the wine was good and the great woodcutter
handed it around generously, no one took more than they
should have, everyone conscious of their job and not wanting
to spoil themselves for the following day's work. So the feast
didn't last long, and although in the middle it had the signs of
growing wild, it ended early and calmly. The woodcutter was

warmly thanked for his hospitality, and it was obvious that he was the natural commander of the whole group, not just because of his means but because of his good heart and sound head.

We received many offers of friendship and help, and I have to admit that these people were more open and cordial than the folk of our region. I saw that Huriel led them one by one to Brulette, introduced them to her by name, and urged them to treat her exactly as they did his sister, which brought her so many courtesies and so much politeness that she had never been so well received in our village.

When the time came for sleeping, the great woodcutter offered to share his room with me. Joey had his own lodge next to ours, but it was smaller and we would have been uncomfortable there. So I followed my host, all the more willingly as I'd been charged with keeping a close eye on Brulette, but I saw when I went into the lodge that she was not in the slightest danger there, for she was to share a bed with fair Thérence, and the mule-driver, faithful to his habits, had already lain down across her door, so that neither wolf nor thief could have come near.

When I glanced into the little room into which the two girls were to retire, I saw that it contained a bed and a few items of furniture, all very clean. Huriel, thanks to his mules, could easily transport his sister's few possessions at no cost, but those of his father can hardly have caused him many problems, for all he had was a pile of dry bracken and a blanket. Even so, the great woodcutter considered this too much, and felt that he would do better to sleep under the stars, like his son.

I was weary enough to do without a bed, and fell fast asleep until daybreak. I thought Brulette had done likewise, for I heard no more noise of movement than if she had been a small stone, behind the plank wall that separated us.

When I got up, the woodcutter and his son were standing together, talking.

'We were just talking about you,' the father said to me, 'and as we must go to work, I want a decision on the matter we're discussing. I've pointed out to Brulette that Joseph needs her company for a little while, and she's told me she would like to be with him as much as possible, so she's promised to stay for at least a week. But she couldn't make any promises for you, and begged us to convince you to stay, too. That's what we'll do, I hope, when we tell you that we're perfectly happy about it, you're no problem to us, and we beg you to treat us exactly as we'd treat you, should the need arise.'

This was said with an air of truth and friendship which obliged me give my promise and, indeed, since I couldn't abandon Brulette to the company of strangers, even though a week seemed very long to me, I was forced to resign myself to her will and Joseph's need.

'Thank you for that, my dear Tiennet,' said Brulette as she came out of Thérence's room. 'And thanks, too, to these good people who have given us such a warm welcome. But if I stay it's on condition that we won't cost you anything and that we'll both be free to pay for our expenses as it suits us.'

'It will be exactly as you want it to be,' said Huriel, 'for if the fear of causing us any expense were to make you leave too early, we'd prefer not to have the pleasure of serving you. But just remember one thing, my father earns money and so do I, and we know no greater delight than to be obliging to our friends and treat them honourably.'

It seemed to me that Huriel seized on any occasion to make his coins ring out, as if to say: 'I'm a good catch.' Nevertheless he immediately behaved like a man who stands to one side, for he told us he was going to leave us.

On that, Brulette was seized by a brief shiver that I alone saw and that she quickly mastered to ask him, without appearing to care very much, where he was going and for how long.

'I'm off to work in the woods of La Roche. I'll be close enough to you to come back and see you if you need me. Tiennet knows how to go there. I'm going this way, first, into the heaths of La Croze in search of my animals and my equipment, and on my way back I'll drop in and say farewell.'

On that he left, and the great woodcutter, urging his daughter to take great care of us and treat us well, went off on his own to work.

So there we were, Brulette and I, in the company of fair Thérence, who, although she served us as actively as if she'd been in our pay, didn't seem eager to make us feel particularly welcome, since she answered by a mere 'yes' or 'no' everything we could think of saying to her. Eventually her indifference rebuffed Brulette, who said to me at a time when we were alone: 'Tiennet, I have the impression that that girl dislikes us. She made room for me in her bed last night exactly as someone would make room for a hedgehog. She flung herself onto the far side of the bed, nose against the wall, and apart from asking whether I wanted more or less of the blanket, she didn't want to say a single word to me. I was so tired I'd have willingly gone straight off to sleep and when I saw she was pretending to sleep so as not to have to talk to me, I pretended, too. But for ages I couldn't close my eyes, for I could hear she was choking back tears. If you take my advice, we won't inconvenience her much longer, but will look for some vacant lodges in another part of the forest, and if there are none, I'll fix things up with the old woman I saw here yesterday, so that she can send her husband to a neighbour's and share her lodge with me. If it's only a herb bed it'll be enough for me. The price of a mattress and pillow is too high if you're received with tears. As for our meals, I'm relying on you, beginning today, to go to Mesples to buy what we need and I'll do the cooking.'

'That's a good idea, Brulette,' I answered. 'I'll do whatever you want. Let's look for a lodge for you and don't worry about me. I'm no more made of salt than the mule-driver is and I can quite well sleep outside across your door. I'd willingly do that for you and I wouldn't be afraid of dissolving in the dew. Nevertheless, listen to me. If we leave the woodcutter's lodge and table like that, he'll think we're angry, and as he's treated us too well to have any cause to reproach himself he'll easily see that it's his daughter who's rebuffed us. He'll probably scold her, and we really ought to see whether or not she deserves it. You say the girl was very good to you, even submissive. Well, if she has some hidden sorrow, do we have the right to criticize her sadness and her silence? Wouldn't it be better to pretend we don't notice anything, to leave her free all day to see or receive her lover, if she has one, and, as to us, we'll keep Joey company, since he's the reason we came here. Don't you think, too, that if we're seen in search of another lodging people will think we're plotting something evil and that's why we're keeping out of things.'

'You're right Tiennet. Very well, I'll be patient with that big sourpuss and watch her gradually come round.'

FOURTEENTH EVENING

Fair Thérence had prepared everything for our breakfast, and seeing the sun rise into the heavens, she asked Brulette if she'd thought to wake Joseph. 'It's time he woke up, he's angry when I let him sleep too late, because the next night he finds it hard to settle back in the old pattern.'

'If you're the one who usually calls him, my dear,' answered Brulette, 'then do it. I'm not used to his habits.'

'Certainly not,' answered Thérence abruptly. 'It's your business to look after him now, since that's why you've come here. As that's the case, I can give myself a break from it and leave it in your hands.'

'Poor Joey!' our Brulette couldn't help exclaiming. 'I can see he's a great problem for you, and that the best he could do would be to come back home with us!'

Thérence turned her back on us without a word, and I said to Brulette: 'Let's both go and call him. I bet he'll be pleased to hear your voice first of all.'

Joey's lodge almost touched that of the great woodcutter. As soon as he heard Brulette's voice, he came running to look at her through the door, and said to her: 'Ah! I was afraid I'd been dreaming, Brulette! So it really is true that you're here?'

When he'd taken a seat on a stump between the two of us, he told us that, for the first time in a long while, he'd slept straight through, and that was obvious from his face, which was worth ten sous more than it had been the day before. Thérence brought him some chicken broth in a bowl, and he wanted to give it to Brulette, who refused all the more firmly because the dark eyes of the maid of the woods seemed furious that the offer had been made.

Brulette, who was too smart to want to give Thérence any reason for resentment, refused, saying she didn't care for broth and that it would be a great pity to have let the nurse go to the bother of making it, if he gained from it neither profit nor pleasure, and she added gently: 'I can see, my lad, that you've been looked after like a plump townsman, and that these fine people have spared nothing to bring you back to health.'

'Yes,' answered Joseph, seizing Thérence's hand and joining it in his own with Brulette's: 'I've been an expense to my master (he always called the great woodcutter his master because he taught him music) and I've wearied this poor sister here. Let me tell you, Brulette, that in addition to you, I've found another angel on this earth. Just as you helped my spirit and consoled my heart when I was a star-gazing child, and more or less good for nothing, she's cared for my poor distressed body when I collapsed here in the misery of fever. I'll never be able to thank her enough for the help she gave me, but there is one thing I can say, and that's that there isn't a third like you two, and on the day when the good Lord brings us to judgement, he'll set aside in heaven his two most beautiful crowns for Catherine Brulet, the rose of Berry, and for Thérence Huriel, the mayflower of the woods.'

Joseph's gentle words seemed to put balm on Thérence's bleeding heart, for she no longer refused to sit down and eat with us, and Joseph sat between these two lovely girls while I, profiting from the easy manners I'd noted in this area, wandered about as I ate, in order to be now near one, now near the other.

I did my utmost to please the maid of the woods with my attentions, and I considered it a point of honour to show her that Berry men are no louts. She answered my courteous words very gently, but I couldn't succeed in making her smile or in getting her to lift her eyes to mine when she answered me. She seemed to me to have a strange temperament, swift to scorn and full of distrust. Nevertheless, when she was still, there was something so good in her appearance and in her voice that you couldn't judge her harshly. But neither in her good moments nor in others did I dare ask her if she remembered that I'd carried her in my arms, and that she'd repaid me with a kiss. I was certain it was she, for her father, to whom I'd spoken about it, hadn't forgotten the encounter, and claimed to have recognized my face without knowing exactly why.

While she was eating her breakfast, Brulette, as she informed me later, began to suspect another truth. That's why she decided to observe and to pretend in order to find out more about it.

'Well then,' she said, 'am I to spend the whole day here with my arms crossed? Although I'm not a great worker, I'm not used to doing nothing but tell my beads between meals, and I beg you, Thérence, to show me some work in which I can help you. If you want to go somewhere I'll look after the lodge for you and do whatever you tell me to; but if you stay, I'll stay, too, provided you put me to work for you.'

'I don't need any help,' said Thérence, 'and you don't need any work to amuse you.'

'Why so, my dear?'

'Because you're with your friend and as I don't want to intrude on all the things you have to tell one another, I'll leave if you want to stay and I'll stay if you want to go out.'

'That won't suit either Joseph or me,' said Brulette with a cunning expression. 'I haven't any secrets to tell him, and everything we have to say to one another we said yesterday. Right now the pleasure we have in seeing each other can only grow in your company and we ask you for it, that is, unless you have company you prefer to us.'

Thérence hesitated, and the glance she cast at Joseph showed Brulette that her pride suffered at the thought of intruding. At that Brulette said to Joseph: 'Well, help me to keep her with us! Wouldn't you like that? Weren't you saying just now that we were your guardian angels? And don't you want your angels to work together to rescue you?'

'That's right, Brulette,' said Joseph. 'Between your two good hearts, I ought to recover more quickly, and if there are two of you who are willing to love me, it seems to me that each of you will love me better, as when you set to work with a good friend who gives you his strength to add to your own.'

'Am I, then,' said Thérence, 'to be the good companion your countryman needs? Well and good! I'll get my work and bring it back here.'

She went in search of some linen cut into the shape of a shirt and began to sew. Brulette wanted to help her, and when she refused, said to Joseph: 'Well then, give me any of your clothes that need repairing. They must be in need of me, for it's a long time since I've had anything to do with them.'

Thérence let her examine Joseph's clothes, but there wasn't a single stitch to be done, not even a button to sew on, so carefully had they been tended. Brulette talked of buying linen at Mesples the following day, to make him some new shirts. But it turned out that those that Thérence was making just then were intended for Joseph, and that she wanted to make them all on her own, just as she had begun them.

Brulette became more and more suspicious, so she pretended to insist on having work to do, and even Joseph was obliged to put his word in, claiming that Brulette was getting bored at having nothing to do. Then Thérence hurled her work down angrily, saying to Brulette: 'Well finish them yourself! I'm not having anything more to do with them.' And she went off to sulk in the lodge.

'Joey,' asserted Brulette, 'that girl is neither capricious nor mad, as I'd imagined she must be. She's in love with you!'

Joseph had such a shock that Brulette could see she'd spoken too quickly. She still didn't realize just how weak and fearful a man is when he's physically ill, as a result of a spiritual malady, and finds he has to think things through.

'Whatever are you saying? What new misfortune has befallen me?'

'Why should it be a misfortune?'

'Are you asking me, Brulette? Do you think it's in my power to return her feelings?'

'Well, then,' said Brulette, trying to calm him down, 'she'll get over it!'

'I don't know if you can get over love,' said Joseph. 'But if,

through ignorance or carelessness, I'd brought misfortune to
the great woodcutter's daughter, to Huriel's sister, to the maid
of the woods, who's prayed so much for me and watched over
me so carefully, I would be so guilty I could never forgive
myself.'

'It never occurred to you, then, that her friendship might
change into love?'

'No, Brulette, never!'

'Well, that's strange, Joey!'

'Why should it be? Haven't I been used ever since childhood
to people pitying me for my stupidity and helping me in my
weakness? Take the friendship you've always shown me,
Brulette, did that ever make me vain enough to believe...'
Here Joseph went as red as fire and couldn't say another
word.

'You're right,' said Brulette, who was as prudent and alert
as Thérence was abrupt and sensitive. 'It's easy to be very
wrong about the feelings one provokes and receives. That was
just a mad idea I had about that girl, and if you don't share it,
the reason must be that it has no foundation in truth.
Thérence must still be, as I am, ignorant of what is called true
love, as she waits for the good Lord to order her to live for the
man He's chosen for her.'

'It doesn't matter,' said Joseph. 'I want to leave this land
and I must do so.'

'We've come to take you home,' I said to him, 'just as soon
as you feel strong enough.'

Contrary to my expectations, he strongly rejected that idea.
'No, no,' he said. 'The only strength I have is my desire to be
a great musician, and to allow my mother to retire with me
and live honoured and sought out in my country. If I leave this
land, I'll go into the high Bourbonnais until such time as I'm
received as a master piper.'

We dared not say to him that it didn't seem likely to us that
he'd ever enjoy healthy lungs.

Brulette spoke to him of other matters. Meanwhile I was
engrossed in the discovery she'd revealed to me about
Thérence, and, I don't know why, concerned about the girl I'd
just seen leaving her lodge and striking out into the woods. I

began to walk in the direction she'd taken, proceeding as if at random, but curious and even eager to meet her.

It wasn't long before I heard stifled sighs which revealed to me where she'd hidden herself. No longer feeling embarrassed with her, given that I'd played no part in her unhappiness, I went up to her and spoke to her resolutely: 'Fair Thérence!' I said to her, seeing that she no longer sobbed but merely trembled and gasped as if she were holding her rage in check, 'I think my cousin and I are the cause of your sadness. Our faces shock you, and especially Brulette's, for I don't think mine is worth so much of your attention. We were speaking of you this morning, and I even stopped her from going away from your lodge, where she truly thought she was a burden to you. Now tell me frankly, and we'll go elsewhere. For even if you do think poorly of us, we're none the less well-disposed where you're concerned, and we don't want to cause you any displeasure.'

Proud Thérence seemed outraged by my frankness, and leapt up from the place where I had sat down beside her. 'So your cousin wants to go away, does she?' she said in menacing tones. 'She wants to bring shame on me? No, she won't do that! or else . . .'

'Or else what?' I asked her, determined to have it out with her.

'Or else I'll leave the woods and my father and my family, and I'll go and die alone in some deserted area!'

She spoke as if in a fever, with an eye so dark and a face so pale that I was afraid. 'Thérence,' I said to her, taking her hand and making her sit down again, 'either you were born unjust, or you have your reasons for hating Brulette. Well, tell me what those reasons are, as a good Christian, for I may be able to clear her of the evil you accuse her of.'

'No, you won't clear her, for I know all about her!' Thérence shouted out, unable to control herself. 'Don't imagine I know nothing about her! I've racked my brains enough and questioned Joseph and my brother enough to judge from her behaviour that she has an ungrateful heart and a deceitful soul. She's a flirt, that's what she is, your Berry girl, and every upright person has the right to detest her.'

'That's a very harsh judgement,' I answered, imperturbably. 'What do you base it on?'

'Well, doesn't she know that there are three boys here who love her, while she just keeps them stringing along? Joseph, who's dying of it, my brother, who's fighting it, and you yourself, who are trying to get over it? Do you really mean to convince me that she knows nothing about it, and that she has a preference for one or the other? No! There's only one person she cares about: she doesn't pity Joseph, she doesn't value my brother, she doesn't love you. Your torment amuses her, and since she has in her village fifty other beaux, she claims to live for all and for none. Well, I don't care about you, Tiennet, since I don't know you. But as for my brother whose work often takes him far from us, and who leaves us at a moment when he could stay . . . and as for Joseph who's been driven ill and almost stupid by it . . . Ah! look, your Brulette is really guilty where those two are concerned, and ought to blush because she can't say a good word to either of them.'

At that moment, Brulette, who'd been listening to us, revealed herself. She wasn't at all used to being treated in such a way, but still she was happy to have heard a reason for Huriel's behaviour. She sat down beside Thérence and took her hand with a serious expression on her face, an expression which contained both compassion and reproach. Thérence was somewhat calmed by this gesture and said to her gently: 'Forgive me, Brulette, if I hurt you. But truly I won't blame myself, if it encourages you to have better feelings. Look, do you agree that you've been false in the way you've behaved, and that you've been hard-hearted? I don't know if it's the custom in your country to arouse desire with the intention of rejecting it, but for all I'm a poor wild girl I think it's criminal to lie, and I can't understand such stratagems. So open your eyes to the evil you're committing. I won't tell you my brother will fall victim to it, since he's too strong and brave, and loved by too many girls who are all your equals, to be unable to make up his own mind. But do take pity on poor Joey, Brulette! You don't know him, although you were raised together. You consider him an imbecile, but on the contrary, he's very intelligent. You think him cold and indifferent, whereas he's devoured by a grief that proves the contrary. But his body is too weak to withstand distress, if you abuse it. Give him your heart as he deserves, I beg you. I'll curse you if you make him die!'

'Do you really believe what you've just told me, my poor Thérence?' said Brulette, looking into the other's eyes. 'If you want to know what I really think, I'll tell you I believe you love Joseph and that, against my will, I'm inflicting on you so much jealousy that you seek out faults of mine to criticize. Well, look closely, and with clearer eyes, my dear. I don't want to make this boy love me, I've never dreamt of doing so, and I'm sorry that he should do so. I'm even absolutely ready to help you cure him, and if I'd known what you have revealed to me, I wouldn't have come here, even though your brother told me the matter was urgent.'

'Brulette, you must think I have very little pride if you believe I love Joseph as you understand it, and that I'd sink to jealousy for your amusement. I'm not the sort to blind myself to the way in which I love him, and I've no reason to be ashamed about it either. If that were true, I would at the very least have pride enough not to let anyone believe I was your rival. But my friendship for him is so strong and so honest that I'll defend him courageously against your traps. So, love him as well as I do, and then instead of resenting you for doing so, I'll love you and admire you. I recognize your rights, which are more longstanding than mine, and I'll help you take him back to your own country on condition that he will be your only friend and your husband. Otherwise you can expect to find in me an enemy who will openly condemn you. I'm not going to let people say that I loved that boy and nursed him when he was ill so that a fine village flirt could come and kill him before my very eyes.'

'Well and good,' said Brulette, who'd recovered all her pride. 'It's more and more obvious to me that you're in love and you're jealous, and that makes me all the more certain I can calmly go away and leave him to your care. That you're honestly and closely attached to him, I have no doubts; I myself don't have, as you do, good reason to be angry and unjust. Still, it surprises me that you want me to stay and that you're willing to seem friendly towards me. That's where your sincerity ends, and I tell you I want to know the reason why, or else I won't do as you ask.'

'The reason for that concerns something you yourself have already mentioned, when you used evil words to humiliate me. You have just said that I'm in love and jealous. If that's the way in which you explain the strength and goodness of my feelings for Joseph you won't fail to make him believe it, too, and that young man, who owes me respect and gratitude, will think he has the right to despise me and mock me in his heart of hearts.'

'You're right, Thérence,' said Brulette, whose heart and mind were too just not to value the pride of the maid of the woods. 'It's my duty to help you keep your secret, and I shall do so. I won't say that I'll do all in my power to win Joseph over; your pride would find that offensive, and I understand why you wouldn't want to receive his friendship as a grace bestowed by me. But I beg you to be just, to reflect, and even to give me the advice that, since I'm softer and more humble than you are, I ask of you for the better guidance of my soul.'

'Ask me, then. I'm listening,' answered Thérence, appeased by Brulette's submission and good sense.

'Well, the thing is that he doesn't love me in the way I want to be loved. I've known Joseph from early childhood. Before coming here he was never particularly pleasant, and he was so withdrawn that I thought him selfish. Now I'm willing to believe that he wasn't selfish in any bad way, but after the conversation we had together yesterday, I'm still sure that I would have in his heart a rival who would quickly crush me, and that he would prefer this mistress to his lawful wife. Don't misunderstand me, Thérence, I'm talking about music.'

'That's sometimes occurred to me, too,' said Thérence, after thinking for a while, and looking consoled enough to show that if she had to fight a rival for Joseph's heart she preferred fighting against music than against the amiable Brulette. 'Joseph is very often in a state I've occasionally noticed in my father, when the pleasure of playing music becomes too much for them and nothing counts in comparison; but for all that, my father is so loving and so lovable that I'm not jealous of the pleasure he feels in music.'

'Well, Thérence, let's hope he'll make Joseph exactly like himself and therefore worthy of you.'

'Of me? Why of me rather than of you? God is my witness that I'm not concerned with myself when I work and pray for Joseph. My fate is of little consequence to me, believe me, Brulette, and I don't understand how anyone can think of herself in her friendship for someone else.'

'Then you're a kind of saint, my dear Thérence, and I feel I'm not your equal, for my own personality counts for something, indeed it counts for a great deal, when I let myself dream of happiness in love. Perhaps you don't love Joseph as I had imagined, but however things may be, please tell me how I should behave towards him. I'm not at all sure that in taking away any hope he may have I'd be dealing him a death blow. Otherwise you wouldn't see me so calm. But he's ill, that's really true, and I must be careful with him. That's where the friendship I feel for him is deep and sincere, and where I'm less of a flirt than you think, for if it were true that I had fifty beaux in my village, what would I gain, what entertainment would I find in coming to the woods to seek out the humblest and least valued of them all? It seemed to me, on the contrary, that you should esteem me all the more because, when the moment came, I felt no regrets in leaving my joyful company behind me to come and help a poor comrade who called on me to remember him.'

Thérence, understanding at last that she was in the wrong, threw her arms around Brulette's neck, without asking her pardon in any way, but showing by her caresses and her tears that she was truly sorry.

That was how things stood when Huriel, followed by his mules, preceded by his dogs, and mounted on his little horse, appeared at the end of the track beside which we were sitting.

The mule-driver was coming to bid us farewell, but nothing in his appearance showed the grief of a man who wants to heal himself, by fleeing from a harmful love affair. On the contrary, he looked in fine form and high spirits, and Brulette thought Thérence had only included him among her lovers in

order to find yet another reason, good or bad, for her initial
bad temper.

She even tried to make him tell her the real reason for his
departure, and as he claimed there was urgent work to be
done, while Thérence, for her part, contradicted him and tried
to make him stay, Brulette, rather piqued by his merriment,
accused him of being bored in the company of Berry folk. He
let her tease him and refused to change any of his plans, which
eventually offended Brulette and led her to say to him: 'Since
I may perhaps never see you again, don't you think, master
Huriel, that the time has come to give me back a pledge that
doesn't belong to you and still hangs in your ear?'

'Indeed,' he answered, 'I believe it belongs to me just as
much as my ear belongs to my head, since it's my sister who
gave it to me.'

'Your sister can't have given you something that belongs
either to Joseph or to me.'

'My sister took her first communion just as you did,
Brulette, and when I gave your jewel back to Joseph, she gave
me hers. Ask her to tell you if that's the truth or not.'

Thérence blushed deeply, and Huriel laughed in his sleeve.
Brulette thought the truth of the matter was that the most
deceived of the three of them was Joseph, who wore like a
relic around his neck Thérence's little silver heart, while the
mule-driver still wore the one that had initially been entrusted
to him. She was unwilling to play a role in this deception and
said to Thérence: 'My dear, I think the pledge Joseph has now
will bring him good luck and it's my opinion that he should
keep it, but since this one is yours, I beg you to ask your
brother to give it back to you so that you can give it to me,
because a gift from you would be something I'd really value.'

'I'll give you anything else you ask me for,' replied
Thérence, 'and I'll do so with all my heart; but that one no
longer belongs to me. When a gift has been given, it's given,
and I don't think Huriel would be willing to give it back to
me.'

'I'll do anything,' said Huriel swiftly, 'that Brulette wants
me to do. Come, are you asking for it?'

'Yes,' said Brulette, who could no longer withdraw, al-

though she was sorry the idea had ever occurred to her, now
that she saw how angry the mule-driver looked. He immediately opened his ear-ring and withdrew from it the pledge,
which he returned to Brulette, saying: 'Let it be as you want it.
I'll be consoled for losing my sister's pledge, if I'm sure you'll
neither give it away nor exchange it.'

'The proof that I'll do neither of those things,' said Brulette
as she attached it to Thérence's necklace, 'is that I'm giving it
to her for safe keeping. And as for you, your ear is free of that
weight now, and anyway, you no longer need a sign in order
to be recognized when you return to my country.'

'That's very good of you,' said the mule-driver, 'but as I've
done my duty where Joseph is concerned, and as you now
know what you need to know in order to make him happy,
I've no further reason to get involved in your affairs. I presume you'll take him home and that I'll never again have any
reason to return to your country. Farewell then, beautiful
Brulette, I wish you all the good fortune you deserve, and
leave you in the care of my family, who can serve you here
better than I could and who'll lead you home whenever you
wish to go.'

On that, he went off, singing:

> One mule, two mules, three little mules
> On the mountain see them go,
> The devil take the lot of them.

But his voice didn't seem as steady as it tried to appear, and
Brulette, whose unhappiness made her want to escape from
Thérence's attention, returned with the two of us to be with
Joseph.

FIFTEENTH EVENING

I won't give you a detailed account of every day we spent in
the forest. At first each day differed little from the others.
Joseph went from strength to strength, and Thérence wanted
us to cheer him in his hopes, although she did support

Brulette's decision not to encourage him to put his feelings into words. That posed no problems, for Joseph had sworn to himself that he would say nothing before the moment when he believed himself worthy of attention, and Brulette would have had to be very coquettish to tear from him a single flirtatious word.

As an extra precaution, she was careful never to be alone with him. She kept Thérence so closely bound to her side, that the maid of the woods soon came to realize not only that she wasn't being deceived, but that we even wanted to leave her entirely in charge of our invalid's health and heart.

These three people were certainly not idle together. Thérence constantly sewed for Joseph, and Brulette, having made me buy a handkerchief of white muslin, set about scalloping the hem and embroidering it as a present for Thérence. For she was a skilful needle-woman, and it was wonderful to watch a country girl create such fine and lovely work. She even pretended in Joseph's presence that she didn't like sewing and mending, so that she could free herself of the need to work for him, and force him to thank Thérence who did such a good job of it; but you know how ungrateful a man is, when he has a woman on his mind! Joseph scarcely glanced at Thérence's fingers, worn bare for him; his eyes were constantly on Brulette's soft hands, and it seemed that, when he watched her plying her needle, every stitch counted as a moment of happiness for him.

I was amazed at how much love could fill his thoughts and occupy his hours, and that he never gave a thought to doing something with his hands. As for me, however much I tried to peel willow and make baskets with it, or make braids for hats with oat stalks, I hadn't been there two full days before I was so intensely bored I felt ill. Sunday is a fine day, because it brings rest after six days of work, but seven Sundays in a week are too much for a man accustomed to put his limbs to good use. I wouldn't have noticed it, had one of those two beauties deigned to pay me any attention; indeed, pale Thérence, with her large, slightly deep-set, eyes and the black mark beside her mouth, would certainly have caught my fancy had she wanted to, but she was in no mood to change her affections. She spoke little, laughed even less, and if you tried the slightest bit of teasing, she looked at you with such an air of surprise that she made you lose all heart for explaining what you were doing.

The result was that, after frittering away two days with these three quiet people around the lodges or sitting with them here and there in the forest, after I had made sure that Brulette was as safe in this country as in our own, I began to look for some work to do, and I offered to help the great woodcutter in his task. He accepted me willingly and I began to enjoy myself in his company, but when I told him I didn't want to be paid and that I was working with him merely in order not to be bored, his good heart no longer restrained him from criticizing my errors, and he began to show me that where work was concerned there was no one less patient than he was. Since this was not my craft, and I didn't know how to make good use of the tools, I irritated him every time I was at all clumsy, and I could see only too well that he tried so hard not to treat me as an imbecile and a blockhead that his eyes almost burst from their sockets and sweat poured down his forehead.

Not wanting to exchange harsh words with a man who in all other respects was so good and pleasant, I spent my time working for the pit sawyers and acquitted myself to their satisfaction. But in doing so, I came to realize that work is hard and heavy when it's done merely as a form of physical exercise, and doesn't bring with it the thought of some kind of profit for oneself or one's loved ones.

On the fourth day, Brulette said to me: 'Tiennet, I can see you're not happy, and I won't hide from you the fact that I have my own share of worries, but it's Sunday tomorrow, and we need to think up some kind of celebration. I know the forest folk gather together in some pretty spot where the great woodcutter plays music for them to dance to. Well, let's buy some wine and food to give them a rather finer Sunday than usual, and bring honour to our own country while we're among these strangers.'

I carried out Brulette's instructions, and the following day we found ourselves on a fine meadow with all the forest workers and several local girls and women whom Thérence had invited to the dance. The great woodcutter played his pipes. His daughter, superb in her Bourbonnais costume, was treated splendidly, although she never abandoned her serious expression. Joey was utterly intoxicated with Brulette's charms as he watched her dance, for she hadn't forgotten to bring some finery with her, and her lovely face and pretty airs charmed everyone. I rushed about, being a good host to everyone and offering refreshments. I'd wanted to do things properly, so I hadn't spared any expense. It cost me a good three crowns out of my own pocket, but I've never regretted them, since everyone showed how much they appreciated what I offered them.

By the time vespers came, everything was going along perfectly, and everyone said that, in living memory, the woodland folk hadn't enjoyed themselves together so much. A mendicant monk even came by and, on the pretext of begging for his monastery, he filled his stomach and drank as deeply as any woodsman or axe-man there. I found this very funny, even though it was at my expense, for this was the first time I'd seen a Carmelite drink, and I had always heard that when it came to raising an elbow they were the best Christianity has to offer.

I was in the act of filling his glass, astonished that I couldn't make him drunk however much I gave him, when there was a great upheaval and commotion among the dancers. So I could watch what was going on, I came out of the log shelter I'd built for myself and where I received those who were thirsty, and I saw a band of three hundred, maybe four hundred, mules following their clairin who had taken it into his head to come straight through the throng of dancers. Thrust aside by everyone with kicks and blows, the clairin was leaping about in fear, so that the mules, those headstrong animals whose bones are very tough, and who are used to pushing through wherever their clairin goes, had struck a course straight through the dancers, not much bothered at being beaten about the rump, thrusting everyone aside, and going straight ahead as if they were in a field of thistles.

These animals didn't move particularly fast, for they were heavily laden, so people had time to move out of their way. No one was trampled or wounded, but many of the lads, warmed up by dancing, were annoyed to find their pleasure

interrupted, and laid about them with sticks, swearing fero-
ciously, so it made quite an amusing spectacle to watch. The
great woodcutter stopped piping and laughed so much he was
bent over double.

But since he knew what tune to play to gather the mules
together, a tune I knew as well from having heard it in the
forest of Saint Chartier, père Bastien played it correctly, and
immediately the clairin and his troop rushed around the
stump on which the woodcutter was standing, making him
laugh even more at the thought of having, instead of a fine
company of dancers, a group of black beasts to play for.

Meanwhile Brulette, who in the midst of all the hubbub had
come across to stand by me and Joseph, seemed apprehensive
and only laughed half-heartedly. 'What's the matter?' I asked
her. 'It may well be our friend Huriel coming back this way
and wanting to dance with you.'

'No indeed,' she answered. 'Thérence, who knows her
brother's mules only too well, says there isn't a single one of
his in this train. Moreover that isn't his horse and those aren't
his dogs. Well, I'm afraid of these mule-drivers, except for
Huriel, and I'd like us to get away from here.'

Just as she was saying this we caught sight of a score or so
of mule-drivers coming out from a nearby wood, to move
their animals out of the way and watch the dancing.

I reassured Brulette, for in full daylight and under so many
eyes I wasn't afraid of an ambush, and I felt quite capable of
defending her. Only I told her not to move away from me, and
I went back to the hut, which I could see the mule-drivers
approaching without a by your leave.

As they shouted out, 'We want to drink! Drinks here!', as if
they thought they were in an inn, I politely pointed out to
them that I wasn't selling wine, but that if they were willing to
ask for it honestly, I'd be happy to give them the evening cup.

'Is it a wedding, then?' asked the biggest of them. I recognized him by his red hair as being the leader of the band with
whom we had had such an unfortunate meeting in the woods
of La Roche.

'Wedding or no,' I answered, 'I'm the host here and I'm
happy to offer wine to anyone who pleases me; but . . .'

Instead of giving me time to finish, he replied: 'We've no

right to be here and you're the boss, thanks for your good intentions but you don't know us and you should keep your wine for your friends.'

He said a few words to the others in his dialect and led them to one side, where they sat down on the ground and began to eat their supper very calmly, while the great woodcutter went to speak to them and treated their leader with much consideration. This redhead was called Archignat and was considered as just a man as a mule-driver can be.

As, moreover, these folk were esteemed just as highly as others by the forest folk, Brulette and I refrained from telling anyone that they disgusted us, and she went back to the dance without any further fears. Apart from the leader, we hadn't recognized among them any of those who had come so close to mistreating us during our journey. And when all was said and done, this leader had saved us from the ill-will of his companions.

Several of those present knew how to play the pipes, not like the great woodcutter, who was unequalled in the entire world and who could have made the stones leap and the oaks of the forest frolic about, had he wanted to do so, but much better than Carnat and his boy, so the pipes went from hand to hand and reached those of the chief mule-driver whom I've named to you as Archignat, while the great woodcutter, who was still young in body and heart, took pleasure in dancing with his daughter of whom he was, rightly, as proud as père Brulet was of his granddaughter in our village.

But just when he called out to Brulette to come and dance with him, an evil-looking devil who'd suddenly arrived on the scene popped up and wanted to seize her by the hand. Although night was beginning to fall, Brulette recognized him straight away as the one who, in the woods of La Roche, had been the most threatening and had even suggested assassinating her two defenders and burying them under some tree that wouldn't breathe a word about it.

Fear and repugnance made her refuse him immediately and come to seek refuge with me, for, having used up all my provisions, I was on my way to dance with her.

'That girl promised this dance to me,' I said to the mule-driver, who was determined to have his own way. 'Leave us alone, and go and find another partner.'

'Very well,' said he, 'but once she's danced this bourrée with you, it'll be my turn.'

'No,' said Brulette, sharply. 'I'd rather never dance again in my life.'

'We'll see about that,' he answered, and he followed us to the dance, standing behind us and criticizing us, I believe, in his own tongue. Each time Brulette went past he uttered words that his evil glances made me believe were insolent.

'Just wait until I've finished,' I said to him, knocking against him as I went by. 'I'll pay you off in a language your back will soon learn to understand.'

But when the bourrée was over, I searched for him in vain. He'd hidden himself so well that I couldn't lay a finger on him. Brulette, seeing just what a coward he was, stopped fearing him and danced with others, all of whom treated her with all due respect. But at a moment when I'd taken my eyes off her, that rascal seized her among a group of other girls, dragged her by brute force into the dance and, taking advantage of the darkness, which prevented anyone else seeing her struggles, he tried to kiss her. At that moment I ran up, not seeing very well, but imagining that I had heard Brulette call out to me. I didn't have time to do myself justice, for, before that ugly, coal-laden face could touch hers, the man was seized so firmly round the throat that his eyes bulged like those of a rat caught in a trap.

Brulette, thinking I was the one helping her, threw herself instantly into her defender's arms, and much amazed she was to find herself in Huriel's embrace.

I wanted to take advantage of the fact that our friend's hands were full to seize the evil rascal on my own account, and I'd have paid him everything I owed him if people had not torn us apart. And as the man poured stupid slander upon us, accusing us of cowardice, and asserting that two of us had attacked him at once, the music fell silent. People gathered around the place where we were quarrelling, and the great woodcutter came with Archignat, the one ordering the mule-drivers, the other commanding the woodsmen not to get involved before the question was cleared up.

Malzac,* for this was our enemy's name (and his tongue was as evil as that of a serpent), made his complaint first, claiming that he'd politely invited the Berry girl, and that in kissing her he'd done nothing more than use the rights and customs of the bourrée, and that two of the girl's suitors, that is Huriel and myself, had treacherously seized him and wickedly struck him.

'That's false,' I answered, 'and I'm only too sorry that I didn't pound him, but the truth is that I arrived too late to grab him either honestly or treacherously, and my hands were seized at the very moment when I was about to strike him. I'm telling you just what happened, but let me go and I'll stop his lies!'

'As for me,' said Huriel, 'I caught him by the collar as you catch a hare, but without striking him, and it's not any fault of mine if his clothes didn't protect his skin. But I owe him a better lesson, and it's for that reason that I came here this evening. Now I request Master Archignat, my boss, and Master Bastien, my father, to reach an agreement, either now or after the celebrations, and to give me full justice if my rights are recognized.'

At that point the monk arrived and wanted to preach Christian peace, but he'd celebrated too well on Bourbonnais wine to control his tongue with any subtlety, and he couldn't make himself heard above the noise.

'Silence!' shouted the great woodcutter, in a voice that would have drowned thunder itself. 'All of you, go away, and leave it to us to judge this matter. You can listen, but you can't speak on the matter. On this side, all the mule-drivers, for Malzac and Huriel, on that side, I and the elders of the forest, acting as sponsors and judges for this boy from the Berry. Speak up, Tiennet, and make your accusation. What were your reasons for bearing a grudge against this mule-driver? If it's because he tried to kiss your fellow countrywoman in the dance, I know you have the same customs as we do. So that wouldn't be sufficient cause for intending to strike anyone. Tell us why you're angry with him. That's the point where we need to begin.'

I didn't need to be asked twice, and although the gathering

of mule-drivers and elders made me a little nervous, I'm a sufficiently good speaker to be able to put into suitable words the tale of the woods of La Roche and to call on the leader, Archignat himself, to bear witness, for I painted him a little whiter than he deserved. But I could see quite well that I shouldn't throw any blame on him if I wanted him to be favourable to my cause, and in doing so, I showed him that men from the Berry are no more stupid than others, nor any easier to put in the wrong.

All those present, who were already well-disposed towards Brulette and me, criticized Malzac's behaviour, but the great woodcutter demanded silence again and asked Master Archignat if anything I had said was false.

This great redhead was a clever and prudent man. His face was as white as a sheet and, however much one might offend him, he never seemed to have a drop more blood in his body. His hazel eyes were fairly gentle and gave no hint of false-hood, but his mouth, half-hidden under his foxy beard, smiled from time to time in a silly way that barely concealed a fair store of ill-will. He had no love for Huriel, but he acted as if he did, and he was generally held to behave as a just man ought to behave. The truth of the matter was that he was the greatest pilferer on this earth, and his conscience placed the interests of his brotherhood above everything else. He'd been chosen as chief because he was so cool and collected, and that allowed him to trick and deceive, and thus enable his band to avoid quarrels and trials, in which he was considered to be as knowledgeable as any attorney.

He made no answer to the great woodcutter's question, and no one could have said whether his silence showed stupid-ity or prudence, for the more alert his wits, the more sleepy he made himself appear, assuming the air of someone lost in day-dreams who doesn't hear the questions he's being asked.

He merely made a sign to Huriel as if to ask him if this description of events conformed with his own, but Huriel who, while you wouldn't call him underhand in his dealings, was just as sharp as Archignat, answered: 'Master, you've been summoned as a witness by this lad. If it's your pleasure to agree with him, I've no business to confirm that you're telling the truth, and if it's your pleasure to accuse him, the customs of the brotherhood forbid me to contradict you. No one here has any business meddling in our affairs, and if Malzac has been wrong, I know in advance that you'll have scolded him. But as far as I'm concerned, there's another issue. In the matter we debated together before you, in the woods of La Roche, the cause of which I'm not required to discuss, Malzac thrice told me I was lying and threatened me personally. I don't know if you were aware of it, but I swear this was so; and as I've been offended and dishonoured, I demand the right of combat, according to the customs of our band.'

Archignat consulted the other mule-drivers in a whisper, and it appeared that all agreed with Huriel, for they formed a circle, and the chief said this one word: 'Start!' At that Malzac and Huriel confronted each other.

I wanted to prevent them, saying that it was up to me to defend my cousin, and that the complaint I'd brought before them was of greater moment than that of Huriel, but Archignat thrust me aside, saying: 'If Huriel is beaten, you can follow him. But if it's Malzac who's trounced, you'll just have to be content with what you'll have seen take place.'

'Get the women out of here!' shouted the great woodcutter, 'they're not needed.' As he said this, he was pale, but he didn't retreat before the danger his son might be facing.

'The women can go if they wish,' said Thérence, who was as pale but as firm as he was. 'As for me, I need to be here for my brother's sake, if there's blood to be stanched.'

Brulette, more dead than alive, begged Huriel and me not to continue with the quarrel, but it was too late to pay any heed to her words. I left her in Joseph's care, and he took her away. Putting my jacket on the ground, I prepared to avenge Huriel, if he were defeated.

I had no idea what kind of combat would ensue and I watched attentively, so I wouldn't be taken unawares when my own turn came. Two resin flares had been lit, and men had measured out the area in which the fight would take place. Each was given a short, knotty, holly stick. The great woodcutter assisted Archignat in all these preparations with a tranquillity that belied the feelings in his heart, and that was painful to watch.

Malzac, who was small and slight, was not as strong as Huriel, but he was quicker in his movements and better versed in that kind of fight, for Huriel, although he was skilled with the stick, was of so kindly a nature that he'd had very little occasion to use it.

This was what was explained to me as they began testing each other out, and I confess my heart was pounding, as much with fear for Huriel as with fury against his enemy.

For two or three minutes, which seemed to me to be each as long as an hour measured by the clock, no blow went home, as each man defended himself well. Finally we began to hear that wood was no longer striking merely on wood and the dull sound made by sticks on bodies made my blood run cold each time I heard it. In our region, battles never take place like that, if the rules are followed, for we use no weapons other than our fists, and I admit that my mind hadn't grown hardened to the idea of split heads and broken jaws. Never had the time seemed to move more slowly, never had I seen worse suffering than at that moment. To see Malzac so skilful, I may well have trembled a little for myself too, but at the same time, I was so furious at not being able to get involved that if I hadn't been held back, I'd have thrown myself into the middle of it all.

The sight of it filled me with disgust, resentment, and pity, and yet I stood there with my mouth and my eyes wide open so as not to miss any part of it, for the wind shook the flares, and at times you could see hardly anything apart from a whitish whirling around the combatants. But suddenly one of the two sighed, as a tree does when it has been snapped in two by a blast of wind, and rolled in the dust.

Which one was it? I couldn't see any more, my eyes were full of dazzling lights, but I heard Thérence's voice saying: 'God be praised, my brother has won.'

I found I could see clearly again. Huriel was standing and waiting, as a loyal companion, for the other to get up again, without approaching him, however, in the fear that his rival might behave with the treachery he knew him to possess.

But Malzac didn't get up again, and Archignat, ordering

everyone to stand still, called him three times. He received no reply, and went up to him, saying: 'Malzac, it's me, don't attack me!'

Malzac didn't seem at all eager to do so, for he lay as still as a stone, and when the chief had leant over him and touched him, he looked at him and called two mule-drivers to him by name, saying to them: 'It's all over with him. Do what has to be done.'

They immediately picked him up by the head and feet, and disappeared, running, followed by the other mule-drivers, who melted into the forest, forbidding anyone not a member of their brotherhood to make any enquiries about how matters had concluded. Master Archignat was the last to follow them, after whispering in the great woodcutter's ear, and receiving this simple reply: 'That's enough. Farewell.'

Thérence had gone to her brother's side and was wiping the sweat from his face with a handkerchief, asking him if he were wounded, and wanting to keep him with her, so she could examine him, but he too whispered in her ear, and at the first word she answered him: 'Yes, yes, farewell.'

Then Huriel took master Archignat's arm, and both vanished immediately into the darkness, for they kicked over the flares as they left, and I felt just as you do when you awaken from a nightmare full of din and bright light to find yourself in the silence and darkness of the night.

SIXTEENTH EVENING

Meanwhile my sight gradually returned, and my feet, which terror had rooted to the ground, allowed me to follow the great woodcutter as he led me in the direction of the lodges. I was then amazed to see that we were alone with his daughter, Joseph, Brulette, and the three or four old folk who had watched the battle. All the rest had evaporated as soon as they saw the cudgels being taken up, so that they wouldn't have to bear witness in the courts if things ended badly. Woodland folk do not betray each other, and to avoid been summoned and tormented by the law, they make sure they know nothing and have nothing to say. The great woodcutter spoke to the old folk in their language, and I saw them return to the area where the combat had taken place, although I couldn't imagine what on earth they were going to do there. I followed Joseph and the women, and we returned to the lodges without exchanging a single word.

As for me, I'd been so unnerved I felt no desire for conversation. When we'd returned to the lodge, we were all so pale that we almost frightened each other. The great woodcutter, who had rejoined us, sat down, and stared morosely at the floor. Brulette, who'd made a great effort not to ask anyone any questions, burst into tears in a corner. Joseph, as if overcome with weariness and anxiety, stretched out full length on the bed of bracken. Thérence was the only one to go back and forth preparing the beds, but she kept her teeth clenched shut, and when she made an attempt to talk it was as if she had suddenly been afflicted with stuttering.

After a few moments of reflection and worry, the great woodcutter stood up and, looking at all of us, he said: 'Well, my dears, what's the matter? A lesson has been given, in accordance with all the rules, to a bad man, who was known wherever he went for his evil behaviour, a man who'd abandoned his wife, leaving her to die of poverty and grief. Malzac has long brought dishonour to the brotherhood of muledrivers, and if he'd died, no one would have wept over him. So why should we be sad and distressed over a few fine blows that my son Huriel gave him in a fair fight? Why are you crying, Brulette? Are you so soft-hearted you're pitying the loser? Don't you think my son did well to avenge his honour and your own? He told me everything that had happened, and I knew that, because your safety was involved, he chose not to punish his colleague's crime immediately. He would even have preferred Tiennet not to talk about it and to stay completely uninvolved. But, because I wanted to be sure that the truth was told in full, I let Tiennet talk as he believed he was honour bound to do. I'm glad he wasn't able to put himself at risk in a battle that would have been very dangerous for someone who doesn't know all the tricks. I'm glad, too, that luck was on my son's side, for when a good man meets a bad one, my heart will always side with the good man, even if he's not my own flesh and blood. So let's give thanks to the good Lord who judged matters well, and ask Him to be with us always, in this and all other matters.'

And the great woodcutter knelt down, and recited the evening prayer with us, bringing us all strength and composure by doing so. Then we parted on good terms to get some sleep.

It wasn't long before I heard that the great woodcutter, whose room I still shared, was sound asleep, although slightly disturbed by dreams. But in the girls' lodge, I could hear Brulette still crying, for what had happened had made her ill and she couldn't get over it. As she was talking with Thérence, I put my ear to the partition, not out of curiosity, but because I was worried to hear her suffer so much.

'Come now, stop crying and go to sleep,' said Thérence firmly. 'It's no use crying over spilt milk, and, as I told you, I just have to go. If you wake my father up, he'll want to go, too, because he doesn't know he's wounded, and that might get him involved in this bad business, whereas I run no risk if I'm caught up in it.'

'You frighten me, Thérence. How can you go in search of the mule-drivers all on your own? Look, they still scare me terribly but I want to go with you all the same. I must go, because I was the cause of the battle in the first place. Let's call Tiennet . . .'

'No, certainly not! Neither you nor he will go! The mule-drivers won't mourn Malzac if he dies, on the contrary. But if he'd been struck down by an outsider and above all by a foreigner, your friend Tiennet would find himself in a bad way by now. Let him sleep. It's bad enough that he wanted to get involved in it, and the best thing he can do now is stay put. As for you, Brulette, you should know that you wouldn't be welcome, since you don't have family interests, as I do, to draw you to them. No one among them would take it into his head to go against my wishes. They all know me, and they're not afraid of letting me into their secrets.'

'But do you think you'll still be able to find them in the

forest? Didn't your father say that they were going into the high country, and wouldn't spend the night in the area?'

'They'll still have to take the time to care for the wounded, but if it turned out that I couldn't find them, I wouldn't worry because that would prove my brother was only slightly wounded and was able to set out with them immediately.'

'Did you see his wound? Please tell me, dear Thérence, and don't hide anything from me!'

'I didn't see it. You couldn't see a thing. He said he hadn't received any serious blows and wasn't giving himself a second thought, but look Brulette, this is the handkerchief I used to wipe his face and that I thought was drenched with sweat. I saw when I got here that it was covered with his blood, and I needed all my courage to hide my shock from my father and from Joseph, who is truly pretty ill.'

There was a silence, as if Brulette, as she looked at the handkerchief or took it in her hands, was unable to speak. Then Thérence said to her: 'Give it back to me. I'll have to wash it in the first stream I come across.'

'Oh!' exclaimed Brulette, 'Let me keep it. I'll hide it away.'

'No, my dear,' said Thérence. 'If the police got wind of any battle they'd come and throw everything here topsy-turvy. They'd even search all of us. They've become very belligerent recently and want us to give up our customs, which are disappearing as it is, without anyone getting involved in it.'

'Alas!' said Brulette. 'Wouldn't it be a good thing if the custom of having battles as dangerous as that were abolished in your region?'

'Yes, indeed, but that depends on many things the king's judges are unable or unwilling to change. They would have to mete out justice, and at present they give it only to those who can pay for it. Is it different in your region? You don't know a thing about it, but I bet it's just the same as here. Only the Berry people are so thick-skinned and put up so patiently with everything evil folk try to do them, that they don't run the risk of making things worse. Here, that's not the case. Those who live in the forests couldn't exist if they didn't defend themselves against evil men in the same way they defend themselves against wolves and other evil beasts. You're not going to tell me that you blame my brother for having demanded justice in front of his own people for insults and threats that, in front of you, he was forced to accept. It may well be that you played some role in the bitterness he felt about that event. Think of that, Brulette, before you accuse him. If you hadn't shown so much grief and distress at the mule-driver's insults, he for his part may perhaps have forgotten them, for there's no one as gentle as Huriel and as willing to forgive. But you felt you'd been insulted and he promised to make things up to you. And he certainly did that. I'm not accusing you, or him either. I may well have been as sensitive as you, and as far as he's concerned, he did what he had to do.'

'No, no,' said Brulette, bursting into tears again. 'He didn't have to expose himself to danger like that for my sake, and I was wrong to let him see my pride had been hurt. I'll never forgive myself, and if anything should happen to him, you and your father who've been so kind to me won't be able to pardon me either.'

'Now, don't distress yourself like that,' answered Thérence. 'Come what may, we won't reproach you for anything. I know you now, Brulette, and I know you're worthy of my highest regard. Come on, dry your eyes, and try to get some rest. I hope I won't have any bad news about my brother to bring you, and I'm sure he will be well on his way to being solaced and cured if you let me tell him how grieved you are at his suffering.'

'I think,' said Brulette, 'that he'll be less touched by that than by your friendship, and that there's no woman on earth he could love as much as so good and brave a sister. That's why I'm sorry, Thérence, that I asked you for the charm you received on your first communion, and if he wanted to have it back again, I think it would be only fitting to let him have it back, since you're wearing it on your necklace.'

'Very well, Brulette,' said Thérence. 'Let me kiss you for those words. Sleep well, I'm leaving!'

'I shan't sleep,' said Brulette, 'but I'll pray to God to help you until you get back home.'

I heard Thérence quietly slip out of the lodge, and I did

likewise, a minute later. I couldn't in all conscience allow that beautiful young girl to go and run such risks all alone at night, while I, fearing for my own skin, failed to give her any assistance. The people she was seeking didn't seem to me as easygoing and such good Christians as she said they were, and besides, they might not be the only ones out in the woods that night. Our dance had attracted beggars, and it's well known that those who ask for charity don't always give it when they've a good opportunity to do ill. And then, I can't explain why the gleaming red face of the Carmelite monk who had feasted so well on my wine came back into my memory. It seemed to me that he hadn't lowered his eyes very often when he went past girls, and I'd no idea what had become of him in the uproar.

But as Thérence had made it clear to Brulette that she didn't want me to go with her in search of the mule-drivers, and since I didn't want to annoy her, I determined to follow her within hearing, but without revealing myself to her, unless she had any need to call for help. To this end, I let her get about a minute ahead of me, but no more, although I would have liked to calm Brulette by telling her what I planned; I would have been afraid to lose time and not be able to find her tracks in the wood.

I saw her cross the clearing and enter the thicket which went down towards the bed of the stream not far from the lodges. I followed her, using the same path, and, as there were many twists and turns on the way, I soon lost her from sight, but I could hear the soft sound of her footsteps as from time to time she broke a dead branch lying on the ground or sent a pebble rolling.

It seemed to me that she was walking quickly, and I did the same in order not to let her get too far ahead. Two or three times, I thought I must be so close to her that I dropped back a little to avoid being seen. In this way I reached one of the roads that traverse the wood, but the shadow of the thicket was so deep, that however hard I looked to left and right I couldn't see a thing that let me know what direction she had taken.

I listened, leaning my ear to the ground, and I could hear on

the path that continued across the road the same sound of
snapping branches that had already guided me. I hurried in
that direction until I reached another track that led me to the
stream, and there I began to think I was no longer following
Thérence, for the stream was wide and muddy, and when I'd
crossed it by wading deep into the water, I no longer found
any established track. There's nothing as deceptive as woodland tracks: in some places the trees are planted in such a way
as to make you think you've found a path; or animals, on their
way to drink at a pond, have made a passage, but suddenly
you find yourself caught in such vicious thorns, or deep in
such unstable terrain that there's just no point in continuing in
that direction. You'd only get even more badly lost than you
already are.

Nevertheless, I persisted, because I could still hear the noise
ahead of me, and it became so clear that I began to run,
tearing myself on thorns and sinking into the worst of the
mire; but a kind of fierce grunting made me realize that what
I was following was a wild boar, which was beginning to tire
of my company and was warning me it had had enough.

Since I had only a club to defend myself, and since I had no
idea how to overcome such a creature, I gave up and backtracked, somewhat worried about the boar, which I imagined
was being polite enough to escort me home.

Fortunately the thought didn't even cross his mind, and I
went back to the first path where, trusting to luck, I went in
the direction that lead to the Chambérat woods where the
party had taken place.

Bewildered though I was, I was unwilling to abandon my
plan, for Thérence ran the same risk as I did of coming across
some wild animal, and I didn't think she knew what she
needed to say to make such an animal listen to her.

I already knew the forest well enough not to be lost in it for
any length of time, and I reached the place where the dance
had been held. It took me a few moments to be sure that it
was the same clearing, for I had counted on finding my
arbour, which I hadn't had time to dismantle, together with
the utensils I'd left in it, and yet I found the place as bare as if
no arbour had ever been there.

Still, by looking closely, I recognized the spot where I had driven in the stake and the area where the dancers' feet had scuffed the grass.

I'd wanted to set out in the direction in which the mule-drivers had led Huriel and carried Malzac, but I racked my brains in vain to remember where it was, I'd been so flurried at that moment that I couldn't imagine where it had been. I was obliged to trust to luck and I walked in this way the whole night long, very weary, as you can well imagine, stopping often to listen, and hearing nothing other than the owls calling in the trees or some poor hare that was more afraid of me than I was of it.

Although, in those days, the Chambérat woods formed a single forest with that of the Alleu, I didn't know it, having been there only once since I'd arrived in the region. It didn't take me long to realize I was lost, but that hardly worried me at all, for I knew that neither one of these woods was big enough to lead me to Rome. Moreover, the great woodcutter had already taught me how to get my bearings, not by the stars, which aren't always visible in the forest, but by the direction of the main limbs, which, in our midland regions, are often thrashed by the northwest wind and prefer to stretch out to the east.

The night sky was very bright, and it was so mild, that if I hadn't been tormented by cares, and physically weary, I would really have enjoyed my stroll. The moon wasn't shining, but the stars gleamed in the sky which wasn't veiled by the slightest cloud, and even under the canopy of the trees I could see very clearly where to go.

My courage was much greater than in the days when I had been afraid in the little forest at Saint Chartier, for, on the contrary, I felt as calm as I would have in our own paths, and when I saw the animals take flight as I approached, I stopped worrying about them. Moreover, I was beginning to recognize that these covered areas, those streams bubbling through ravines, that fine grass, those sandy tracks, and all those magnificent tall trees could make its inhabitants love this country. There were large flowers whose names I've never discovered, looking like white throats with yellow borders, and with a perfume so intense and so delightful that from time to time I could have believed myself in a garden.

I continued walking towards the west, and reached the heathland. For a long time I followed along the forest edge, listening and looking in all directions. But nowhere could I find any sign of people, and I turned back at daybreak, without having found either Thérence or anyone else to speak to.

As I'd had enough, and no longer held out any hope of being useful, I went back into the woods, and cutting directly across, I came to a very wild place, where at long last, under a great oak, I saw something that seemed to me to be someone. The dawn light was turning even the bushes grey, and I walked on without making any noise until I was close enough to recognize the habit of the Carmelite monk. This poor man, of whom I'd been so suspicious, was kneeling in pious devotion and praying without apparently having the slightest thought of any evil.

As I drew near, I cleared my throat in order to let him know I was there and to avoid alarming him, but in fact I could have saved myself the trouble, for this monk was quite tough, fearing only God, and being quite unafraid of men or the devil.

He raised his head, looked at me without any astonishment, and, covering his head with his hood, continued mumbling his prayers under his breath. All I could see was his beard, which danced with each word he said, like that of a goat chewing salt.

When he seemed to me to have finished, I wished him good morning, hoping he'd have some news for me; but he signalled for me to be quiet, stood up, picked up his pack, looked closely at the place where he'd been kneeling, smoothed the grass with his nearly-bare foot, and levelled the sand that had been scuffed about. Then, he led me some distance away and said to me in a low voice: 'Because you know what's up, I'm glad to have the chance to talk to you before I set out again.'

Seeing he was in a mood to talk, I was careful not to question him, which may perhaps have made him more suspicious. But at the moment he opened his mouth, Huriel appeared before us, and seemed so surprised and even annoyed to find me there that I for my part was embarrassed, as if I had been caught doing something wrong.

It must be said that Huriel might well have frightened me if I'd met him all alone in the morning mist. He was more thickly covered with coal black than I'd ever seen him before, and a kerchief, bound over his head, hid his hair and his brow so completely that all you could see of his face were his great eyes, which seemed sunken and lacking their usual fire. He looked like his own ghost rather than his physical self, so softly did he slip over the ferns, as if afraid to awaken even the crickets and the midges hidden in the grass.

The monk was the first to speak, not in the way of a man who accosts another, but as one who continues a conversation after a brief interruption: 'Since he's here,' he said, pointing to me, 'it will be useful to give him some serious advice, and that's what I was doing.'

'Well, if you've told him everything,' broke in Huriel reproachfully.

In my turn I interrupted Huriel to tell him I knew nothing yet, and that he was free to hide from me whatever he had on the tip of his tongue.

'It's good of you,' said Huriel 'not to want to know more than you need to; but if that's the way you keep so important a secret, Brother Nicholas, I'm sorry I trusted you.'

'You've nothing to fear,' said the monk. 'I thought this young man was as deeply compromised as you were.'

'He's not compromised at all,' said Huriel. 'Thank goodness! It's enough that I should be.'

'All the better for him if his sin was merely one of intention,' replied the monk. 'He's your friend and you've nothing to fear from him. But as far as I'm concerned, I'd be most grateful if he said nothing to anyone about my spending the night in the woods.'

'What difference can that make to you?' asked Huriel. 'A mule-driver was wounded in an accident, you looked after him and thanks to you he'll soon recover. Who can criticize you for that act of charity?'

'Yes, yes,' said the monk. 'Keep the bottle and use it twice a day. Wash the wound carefully in running water as often as you can. Don't let your hair stick to it, and keep it covered from dust. That's all that's needed. If you happen to get a fever, get yourself well bled by the first monk you come across.'

'No thanks,' said Huriel. 'I've lost enough blood as it is, and it's my belief you can never have too much. My thanks to you, Brother, for your kind help. I didn't really need it, but I'm grateful all the same. And now farewell, for day is coming and your prayers may have kept you here too long.'

'No doubt,' said the monk. 'But are you going to let me go without making a brief confession? I've cared for your skin, since that was the most urgent; but is your conscience in any better state? Don't you think you're in need of absolution, which acts on the soul as ointment acts on the body?'

'I stand in great need of it, Father, but you'd be wrong to give it to me. I won't be worthy of it until I've carried out acts of penitence, and as for my confession, you've no business to preach to me about it, for you saw me commit a mortal sin. Pray for me, that's all I ask, and have many masses said for . . . those who let themselves be carried away by anger.'

I had thought at first that the mule-driver was joking, but the sadness with which he spoke, and the money he gave the monk when he stopped speaking, showed me he was serious.

'You can count on being treated as generously as you have treated me,' said the monk, putting the money away in his begging bowl, and he added in a tone that had no hint at all of the sanctimonious: 'Master Huriel, we are all sinners and there is but one just judge. He alone who has never committed any evil has the right to condemn or absolve the faults of men. Recommend yourself to His care, and know that in His pity He will take into account everything that is in your favour. As for the earthly judges, anyone who wanted to send you before them would be very stupid and very cowardly, for they're as weak or as hardened as all fragile creatures. Repent, that's the right course for you, but do not betray yourself, and when you feel grace calling you to the tribunal of penitence, choose only a good priest, in other words, a barefoot Carmelite monk like Brother Nicholas.

'And you, my child,' he went on, for he was in a mood to

preach and also wanted to shake his censer over me, 'learn to moderate your appetite and control your passions. Avoid opportunities to sin and keep away from quarrels and bloody battles . . .'

'That's enough, that's enough, Brother Nicholas,' said Huriel, interrupting him. 'You're preaching to the converted and you've no need to impose any penitence on a man whose hands have stayed pure. Farewell, leave, I tell you, the time has come to part.'

The monk left after giving each of us his hand, with an air of great openness and kindness. When he was far off, Huriel, taking me by the arm, led me to the tree where I had seen the monk in prayer.

'Tiennet,' he said, 'I trust you completely and if I seemed to stop that good monk from talking, it was to make sure he'd be prudent. In any case, there's little danger from him. He's the uncle of our chief, Archignat, and, moreover, a man in whom one can trust, always on good terms with the mule-drivers, who often help him transport what he's collected from one spot to another; but the fact that I've nothing to fear from him or from you is no reason for me to tell you what you've no need to know, unless you choose to hear it so you'll have no doubts about our friendship.'

'Do whatever seems right to you,' I answered. 'If it will help you to let me know the outcome of your fight with Malzac, tell me, even if I'll be sorry to hear it; if not, I'd just as soon not know too much about what happened to him.'

'What happened to him!' repeated Huriel, whose voice seemed stifled by a violent indisposition, and he stopped me at the first branches that the oak spread over us, as if he were afraid to walk on earth where I could see no trace of what I was beginning to fear. Then he added, looking around with eyes dimmed with sorrow, and speaking of what he wanted to keep silent, as if something forced him to betray himself: 'Tiennet, you remember those spine-chilling words he said to us in the woods of La Roche? "There's no shortage of ditches in the woods to bury the foolish, and neither stones nor trees have tongues to tell of what they have seen!"'

'Yes,' I replied, feeling a cold sweat run all over my body. 'It seems that ill words tempt ill luck, and bring misfortune to those who say them.'

SEVENTEENTH EVENING

Huriel crossed himself with a sigh; I did likewise, and we turned our backs on that ill-starred tree and set out on our way.

I would like to have been like the monk, and say something reassuring to him, for it was all too obvious that he was in mental distress; but not only was I too ignorant to preach, but I also felt that, in my own way, I, too, was guilty. I kept thinking, for instance, that if I hadn't narrated the whole story of the La Roche woods, Huriel may well not have remembered so clearly that he'd promised Brulette to avenge her, and if I hadn't defended her first before the mule-drivers and the forest elders, Huriel wouldn't have been so eager to have the same honour.

Hounded by these ideas, I couldn't help voicing them to Huriel, and accusing myself before him, as Brulette had accused herself in Thérence's presence.

'My dear friend Tiennet,' the mule-driver answered, 'you're a stout heart and a fine lad. I really don't want you to go on feeling troubled in your mind, over a matter that God on Judgement Day will not lay at your feet or even perhaps at mine. Brother Nicholas is right, He is the sole judge who can mete out true justice, because He alone knows the truth of all things. He has no need to summon witnesses, and to carry out enquiries into the truth. He reads what lies in the depths of each heart, and he knows full well that mine never swore or plotted to kill any man at the moment I took up the club to punish that unfortunate soul. Such weapons are evil; but they're the only weapons our customs allow us in such a case, and I'm not the person who invented that rite. Of course it would be better if we used only the strength of our arms and the power of our fists, as you and I did one night in your meadow over a mule of mine and some oats of yours. But you need to know that a mule-driver has to be as brave and as jealous of his reputation for honour as the greatest gentleman who has ever worn a sword. If I'd swallowed Malzac's insult without seeking redress, I'd have deserved to be driven from my brotherhood. It is of course true that I didn't seek redress in cold blood, as one ought to do. I met Malzac yesterday morning, one to one, in those very same woods, where I was working away calmly without sparing him a thought. He attacked me yet again with his stupid words, claiming that Brulette was a mere gatherer of dead wood, by which the forest folk mean a phantom that roves abroad at night. It's a belief that often serves girls who are no better than they should be and want to remain unrecognized, for people here are deeply afraid of such elfish sprites. So, for mule-drivers, who aren't superstitious, such an expression is a terrible insult.

'All the same, I put up with it as far as I could, but in the end he pushed me to my limits, and I threatened him just to get him off my back. He replied that I was a coward, that I'd make evil use of my own strength in a secluded spot like that, but that I wouldn't dare defy him to a combat with clubs, in accordance with the rules and before witnesses. He added that everyone knew perfectly well that I'd never had occasion to put my courage to the test, and that, whenever I was with others, I always fell in with everyone's tastes, so that I could avoid showing my true colours in an equal match.

'On that note he left me, saying that there was a dance on in the Chambérat woods, that Brulette was the hostess, and that she could easily afford to be so because she was the mistress of a big property-owner from her own country. For his part, he was going there to enjoy himself and pay court to the lady under my very eyes, if I was brave enough to come and see for myself.

'You know, Tiennet, that it was my intention not to see Brulette again, for reasons I may perhaps tell you about later on.'

'I know,' I replied, 'and I can see you met your sister last night. There on your ear is a pledge that hangs down below your kerchief and proves to me something I already suspected.'

'If you know I love Brulette and that I value her pledge,'

answered Huriel, 'then you know as much as I do, but you can't know any more, because I'm sure only of her friendship and as for the rest . . . But that's not what we're talking about. I wanted to tell you how misfortune led me back here. I didn't want Brulette either to see me or to speak to me, because I'd noticed how much Joseph was suffering through me, but I knew Joseph wasn't strong enough to defend her, and I knew Malzac was cunning enough to escape from you, too.

'So I came here at the beginning of the merry-making, and remained hidden in the area around the dance, promising myself I'd leave without letting anyone see me, if Malzac didn't turn up after all. You know the rest, up to the point when we took up the clubs. At that moment, I was furious, I own it; but how could it be otherwise for anyone who wasn't a saint in paradise? Nevertheless, all I wanted to do was punish my enemy and stop him saying, particularly at a time when Brulette was in the region, that I was so gentle and patient that I didn't have the courage of a hare.* You saw how my father, who's fed up with such talk, didn't prevent me from proving I was a man; but I must have been born under an unlucky star, because at my first fight and almost at my first blow . . . Oh! Tiennet! it doesn't matter that you were forced to do it, that you yourself feel gentle and humane, it won't be easy to find consolation, I fear, for having had so fell a hand! A man's a man, however bad mannered and foul mouthed he might be. That one didn't have much good in him, but he might have had the time to improve, and now I've sent him to render his accounts before he'd had time to put them in order. So, Tiennet, you can take my word for it that I'm truly disgusted with the profession of mule-driver. I now recognize that Brulette was right to say that it's hard for a man who's just and God-fearing to be a mule-driver, and still maintain his esteem in his own judgement and in that of others. I'm obliged to spend a little more time as a mule-driver, because of commitments I've undertaken, but you can be sure that as soon as I can I'll get out, and take up some other, more tranquil occupation.'

'And that's what you want me to tell Brulette, isn't it?'

'No,' answered Huriel, with great self-assurance, 'unless

Joseph is so well cured of his love and his illness that he can give her up. I am as fond of Joseph as you are, my dears, and what's more, he confided in me, he took me as adviser and supporter. I've no wish either to deceive him or to go against his wishes.'

'But since Brulette doesn't want him as a lover and a husband, the best solution may well be for him to realize that as soon as possible. I'll undertake to talk him round if the others don't dare do so. Moreover, there is someone here who could make Joseph happy, whereas Brulette cannot do so. It doesn't matter how long he waits, the more he deceives himself, the harder the blow will be when it finally falls. But if he only opened his eyes to the true attachment he could find elsewhere . . .'

'Let's drop that subject,' said Huriel, with a frown that made him wince, like a man who suffers from a great hole in the head, as indeed he did have a very recent hole under his red kerchief. 'Everything is in God's hands. And in our family no one is in a hurry to seize happiness at the cost of other people's happiness. As for me, I must leave, for I'd be hard put to answer those who asked where Malzac had gone, and why he's no longer seen around here. Let me say one more thing about Brulette and Joseph. It would be pointless to tell them the misfortune I've brought about. Apart from the mule-drivers, there's only my father, my sister, the monk, and you, who know that when the man fell, he was never to rise again. I only had time to whisper to Thérence: "He's dead. I have to leave the country." Master Archignat said as much to my father; but the other woodcutters knew nothing about it and don't wish to know. The monk himself would have been completely hoodwinked, if he hadn't followed us to give succour to the wounded. The mule-drivers were eager to send him away without telling him anything, but the chief took responsibility for him, and as for me, even if it meant risking my neck, I didn't want the man to be buried like a dog, without any Christian prayers said over him.

'Now it's in God's hands. Besides, you can understand that a man threatened with a dangerous case, as I am, can't think of paying court to a girl as sought after and precious as

Brulette, or at least not for some considerable time. Only, as you love me, you might not tell her how things stand with me. I want her to forget me, but I don't want her to hate or fear me.'

'She certainly wouldn't have the right to do that, since it was for love of her . . .'

'Ah!' said Huriel with a sigh, as he put his hand over his eyes, 'that's a love that cost me dear!'

'Come on,' I said. 'Take heart! She'll know nothing of this, you can count on my promise. And everything I can do to make her recognize your true value when the time is ripe, I shall do.'

'Calm down, Tiennet, calm down. I'm not asking you to take up the cudgels for me, as I've taken them up for Joseph. You don't know me well enough, you don't owe me the same degree of friendship, and I know how it feels to push someone into the very place you'd like to occupy yourself. You love Brulette, too, and we must make sure that out of the three suitors, two behave in a just and reasonable way when the third is chosen. And we don't even know that we won't be outdone by a fourth. But, however it turns out, I hope we three will remain friends and brothers.'

'You must strike me out of the list of suitors,' I said, smiling without any sense of bitterness. 'I was always the least passionate, and by now I am as calm as if I'd never given it any thought. I know the girl's secret; I think she's made the right choice, and I'm happy about it. So farewell, Huriel, God be with you! Try to find the heart to forget this evil night!'

We embraced each other in farewell, and I asked where he was heading.

'I'm going as far as the Forez* mountains. You can write to me at the town of Huriel, where I was born, and where we have relatives. They can send letters on.'

'But can you travel so far with that wound in your head? Isn't it dangerous?'

'No, no, it's nothing. I only wish that *my rival* had a head as hard as mine.'

When I was alone, I felt amazed at the thought of everything that had happened in the forest without my hearing the slightest sound, or coming across the smallest clue. And I was all the more astonished when, in broad daylight, I crossed the place where we'd held the dance, and saw that since midnight someone had mown the grass and dug the ground to remove all traces of the calamity that had taken place. Thus, twice, someone had come to rearrange things in this place, and, what's more, Thérence had communicated with her brother, while in the midst of all this a burial had taken place, and all the time, despite the brightness of the night and the calm of the woods, and although I'd followed those woods along their entire length, paying the closest attention, I hadn't been warned by the slightest glance or the softest sigh. That certainly gave me food for thought concerning the different habits, and therefore the different natures, of the forest people and those who farm the open country. On the plains, good and evil are too clearly visible for people not to learn from an early age to submit to the laws and to be prudent in their behaviour. In the forests you feel you can hide from the gaze of your fellow human beings, and you place yourself in the hands of God or the devil, depending on whether your intentions are good or bad.

When I got back to the lodges the sun had risen; the great woodcutter had left for work, Joseph was still asleep, and Thérence and Brulette were chatting together under the lean-to. They asked me why I'd got up so early in the morning and I saw Thérence was worried about what I might have seen and unearthed. I acted as if I'd detected nothing and hadn't gone further than the Alleu wood.

Joseph soon came to join us, and I remarked that he looked much healthier than he had when we first arrived.

'Yet I hardly slept a wink,' he answered. 'I felt worried until daybreak, but I think that's because the fever, that has tormented me so, left me at last yesterday evening, for I feel stronger, and in better form, than I have for a long time.'

Thérence, who knew fevers well, checked his pulse, and her face, which was very tired and showed signs of distress, suddenly lit up.

'Well!' she said. 'The good Lord has at least sent us this good fortune, for here's our invalid well on the road to recovery. The fever has gone, and his blood is already recovering strength.'

'If I tell you what I felt,' answered Joseph, 'then you mustn't tell me it was all a dream. This is what happened. But first tell me if Huriel was unharmed and his rival suffered no more than he needed to. What news have you had from the Chambérat woods?'

'Yes, yes,' Thérence replied swiftly. 'They both went off to the high country. Say what you have to say.'

'I don't know if you two will understand it,' said Joseph, talking to the two girls, 'but Tiennet here will grasp it perfectly well. Yesterday, when I saw Huriel fighting so resolutely, my legs failed me, and feeling weaker than a woman, I was on the point of fainting. But at the same time as my body was losing strength, my heart felt warm, and my eyes couldn't stop staring at the battle. When Huriel knocked his man to the ground while he remained on his feet, I was seized with giddiness, and, had I not restrained myself, I would have shouted out "Victory", and even sung like a madman or a drunkard. If I could have, I'd have run to embrace him, but everything faded away, and as I came back here I felt as if all my bones were broken, exactly as if I'd been the one who'd given and received the blows.'

'Don't think about it any more,' said Thérence. 'Those are evil things to think about and remember. I bet you had nightmares about it this morning?'

'I didn't dream about it at all; I thought about it, and little by little, I felt my mind completely revived and my body in full health again, as if the time had come for me to pick up my bed and walk, like the cripple the Bible talks about. I saw Huriel standing before me, surrounded by light, and reproaching me for my illness, as if it were a form of mental cowardice. He seemed to say to me: "I'm a man and you're nothing but a child; while you tremble with fever, my blood is on fire. You're worthless and I'm worthy of everything for myself and for others! Come now, listen to this music . . ." And I heard music that howled like a storm and picked me up from my bed, as the wind picks up fallen leaves. Look, Brulette, I think I've finished being cowardly and sickly, and I'm sure that now

I could go home, kiss my mother, and pack my bags to leave, for I want to travel, I need to learn, and make myself into what I must be.'

'You want to travel?' said Thérence, who had glowed with happiness like a sun, but who was now as pale and lack-lustre as an autumn moon. 'You hope to find a better master than my father, and better friends than the people around here? Go and see your family, that would be good, if you're strong enough to do so. But, unless you want to die far away from us . . .'

Unhappiness and sorrow made it impossible for her to say any more. Joseph, who'd been watching her, suddenly changed his expression and his words.

'Don't pay any attention to what I dreamed this morning, Thérence,' he said to her, 'I'll never find a better master or better friends than here. You told me to tell you my dreams, and I told you, that's all. When I'm cured, I'll ask all three of you for your advice, as I'll ask your father. Until then, let's not give any more thought to what might go through my mind, but just enjoy the time we have to spend together.'

Thérence calmed down, but Brulette and I, who knew how determined and pig-headed Joseph could be, despite his gentle airs, and who remembered how he'd left us, without arguing and without letting anyone change his mind about anything, thought he'd made his decisions, and that no one was going to change them for him.

Over the next two days, I began to grow bored again, and so did Brulette, although she devoted herself to completing the embroidery that she wanted to give to Thérence, and frequently went to see the great woodcutter, as much to leave Joseph in the hands of the maid of the woods, as to talk about Huriel with his father, and console that good man for the grief and fear the battle had caused him. The great woodcutter, moved by this display of friendship, trusted her enough to tell her the whole truth about Malzac, and Brulette, far from holding it against Huriel, as Huriel himself had feared, was all the more attracted to him through concern and gratitude.

On the sixth day we began to talk of parting, for the time was coming when we needed to think of leaving. Joseph was

improving visibly; he worked a little and did his utmost to test
out and restore his strength as quickly as possible. He had
decided to accompany us and spend a few days at home,
saying that he would return to the Alleu woods immediately,
a promise that didn't seem at all certain to us, or to Thérence,
and she began to worry almost as much about his good health
as she had about his illness. I don't know if it were she who
persuaded the great woodcutter to accompany us for half of
the way, or if the idea was his own, but he made the suggestion, and it was very quickly accepted by Brulette, although
Joseph was only partly pleased by it, however much he hid his
feelings.

This little journey could only help the great woodcutter to
forget his worries, and, as he prepared for it the evening
before we left, he regained a good part of his high spirits. The
mule-drivers had left the region without encountering any
difficulties, and no questions were raised about Malzac, who
had neither family nor friends to ask after him. The law might
well not begin worrying itself about what had happened until
a year or two had passed; indeed it might well not take it into
its head to worry about it at all, for in those days the French
police force was not large, and a man of low rank could
disappear without anyone taking any notice.

Moreover, the great woodcutter's family were to leave that
area at the end of the season, and, as neither father nor son
remained in any one spot for more than six months, you'd
have to have been pretty clever to know where to find them.

For all these reasons, when the great woodcutter, who
feared only the first repercussions of the event, saw that the
secret was not being bruited abroad, he regained confidence
and that revived our spirits too.

On the morning of the eighth day, we all climbed into a
little, low cart he had borrowed, together with its horse, from
one of his forest friends, and seizing the reins, he led us by the
longest but safest route as far as Sainte Sévère* where we were
to take our leave of him and of his daughter.

Brulette was secretly sad to cross new territory where she
could not see again any of the spots in which she had travelled
with Huriel. As for me, I was delighted to travel and to see

Saint Palais in Bourbonnais, and Préveranges, two small towns standing on great stone outcrops; then Saint Prejet and Pérassay,* two other towns, which we met as we followed the course of the Indre; and as we were following this stream almost from its source, and as it's a river that travels through our region, I no longer felt so foreign and no longer considered myself to be in a lost land.

I felt completely at home when we reached Sainte Sévère, which is no more than six leagues from our region, and which I'd already visited. There, while those who'd accompanied us talked of bidding us farewell, I went to find a vehicle to hire so that we could continue our journey. I could find one only for the following day, but then it could leave as early as we liked.

When I returned with this news, Joseph flew into a rage. 'What do we need with a cart?' he asked. 'Can't we simply walk back home in the cool, and arrive late in the evening? Brulette has often walked further than that to attend a dance, and I feel quite capable of doing as much as she does.'

Thérence remarked that such a long walk would bring back his fever, but that only made him more obstinate. Brulette, however, could see Thérence's sorrow, and broke in to say that she felt weary, and would be happy to spend the night in the inn, and then to travel on by cart.

'Very well,' said the woodcutter. 'In that case, we'll do the same. We'll let the horse rest overnight and we'll set out when you do tomorrow morning. And if you take my advice, instead of dining in this inn, which will be full of flies, we'll carry our meal under some leafy boughs or beside the water, and we'll spend the evening chatting until it's time to sleep.'

That indeed is what we did. I booked two rooms, one for the girls, the other for the men, and because, just for once, I wanted to treat père Bastien, having seen that on the right occasion he had a fine appetite, I filled a great basket with the best there was to be found in the way of pâtés, white bread, wine, and brandy, and we carried it beyond the town. It's just as well that the habit of drinking coffee and beer hadn't yet become established, for I wouldn't have given a thought to economy, and would have paid out every last coin in my purse.

Sainte Sévère is a lovely area, cut by well-watered ravines, and a delight to look at. We chose a high hillock where the air was so bracing that there remained of our meal not even a crust of bread or a mouthful of drink.

After that, the woodcutter felt in such good spirits that he took his bagpipes, which he never left behind, and said to Joseph: 'My boy, there's no knowing who will live and who will die; you say we're parting only for a few days, but I suspect you're thinking of a longer separation, and it may be that the good Lord will arrange things so that we never meet again. That's what you always ought to tell yourself when, at the crossing of the roads, each one goes their separate way. I hope you're leaving us content with me and my children, just as I'm happy with you and these friends of yours. But I'm not forgetting that the main purpose was to teach you to play music, and I'm sorry that two months of illness forced you to stop. Now, I'm not claiming I could have made a great scholar of you. I know there are some folk in the towns, men and women, who play instruments we don't know about, and read written music, as one reads words written in books. Apart from plainsong, which I learned in my youth, I know little of that music, and I showed you all I know, that is, the keys, the notes, and the beat. When you want to know more about that, you should go to the cities where the violinists will teach you minuets and contredances. But I'm not sure that that will be of much use to you, unless you want to leave your home and your peasant status behind you.'

'God forbid!' said Joseph, looking at Brulette.

'Well then,' went on the woodcutter, 'you can find elsewhere the instruction you'll need to play the pipes and the hurdy-gurdy. If you want to return to me, I'll help you play them; if you think you can find new things in the lands out there, then you must go there. All I would have liked is to lead you gently until such time as you can find your breath without effort, and your fingers no longer make mistakes, for as far as the musical imagination is concerned, that lies in no one's gift, and you have your own share, which I know is of high quality. I didn't stint in sharing with you what I have in my head, and what you've retained you can use if you want to do so; but as it's your desire to compose, you can do no better than travel a while, so that you can compare what you already know with what others have. You should go up to the Auvergne and to Forez so that you can see how fine and large the world is, on the far side of our valleys, and how the heart swells, when, from the top of a real mountain, you find wild water drowning the sound of human voices and covering trees with a green they never lose. But don't go down to the plains of other lands. There you'd only find what you've left in your own. Now the moment has come to give you a lesson you mustn't ever forget. So listen carefully.'

EIGHTEENTH EVENING

The great woodcutter, having checked to see that Joseph was paying close attention, went on to say:

'Music has two modes that the scholars, or so I've heard tell, call the major mode and the minor mode, and that I myself call the clear mode and the muddy mode; or, if you prefer, the blue-sky mode and the grey-sky mode; or else, the mode of strength and joy, and the mode of sorrow and reverie. You can spend an entire day and still not find all the contrasts that exist between these two modes, any more than you would find a third mode. For everything, on earth, is shadow or light, leisure or labour. Now keep listening closely, Joseph! The plains sing in the major mode, and the mountains in the minor mode. If you'd stayed in your own country, you'd still be thinking in the clear, calm mode, and when you return to it, you'll see what advantages a mind like yours can extract from such a mode, for neither is lesser or greater than the other.

'But, because you felt you were a complete musician, you were tormented when you couldn't hear the minor mode ringing in your ears. Your minstrels and singers have learnt it for form's sake, because songs are like the air that blows everywhere, and carries the seeds of plants from one horizon to the other. But since nature did not make them passionate, deep thinkers, the people of your country make a poor showing in the sad tones, and corrupt them when they use them. That's why you felt your bagpipes were playing out of key.

'So, if you want to know the minor mode, go and seek it out in sad and wild places. You should realize that you'll have to shed tears from time to time, before you'll be able to make full use of a mode that was given to man to allow him to lament his suffering, or at the very least to sigh out his feelings of love.'

Joseph understood the great woodcutter so well that he begged him to play the last tune he'd invented, to give us a sample of this sad, grey mode that he'd called the minor key.

'Willingly, my lad,' said the woodcutter. 'So you overheard it, did you, that air I've been trying to fit to words for at least a week? I really thought I'd been singing it to myself alone, but because you were eavesdropping, this is how I plan to leave it.'

And, dismantling his bagpipes, he took the chanter, on which he played a very sweet air, that without being the sort that makes one sad, nevertheless made us remember or envision all kinds of things, depending on the personality of each one who listened.

Joseph was overjoyed at the beauty of the tune, and Brulette, who listened to it without moving, seemed to awaken from a dream when it was over.

'What about the words?' said Thérence. 'Are they sad, too, father?'

'The words are like the tune, they're a little perplexing, and they demand reflection. It's a story about the problems of three suitors each in love with the same girl.'

And he sang a song which, today, is well known in our region, although the words have since been greatly altered. Here it is as the great woodcutter performed it:

> There were once three woodsmen,
> In the springtime, on the meadow.
> (I hear the nightingale),
> Three woodsmen there were,
> All speaking to a lass.
>
> The youngest one declared,
> (In his hand he held a rose);
> (I hear the nightingale),

The youngest one declared:
I love but do not dare.

The oldest one cried out:
(In his hand he held an axe),
(I hear the nightingale),
The oldest one cried out:
When I love, I command.

The third one sang a song,
In his hand some almond blossom,
(I hear the nightingale),
The third one sang a song:
When I love, I ask.

My friend you will not be,
You who hold the rose;
(I hear the nightingale),
My friend you will not be,
If you don't dare, can I?

My master you'll not be,
You who hold the axe,
(I hear the nightingale),
My master you'll not be,
Love cannot be commanded.

My lover you will be,
You with the almond spray,
(I hear the nightingale),
My lover you will be,
One gives to him who asks.

I liked the tune much better when I heard it set to words than I had the first time, and I was so pleased with it that I asked for it again on the bagpipes, but the woodcutter, who wasn't the sort to be vain about his works, said it wasn't worth the trouble, and played us other tunes, sometimes in one mode and sometimes in the other, and even using both in the same song, teaching Joseph how to move appropriately from major to minor, and from minor to major.

The stars had long been blazing down and yet we felt no need to go to bed. People from the town and the area around had gathered in the valley to listen, to the great delight of their ears. Several even said: 'It's a player from the Bourbonnais and, what's more, a master player. Just listen to how much he knows! There's not a single one of our people to rival him.'

As we returned to the inn, père Bastien continued teaching Joseph, while the latter, who could never weary of the subject, remained a little behind us to listen to him and ask questions. That meant I was walking ahead with Thérence, who, very helpful and willing, as always, helped me carry back the baskets. Brulette, between the two pairs, walked alone, dreaming of something or other, as she'd fallen into the habit of doing over the last few days. Thérence frequently turned as if to look at her, but in reality she was checking that Joseph was following us.

'Look closely at him, Thérence,' I said to her at a moment when she seemed greatly disturbed, 'for your father said truly: When one parts for a day, it may be for all one's life.'

'Yes,' she replied, 'and, also, when you think you're leaving someone for ever, it may be that it is only for a day.'

'You remind me,' I said, 'that when I saw you once disappear as if you were a day-dream, I really thought I would never see you again.'

'I know what you mean. My father refreshed my memory, yesterday, in talking to me about you. For my father is very fond of you, Tiennet, and values you highly.'

'I'm pleased and honoured that it should be so, Thérence, but I really don't know how I deserve it, for there's nothing in me that announces a man who's any different from the others.'

'My father's never mistaken in his judgements, and however he judges you, I'll judge you too. But why does that make you sigh, Tiennet?'

'Did I sigh? I didn't mean to.'

'It may well have been unintentional, but that's no reason to hide your feelings from me. You love Brulette and you're afraid . . .'

'It's true that I'm very fond of Brulette, but not in a way that makes me sigh with love, or worry about what she thinks at this particular moment. My heart is fancy free, since there's no point in loving her.'

'Oh, how lucky you are, Tiennet, to be able to control your thoughts with your reason.'

'I'd be worth more, Thérence, if, like you, I controlled them with my heart. Yes, yes, I can guess what you're thinking and I know your feelings, indeed I do, for I've watched you and I've guessed the secret behind your behaviour. I've seen over the last week how you've stepped aside to let Joseph recover more quickly, and how you've cared for him in secret, without letting him catch sight of so much as the tips of your fingers. You want him to be happy, and you didn't lie when you told us that, provided one does good to the person one loves, there's no need to get any benefit from it. That really is the sort of person you are, and although jealousy sometimes whips up your blood a little, you recover immediately and so perfectly that it's wonderful to see how kind and strong you are! Surely you must agree that if either of us owes the other respect, then it's I who should respect you, and not the other way round. I'm a fairly rational boy, that's all, and you are a big-hearted girl who knows how to control herself.'

'Thank you for thinking so well of me, but it may be that I'm not as deserving of praise as you think, my dear boy. You want to presume that I love Joseph, but that just isn't the case! As true as God is my judge, I never considered being his wife, and the feelings I have for him are those of a sister or a mother.'

'Well, as far as that's concerned, I'm not sure you aren't deceiving yourself. You've a passionate nature!'

'That's the very reason why I'm not deceiving myself. I love my brother and father fiercely and almost madly. If I had children I would defend them like a she-wolf, and brood over them like a hen. But what people call love, what for instance my brother feels for Brulette, a desire to please, and something that makes you sad when you're alone, and that makes you suffer whenever you think of the one you love . . . I don't feel that and I don't let it bother me. Joseph can leave us forever, if that's what will do him good, and I'll give thanks to God and will be sad only if it makes him fall ill.'

The way Thérence saw these matters gave me much food for thought. I no longer felt I understood much about it, so far did she seem above everyone else and above me too. I walked beside her a little further without saying anything, and hardly knowing where my thoughts were, for I was seized with great waves of friendship for her, as if I were about to embrace her most willingly and without any evil thoughts. Then I suddenly saw how lovely and young she was, and that filled me with shame and fear. When we reached the inn, I asked her, I don't know why, exactly what her father had told her about me.

'He said you were the most sensible man he'd ever met.'

'You may as well say a great fool, wouldn't you say?' I answered with a laugh, feeling somewhat mortified.

'Not at all. These are my father's very words: "He's the man who sees things most clearly and who acts with the greatest justice." Well, good sense means kindness and I don't believe my father is mistaken.'

'In that case, Thérence,' I cried, somewhat shaken in the depths of my heart, 'give me a little of your friendship!'

'A great deal!' she answered, seizing my hand as I stretched it out to her. But she said it with an open, comradely air, that set aside all misunderstanding, and I fell asleep on it without imagining any more in it than was really there.

The next day, when the time came to part, Brulette wept as she embraced the great woodcutter, and made him promise to come and see us with Thérence in our own homes. Then, those two lovely girls embraced each other so warmly, and made such professions of friendship, that they were scarcely able to leave each other. Joseph thanked his master for giving him so many advantages and helping him so greatly. When it was Thérence's turn, he tried to treat her in the same way, but she looked at him openly and frankly in a way that disturbed him, and as they shook hands they hardly said anything more than: 'Look after yourself, until we meet again.'

Without feeling too embarrassed, I asked Thérence's permission to kiss her, thinking that in doing so I'd give a good example to Joseph, but he took no advantage of it and swiftly leaped on to his horse to cut the embraces short. He seemed discontent with himself and with everyone else. Brulette sat right at the back of the cart, and as long as she could see our Bourbonnais friends, she followed them with her eyes, while

Thérence, standing against the door, seemed lost in thought rather than filled with grief.

We covered almost the whole of what remained of our journey pretty cheerlessly. Joseph didn't utter a single word. He may perhaps have hoped that Brulette would fuss over him a little, but as Joseph had regained his strength, Brulette had taken back her freedom to think of whomever she wanted to, and, full of friendship for Huriel's father and sister, she thought about them, and talked about them with me, in order to praise them and yearn for them. And as if she'd left all her thoughts behind her, she also missed the land we'd just left. 'It's bizarre,' she said to me, 'how I feel that the closer home we come, the smaller the trees seem, the yellower the grass, the sleepier the water. Before I ever left our plains, I never imagined I could bear three days in the woods, and now it seems as if I could spend my life there just as well as Thérence does, if I had my old grandfather beside me.'

'I can't say the same on my own account, cousin,' I answered. 'Still, if it were necessary, I think it wouldn't kill me. But let the trees be as tall, the grass as green and the water as lively as they can, I prefer a nettle in my own land to an oak in foreign country. My heart leaps with joy at every stone and bush I recognize, as if I had been away for two or three years, and when I see the church steeple, I really want to sweep my hat off to it.'

'And how do you feel, Joseph?' asked Brulette, who at last took note of our companion's pained expression. 'You've been away more than a year, aren't you glad to be coming near home?'

'I'm sorry, Brulette,' said Joseph, 'I don't know what you're talking about. I was remembering the woodcutter's song, and in the middle there's a pretty refrain I can't recall.'

'Oh!' said Brulette. 'That's when the song says: "I hear the nightingale".'

And as she said it, she sang it perfectly, which made Joseph leap with joy and clap his hands as if he'd suddenly woken up.

'Ah Brulette! How lucky you are to have such a good memory. Sing it again, sing "I hear the nightingale".'

'I'd rather recite the whole song,' she said, and she sang it right through without omitting a word, a feat that filled Joseph with such joy that he clasped her hands and told her, with a display of courage of which I wouldn't have believed him capable, that only a musician deserved her friendship.

'To tell the truth,' said Brulette, who was thinking of Huriel, 'I'd like him to be both a good singer and a good player.'

'It's rare to be both,' said Joseph. 'Playing breaks the voice, and apart from the woodcutter . . .'

'And his son!' said Brulette, who spoke without thinking.

I kicked her ankle, and she changed the subject, but Joseph, who wasn't free of jealousy, brought us back to the song.

'I believe,' he said, 'that when père Bastien set it to words, he was thinking of three boys we all know, for I remember a conversation we had with him one supper-time, the day you arrived in the woods.'

'I've forgotten,' said Brulette with a blush.

'Well I certainly haven't,' replied Joseph. 'We were talking about girls' love, and Huriel was saying you couldn't win it by playing heads or tales. Tiennet asserted with a laugh that sweetness and submission did no good, and that to be loved it was better to make yourself feared than appear too kind. Huriel contradicted him, and I listened without saying anything. Who else could it be who "has the rose in his hand"? "The youngest of the three. He loves but does not dare." Sing the last couplet Brulette, since you know it so well! Isn't there a line: "One gives to him who asks"?'

'Since you know it as well as I do,' said Brulette, somewhat offended, 'remember it, and sing it to the first sweetheart you have. If the woodcutter enjoys putting to music conversations he hears, it's not up to me to accept the consequences. For my part I still don't understand it at all. But I have pins and needles in my feet, and while our horse walks up this hill, I want to stretch my legs a little.'

Without waiting for me to take the reins and stop the horse, she leapt on to the path and began striding ahead, as light as a sparrow. I was about to get down, too, but Joseph held my arm and, still following his own thoughts, said: 'Isn't it true that those who show their desires too openly are despised as much as those who keep them hidden?'

'If that's meant for me . . .'

'It's not meant for anyone. I'm continuing the conversation we had in the forest, the conversation that was turned into a song attacking your words and my silence. It seems it's Huriel who won the trial with the lass.'

'What lass?' I asked impatiently. For Joseph hadn't confided in me before that moment, and I wasn't pleased that he should trust me only out of spite.

'What lass?' he echoed with an air of sad mockery. 'The lass in the song!'

'Well, what trial did Huriel win? Does that lass live far away, since the poor boy has set out for the Forez?'

Joseph remained lost in thought for a moment, then he replied: 'It's true all the same that he was right when he said that between command and silence was prayer. That still comes back to what you first said, which was that in order to be heard it was essential not to love too deeply. He who loves too much is fearful, he can't extract a single word from his heart, and he's considered stupid because he's paralyzed with desire and shame.'

'No doubt,' I answered. 'I've been in that quandary many times, but sometimes I spoke so badly that I would have done better to say nothing at all: I could have deluded myself a little longer.'

Poor Joseph held his tongue and didn't say another word. I was sorry to have made him angry, and yet I couldn't help feeling that his jealousy was ill-placed where Huriel was concerned, for I knew quite well that Huriel had served Joseph to his own detriment, and from that moment I despised jealousy so much that I've never since felt its bite, and wouldn't have felt it at all, I believe, unless I was sure I had reason to feel it.

Still, I was on the point of talking to him calmly, when we saw that Brulette, who was still walking in front of us, had stopped beside a path to speak to a monk, who seemed to me as fat and short as the one we'd met in the Chambérat woods. I whipped up the horse and made sure it was indeed the good

Brother Nicholas. He'd asked Brulette if our village was far off, and as there was still some distance to travel, and as he complained of being weary, she'd invited him to share our cart.

We made room for him, as well as for a large, covered basket he was carrying, which he carefully set on his knees. None of us thought of asking him what was in it, except perhaps for me, since I'm naturally a little inquisitive. But I'd have been afraid to show him less courtesy than I owed him, for the mendicant brothers collect in their wanderings all manner of things that merchants give them out of devotion, and that they then sell for the benefit of their monastery. Everything was a source of profit to them, even women's adornments, which one sometimes felt really amazed to find in their hands, and which some of them did not dare to sell openly.

I made the horse start trotting again and soon we caught sight of the steeple, and then the old elms around the square, and then all the houses, big and small, but they didn't bring me as much pleasure as I'd promised myself, for the encounter with Brother Nicholas had aroused within me sad memories that still gave me some cause for worry. Nevertheless, I saw that he was as much on his guard as I was on mine, for in front of Brulette and Joseph he said not a word to me that could have given them any grounds to believe we'd seen each other since the day of the feast, and that he and I knew more than many others about what had transpired there.

He was a pleasant and jovial man, who at any other time would have amused me, but I was eager to arrive and to be alone with him, to ask him if he, for his part, had any news about what had happened. At the edge of the town, Joseph leapt down from the cart and, despite whatever Brulette could say to him to urge him to come and rest at her father's place, he took the path for Saint Chartier saying he'd come and pay his respects to père Brulet when he had seen and embraced his mother.

It seemed to me that the monk was urging him on, as if it were his primary duty, but really just wanting him to leave. And then, instead of accepting my invitation to come to my house to dine and sleep, he told me he'd merely spend an hour in père Brulet's house, for he had business there.

'You'll be welcome,' said Brulette, 'but do you know my grandfather, then? I've never seen you at our place, have I?'

'I know neither this area nor your family,' replied the monk, 'yet I'm charged with a commission I can talk about only in your house.'

It occurred to me once more that he had in his basket laces or ribbons he wanted to sell, and that having heard in the area around the town that Brulette was the best-adorned girl in the region, and having seen her in all her finery at the Chambérat feast, he wanted to show her his merchandise without exposing himself to criticism, which in those days spared neither the good monks nor the bad ones.

I thought that was also what Brulette assumed, for when she alighted before her door, she reached out her hands to take the basket, saying to him: 'Don't worry, I can guess what's in there.' But the monk refused to be separated from it, saying, for his part, that it was worth a great deal and he feared breakages.

'I can see, Brother,' I said to him softly, holding him back a little, 'that you've got plenty on your hands. I don't want to bother you, and that's why I'd like to ask you to tell me quickly if there's any news about what happened over there.'

'Not that I know of,' he replied, just as softly, 'but no news is good news.' And shaking my hand in friendly fashion, he went into Brulette's house, where she was already clinging to her grandfather's neck.

I thought that the old man, who was usually very courteous, owed me a warm welcome and hearty thanks for the great care I'd taken of her, but instead of detaining me for a moment or two, he seemed even more eager to see the monk than to see us. He took him by the hand and led him into the house, telling me to forgive him, but he needed to be alone with his granddaughter for important matters.

NINETEENTH EVENING

I'm not easily shocked, and yet I did feel shocked to be as poorly received as that, so I took myself off home to put my cart away and find out how my family was. By then, it was too late in the day to get down to work, so I went into the town to see if everything was in its accustomed place, and I found that nothing had changed, except that one of the trees on the village green, the one that had stood in front of the clogmaker's store, had been cut up for clogs, and that père Godard had trimmed his poplar and put new tiles on his roof.

I'd thought my journey into Bourbonnais would have aroused more interest, and I was expecting so many questions that I'd be hard put to answer them all, but our folk are far from inquisitive, and for the first time I realized they were even rather sleepy as regards everything foreign, for I was forced to tell several people that I'd been away at all. They hadn't even known I'd been gone.

Towards evening, as I was returning home, I met the monk on his way to La Châtre, and he gave me a message from père Brulet, inviting me to supper.

Who was amazed on entering Brulette's house? I was, for there I found the grandfather sitting on one side of the table and Brulette on the other, looking at the monk's basket, which lay on the table between them, and which was now open to reveal a plump baby boy of about a year old, sitting on a cushion and trying to eat black plums, which turned his face completely black!

At first Brulette seemed to me very thoughtful and even sad, but when she saw my amazement, she couldn't help bursting out laughing, after which she wiped her eyes, but it seemed to me that if she had shed tears, they were tears of sorrow and pain rather than tears of mirth.

'Come on,' she said at last, 'shut the door and listen to what we have to tell you. My grandfather wants you to know about the fine present the monk brought us.'

'Let me tell you, nephew,' said père Brulet, who never laughed at anything amusing, any more than he worried over anything. 'Here we have an orphan child that we've arranged with the monk to care for, in return for a pension. We know nothing about the child's father or mother or country or anything at all. His name is Charley and that's all we know. It's a good pension, and the monk chose us because he'd met my granddaughter in Bourbonnais, and as he'd heard where she came from, and that she was a reliable person who wasn't wealthy but wasn't burdened with poverty either, and was free to spend her time as she chose, he thought it would give her pleasure and would be a service he could pay her, if he put her in charge of this child, with the benefits that come with such a responsibility.'

Although it was a rather amazing thing, I wasn't really amazed by it in the first few moments, and only asked if the monk had already met père Brulet at an earlier point, for Brulet to have had such confidence in the monk's words where the pension was concerned.

'I hadn't seen him,' père Brulet told me, 'but I know he has come to this area several times, and that he's known by people in whom I trust, people who, a few days ago, had already told me on his behalf what it was he wished to discuss with me. Moreover, twelve months of the pension are paid in advance, and if the money doesn't come in the future, that'll be the time to worry about it.'

'Well and good, uncle. You know what you should do. But I wouldn't have expected that my cousin, who's so fond of her freedom, would embrace a kid who has nothing to do with her, and who, and I mean no offence by this, doesn't look particularly attractive.'

'Well, that's what upsets me,' said Brulette, 'and I was just saying so to my grandfather when you came in.' And she added as she rubbed the child's face with her handkerchief, 'it doesn't matter how hard I rub, it won't make his mouth better shaped, and yet I'd have liked to do my apprenticeship with a child that was a pleasure to caress. This one seems bad tempered and doesn't respond to any smiles. All he cares about is food.'

'Bah!' said père Brulet. 'He's no uglier than any child of his age, and as for becoming sweet, well, it's up to you to make him so. He's tired after his travels and he doesn't know where he is or what we want of him.'

When père Brulet went out to get a knife he'd left with the neighbour, I began to feel more surprised now that I found myself alone with Brulette. She seemed irritated at times and even really unhappy.

'What distresses me,' she said, 'is that I don't know how to care for a child. I wouldn't want to cause suffering to a poor creature who can't help himself at all, but I feel so clumsy, that I'm sorry that up until now I've taken so little notice of small children.'

'It's true that you don't seem to have been destined for such a task, and I can't understand why your grandfather, whom I've never known to be rapacious, should impose such a duty on you for the sake of having a few more crowns at the end of the year.'

'You're talking like a rich man! Remember I have no dowry, and it's the fear of poverty that has always put me off marriage.'

'That's a bad reason, Brulette; for you've been sought out in the past, and will be in the future, by men richer than you, who love you for your beauty and your pretty voice.'

'My beauty will fade, and my pretty voice won't help me when my beauty has gone. I don't want to be criticized, at the end of a few years, for having spent my dowry on ornaments and brought nothing solid into the relationship.'

'Does this mean you've begun to think seriously of marriage, since we've returned from Bourbonnais? This is the first time I've heard you make any plans to save money.'

'I'm not giving it any more thought than I did in the past,' she said looking less assured than usual, 'but I never said I wanted to stay an old maid.'

'It's true, it's true, you're thinking of settling down,' I said to her, laughing. 'You don't need to hide it from me, I won't ask any more questions, and what you're doing in burdening yourself with that unfortunate little rich kid there who has money but no mother, is proof enough for me that you're planning to start your glory-box. If it weren't for that, your grandfather, whom you've always been able to twist round your little finger as if he were your grandson, wouldn't have pushed you into taking charge of such a boy.'

Brulette picked up the child to remove him from the table and set the places for dinner, and as she carried him to her grandfather's bed she looked at him with the saddest expression.

'Poor Charley!' she said. 'I'll certainly do the best I can for you. It's a pity you were ever born, and it's my opinion you weren't welcome.'

But her gaiety soon returned and she even smiled broadly at supper as she fed Charley, who had the appetite of a little wolf, and responded to all her care by trying to scratch her face.

Towards eight in the evening, Joseph came in and was warmly welcomed by père Brulet, but I saw that Brulette, who'd just put Charley back on the bed, quickly pulled the bed curtain to hide him and seemed perturbed all the time Joseph stayed in the house. I also saw that not a word was said to him about this strange windfall, neither by the old man nor by Brulette, and I thought I should remain silent about it to please them.

Joseph was down-hearted and gave the briefest possible answers to my uncle. Brulette asked him if he'd found his mother in good health and if she'd been much surprised and pleased to see him. And as he just said 'yes' and no more to all her questions, she asked him if he weren't too tired after going to Saint Chartier and back on foot.

'I didn't want to spend the whole day there,' he said, 'without paying my respects to your grandfather. Now I feel really tired and I'll go and spend the night at Tiennet's, if he doesn't mind.'

I replied that it would be a pleasure for me, and took him to the house, where, when we'd gone to bed, he said to me: 'Tiennet, I've no sooner arrived than I'm about to leave again. I only came here to get away from the Alleu woods, which had become a place of unhappiness for me.'

'But you're wrong to leave, Joseph; there you had friends who replaced those you'd left . . .'

'Anyway, that's how I feel,' he said rather sharply. But in a gentler tone he added: 'Tiennet! Tiennet! There are things you can talk about and others you have to keep silent about. You hurt me today when you let me know that Brulette would never accept me.'

'Joseph, I never said anything of the sort, for the reason that I don't know if you're even thinking of such a thing.'

'You do know I am, and I'm wrong never to have talked about it openly with you. But what could I do? I'm not the sort that finds it easy to confess, and the things that cause me most pain are those I find the hardest to explain to myself. It's my misfortune, and I believe that the only illness I suffer from is that my mind always runs on the same course, and always goes into eclipse the moment I have the words on the tip of my tongue. Just listen, then, while I talk, for God knows how long it'll be before I can speak again. I'm in love, and I can see I'm not loved in return. Things have been like that for so many years (for I've loved Brulette since she was a child) that I've grown used to suffering from it. I never flattered myself that she liked me, and I lived in the belief that she would never pay any attention to me. Now I can see that the fact that she came to the Bourbonnais proves I was of some importance to her, and that's what gave me the strength and the courage not to die. But I know only too well that in that country she saw someone who would suit her better than I would.'

'I know nothing of that,' I answered, 'but if that were the case, that person hasn't given you any cause for complaint or reproach.'

'That's true,' admitted Joseph, 'I know I'm being unjust. All the more so since Huriel, who knows Brulette to be an honest girl, and who isn't in a position to marry her, as long as he's one of the mule-drivers, freely chose to do all he ought to do in going far away for a long time. That means I can have some hope of being able to return and present myself to Brulette with a little more merit than I now have. At present I can't bear to be here, for I can see I'm not bringing anything I didn't have in the past. There's something in the air I breathe and in the words everyone says that tells me: "You're ill, you're thin, and you've learnt nothing new or good that would make us take an interest in you!" Yes, Tiennet, what you said is true enough: my mother seemed afraid of my appearance when I turned up, and she shed so many tears as she embraced me that it brought as much pain as joy. This evening, too, Brulette seemed embarrassed at seeing me in her home, and her grandfather, although he's a fine man and a good friend to me, seemed uneasy at the thought that I might make him stay up any longer than he wanted. Don't tell me I imagined all that. Like all those who don't talk a lot, I see a great deal. My time has not yet come: I have to leave, and the sooner the better.'

'I think you should at least take a few days to rest, because I have the feeling that you want to go far away from here, and I don't think it's an act of friendship for you to inflict on us worries you could easily spare us.'

'Don't fret, Tiennet. I have the strength to do it, and I won't be ill any more. I know one thing, now, and that is that feeble bodies, to which God has given no great strength, have a will power that controls them better than the good health of other people. I wasn't making anything up when I told you in the woods that I'd been, so to say, renewed when I saw Huriel fight so boldly, and that when I was wide awake in the night I heard his voice saying to me: "Go to it! I'm a man, and as long as you're not a man, you'll count for nothing." So now I want to change my poor nature and come back here as fine to look at and as pleasant to listen to as any of Brulette's beaux.'

'But what if she makes her choice before you get back? She's almost nineteen now, and for a girl who has as many suitors as she has, it's time for her to make up her mind.'

'The only decision she'll make is between Huriel and me,' said Joseph in less assured tones. 'There's only him and me who could give her real love. Forgive me, Tiennet, I know or at least I guess that you too thought of her . . .'

'Yes, but I no longer think of her.'

'And you do well not to, for you wouldn't have been happy with her. She has tastes and ideas that are not native to the land in which she blossomed, and she needs another wind to shake her. The wind that blows here isn't subtle enough and can only dry her out. She's all too aware of it, although she can't put it into words, and I promise you that if Huriel doesn't betray me, I'll find her still free in a year's time or even in two.'

On that Joseph, as if exhausted from having spoken openly for such a long time, let his head drop back on the pillow and fell asleep. I'd been struggling for more than an hour not to set him an example in this for I was utterly exhausted, but when at daybreak I called Joseph there was no answer. I looked for him and saw he'd gone without waking anyone.

The next day Brulette went to see Mariton, saying she wanted to break the news about Charley to her gently, and find out what had happened between her and her son. She didn't want my company to make this visit, and told me, when she came back, that she hadn't got much out of her because her master, Benoît, was ill, and even in some danger from a burst blood vessel. I guessed that Mariton, obliged to look after her boss, had been unable the day before to pay as much attention to her son as she would have liked, and that Joseph had, in accordance with his nature, been smitten with jealousy yet again.

'That's true,' said Brulette. 'The more intelligent Joseph has made himself through his ambitions, the more demanding he's become, and I think I liked him better when he was simple and submissive than the way he is now.'

And as I told Brulette all that Joseph had told me the previous evening before we fell asleep, she replied: 'If he has such a fine desire, we'd only irritate him by worrying about him more than he wants us to. So let him go with God's protection! If I were the wicked flirt you've sometimes accused me of being, I'd be proud to be the reason for this boy trying so hard to improve his mind and his lot, but that's not the case, and I'm sorry he's not doing it for his mother's sake or for his own sake.'

'But he is right, isn't he, when he says that you can choose only between Huriel and him?'

'I've plenty of time to think about that,' she said, with a laugh that came only from the lips and didn't brighten her face, 'since here we have the only suitors Joseph allows me fleeing from me as fast as their legs can carry them.'

For a week, the arrival of the child monk had brought

to Brulette's house was the news of the town, and the torment of the curious. So many stories were told about it that it wouldn't have taken much for Charley to become the son of a prince, and everyone wanted to borrow money or sell goods to père Brulet, thinking that the pension that had been able to persuade his daughter to take up a task so contrary to her tastes must be at the very least equal to the revenue of an entire province. Everyone was soon amazed to see that Brulette and her grandfather made no alterations to their lives as poor people, didn't leave their little home, and merely added to it a crib for the child, and a bowl for his soup. So the estimates had to be brought down, but gossips, who didn't want to have been proved wrong, began to criticize my uncle for his avarice and even to attack him, saying that not everything was being done to care for the child that was due to him, given the enormous profits the Brulets were making.

The envy felt by some and the discontent felt by others made Brulet enemies that he'd never had, much to his amazement, for he was a simple man and so good a Christian that he hadn't foreseen that such a matter would make people talk so much. But Brulette merely laughed about it and persuaded him not to pay it any further attention.

Meanwhile the days and weeks went by without there being any news of Joseph or of Huriel, of the great woodcutter or Thérence. Brulette wrote letters to Thérence, and I wrote to Huriel, and we received no reply. Brulette was saddened by this and even rather hurt, so much so that she told me she didn't want to give any more thought to these strangers who didn't even remember her and didn't return the friendship she'd offered them.

So she began to dress up again and to appear at dances, for her beaux were distressed by her air of sadness and the headaches of which she often complained since her return from Bourbonnais. The journey itself had even aroused a few criticisms, and people had said that she had some hidden love either for Joseph or for someone else. They wanted her to appear even more friendly than usual so they could forgive her for absenting herself without consulting anyone.

Brulette was too proud to get out of this difficulty by

softening people up, but, since her taste for pleasure led her in that direction, she tried to entrust the care of Charley to her neighbour, mère Lamouche, and to give herself, as she had in the past, the pleasure of light-hearted enjoyments.

Well, one evening when I was returning with her from the Vaudevant pilgrimage, which is a great feast, we heard Charley bellowing, from further away from the house than we were able to run. 'That damned boy!' said Brulette. 'He never gives up being naughty, and I don't know anyone who could control him.'

'Are you sure that mère Lamouche looks after him as she promised you she would?'

'Surely she does. That's all she has to do, and I recompense her enough to please her.'

But Charley was still bellowing and the house seemed to us to be closed, as if everyone had gone away.

Brulette began to run and although she pounded on the neighbour's door, no one answered, except for Charley, who screamed even more, either from fear or from boredom or rage.

I had to climb up to the thatch roof, and drop into the bedroom through the trap door in the attic. I swiftly opened the door for Brulette and we saw Charley all alone, rolling in the ashes, where fortunately there remained very little fire, and as red as a beetroot from howling so much.

'Hey there,' said Brulette. 'So that's how this poor unfortunate little boy is being looked after. Come! Whoever accepts a child accepts a master. I should have known it, and should either not have accepted this child or renounced all pleasure when I did so.'

She carried Charley off to her house, partly pitying, partly impatient, and having washed him, fed him, and consoled him as best she could, she put him to sleep and sat down deep in thought, her head between her hands. I tried to tell her that it wasn't hard, if she sacrificed some of the money they were getting, to entrust the child to a gentle and caring woman.

'No,' she answered. 'He needs constant watching, since I've accepted responsibility for him, and you can see what watching him means. The one day you think you can relax your guard is precisely the day that you should have been there. Moreover, it's just not possible,' she added, in tears. 'It'd be bad and I'd reproach myself my whole life long.'

'You'd be wrong, if it's in the child's interest. He isn't happy with you and he could be happy elsewhere.'

'What do you mean he isn't happy? I hope he is, except on those days when I'm not here. Well, I'll be here all the time from now on.'

'I tell you he's hardly happier on those days than when you're not here.'

'What do you mean? What do you mean?' Brulette said again, clapping her hands in fury. 'Where ever do you get that from? Have you seen me mistreat him, or even threaten him? Can I help the fact that he's not naturally pleasant and that he's so bad tempered? Even if he were my own child I could do nothing more with him.'

'Oh, I know you don't hurt him and don't let him suffer at all, because you're a good Christian. But the point is, you can't love him, that isn't something you can control, and although he doesn't know it, he feels it so much that he's not moved to love or caress anyone. Animals know whether we like them or not, so why should small humans not have the same knowledge?'

TWENTIETH EVENING

Brulette blushed, sulked, shed some more tears and made no answer; but the next day I found her taking her flock to the fields and, contrary to her general practice, carrying plump Charley in her arms. She sat down in the middle of the pasture field and set the child down on her dress, saying: 'Tiennet, you were right yesterday. Your chiding gave me food for thought, and I've made up my mind. I can't promise to love Charley very deeply, but at least I can behave as if I do, and perhaps God will reward me one day in giving me children who are somewhat sweeter than he is.'

'Ah, my dear, I don't know where you've dug all that up. I

didn't chide you, and I've no criticism to make, except as regards your determination to bring this wretched lad up all by yourself. Come on, do you want me to have a letter sent to the monk, or would you like me to go and find him, to make him seek out another family? I know where to find his monastery, and I'd prefer to make another journey rather than see you condemned to such penal servitude as this.'

'No, Tiennet, no. You mustn't even think of changing what has been decided. My grandfather promised on my behalf and I had to approve his decision. If only I could tell you . . . but I can't. Just let me tell you one thing. Money plays no role in this, and neither my grandfather nor I would be willing to accept a penny in payment for the duty we've been urged to carry out.'

'Now you're amazing me more and more. Whose child is this, then? Does he belong to relatives of yours? And to me, as a result?'

'That may be. We have family who live far from here. But allow me not to tell you anything, since not only am I unable to, but in any case I'm not permitted to. Just behave as if this kid is a stranger to us, and we've been paid for his care. Otherwise the gossips may well accuse people who don't deserve it.'

'Devil take it! You're really intriguing me. I just can't guess . . .'

'Right, well, don't guess. I forbid you. Even though I'm sure you'll never guess right.'

'Well and good. But are you really going to wean yourself of amusements, as this child is being weaned of his nurse's milk? A curse on your grandfather's promise!'

'My grandfather did the right thing, and had I gone against his wishes, I'd have been a heartless ingrate. So I'm telling you again that I don't want to go into it in a half-hearted way, even if it makes me die of boredom . . .'

Brulette had a mind of her own. From that day on there took place in her such a change that she was hardly recognizable. She no longer left the house for any reason other than to take her flock to pasture, and she always took Charley with her. And when she'd put him to bed each evening she took her sewing or did the housework. She no longer went to any dances and didn't buy any finery, having no further reason to dress up in it.

As a result of this harsh task, she grew serious and even sad, for she soon found herself abandoned. There's no girl so pretty that if she wants to be surrounded by friends, she must make herself amiable, and when Brulette no longer showed any desire to please, she was judged bad tempered and people assumed she'd already frittered away all the wit she'd been given.

To my mind, she'd changed for the better since, as she'd never been flirtatious with me but had merely acted as a princess might, she seemed to me softer in her way of talking to me, more sensible and more interesting in what she did, but she wasn't generally judged like that. She'd held out enough hope to all her beaux for each of them to feel as offended at being dropped by her as if he had some rights over her. And although her flirtations had been very innocent, she was punished for them as much as if she'd spoilt the chances of other girls, which to my way of thinking just proves that men have at least as much vanity as women have, and maybe more, and they don't consider that anyone ever does enough to please or soothe the esteem in which they hold themselves.

At the very least, what's certain is that there are plenty of unjust people, even among those young men who seem such good friends and such happy servants as long as they're in love. Several of them became really bitter, and more than once I exchanged words with them to defend my cousin against the criticisms they directed at her. Unfortunately, they were supported by the old gossips and those who were envious of père Brulet's imagined fortune, and the result was that Brulette, when she heard about these unkind stories, was obliged to refuse admittance to those inquisitive and ill-intentioned people as well as to those cowardly friends who, through weakness, repeated what they'd heard others say.

So it came to pass that in less than a year the queen of the village, the rose of Nohant, was cut down by the malicious and abandoned by the fools. People made such black accusations against her character that not only did I tremble that she might learn about them, but I myself was sometimes attacked and had no idea how to respond.

The worst of these lies, but it was one père Brulet really should have anticipated, was that Charley was neither a poor abandoned foundling nor a prince's son to be raised in secret, but in reality Brulette's child. It was in vain that I protested that she'd always lived openly under the eyes of all and sundry, and that she'd never made a favourite of any man, and that she could therefore not have committed a sin so difficult to hide. People would refer to this or that girl who'd boldly concealed her condition until the last moment, and had reappeared almost the following day, as calm and lively as if nothing had happened, and had even been able to hide the consequences until after she'd married either the author or the dupe of her sin. That had unfortunately occurred several times in our village. In our little country towns, where the houses are all dotted through the gardens, and separated from each other by hemp fields, lucern fields, and even fairly extensive meadows, it's no easy matter to see and hear at every hour of the night what is happening in other houses, and from time immemorial things have happened there that the good Lord alone can judge.

One of the fiercest tongues was that of mère Lamouche, since the time Brulette had caught her out and had taken the child out of her care. She had for so long been Brulette's servant and lapdog that she couldn't get used to receiving nothing from her and so, to exact revenge, she invented whatever people hoped to hear her say. She therefore recounted, to anyone who wished to hear it, that Brulette had forgotten what she owed her honour with *that feeble lad Joseph*, and that she'd been so filled with shame that she'd ordered him to leave. Joseph was said to have obeyed on the promise that she wouldn't marry anyone else, and he'd gone to seek his fortune far away, with the sole aim of marrying her. The child, according to mère Lamouche, had been taken to Bourbonnais by messengers mired with black who were said to be mule-drivers and with whom Joseph had long been acquainted under the pretext of buying a set of bagpipes from them. But, the story went, there had never been any other bagpipes in question than that boisterous little Charley. Finally, about a year after he was born, Brulette had gone to see her lover and her child, accompanied by me and a mule-driver who was as ugly as the devil. It was there that we met the mendicant monk, who'd agreed to carry the baby for us, as a result of which we'd got together to concoct the story of the rich man's child which was all the more false, as that rich man's child had never brought in an extra sou to my uncle's home.

When mère Lamouche had invented this explanation in which, as you can see, lies mingled with truth, her word prevailed over that of everyone else, and the visit that Joseph had made to the country, a visit so short and so nearly secret, was the final point needed to persuade everyone.

Then everyone smirked about it, and Brulette was called Josephine, as a kind of nickname.

Despite my anger at all these nasty words, Brulette made so little attempt to defend herself, and revealed through the care she took of the child so much contempt for what people said, that I began to get confused myself. Why, after all, was it completely impossible that I should have been duped by all this? At a certain time, Brulette's friendship for Joseph had caused me some jealousy. However well-behaved and self-controlled a girl may be, and however embarrassed a boy may be, love and ignorance have caught out many another, and there are couples so young that they don't know the evil they're committing until they've succumbed. Just because she'd been silly on one occasion didn't mean that subsequently Brulette couldn't be an intelligent girl, capable of hiding her misfortune completely, too proud to confess to it, and yet just proud enough not to want to deceive anyone. Was it because she'd commanded him to do so, that Joseph longed to show himself worthy of being a handsome husband and a good father? That showed a sensible and patient desire. But was I mistaken in thinking that she was attracted to Huriel? I was quite capable of being wrong, and even if that attraction had come to her despite herself, the fact that she'd barely yielded to it meant she wasn't greatly in the wrong towards Joseph. Finally, was it because of the voice of her conscience or because of a long-lasting friendship that she'd gone to help the poor invalid? In either case, it was her right to do so. And if she was a mother, she was a good one, even though her own nature didn't perhaps lead her in that direction. All women can have children, but that doesn't mean that all women are curious about children, and Brulette was all the more praiseworthy in returning to her child despite her taste for company and the doubts that she allowed to gather about the truth.

All things well considered, I could see nothing in the worst that I could imagine that would make me feel less friendship for my cousin. The only thing was that she'd been so inconsistent in what she said about the topic, that my faith in her was a little shaken. If it were true that she loved Joseph, that showed she was too well-versed in the art of deception, and if she didn't love him, she'd been too lax and forgetful for a person resolved to do as duty bids.

Had she not been so ill-treated, I'd have visited her less often, so uneasy had my doubts made me in her company, but, on the contrary, I forced myself to go and see her every day, and not to show her the slightest distrust in what I said to her. Nevertheless, I was constantly amazed at how hard she found it to carry out her duties as a mother. Despite the weight of sorrow I felt she carried in her heart, she constantly experienced the return of that fine youthfulness that still flourished throughout her being. If she no longer made a show of silks and laces, she nevertheless kept her hair silky, her white stockings nicely drawn, and her attractive feet longed to leap about when she saw a fine green space or heard the sound of the pipes. Sometimes, in the house, when she remembered a Bourbonnais bourrée, she would set Charley on her grandfather's knees and make me dance with her, singing, laughing, and strutting as if all the parish could see her, but after a moment, Charley would cry and want to go to bed, or to be carried, or to eat, although he wasn't hungry, or drink, although he wasn't thirsty. She would take him back with tears in her eyes, like a dog having its collar put back on, and with a sigh she would rock him or sing him a nursery song or let him suck a biscuit.

Seeing how much she missed her days of happiness, I tried

to offer her my sister to look after the child while she danced at Saint Chartier. I should tell you that in those days there was in the old castle, of which nowadays there remains only the carcass, an old, good-natured spinster who used to arrange balls for all the local people. Middle-class or upper-class, peasants or artisans, anyone who wanted to could go; the castle's rooms were so large that they could never be too full. You used to see ladies and gentlemen going there mounted on horses or asses in the depths of winter, through dreadful roads, wearing silk stockings, silver ear-rings, and wigs powdered with white as the trees along the route were often white with snow. People used to enjoy it so much that nothing would stop the dancers, rich and poor, who saw themselves heartily treated from midday to six in the evening.

The dowager lady of Saint Chartier, who had noticed Brulette in the dances on the square the year before and who was eager to attract pretty girls to her day-time balls, invited her, and at my suggestion she did go once. I thought I was performing a good deed, for I felt she was allowing herself to fall too low in not responding to the evil minds. She always looked so well and spoke so well that it didn't seem possible to me that people wouldn't change their minds when they saw how lovely and well-behaved she was.

When she entered on my arm, people whispered at first, without daring to do anything more. I danced with her for the first dance, and, as she was so graceful that people couldn't help being affected by her, others came and invited her, boys who may have been tempted to joke with her but didn't dare risk it. Everything was going smoothly, when some middle-class people came into the room where we were. I should explain that the peasants had a separate ball and mingled with the rich only towards the end, when the ladies, irritated at being abandoned by their partners, decided to mix with the country girls, who more easily attracted boys from all walks of life through their cheerful talk and their fresh good health.

Brulette was at first sought after as the finest piece on display, and the silk stocking brigade treated her so well that the woollen stockings could hardly get near her. Through sheer contrariness, having torn her apart for six months, these boys all became jealous of her again in an hour, and even more in love than before. The result was that there was a kind of battle to see who could ask her to dance, and boys would almost have fought each other to give her the kiss that accompanies the entrance to the dance.

The girls and women sulked, and the women from our village accused their menfolk of being unable to maintain their rancour; but they may as well have been singing hymns, so much more balm does a beauty's gaze contain than an ugly woman's tongue has venom.

'Well, Brulette,' I said to her as I escorted her home, 'wasn't I right to shake you out of your unhappiness a little? You can see the game is never lost when you know how to play with all your heart.'

'I'm grateful to you,' she answered. 'You're the best of friends, and I truly think you're the only faithful and certain friend I've ever had. I'm glad I triumphed over my enemies, and now I won't be bored at home any longer.'

'Gracious! You move quickly. Yesterday, it was all clouds and today it's all joy! So you're going to reclaim your title as queen of the village?'

'No. You haven't understood me. That was the last party I'll go to, as long as I have Charley, for, to tell you the truth, I didn't enjoy it a bit. I put a good face on things to please you, and I'm glad now to have passed the test, but the whole time I was there I thought only of my poor little lad. All the time I saw him crying and complaining, however kindly he was treated at your home, and he's so awkward at making himself understood that he'll have grown cross in making the others cross.'

Brulette's words froze my blood. I'd quite forgotten Charley when I saw her dancing and laughing. The love she felt for him and that she no longer hid reminded me of everything that in the past had seemed lies, and I believed I could rightly consider her a master-mind who was without equal and who was tired of forcing herself.

'So you love him with all your being?' I asked her, without giving too much thought to the words I was using.

'With all my being?' she asked, in astonishment. 'Well, perhaps one loves all children like that when one thinks of what one owes them. I never pretended, like many girls whom I've known to be eager for marriage, that I had the instinct of a good brood hen. It could be that I'm too much of a harum-scarum to deserve having a family early in my life. There are some who can't reach the age of sixteen without losing sleep over it. As for me, I'd be happy to turn twenty unmarried, and I wouldn't feel I was behindhand. If that's wrong, it's no fault of mine. I am as God made me, and I've gone in the direction in which he pushed me. To tell the truth, a small child is a harsh master, as unjust as an insane husband and as obstinate as a starving animal. I love reason and justice, and I'd have been happy with a gentler and better-behaved companion. I like cleanliness, too, and you've often teased me when a grain of dust on the dresser tormented me, or when a fly in my glass took away my thirst. A little child always seeks out dirt, however much you discourage him. Besides, I love to think and day-dream and remember, whereas the little child wants you to think only of him, and is cross as soon as you stop looking at him. But all that doesn't amount to anything, Tiennet, when the good Lord takes a hand. He's invented a kind of miracle that takes place in our minds when it's called for, and now I know something I didn't believe in before it happened to me. That is that any child at all, even if he is ugly and wayward, can easily be bitten by a wolf or trampled by a goat, but never by a woman, and that the child will come to control her, unless she is made of a different substance than other women.'

As she said that, we were going into my home, where Charley was playing with my sister's children. 'Oh thank goodness, I'm glad you're here,' said my sister. 'You have the wildest boy on this earth. He hits my children, he bites them, he swears at them, and he needs forty cartloads of patience and compassion.'

Brulette went up, laughing, to Charley, who never made a fuss over her, and, watching him play in his own way, she said to him as if he were capable of understanding her: 'I was sure you wouldn't win the hearts of these good people who put up

with you. There's only me, my poor little owl, who's used to
your beak and your claws!'

Although Charley was hardly more than eighteen months
old at that stage, he seemed to understand what Brulette said
to him, for he got up, after looking at her thoughtfully for a
moment, then hopping up to her, he began to cover her hands
with kisses as if he wanted to eat her.

'Oh!' said my sister. 'So he does have some good moments,
apparently.'

'My dear,' said Brulette, 'I'm as amazed as you are, for this
is the first time I've seen him like this.' And kissing Charley on
his big round eyes, she began to cry with joy and tenderness.

I don't know why I was as shaken by that little scene as if
it had been a miracle. And indeed if that boy were not hers,
then Brulette at that moment really rose in my estimation.
This girl, so proud that she wouldn't have wanted to serve the
king's cousin six months before, and who that very morning
had been served by all the youth of the area, rich and poor
alike going down on their knees to her, had put so much pity
and Christianity in her heart that she considered herself rewarded for all her pains by the first caresses of an unattractive
and grubby little boy, who hadn't a spark of gentleness and
almost no awareness.

It brought a tear to my eye, when I thought of what those
caresses cost her, and lifting Charley on to my shoulders, I
took them both back to her home.

Twenty times it was on the tip of my tongue to ask her to
tell me the truth, for if she'd committed a fault that had led to
Charley, I was perfectly willing to absolve her of her sin, and
if, on the contrary, she was accepting the burden of someone
else's sin, I would have liked to kiss the tips of her feet,
considering her the sweetest and most patient winner of paradise.

But I dared not ask her any questions and when I repeated
my doubts to my sister, who has never been a fool, she
answered: 'If you can't find the courage to talk to her about it,
that's because, in the depths of your heart, you feel she's
innocent. And what's more, such a lovely girl would've made
a finer boy. He's no more like her than a potato is like a rose.'

Winter passed and spring came, and still Brulette made no attempt to return to any kind of amusement. She didn't even feel any regrets about it, because she realized that she could make herself mistress of men's hearts again whenever she chose to do so, but she said that so many male and female friendships had betrayed her that she no longer valued numbers and would henceforth value quality. The poor child didn't yet know all the wrong that had been done to her. Everyone had decried her, but none had had the courage to insult her. When you looked at her, you could find honesty written all over her face, but behind her back, people took their revenge, in what they said, for the esteem they hadn't been able to prevent themselves feeling for her, and from a distance they would snap around her heels, like cowardly dogs who don't dare leap at your face.

Père Brulet was getting on in years, becoming a little deaf, and thinking more often of himself, as old folk do, than of what the world was saying. So grandfather and granddaughter weren't as unhappy as people would have liked them to be, and my own father, as well as the rest of the family who were wise in Christian values, gave me the advice and the example of not tormenting their minds, for they said that truth would out, and the time would come when the ill-natured gossips would be punished.

Time, which is also a great leveller, began of its own accord to carry away that evil dust. Brulette would have scorned to exact vengeance, and never wanted any revenge other than to receive very coldly any advances anyone made to return to her good graces. What happened is what always does happen, for she found friends among those who had not been her suitors, and those friends, being uninvolved and not being hurt, defended her at the time when she least expected it. I'm not speaking of Mariton, who was like a mother to her, and who, in her tavern, came close, on more than one occasion, to hurling jugs at the heads of the drinkers, when they allowed themselves the liberty of singing *Josephine*, but I'm referring to people whom one couldn't accuse of being blind and who for all that made the slanderers ashamed.

Brulette, then, had knuckled under, at first with difficulty, but little by little with pleasure, accepting a calmer life than had been hers in the past. Those who befriended her were the most rational people, and she often came to our place with Charley, who, once winter was over, lost the redness of his heated little face and became more gentle in his behaviour. The child was not so much ugly as stubborn, and when Brulette's gentleness and kindness had slowly but surely tamed him, you realized that his large black eyes were not lacking in intelligence, and that when his large mouth was willing to smile, it was comical, rather than unsightly. He'd suffered from a teething rash which Brulette, who in the past had been so fussy, had treated and cared for so well that he'd become the healthiest, the most inviting and the tidiest child in town. Of course his jaw was still too large and his nose too short to be pretty, but as what counts with a child is good health, you couldn't help exclaiming at his size, his strength, and his air of determination.

But what made Brulette even more proud of her handiwork was that Charley grew daily more appealing in what he said and more open-hearted in what he did. When she'd first taken him under her wing, the few words he'd been able to say were oaths that would have made a regiment recoil, but she'd made him forget all that, and had taught him sweet prayers, and many little jokes, and pretty sayings that he arranged in a way that delighted everyone. He was not naturally affectionate, and didn't cover all and sundry with caresses, but he had for his dearie, as he called Brulette, such violent affection that whenever he was naughty, cutting up his overalls to make some ties, or putting his clogs in the soup pot, he would anticipate her reproaches by hugging her so hard around the neck that she didn't have the heart to reprimand him.

In the month of May, we were invited to a cousin's wedding. The wedding was to take place at Le Chassin,* and, the day before, she'd sent a cart to carry us, sending word to Brulette that if she didn't come with Charley it would cast a blight on her wedding day.

Le Chassin is a pretty spot on the Gourdon river, about two leagues from where we live. The country bears some resemblance to Bourbonnais, and Brulette, who didn't have a big appetite, left the noise of the wedding, and went for a walk outside to amuse Charley. She told me she wanted to take him to some quiet, shady spot, for it was his nap time and the noise of the festivities was preventing him from sleeping. If he didn't get his nap, he'd be uncomfortable and bad tempered until evening.

As it was very warm, I offered to accompany her to a little wood that in the past had been cultivated as a rabbit warren, and stood next to the ruined castle. Still closely bordered by thorns and ditches, it's a well sheltered and secluded place. 'Let's go there then,' she said. 'The child can sleep on my lap, and you can come back here and amuse yourself.'

When we reached the place, I begged her to let me stay with her.

'I'm not as eager for parties as I used to be,' I told her, 'and I'd be just as happy, if not more so, chatting with you. You get unhappy when you're not in your rightful place and when you've nothing to do, and you'd be unhappy here; and perhaps you might be accosted by someone who doesn't know you and who would cause you another sort of unhappiness.'

'Very well, but I can see only too clearly, my poor cousin, that I'm always a problem for you, and yet, you accept it with such patience and such good nature that I can't get used to doing without your help. But the time will come when I shall have to do so, for you're now at the age when you'll be settling down, and your wife may well think poorly of me, as so many others do, and won't want to believe that I deserve your friendship and hers.'

'It's too early to worry your head about that,' I said, settling plump Charley on my smock, which I'd spread out on the grass, while she sat beside him to wave any flies away from him. 'I haven't any thoughts of marriage, and if I do happen to enter on that path I promise you my wife will become a friend of yours, or she'll no longer be a friend of mine. She'd have to have her heart set in upside down if she didn't realize that what I feel for you is the most honest of friendships, and that, having followed you in your joys and pains, I've grown used to your company as if you and I were one. But what about you, Brulette, do you have no thoughts of marriage, or have you closed that chapter off?'

'Oh! As for me, Tiennet, I think that, unless the good Lord wills it otherwise, I've now nearly attained my majority and it seems that by waiting until I wanted to marry I've let the time to marry slip by without noticing it.'

'But it's more likely that the time to marry is near at hand, my dear. You're losing your taste for pleasure, you've found that you can love children, and I can see that you've accepted the quiet life of the household. But all the same you're still in the springtime of your life, like the earth around us with its flowers. You know that I don't flirt with you these days, so you can believe me when I tell you that you have never been as pretty as you are now, even if you have grown a little pale, just like lovely Thérence, the maid of the forest. And you've also got a little sad look that reminds me of her, and that goes fairly well with your plain head-dresses and your grey dresses. In a word, I think your character has changed, and that if you don't fall in love you'll become devout.'

'Don't talk to me about that, dear Tiennet,' exclaimed Brulette. 'A year ago I could have turned towards love or towards heaven. I felt that I was, as you say, changed in character, but now I'm attached to the suffering of this world, without finding in it either the sweetness love brings or the strength religion offers. I feel I'm harnessed to a yoke and push forward with my head without knowing what plough I draw behind me. You can see I'm none the sadder for that, and it doesn't make me want to die; but I confess I miss something in my life, not something I've already had, but something that might have been.'

'Come, Brulette,' I said, sitting beside her and taking her hand, 'this may be the moment for confidences. Now you can tell me everything without fear of causing me jealousy or pain. I've got over wanting from you anything you can't give me. Give me, then, something which is truly due to me, tell me what's making you so sad.'

Brulette blushed, made an effort to speak, but couldn't utter a word. It was as if I were forcing her to confess to herself, and that she'd forbidden herself to do so for so long that now she was unable to.

She lifted her fine eyes to the landscape around us, for we were sitting at the edge of the wood on a grassy, terraced spot overlooking a pretty valley embossed with little hillocks covered with crops.

Below our feet flowed the little stream, and on the other side, the land rose up steeply under a fine thicket of oaks, which, while not very extensive, was so rich in great trees that you might have taken it for a corner of the Alleu forest. I saw in Brulette's eyes what she was thinking about, and taking her hand again, which she'd removed to cover her heart, like someone who's suffering from heartburn, I said to her: 'Is it Huriel or Joseph?' in a tone that had no trace of mockery or teasing.

'It's not Joseph!' she said sharply.

'Then it's Huriel. But are you free to follow where your heart leads?'

'How could my heart lead,' she said, blushing more and more, 'towards someone who doubtless has never thought of me in that way?'

'That's no reason!'

'It is indeed,' she answered.

'No, I swear it isn't. My heart certainly led me to you!'

'But you abandoned those thoughts.'

'And you're finding it hard to abandon yours, and that means you still feel like that. But what of Joseph?'

'Well, what of Joseph?'

'You never pledged your word to him?'

'You know I didn't!'

'But . . . Charley?'

'Well, what of Charley?'

As my eyes had fallen on the child, hers turned in that direction, too, and then returned to me, so amazed, so clear and innocent, that I was as ashamed of my doubts as if they had been a kind of insult. 'Nothing,' I said quickly. 'I said "And Charley" because I thought I noticed him waking up.'

At that moment the sound of bagpipes could be heard on

the far side of the water among the oak trees, and Brulette was shaken by it as a leaf is shaken by a gust of wind.

'Listen,' I said to her, 'they're about to start dancing at the wedding. It looks like they're sending the music to seek you out.'

'No! No!' said Brulette, who had grown pale. 'Neither the tune nor the pipes come from this region. Tiennet, Tiennet, either I'm mad . . . or the person playing over there . . .'

'Can you see him?' I asked, moving to the front of the terrace and looking as hard as I could. 'Could it be père Bastien?'

'I can't see anyone,' she said, following me, 'but it's not the great woodcutter . . . It's not Joseph either. It's . . .'

'Huriel, perhaps! That seems less sure than the river between us, but let's go there anyway. We'll find a ford, and if he is over there we must catch that fine mule-driver as he travels through, and find out what he thinks.'

'No, Tiennet, I don't want to leave Charley or disturb him.'

'To the devil with Charley! Well, wait for me here; I'll go alone.'

'No, no, don't! Tiennet,' Brulette cried out, holding me back with both hands. 'It's a dangerous place to go down.'

'Even if I break my neck doing it, I want to help you out of your misery,' I cried.

'What misery?' she asked, still holding me back, and recovering from her first emotion, but through an effort of pride. 'What is it to me, whether it's Huriel or someone else passing through the wood? Do you think I want to run after someone who, if he knew I was here, might well pass by even further away?'

'If that's what you think,' said a soft voice behind her, 'perhaps we should go away?'

We'd swung around at the first word: fair Thérence stood before us.

When she saw her, Brulette, who'd so criticized her for her forgetfulness, was overwhelmed, and fell into her arms, shedding floods of tears.

'Now then, now then,' said Thérence, hugging her with the strength of the true woodsman's daughter that she was, 'did you think I was a fair-weather friend? Why think ill of people who haven't passed a day without thinking of you?'

'Say quickly if your brother is there, Thérence,' I cried out, 'for . . .'. Brulette, turning around, put her hand on my mouth and I caught myself up quickly with a laugh, 'for I'm very eager to see him.'

'My brother is here, but he doesn't know you're so close . . . Listen, he's going away. His music can hardly be heard any more.'

She looked at Brulette, who grew pale again, and added with a laugh: 'He's too far away for me to call him, but it won't be long before he comes back this way to come to the old castle. So if you don't despise him too much, Brulette, and unless you don't want me to, let's give him a little surprise that he'll scarcely be expecting. He thought he wouldn't be able to greet you until this evening. We were planning to visit your town. It's sheer good luck that we've met you here, and so don't have to wait any longer to be with you again. Let's go into these woods, for if he caught sight of you from over there, he'd be quite capable of drowning himself crossing the river, whose fords he doesn't yet know.'

We went back to sit down around Charley, whom Thérence looked at, and asked with her open and simple air if he were mine. 'Unless I were married long ago,' I told her, 'which is not the case . . .'

'It's true,' she said, looking at him more closely, 'that he's already quite a little man, but you could have been married when you came to us.' Then she confessed with a laugh that she'd only a vague idea of how quickly children grow, hardly seeing any in the woods in which she still lived, since people don't usually bring their families to the forests to raise them. 'You find me as wild as when you left me, but less prickly, and I hope my sweet girl from the Berry won't have to complain of my bad temper again.'

'It's true,' said Brulette, 'that you seem to me happier and more healthy and so much more beautiful that my eyes are dazzled from looking at you.'

That was an observation that had struck me from the very moment I'd set eyes on her. Thérence had greatly improved in health, freshness and brightness in her face, and looked another woman. If her eyes were still somewhat deep-set, her black brows no longer twisted to hide their flame, and if there was still pride in her laughter, there was also a fine gaiety that, at times, made her teeth gleam like dew drops in a flower. Her cheeks no longer astonished you by their feverish pallor, the May sun had tanned her a little during the journey, and there was about her something young, strong, and valiant that made my heart leap at an idea that came into my mind, I don't know how, when I looked to see whether the velvety black mark she had at the corner of her mouth was still there in its proper place.

'My friends,' she said, smoothing back her fine curly hair, which was clinging to her forehead in the heat, 'since we've a moment to talk before my brother arrives, I want to tell you my own tale, without grimacing and without feeling ashamed, for on that tale hangs that of many another person. But tell me first, Brulette, if I'm right in thinking that this Tiennet, whom in the past you valued so highly, is still just the same, and if I can take up my conversation with you where we left it, a year ago come harvest time?'

'Yes, my dear Thérence, you can,' replied Brulette, glad to be addressed with the informal 'you' for the first time.

'Well, Tiennet,' Thérence said, with her unequalled courage and good faith, that made her so different from the restrained and timid Brulette, 'I won't be telling you anything you don't already know when I say that last year, before you visited us, I'd grown attached to a poor, sad, sickly lad in the same way a mother is attached to her child. I didn't know then that he was in love with someone else, and he, when he saw my friendship, which I didn't hide, hadn't the heart to tell me that he couldn't return my feelings. Why did Joseph, for I can call him by his name, and you can see, my friends, that doing so doesn't make me change colour, why did Joseph, whom I'd asked so often, when he was weak with illness, to tell me why he was suffering so much, swear to me that the only reason for his unhappiness was his homesickness for his mother and his country? He must have thought me a real weakling, and he really insulted me, because if he'd been open with me, I'd have gone in search of Brulette, without making any fuss, and without falling into the error of judging her harshly, as I did in fact do, for which I confess I was wrong and ask your pardon.'

'You've already done so, Thérence, and there's no need for pardon when friendship is already present.'

'Yes, my child,' replied Thérence, 'but if you've forgotten my faults, I remember them, and I'd have given the world to make it up to Joseph by continuing to give him my care, my friendship, and my good humour after you left. Just think, dear friends, that I'd never lied, and that from my earliest childhood, my father, who's an expert in this regard, had nicknamed me Thérence the sincere. When we were on the banks of your river Indre, the last time I saw you, half way back to your village, I spoke alone with Joseph for a moment, begging him to come back with us and promising him that there'd be no changes in the way I cared for his rest and health. Why did he refuse in his heart to believe me? And why, when he promised with his lips to come back, a lie which didn't deceive me, why did he withdraw from me forever, despising me, as if I were a careless girl who felt no shame in tormenting him because of some stupid folly of love?'

'What?' I asked. 'Do you mean that Joseph, who spent only a day with us, didn't go back to you, at the very least to tell you of his plans and to make his farewells? Since he left us we've had no news of him.'

'If you haven't had any news,' Thérence answered, 'then I can give you some. Joseph returned to our woods without calling on us, without speaking to us. He came by night like a thief ashamed of the sun. He came into the lodge to take his bagpipes and his belongings, and he left without greeting the threshold of my father's cabin, without even turning his head in our direction. I saw him, I wasn't asleep. My eyes followed all he did, and when he'd gone into the woods I felt as numb as if I had died. My father warmed me again in God's good sunlight and with his own warm heart. Taking me with him to the heath, he spoke to me for a whole day, and then a whole night, until he saw me pray and sleep. You know my father a little, my friends, but you can't know how much he loves his children, how he consoles them, how he can find all he needs to say to them to make them grow like him. He's an angel from heaven hidden under the bark of an old oak.

'My father restored me to health; without him, I would have despised Joseph. Now I don't love him any longer and that's all!'

And with those words, Thérence again wiped her fine brow, which was damp with perspiration, and drew breath, kissing Brulette, and holding out to me, with a laugh, a long, white hand, beautifully formed, with which she shook my own hand as frankly as a boy might have done.

TWENTY-SECOND EVENING

I could see Brulette was inclined to criticize Joseph very severely and I thought I should stand up for him a little.

'I'm far from approving him for treating you so ungratefully,' I said to Thérence, 'but since you've returned to your senses enough to see what's just, you must agree that his underlying thought was one of respect for you and a fear of deceiving you. Not everyone is like you, my woodland beauty. I'd even go so far as to say that few people are pure enough of heart and open enough in their courage to go straight to the point and say, as you did, what the case really is. And then, you have a fund of strength and virtue that Joseph and many others in his place might well not feel they possessed.'

'I don't understand you,' said Thérence.

'But I do,' answered Brulette. 'Joseph was no doubt afraid to risk being enchanted by your beauty, and loving you for it without being able to give you his whole heart as you deserve.'

'Oh!' replied Thérence, blushing with hurt pride. 'That's exactly what I'm complaining about! Joseph was afraid he might lure me into some fault, you can say the word. He didn't count on my good sense and my honour. Well, if he'd respected me, that would have consoled me, whereas his doubts are humiliating for me. Never mind, Brulette, I forgive him for everything, because I no longer suffer from it, and I consider I'm above him; but in the depths of my heart there'll always be the thought that Joseph was ungrateful in the way he treated me, and that he had a paltry view of what his duty was. I'd say to you: let's not mention the matter ever again, were I not obliged to tell you the rest; but I must do so, otherwise you won't know what to think of my brother's behaviour.'

'Ah! Thérence,' said Brulette, 'I'm really longing to hear from you that there were no consequences to a misfortune that caused us such pain when we were with you.'

'My brother didn't do what people thought he would. Instead of hiding his unfortunate secret in far-off lands, he retraced his steps after a week. He sought out the monk in his monastery, which is near Montluçon, where he knew he'd find him back from his voyage.

' "Brother Nicholas," he said to him, "I can't live with so heavy a lie on my heart. You told me to confess my sins to God, but there is justice on earth, and while it may not always be exacted, it is none the less a law that comes from Heaven. I must therefore confess to man as well as God, and endure whatever suffering and blame I may merit."

' "Just a moment, my son," the monk replied. "Men have invented the death penalty that God condemns, and they may kill you in cold blood, for having killed by mistake."

' "That's not possible," my brother said. "I had no wish to kill and I can prove it."

' "You'll prove it by calling on witnesses," said the monk, "and then you'll compromise your companions, your leader, who is my nephew and who no more planned to be an assassin than you did; you'll expose them to harassment and you'll find yourself tricked into betraying the oaths you've made to your brotherhood. Listen, stay in my monastery and wait for me. I'll take it on myself to settle everything, provided you don't ask me too many questions."

'So saying the monk went in search of his abbot, who sent him to the bishop, the one who is Bishop of Montluçon and whom, in our country, we call the great priest, as in the olden times. The great priest, who has the ear of the highest judges, said and did things that we can't know about, then he summoned my brother before him and said: "My son, make your confession to me as you would to God." And when Huriel told him the truth from beginning to end, the bishop said to him: "Do penitence for this, my son, and repent. Your case has been settled as far as men are concerned, and human justice will never worry you on that score, but you must appease the displeasure of the Lord, and to that end, I engage you to leave the company and brotherhood of the mule-drivers, who are men without faith and whose secret practices are contrary to the laws of heaven and of earth." When my brother humbly remonstrated with him, protesting that there were honest people among the mule-drivers, the great priest replied: "That's too bad. If the honest men among them refused the oaths that have to be taken, evil would abandon that society, and it would be an association of workers as estimable as any other."

'My brother reflected on the great priest's words, and would have liked to reform the evil practices of his companions, something that struck him as more useful than abandoning them. So he went in search of them, and spoke to them very eloquently about the subject, or so I was told; but after they'd listened to him very calmly, they told him they were unwilling and unable to give up their practices. On that, he paid them the agreed forfeit, sold all his mules and kept only the clairin for our use. As a result, Brulette, it's not a mule-driver you're about to see, but a good and solid woodcutter who works with his father.'

'He must have had some difficulty getting used to that, I imagine,' said Brulette, struggling to hide the pleasure she felt on hearing this news.

'If he found it hard to change his work,' Thérence answered, 'he consoled himself with the thought that you were afraid of the mule-drivers, and that in your region they're held in abomination. But since I've satisfied your impatience to know how my brother got out of his difficulties, you must listen again while I talk of Joseph, for I have something to tell you that may perhaps anger you, lovely Brulette, and will surprise you even more than it angers you.'

Since Thérence said this rather teasingly and gaily, Brulette wasn't concerned, but begged her to explain what she meant.

'Well, then, you must know that we've spent the last three months in the forest of Montaigu,* where we met Joseph in good health, but still sombre and withdrawn; and if you want to know where he is, I'll tell you that we left him over there with my father, who's helping him to be received as a master piper. You know, or perhaps you don't know, that they too form a brotherhood, and that, to be accepted, there are practices that are kept secret from us. Joseph was at first embarrassed when he saw us. He felt ashamed to speak to me, and may well have avoided us if my father, after he'd reproached him for his lack of trust and friendship, hadn't held him back, knowing full well Joseph still needed him. When he was sure I was calm and bore him no ill will, Joseph took courage and asked if we could be friends again, and even attempted to excuse himself for the way he'd behaved. But my father, who didn't want to let him put his finger on the wound, turned the subject into a joke, and made him work the wood and the music just so he could achieve his goals more quickly.

'Well, as he didn't tell us anything about you, I was amazed, and asked him question after question without succeeding in extracting a word from him. Neither my brother nor I had received any news of you, it was only last week, when we passed through our land of Huriel, that we heard anything. So we were very concerned about you, and when my father said rather sharply to Joseph that if there were letters from his country he should at the very least tell us who was still alive and who had died, Joseph answered: "Everyone is well and so am I." But he said that in a rather hollow voice.

'My father makes no bones about anything, so he just ordered him to speak, but Joseph merely answered abruptly: "I tell you, my master, that all our friends there are happy and that if you are willing to grant me your daughter's hand in marriage, I shall be as happy as they."

'At first we thought he'd gone mad, and we only answered him by laughing, although his expression astonished us. But he returned seriously to the topic two days later, and asked me if I felt any friendship for him. I had no wish to extract revenge from an offer that came so late, other than in saying to him: "Yes, Joseph, I feel friendship for you, just as Brulette does."

'He closed his mouth, bowed his head and didn't return to the subject. But my brother raised it with him on another occasion and received this answer: "Huriel, I no longer think about Brulette in that way, and I beg you never to speak to me of it again."

'We were unable to draw anything else from him, except that, as soon as he was received as a master piper, he wanted to go and practise for a while in his own country, to show his mother that he was in a position to support her, after which he would settle down with her in the Marches or in the Bourbonnais if I were willing to be his wife.

'Then there were great discussions between my father, my brother and myself. Both of them wanted to make me admit that later I would perhaps consent; but Joseph had raised the question too late for me, and I had thought too much about him. I refused calmly, for I felt nothing for him any more, and I was sure he had never loved me. I'm too proud a girl to want to serve as a remedy for disappointment. I thought you must have written to him to remove any hope he might have had . . .'

'No,' said Brulette, 'I didn't do so, and it's simply thanks to the good Lord that he's forgotten me. It may be that he knows you better, dear Thérence, and therefore . . .'

'No, no,' the maid of the woods replied in resolute tones. 'If he's not acting out of pique because of your indifference it's because he's piqued at seeing me cured. He values me only because I no longer value him enough! If that's what he means by love, it won't be my view of love, Brulette! All or nothing; *yes* for all time in complete frankness or *no* for all time in complete liberty!

'But now the child is waking up and I want to take you to where I'm staying, in this old castle of Le Chassin.'

'Won't you at least tell us,' said Brulette, deeply intrigued by all she had heard, 'how and why you're here?'

'You're too eager to know. Just be a little more eager to see!'

And putting her fine, bare arm, all brown from the sun,

around Brulette's neck, she led her off without giving her time
to pick up Charley, whom Thérence seized like a goat kid
under her other arm, although he was already as heavy as a
little bullock.

In the past, so I've heard, the fief of Le Chassin was a castle
with seigniorial justice and rights; but at that time, all that
remained was the porch which is a room of some size, solidly
built, and so thick that there are habitable bedrooms on the
sides. It even strikes me that the building I've termed a porch,
and whose use is hard to explain today, from the manner in
which it's been constructed, was a vault serving as an entry
into other buildings, for those that remain around the
meadow and are merely shabby stables and dilapidated barns,
could hardly have provided any defence or offered any comfort. There still was, at the time of which I'm telling you, three
or four bare bedrooms that seemed to be of ancient date, but
if ever a great lord had lodged in them for his pleasure, then
he needed very little to give him that pleasure.

Yet it was in that ruin that happiness awaited some of those
whose story I'm narrating to you, and as if there were something hidden in individuals that delights them in advance by
the promise of joy to come, Brulette and I found nothing ugly
or sad in that place. The grassy meadow, surrounded on two
sides by ruins, and on two others by the little wood we'd just
left; the high hedge in which I'd already felt surprised to see
shrubs generally known only in the gardens of the rich, proving that the place had been cared for and decorated; the thick,
heavy door, cluttered with rubbish, in which one could nevertheless find stone seats, as if in the past some watchman had
been charged with protecting this clutter when it was considered precious; thorns so long that they ran from one end to the
other of this frail enclosure; all that, while it resembled a
locked prison, as steeped in oblivion and abandonment as it
had in the past been full of war and distrust, nevertheless
seemed to us as pleasant as the spring sun which pierced the
fences and dried out the dampness. It may also have been that
the sight of our old acquaintance, Huriel's clairin, who wandered about there in complete freedom, was a foretaste of the
presence of a true friend. I believe he recognized us, for he

came to be patted, and Brulette couldn't refrain from kissing the white crescent he had on his forehead.

'This is my castle,' said Thérence, as she led us to a bedroom in which were already installed her bed and her few pieces of furniture. 'And on this side you can see the room belonging to my brother and my father.'

'So, the great woodcutter's going to come, is he?' I exclaimed, leaping with pleasure. 'Well that's a delight! I can't think of anyone I'd rather see.'

'And you're right to think so,' said Thérence, tapping my ear in a gesture of friendship. 'He likes you, too. Well, you'll see him, if you're willing to come back next week and even . . . But it's too soon to talk to you of that. Here's the boss arriving.'

Brulette blushed again, thinking it was Huriel that Thérence called by that name, but it was merely an unknown landowner who had acquired the forest of Le Chassin.

I call it a forest because without doubt it had been one in the past, and had included that small, fine copse of oaks we'd seen from the other side of the water. When a name has been preserved, that must prove it wasn't given in vain. Through the conversation between the landowner and Thérence, we were soon brought into the picture. He was a man of Bourbonnais who had long known the woodcutter and his family as people who worked hard and kept their word. Since he was trying to fulfil the demands made of a man of his status for fine trees for the king's navy, he had discovered this virgin copse, a rare thing in these lands, and had entrusted père Bastien with the felling and cutting, and the woodcutter had agreed all the more readily in that his son and daughter, knowing the area to be close to our own region, were delighted at the thought of coming to spend all the summer and perhaps part of winter near us.

So the great woodcutter was in charge of choosing and overseeing his workers through a contract with the company that provided the state's roads. To facilitate the operation, the company had persuaded the owner of the forest to allow him free use of the old castle. Since the owner was a merchant, he would have considered himself very poorly housed in this castle, but, late in the season, a woodcutter's family would be better off there than in cabins made of staves and brushwood.

Huriel and his sister had arrived only that morning; Thérence had begun settling in while Huriel had gone to explore the wood, the terrain, and the local people.

We heard the buyer, in a way that showed he was well versed in all that concerned woodcutting, remind Thérence of a condition in his agreement with père Bastien. This was that he would employ only workers from Bourbonnais for the cutting up of the branches, for they alone knew how to do it, while the locals would spoil his best trees.

'Very well,' replied the maid of the woods, 'but for the faggots we'll use whomsoever we want. We've no wish to take work away from the local people, who'd attack us and hate us. They're already sufficiently antagonistic towards all those who don't come from their neck of the woods.'

'Well, Brulette,' she said, on the departure of the boss who had taken up residence at Sarzay, 'it seems to me that if nothing keeps you in your village, you could give your grandfather a very pleasant summer. You told me he was still a good worker, and he would be dealing with a good master in my father, one who'd let him take his time. You could live here without spending anything and we could keep house together . . .'

As Brulette was dying to say yes and didn't yet want to give herself away, Thérence added: 'If you make a fuss, you'll make me believe that your heart is engaged somewhere, and that my brother will get here too late.'

'Too late?' cried a fine voice that came from the little window, which was criss-crossed with ivy. 'God forbid that such a statement might be true!'

Huriel, handsome and fresh as the attractive man he was when the charcoal no longer played him false, came in quickly and lifted Brulette up in his arms to kiss her soundly on the cheeks, for he wasn't one to stand on ceremony, and didn't conform to the rather icy restraint of people from our area. He seemed so pleased, shouted so loudly, and laughed so joyously that there was no way in which she could take offence. He kneaded me, too, as if I were a loaf of bread, and leapt around the room as if joy and friendship were working on him like new-made wine.

But suddenly, having caught sight of Charley, he stopped, looked in the other direction, forced himself to say two or three words which had nothing to do with the child, sat down on his sister's bed, and went so pale that I thought he was going to faint.

'What's the matter with him?' Thérence cried out in astonishment, and touching his face, she said: 'Oh, good heavens! You're covered with icy sweat! Do you feel ill?'

'No, no,' said Huriel, standing up and shaking himself. 'It's just joy and shock . . . It's nothing.'

At that moment, the bride's mother came to ask why we hadn't returned to the wedding, and if Brulette or the child were ill. Seeing we'd been detained by strangers, she very warmly invited Huriel and Thérence to come and amuse themselves with us, at the meal and at the dance. This woman, who was my aunt, being my father's sister and also the sister of Brulette's dead father, seemed to me to know the secret of Charley's birth for she'd never raised any questions about him, and had taken great care of him in her home. She'd even told her family he was a little relative, and the people of Le Chassin had never felt the slightest suspicion about him.

Huriel, who was still troubled in his mind, thanked my aunt without reaching any decision, but Thérence aroused him by saying that Brulette was obliged to return to the wedding, and that if he didn't go with her, he'd lose the chance to take her to something that both of them desired. But Huriel had become anxious and rather hesitant, so Brulette asked him: 'Don't you want to dance with me today?'

'True, Brulette?' he said, looking her in the eyes, 'you truly want me as your partner?'

'Yes, I remember you as a fine dancer.'

'Is that your only reason?'

Brulette was embarrassed, finding that the young man was very eager to make her explain herself, and yet not daring to return to the little disdainful ways she'd used in the past, so deeply did she fear they'd make him cross or discouraged again. Thérence tried to rescue her by chiding Huriel for asking too much on the first day.

'You're right, sister,' he answered. 'And yet, I can't behave differently. Listen to me, Brulette, and forgive me. You must promise me not to dance with anyone else but me at this party, or I won't go.'

'Well, what a strange boy!' said my aunt, a gay little woman who looked on the bright side of things. 'I can see perfectly well, my Brulette, that you have a suitor there, and it seems to me that he isn't doing things by halves; but you should know, my child,' she said to Huriel, 'that in our country it's not the done thing to show so clearly what you feel, and that you dance several times only with a girl whose heart and hand are promised to you.'

'Your customs are our customs, my good mother,' answered Huriel, 'and yet, whether or not she promises me her heart, Brulette must promise me her hand for the entire dance.'

'If that suits her, then I won't prevent it,' said my aunt. 'She's a reasonable girl and knows perfectly well how to behave. But it's my duty to warn her that tongues will wag.'

'Brother,' said Thérence, 'I think you've gone mad. Is that the way to treat this Brulette, whom you know to be so prudent and who hasn't yet given you the rights you're demanding?'

'Oh! that I'm mad or she's prudent, that may all well be true, but my madness must prevail and her prudence must go under today straight away. I don't ask anything else of her than that she suffer me to stay next to her until the end of the wedding. If after that she doesn't want to hear another word about me, that will be her privilege.'

'Very well,' said my aunt, 'but the wrong you'll have done her, if you abandon her, who'll repair that?'

'She knows I'll not abandon her.'

'If you know that,' my aunt said to Brulette, 'then you should explain yourself, for this is an affair in which I understand nothing. Did you promise your hand to this lad when you were in Bourbonnais?'

'No,' answered Huriel, without leaving Brulette the time to

answer. 'I've never asked anything of her! What I'm asking her now, she alone, and without anyone's advice, she alone must know whether she can grant it to me.'

Brulette, trembling like a leaf, had turned to the wall and hid her face in her hands. If she was pleased to see Huriel so persistent in the way he treated her, she was also angry that he should take her timid and hesitant nature so little into account. She was not made like Thérence, who could have pronounced a fine yes immediately in front of everyone; so, not knowing how to get out of her predicament, she burst into tears.

TWENTY-THIRD EVENING

'What a madman you are!' my aunt said to Huriel, giving him a gentle cuff to make him move away from Brulette, whom he'd approached, deeply moved. Taking her niece's hands, she comforted her, begging her gently to tell her what it all meant.

'If your grandfather were here,' she told her, 'he'd be the one to tell me what's going on between you and this stranger, and we'd have his judgement to draw on, but since in these circumstances I have to act as your father and your mother, I'm the one you'll have to trust. Do you want me to free you from being pursued in this way? Instead of inviting this joker or this ruffian, for I don't know how to describe him, do you want me to beg him to leave you in peace?'

'Well,' exclaimed Huriel, 'all I ask is that she says what she wants, and I'll obey her without the slightest resentment, and without feeling any less esteem or friendship for her. If she thinks me either a joker or a ruffian, then she can refuse to see me ever again. Speak up, Brulette: I'll always be your friend and your servant, you know I will.'

'Be whatever you want to be,' Brulette said at last, standing up and giving him her hand. 'You defended me in a situation that was so dangerous, and you've suffered so many difficulties because of me, that I'm neither able nor willing to refuse you so small a matter as to dance with you as much as you like.'

'Give some thought to what your aunt told you,' Huriel said to her, as he held her hand. 'People will talk about it, and if nothing good comes of it for the two of us, as is still possible where you're concerned, then any arrangement or project you might have for another marriage will be spoilt or delayed.'

'Well, that won't be as bad,' answered Brulette, 'as the situation into which you threw yourself on my account, without any fear or reflection. Aunt, forgive me if I can't explain all this to you straight away, but believe that your niece loves you, respects you and will never have any cause to reproach herself before you.'

'I'm sure of that,' said the good aunt, hugging her, 'but how will we answer the questions that will be asked?'

'We'll say nothing, aunt,' replied Brulette resolutely, 'nothing at all! I've learnt not to take any notice of questions, and you know I'm used to them.'

Then Huriel kissed her hand five or six times, saying to her: 'Heart's love, thank you. You won't have any cause to regret what you're granting me.'

'Well, are you coming, you obdurate man?' my aunt asked him. 'I can't delay any longer, and if I don't bring Brulette soon, the bride is capable of leaving her guests to come here and insist that she return.'

'Go on then, Brulette,' said Thérence, 'and leave the child to me. I promise you I'll take good care of him.'

'Aren't you coming, then, fair maid of Bourbonnais?' asked my aunt, who kept gazing at Thérence as if she were a miracle. 'I'm counting on you, as well.'

'I'll come later on,' said Thérence. 'For now, I want to find clothes for my brother that are fit to honour you as you deserve, for the two of us are still in our travelling gear.'

My aunt led Brulette away, still longing to take Charley, although Thérence insisted that she wanted to look after him, for she longed to give her brother some time with his friend, without the trouble and interference of this little child. That wasn't what suited Charley, who, when he saw his dearie being taken away, began to howl and struggle in Thérence's arms; but she looked at him with a serious and determined gaze and said to him: 'Now you're going to stop that noise, my boy. You just have to do it and that's all there is to it.'

Charley, who had never before been ordered to do anything, was so amazed by such a tone that he fell silent immediately; but as I saw Brulette was distressed at leaving him in
the care of a girl who, in all her life, had never touched a child,
I promised her I would bring him to her myself if it proved
necessary, and pushed her after our aunt, who was beginning
to grow impatient.

Huriel, pushed in his turn by his sister, went into his room
to shave and wash, while I, alone with Thérence, helped her to
unpack the trunks and unfold the clothes, while Charley,
stunned, stared at her in astonishment. When I'd taken Huriel
the clothes Thérence piled into my arms, I came back to ask
her if she wasn't going to dress, too, and to offer to take the
child for a walk while she did so.

'As for me,' she replied as she put her possessions on the
bed, 'I'll go if it bothers Brulette, but if she can forget me for
a while, I confess I'd prefer to stay quietly here. In any case, I
can be ready in a moment, and I don't need anyone to escort
me. I'm used to seeking out and preparing dwellings when we
travel, just like a true sergeant on campaign, and nothing
worries me, wherever I may be.'

'You don't like dancing, then? It can't be because you're
ashamed of your new acquaintances that you choose to remain alone in the castle?'

'No, I don't like dancing,' she replied, 'I don't like the noise
or the food, and above all I dislike wasting time since it makes
me feel bored.'

'But it isn't always dancing for dancing's sake that people
like. Are you afraid or disgusted at the things boys say to
girls?'

'I'm neither afraid nor disgusted,' she answered simply. 'It
just doesn't amuse me, that's all. I don't have Brulette's wit. I
can't answer appropriately, I can't joke, I can't encourage
others to chat. I'm stupid and dreamy, and I feel I'm as out of
place in company as a wolf or a fox would be if they were
invited to a dance.'

'You don't look like a wolf or any other cunning beast, and
you dance as gracefully as the branches of a willow when the
wind caresses them.'

I would have said more to her about it, but Huriel came out of his room, handsome as the sun, and more eager to go than I was, for I would have been very happy to remain in his sister's company. She held him back a little, while she arranged his cravat and tied his garters, for she could never consider him fine enough to be worthy of dancing a whole wedding with Brulette. As she did so she said: 'Will you tell us why you appeared so jealous that you wouldn't allow her to amuse herself with anyone but you? Aren't you afraid to distress her by making such a sudden command?'

'Tiennet!' said Huriel, who suddenly stopped arranging himself and picked up Charley, whom he placed on the table so that he could gaze at him to his heart's content. 'Whose child is this?'

Thérence, astonished, asked him first why he should ask such a question, and then asked me why I didn't answer.

The three of us looked at each other like three idiots, and I would have given a great deal to be able to answer, because it was perfectly clear to me that a rock was threatening to fall on our heads. At last I took heart when I remembered what honesty and truth I'd seen in my cousin's eyes, that very day, when I'd asked her a similar question, and, plunging right in, I answered Huriel in these terms: 'Comrade, if you come to our village, many people will tell you that Charley is Brulette's child . . .'

He didn't let me continue, but picked the child up, touching him and turning him about like a huntsman examining a game animal he has stumbled across. Fearing he was in a rage, I wanted to take the child away from him but he held on to him saying: 'Don't be afraid for the innocent child's sake. I'm not evil at heart, and if I found any resemblance with her I might detest my fate but I couldn't refrain from kissing that resemblance. But he isn't at all like her, and however much I ask my blood, this child in my arms makes me neither hot nor cold.'

'Tiennet, Tiennet, answer him!' exclaimed Thérence, as if she were coming out of a dream. 'Answer me, too, for I've no idea what all this might mean, and it's driving me mad to think about it. There's no stain in our family and if my father were to think . . .'

Huriel interrupted her. 'Just a minute, Thérence. Least said, soonest mended. It's up to Tiennet to answer. Once, twice, Tiennet, for you're an honest man, tell me whose is this child.'

'I swear to God, I do not know,' I answered.

'If he were hers, would you know?'

'I don't believe she could hide it from me.'

'Has she ever hidden anything from you?'

'Never.'

'Does she know who the child's parents are?'

'Yes, but she doesn't even want anyone to ask her about them.'

'Does she deny that he's her child?'

'No one has ever dared ask her such a question!'

'Not even you?'

I told them in a few words all I knew about it, and what I believed to be the case, and I finished by saying: 'Nothing offers me any proof either for or against Brulette; but, however hard I try, I can't suspect her.'

'Well then, neither can I!' said Huriel. Giving Charley a kiss, he put him back on the floor again.

'Nor can I,' said Thérence. 'But why did other people have such an idea, and how did you come to think it, Huriel, when you looked at this child? I didn't even think of asking if he were Brulette's nephew or her cousin. I just thought he was obviously related to her, and I only needed to see him in her arms to want to take him in my own.'

'Well, I should explain to you,' said Huriel, 'even though the words burn my mouth. Well, yes, I prefer to say it aloud! It will be the only time, I've made up my mind, whatever the case may be and whatever may happen! You should know, Thérence, that three days ago when we left Joseph at Montaigu . . . you know how I set out with a free and happy heart! Joseph was cured, Joseph renounced Brulette, Joseph asked for your hand in marriage, and Brulette was not married, so he said. He considered her to be free, too, and to all my questions he replied: "Do as you like, I'm no longer in love with her; you can love her without affecting me."

'Well, dear sister, the moment he left us, he seized hold of my arm and said to me, as I stepped into the cart: "Is it true then? Have you decided to go to our region? And is it your plan to court the girl I loved so deeply?"

'"Yes," I told him, "if you must know, it is so. That's my plan, and you don't have the right to go back on what you told me, or I'll believe you were merely mocking me when you asked for my sister."

'"That's not what I mean," said Joseph, "but I believe I'd be betraying you now if I let you go without telling you some sad news. God is my witness that such words wouldn't have left my lips against someone whose grandfather brought me up, if you weren't on the brink of committing a blunder. But, as your father brought me up too, educating my mind, just as the other cared for and nourished my body, I believe I'm obliged to tell the truth. You should know, then, Huriel, that at the time I left Brulette because of my love for her, Brulette had already, unknown to me, loved another and today there is a proof of this love, a living proof that she doesn't even bother to hide. Now you can do whatever you like, I don't want to give it another thought."

'On that, Joseph turned his back and disappeared into the woods.

'He seemed so agitated, and I felt such love and trust in my heart, that I accused that ill-starred young man of an act of insanity and vicious rage. You remember, Thérence, that you found me altered, and that you thought I was ill when we went to Huriel town. When we got there, you found the two letters from Brulette, and I found three from Tiennet, all very old, letters that hadn't been forwarded to us, although people had promised to do so. Those letters were so simple, so good, and revealed such true friendship, that I said: "Let's go!", and Joseph's words left my mind like a bad dream. I was ashamed on his behalf, and didn't want to remember. And when, just now, I saw Brulette there, looking so gentle, and with the modesty I found so charming in the past, I swear to God that I'd forgotten everything, forgotten it as deeply as if it had never happened. The sight of this child nearly killed me! That's why I wanted to know if Brulette was free to love me. She is free, since she's promised that for my sake she'll expose herself to criticism and to being abandoned by others. Well, since she isn't dependent on anyone else, if she's had a misfortune in her life . . . and I can hardly believe that, or indeed I don't believe it at all . . . whether she confesses or justifies herself . . . it's all the same to me: I love her!'

'Could you love a girl who had dishonoured herself?' exclaimed Thérence. 'No, no! Think of your father, of your sister! Don't go to this wedding before we know the truth. I don't accuse Brulette, I don't believe Joseph. I'm sure Brulette is pure but still she needs to say so and she'll do better, she'll prove it. Go and get her, Tiennet. She must explain things immediately, before my brother takes a step that for an honest man would be irretrievable.'

'Don't go, Tiennet, I forbid you. If, as I believe, Brulette is as innocent as my sister Thérence, she'll not be insulted by any questions before I for my part have had the honour of giving her my word.'

'Think about it . . .' said Thérence again.

'Sister,' said Huriel, 'you're forgetting something. If Brulette has committed a fault, I for my part have committed a crime, and if love led her to bring a child into the world, love led me to put a man under the earth!'

When Thérence insisted, he said, embracing her and putting her aside: 'Enough! Enough! I have much to be pardoned for before I start judging others! I killed a man!' So saying he fled without waiting for me, and I saw him running towards the bride's house, which was smoking from all the cooking, and bursting with din among all those of the village.

'Ah!' said Thérence as she watched him go. 'My poor brother hasn't forgotten his misfortune! Perhaps he'll never be consoled for what he did!'

'He'll find consolation, Thérence,' I told her, 'when he finds he's loved by the girl he loves, and I can promise you she's already loved him for a long time.'

'I think so, too, Tiennet; but what if she weren't worthy of him?'

'Come, my lovely Thérence, are you so severe that you'd consider a misfortune that happened to a child to be a mortal sin? Who knows? She may have been surprised or forced into it.'

'It's not so much the misfortune or the fault that I'd blame, but the lies she's told or the deceits she's practised as a result of it. If, from the first day, your cousin had said to my brother: "Don't seek me out, I've been betrayed or raped," I'd have understood if my brother had taken no notice and pardoned her for her frank confession. But to let yourself be courted and admired without saying anything . . . Come, Tiennet, do you really know nothing? Can't you at the very least guess or imagine some story that could calm my fears? I'm so fond of Brulette that I don't feel I have the heart to condemn her. And yet, what will my father say if he thinks I should have done all in my power to hold Huriel back from such a danger?'

'Thérence, I can't tell you anything except that I suspect Brulette less than I ever did. For if you want to know who the only person was that I could have suspected of having abused her, and about whom people's accusations seemed to have a shred of truth, I'll tell you it was Joseph, who seems to me to be as pure as the driven snow in this regard, from what your brother has just told us. Well, in the whole world there was only one other boy, as far as I know, who was, I won't say capable, but in a position through his friendship with Brulette, to lead her away from the paths of honour through evil temptation. And that boy is me. Well, Thérence, do you believe that of me? Look me in the eyes before you answer. No one, as far as I know, has ever accused me of it, but I could be the culprit for all that, and you don't know me well enough to be sure of my honesty and my word. That's why I tell you, look at my face to see if lies and cowardice can live there comfortably!'

Thérence did as I asked her to, and looked at me with no show of embarrassment, then she said to me: 'No, Tiennet, you're not capable of lying like that. And if your mind's at rest about Brulette, I feel I should be, too. Come, my lad, off to the wedding with you. I don't need you here any more.'

'But you do,' I answered. 'That child is going to give you problems. He's not very cooperative with people he doesn't know, and I'd like either to take him off your hands or help you look after him.'

'He's not co-operative?' asked Thérence, taking him on her

lap. 'Bah! What's so hard about controlling a little child like this? I've never tried but it doesn't seem to me that you need a lot of cunning. Come, my big boy, what do you need? Don't you want something to eat?'

'No,' said Charley, who was sulking without daring to show that he was.

'Very well, just as you please! I won't force you, but when you'd like your soup, just ask for it. I'm happy to serve you and even play with you if you're bored. Tell me, do you want to play with me?'

'No,' said Charley, glowering proudly.

'Well, play on your own,' said Thérence calmly, putting him on the floor. 'I'm going to look at the lovely little black horse that's feeding in the courtyard.'

She made as if to go, and Charley burst into tears. Thérence pretended not to hear him until he went up to her.

'Well, what's the matter with you?' she said, as if she were surprised. 'Hurry up and tell me, or I'll go away. I don't have time to wait.'

'I want to see the lovely little black horse,' said Charley, sobbing.

'In that case, come along, but stop crying, because he runs away when he hears children crying.'

Charley swallowed back his sobs, and went to stroke and admire the clairin.

'Do you want to sit on him?' asked Thérence.

'No, I'm afraid,' said Charley.

'I'll hold you.'

'No, I'm afraid.'

'Very well, don't sit on him.'

After a minute, he wanted to sit on the horse.

'No,' said Thérence, 'you'd be frightened.'

'No, I wouldn't.'

'Yes, you would.'

'I wouldn't!' said Charley.

She put him on the horse whom she led around while holding the child very cleverly, and when I'd watched them for a moment or two, I was sure that Charley's whims would have no power over a will-power as unshakeable as that of

Thérence. From the very first day she took just as well to looking after a child who was by nature difficult, as Brulette after a year of patience and weariness. You could see that the good Lord had made her to be a fine mother without any need of apprenticeship. She could guess the tricks and strengths of the task, and lent herself to them without any suffering, astonishment, or impatience.

Charley, who thought he could boss everyone around, was amazed to see that, with her, all he could do was sulk, and that she took so little notice that sulking was a complete waste of his time. So, at the end of half an hour, he became completely gentle, asking of his own accord for what he wanted, and accepting quickly what was offered to him. Thérence fed him and I admired how she used her own judgement to measure out what he needed without giving him too much or too little. I admired, too, the way she could keep him occupied beside her while she went about her own tasks, chatting with him as she would to any rational person, and inspiring in him such trust without appearing to ask him questions that he had soon unrolled for her his whole bag of little sayings, whereas usually you had to beg him to do so if you showed that you were at all eager to hear them. What's more, he seemed so happy with her and so proud to know how to talk that he grew impatient with words he didn't know, and expressed himself with words he'd made up, words that were neither silly nor ugly.

'What are you doing there, Tiennet?' she said to me suddenly, as if to let me know I'd stayed too long.

And as I'd invented fifty little stories to avoid leaving her, I found I'd run out of excuses and didn't know what to say to her, except that I was just looking at her.

'You enjoy that?' she asked.

'I don't know. You may as well ask wheat if it's happy to feel itself growing in the sunshine.'

'Oh! Oh! It seems you've learnt the art of turning compliments. But just remember it's a waste of time with me, for I know nothing about compliments, and I don't know how to respond to them.'

'I don't know anything about them either, Thérence. All I

want to tell you is that in my opinion there's nothing more beautiful and healthy than seeing a young girl delighting in the chatter of a little child.'

'But isn't that perfectly natural? It seems to me I'm returning to the world of God's truth when I look at that little boy and listen to him talking. I know I don't live as women generally like to live, but I didn't choose my lot, and the travelling, abandoned way of life which is mine is my duty, since I'm my father's support and joy. So I don't complain and I don't wish for a life that wouldn't be like his, but I understand other people's pleasure perfectly well. I understand Brulette's delight in the company of her Charley, whether he's hers or the good Lord's, and I'd feel the same delight if I were in her shoes. I haven't often had the chance to enjoy so pleasant an entertainment, and I can certainly take it where I find it. He truly is a pleasant companion, this little man, and I'd no idea children could be so clever and knowledgeable.'

'Yet, my sweet, this Charley is friendly only because of the great care Brulette has taken of him, and he had to improve greatly in order to be as well behaved as God made it in his nature to be.'

'But that's very surprising,' said Thérence. 'If there are children who are better behaved than he is, their people are only too lucky to be able to live with them. But that's enough, Tiennet. Off with you, or people will come in search of you and will want to take me too and that, I confess, would annoy me, for I'm a little weary, and I'm so contented to stay here quietly with the child that it would be doing me a disservice to disturb me so soon.'

There was nothing for it but to obey her, and I went off with a full heart, and a mind shaken by the ideas that Thérence had put there.

TWENTY-FOURTH EVENING

It wasn't just Thérence's astounding beauty that filled my mind, but something indefinable that made her appear in my eyes above all other women. I was surprised I loved Brulette so much, for she bore little resemblance to Thérence, and I asked myself whether one of the two was too open and the other too reserved. In my judgement, Brulette was more congenial, always having something pleasant to say to her friends, and knowing how to keep them around her by making countless little requests that flatter boys because they like to feel they're needed. Thérence, on the contrary, showed you openly that she didn't need you, and even seemed surprised or irritated if you paid her any attention. Nevertheless, each of them knew her own worth, but whereas Brulette bothered to make you feel important too, Thérence seemed to want to be valued only as much as she could value you. And somehow or other that element of pride, more deeply hidden in her, struck me as a kind of lure that was as tempting as it was terrifying.

I found the dance in full swing, and Brulette swirling like a butterfly in the hands and arms of Huriel. Their faces were so inflamed, and she seemed so inwardly intoxicated while he appeared so outwardly intoxicated, that they neither saw nor heard anything around them. The music lifted them away, but I truly believe they didn't feel their feet touch the ground, and their spirits were dancing in paradise. Since, among those who dance the bourrée, there are very few who aren't either in love or have great dreams, no one even took any notice of them, and there was so much wine, noise, dust, song, and happy talk in the warm party air, that dusk fell without the guests paying much attention to any individual's own happiness.

Brulette drew away only to ask me how Charley was, and why Thérence wasn't coming, but my answers easily calmed her, and Huriel didn't give her time to listen long to how her little boy was behaving himself.

I felt no desire to dance, for as it happened none of the girls there struck me as pretty, although there were pretty girls at that wedding. But not one of them resembled Thérence, and I couldn't get Thérence off my mind. I sat in a corner to watch her brother so I could talk to her about him when she asked me. Huriel had so completely forgotten his suffering that he was full of joy and youth. He was well matched with Brulette, for he loved noise and pleasure as much as she did, when he put his mind to it, and he had the advantage over all the other boys, in that he never grew tired of dancing. Everyone knows that, in all lands, it's the women who dance the men into the ground, and still want to go on when we're dead of thirst and heat. Huriel had no desire to eat or drink, and it was as if he had sworn to satisfy Brulette in her favourite entertainment. But, when I thought about it, it was clear that he also took pleasure in it, and that he could have walked all the way round the world, provided that light-footed dancer was on his arm.

Finally, several boys, irritated because Brulette had turned them down, noticed that there was a stranger to whom she gave many favours, and tongues began to wag at all the tables. I have to tell you that Brulette, who hadn't expected to enjoy herself so much, and who now felt some scorn for all the local gallants, because of the poor conduct of their tongues, hadn't put on her finest attire. She looked more like a little nun than our local queen; and as there were great party dresses present, she hadn't made such a great impact as she had done in the past. Nevertheless, when she'd been warmed up by dancing, everyone had to acknowledge that no one could compete with her, and when those who didn't know her had questioned those who did, much good and much evil was said about her around me.

I lent an ear to it, for I wanted to get to the bottom of things, and I didn't let on that I was related to her. At last I heard them tell the story of the monk and the child, of Joseph and the Bourbonnais boy, and people said that perhaps Joseph wasn't the perpetrator of that sin, that it might well be this great lad, who was so eager to keep her, and seemed so sure of himself that he wouldn't allow anyone else near her.

'Well,' said one of them, 'if he's the one and he's come to makes things right, it's better late than never.'

'I have to say,' remarked another, 'that she hasn't chosen badly. He cuts a superb figure, and seems a pleasant lad.'

'After all,' said a third, 'they'll make a fine couple, and once the priest has joined them, they'll make as good a household as any other.'

I could see from all this that a woman is never lost as long as she's well protected, but that such protection has to be open and complete, for a hundred protectors aren't worth a sou, and the more that get involved, the more they drag her down and injure her reputation.

At that moment, my aunt took Huriel aside, and leading him over to me, she said: 'I want you to drink a glass of wine to my health, for you delight my soul, you dance so well, and you've given such an excellent lead to my guests.'

Huriel was sorry to leave Brulette even for a moment; but the mistress of the house was very determined, and there was no way in which he could refuse her kind offer.

So they sat down at the end of the table, which happened to be empty, a candle between them, and looking each other in the face. My aunt Marghitonne was, as I've told you, a small woman who'd quite forgotten how to be foolish. She had the funniest face you could ever wish to see, very white and very fresh, although she was fifty and had given birth to fourteen children. I've never seen such a long nose, with such small eyes, set deep on each side of her face as if with a drill, but so bright and so cunning that you couldn't look at them without wanting to chatter and laugh.

Nevertheless, I could see Huriel was on his guard, and he was wary of the wine she poured for him. He found in her expression something mocking and inquisitive, and without having any clear idea why, he remained on the defensive. My aunt, who hadn't rested a minute since morning but had been moving and chatting all the time, was truly very thirsty, and hadn't swallowed three small sips before the tip of her nose turned as red as a berry and her large mouth, where there were enough white, close-packed teeth for three people rather than one, was grinning all the way to her ears. Still, her judgement was unaffected, for no woman ever outdid her in being gay without excess and in teasing without being unkind.

'Well then, my lad,' she said, after a lot of idle chatter that merely allowed her to deal with her initial thirst, 'are you truly engaged to my Brulette? You can't go back on it now, for what you wanted has happened. Everyone is talking about it, and if you could hear as I do what they're saying all round the room, you would see that they're burdening you with my pretty niece's future as well as her past.'

I could see this expression drove a dagger into Huriel's

heart, and sent shivers down his spine, but he put a good face on it and said with a laugh: 'I'd like to have had that past, my good lady, for everything connected with her can only have been beautiful and good; but if all I get is the future, I'll consider God has done very well by me.'

'And that will be sensible,' retorted my aunt, still laughing and looking at him so closely with her little, green, short-sighted eyes that she seemed to be trying to pierce his brow with her sharp-tipped nose. 'When you love, you love every-thing and you're not put off by anything.'

'That's just how I want it,' said Huriel, in an abrupt manner that didn't disturb my aunt.

'And that's all the better on your part, since poor Brulette has more method than money. No doubt you know that her entire dowry would easily fit in your glass, and leave room to spare, and there are no golden sovereigns in what she'll bring you.'

'Well, all the better,' said Huriel. 'We'll do the addition all the faster, and I don't like wasting my time in doing sums.'

'Moreover, a child that's already raised is one problem the less in a household, especially if the father does his duty, as he will, I can promise you that!'

Poor Huriel went hot and cold, but thinking this was some kind of test, he accepted it, and said: 'The father will do his duty and so shall I, I can answer for that! For there will be no other father than I for all the children already born or yet to come.'

'Ah! as for that, it's not in your hands, I can assure you!'

'I hope it is,' he answered, grasping his glass as if he wanted to crush it between his fingers. 'Anyone who abandons his possessions has no right to come and fish them out again, and I'm a sufficiently faithful guardian not to allow any marauders.'

My aunt stretched out her thin little hand and touched Huriel's brow. She felt the sweat, although he was very pale, and suddenly changing her expression from that of a cunning devil to that of the good, open woman she really was, she said: 'My boy, put your elbows on the table and come close to my mouth. I want to give you a good kiss on the cheek.'

Huriel, astonished at her tender expression, did as he was bid. She lifted the thick hair from his temple and caught sight of Brulette's pledge, which he still wore, and which she no doubt recognized. Then, bringing her large mouth near him as if she wanted to eat him, she slipped four or five words in his ear, but so low, so low that I could hear nothing. Then she added aloud, as she pinched the tip of his ear:

'There! That's a very faithful ear, but you must agree it's been well rewarded.'

Huriel leaped over the table, overturning the glasses and the candle that I only just had time to pick up. He flung himself down by my little aunt and hugged her as tight as if she'd been the mother who'd given him birth. He seemed mad, crying and singing, drinking and wishing her good health, and my little aunt, laughing like a small grasshopper, said to him as she clinked glasses with him: 'To the health of your child's father!'

'And all that proves,' she added immediately, turning round to me, 'that the cleverest people are sometimes those who are considered the stupidest, just as the stupidest are often those who think themselves the smartest. You can tell yourself that, too, my Tiennet, for your heart is sound, and you're a faithful friend to your own kin, and I know you've treated your cousin as if she were your own sister. You deserve to be rewarded for it, and I'm sure the good Lord won't renege on what He owes you. One day or another, He will give you, too, exactly what you need to make you happy.'

At that she went away, and Huriel, throwing his arms around me, said: 'Your aunt is right. She's the best of women. You're not privy to the secret, but that doesn't matter. You're just a better friend for all that, so . . . Give me your promise, Tiennet, that you'll come and work here all summer with us, for I have my own plans for you and if God helps me, you'll thank me heartily for what I'll have done for you.'

'If I understand you aright,' I answered, 'you've just drunk your wine without any water, and my aunt has removed the piece of straw that would have made you choke. But as for your plan for me, that strikes me as hard to satisfy.'

'Friend Tiennet, happiness is infectious and unless you have plans which are contrary to mine . . .'

'I'm afraid they're only too close to yours, but it isn't enough just to have plans.'

'No doubt of that. But nothing ventured, nothing gained. Are you so much of a Berry man you don't want to try your luck?'

'You've set me too good an example for me to be a coward, but do you really think . . .'

Brulette came and interrupted us, and we could see from her expression that she still had no inkling of what had happened.

'Sit down here,' said Huriel, pulling her on to his knees, as is the custom with us, and no one sees anything wrong in it. 'Tell me, my dear sweetheart, wouldn't you really rather dance with someone other than me? You've given me your promise and you've stuck to it, and that's all I needed to remove the sorrow that was weighing on my heart. But if you think people will talk about it in a way that'll vex you, I'm ready to submit to your pleasure, and I'll dance only when you order me to do so.'

'Can it be then, master Huriel,' replied Brulette, 'that you're tired of my company and want to meet some of the other girls at the wedding?'

'Oh! If you take it like that,' cried Huriel, overwhelmed with joy, 'so be it! I don't even know if there are other girls apart from you, and I've no wish to know.'

Then he offered her his glass, begging her to touch it with her lips, and then he drank from it most willingly. After that, he broke the glass so no one else could use it, and took his fiancée off to dance, while I meditated on what he had implied, feeling deeply shaken by his suggestion.

Up until then, I hadn't much explored my own feelings in that regard, and it had never seemed to me that my nature was ardent enough for me to fall lightheartedly in love with a girl as serious as Thérence. I'd avoided feeling hurt at not attracting Brulette, by being merry and delighting in all manner of distractions, but I couldn't think of Thérence without a kind of trembling in the marrow of my bones, as if I'd been invited to cross the wide ocean, I, who had never so much as set foot on a river boat.

'Is there the remotest chance,' I wondered, 'that I can have fallen in love today without realizing it? It must be so, since here's Huriel driving me to it, and his eyes have clearly read the truth in my face, but I'm not sure of it, because I feel as if I've been suffocating ever since this afternoon, and love ought surely to be something that's more cheerful than that!'

As I meditated on this, I found that, without quite knowing how, I'd returned to the old castle. That old pile of stones was sleeping under the moon as silent as those who had built it. Only a little area of light coming from Thérence's room fell on the meadow to show that the dead were not its sole guardians. I approached very quietly, and, looking through the leaves around the small window which had neither glass nor wood, I saw the fair maid of the woods praying, on her knees, beside the bed on which Charley was lying fast asleep.

Were I to live a hundred years, I'd never forget the expression on her face. She looked like an image of a saint, as tranquil as those sculpted in stone on churches. I'd just seen Brulette, glowing like a summer sun, in the joy of her love and the movement of the dance. Thérence was there, alone and happy, as white as the moon in the bright spring night. In the distance could be heard the music of the wedding party, but that said nothing to the ear of the maid of the woods, for I think she was listening to the nightingale singing the loveliest of songs to her from a nearby bush.

I don't know what happened in my heart, but suddenly, I thought of God, a thought that may well not have come to me often enough in those days of my forgetful youth, but I bent my knees as if through a secret command, and my eyes filled with tears that fell like rain, as if a heavy cloud had just burst in my head.

Don't ask me what I prayed to the good angels of heaven. I didn't even hear it myself. I wouldn't yet have dared to ask God to give me Thérence, but I do believe I asked Him to make me more worthy of so great an honour.

When I raised my head again, I saw that Thérence had finished her prayers and was preparing for bed. She'd removed her head-dress, and I saw that her black hair fell in great tresses to her feet. But before she'd removed the first pin from her clothes, believe me or not as you please, I'd already taken flight, as if I were afraid of committing a sacrilege. Nevertheless, I was no stupider than any other boy, and I wasn't accustomed to rejecting the devil's gifts, but Thérence exacted as much respect from me as if she had been first cousin to the Virgin Mary.

As I left the old castle, a man, who had been hidden from me by the shadow of the doorway, surprised me by addressing me: 'Hey, friend, tell me if I'm right in thinking that this is the former castle of Le Chassin?'

'The great woodcutter!' I exclaimed, recognizing his voice. And I hugged him so enthusiastically that he was astonished, for he didn't remember me as well as I remembered him.

But as soon as he had recalled me to his mind, he treated me in a very friendly fashion, and said: 'Tell me quickly, lad, if you've seen my children or if you know whether they've arrived here yet.'

'They've been here since this morning,' I answered, 'and so have I and my cousin Brulette. Your daughter Thérence is there, very peacefully, while my cousin is nearby at another cousin's wedding, together with your good son Huriel.'

'Thank goodness! Then I haven't got here too late, and Joseph is by now on the road to Nohant, where he's confident he'll find them together.'

'Joseph? Has he come with you? We weren't expecting the two of you for another five or six days, and Huriel was telling us . . .'

'You'll have to learn how things go in this world,' said père Bastien, drawing me down the path a little, so none but I could hear him. 'Of all things that blow with the wind, the mind of lovers is the lightest. Has Huriel put you in the picture about Joseph?'

'Yes, completely, I think.'

'When Joseph saw Huriel and Thérence setting off for these regions, he whispered something in Huriel's ear. Do you know what he said?'

'Yes, I do know, père Bastien, but . . .'

'Silence! For I know it, too. Seeing my son change colour, and Joseph rush off into the woods with a strange expression, I went after him and ordered him to tell me what secret he'd just told Huriel. "Master," Joseph said, "I don't know whether I've done well or ill, but I thought it my duty. This is what I said, for it is my duty to tell you too." At that he told me he'd received a letter in which he'd been informed that Brulette was raising a child that could only be her own. Telling me this with much pain and suffering, he urged me strongly to run after Huriel to prevent him from committing a great folly or incurring intense shame.

'When I'd questioned him about the child's age, and he'd let me read the letter that he still carried with him, as if he'd wanted to retain this remedy for the wound inflicted on his love, I didn't feel at all convinced that he hadn't been the butt of someone's joke, all the more so in that Carnat's son, who wrote this to him, in answer to an application Joseph had made to have himself honestly accepted as a piper in his own land, seemed to have plotted to prevent his return. Then, when I remembered how decent and modest little Brulette had been, I grew more and more convinced that she was being misjudged, and I chided Joseph for believing so easily in so evil an affair.

'I would doubtless have done better, my good Tiennet, to have left him, error or no error, in the belief that Brulette was unworthy of his affection; but, blame me or not as you will, the spirit of justice led my tongue, and stopped me from thinking of the consequences. I was so unhappy at seeing a poor honest girl defamed, that I spoke as I felt. That had more effect on Joseph than I'd have believed. He suddenly spun completely around, and shedding tears like a baby, he fell to the ground, tearing his clothes and pulling out his hair, with such sorrow and rage at himself, that it was only with the greatest difficulty that I managed to soothe him. Fortunately his health has become as sound as your own, for a year earlier any despair that shook him so greatly would have killed him.

'I spent the rest of the day and all the night alone with him trying to restore him to good spirits. I found it no easy task. On the one hand, I know that my son, from the very first day he saw Brulette, fell unswervingly in love with her, and that he felt at ease with life again only when Joseph ceased to block his hopes. On the other hand, I'm very fond of Joseph, and I know Brulette has been in his thoughts his whole life long. I had to sacrifice one of the two, and it occurred to me that I might be an egoist if I decided in favour of my son's happiness to the detriment of that of my pupil.

'Tiennet, you don't know Joseph any more, and perhaps you never knew him well. My daughter Thérence may have spoken of him very harshly. She doesn't judge him as I do. She thinks him selfish, hard, and ungrateful. There's some truth in that, but what excuses him in my eyes cannot excuse him in the eyes of a girl like her. Women, my little Tiennet, ask us only to love them. It's in their hearts alone that they draw sustenance for their lives. God made them like that and for us it's a source of happiness, when we're worthy of understanding it.'

'It seems to me,' I said to the great woodcutter, 'that I understand it now, and that women are perfectly right to want nothing from us but our hearts, for that's what's best in us.'

'Of course, dear boy, of course! I've always thought so. I loved the mother of my children more than money, more than talent, more than pleasure and glory, more than anything on earth. I can see that my son Huriel is built the same as me, since he's changed his condition and his tastes without any regrets to put himself in a position to claim Brulette. And I believe you're of the same opinion, since you say so in such an open way. But talent is, after all, something God also values, since He doesn't give it to everyone, and one must respect and help those whom He's marked as His chosen flock.'

'Don't you think then that your son Huriel has as much wit as our Joey, and more musical talent?'

'My son Huriel certainly does have wit and talent. He was accepted as a master piper at the age of eighteen, and even though that's not his trade, he has the knowledge and the facility to make it so. But there's a great difference, Tiennet my friend, between those who remember and those who invent; there are those who, with nimble fingers and a good memory, repeat in a pleasant way everything they've been taught, but there are those who are not happy with any lesson and go further than their teachers, seeking out ideas and giving all the musicians of the future the gift of their discoveries. Well, let me tell you that Joseph is one of those, and that there are two remarkable natures in him: the nature of the plain, in which he was born and which has given him strong, gentle, tranquil thoughts, and the nature of the woods and hills, which opened his understanding and have given him tender, lively, sensitive thoughts. So, for those who have ears to hear he'll be something more than a country minstrel. He'll be a true master piper of the type we had in days gone by, one of those whom the best listen to attentively and who command changes in people's customs.'

'Do you think, then, père Bastien, that he'll become the second great woodcutter of your brotherhood?'

'Oh, my poor Tiennet,' answered the old piper with a sigh. 'You don't know what you're talking about, and I'd probably have a hard time trying to explain to you.'

'Try anyway, I like listening to you, and it's not good for me to go on being as simple as I am now.'

TWENTY-FIFTH EVENING

'Let me tell you, then,' said the great woodcutter, forgetting his story just as I had (for he loved talking when he realized people wanted to listen to him), 'that I could have been something, if I'd devoted myself entirely to music. I could have done it, if I'd become a minstrel as I'd planned to do when I was young. It's not that you become any more talented by bellowing for three whole days and three whole nights at a wedding, like that ill-starred wretch I can hear even this far away crippling our mountain dance. It wearies you, and your voice grows rusty when all you're thinking about is how much you're earning. But it does provide the musician with a livelihood for his body, without destroying his soul at the same time. As even the smallest feast brings in two or three pistoles, you can accept however many you like, live frugally, and travel for pleasure and instruction.

'That's what Joseph wants to do and what I've always advised him to do. But this is what happened to me. I fell in love, and the mother of my dear children had no intention of being the wife of a minstrel with neither hearth nor home, always living outside, spending the nights in uproar, sleeping through the days, and dying in a state of debauchery. For, unfortunately, it's rare for someone to stay sober in such a profession. She made me choose the life of a woodcutter and that was that. I never regretted abandoning my talent while she was still alive. As far as I'm concerned, I've already told you that love is the most beautiful music imaginable.

'I was widowed when I was still young, and had the care of two small children, to whom I devoted myself completely. But my knowledge of music grew rusty, and my fingers became hooked and clumsy from constant use of the sickle and the axe. So, I have to confess, Tiennet, that if my two children were happily married to people they loved, I'd abandon this heavy task of lifting iron and cutting wood, and I'd take myself off, delighted and rejuvenated, to live according to my own lights, and seek out the conversation of the angels until old age drew me back, stiff and content, to sit by the family fire.

'Besides, I'm tired of cutting trees. Do you know, Tiennet, I love them, those graceful old companions of my life, who have told me so many things in the whispering of their leaves and the cracking of their branches! And I, less wholesome than the fire of heaven, I thank them for what they tell me by driving my axe into their hearts, and laying them at my feet, like so many dismembered corpses! Don't laugh at me, but I've never seen an old oak or even a young willow fall without trembling with fear and pity, as if I were an assassin who'd killed one of the good Lord's creations. I'm longing to walk under shade that will no longer drive me away as an ingrate, but will at long last tell me secrets I've not yet been worthy of.'

The great woodcutter, who'd grown more and more impassioned as he spoke, stopped for a moment, lost in thought, and I did, too, astonished not to find him quite as mad as anyone else would have had they been in my shoes, either because he was able to convey his ideas to me, or because I thought just as he did.

'You probably think,' he went on, 'that all this has taken us far from Joseph, but you're wrong. We're all the closer to him. Now you can understand why I decided, after a moment's hesitation, to tread on the poor lad's corns. I thought to myself, and it was all too obvious from the way he was grieving, that he'd never make a woman happy, and that as a result he himself would never be happy with a woman, except if she were filled with pride in him. For you have to admit that Joseph doesn't need friendship so much as encouragement and praise. The reason why he fell so deeply in love with Brulette is that from an early stage she listened to him and urged him to play his music. What prevented him from loving my daughter (for he turned to her only on the rebound) is that she asked him for more affection than skill, and treated him as a son more than as a man of talent.

'Now I think I've the right to say that I read the boy's heart, and I could see that his entire plan was to astonish Brulette, one day or another. And while Brulette was considered the queen of beauty and pride in her region, she'd bring him all the royalty he could ever want, but a Brulette, spoilt by a sin she'd committed, or at the very least lowered in his estimation, a Brulette mocked and criticized, was no longer the woman of his dreams. And I, who also knew my son Huriel's deepest longings, I knew that he wouldn't condemn Brulette without close examination, and that if she'd done nothing worthy of blame, then the more others misjudged her, the more he'd love and support her.

'That's what finally decided me to fight Joseph's love, and advise him not to give any more thought to marriage. And I even tried to make him understand something I was pretty much certain about, which is that Brulette preferred my son to him.

'He seemed to accept my arguments, but I think he did so only to get rid of me, for yesterday at daybreak, I saw him preparing to leave. Although he thought he was cleverer than me, and was sure he could decamp without anyone guessing,

I clung on to him until he lost patience and showed me what he really thought. That's when I learnt how deep his resentment lay, and that he'd decided to follow Huriel, in order to challenge his right to Brulette, should Brulette seem to him to be worth fighting over. And as he wasn't quite certain about that last point, I thought I should reproach him, and even mock his love, which seemed to me to be a form of jealousy without any esteem for the other, what you might call greed without appetite.

'He admitted I'd hit the nail on the head, but he left all the same, showing me just how obstinate he is. At a point when he'd mastered his art, and had set a time for an examination over towards Ausances,* he abandoned everything, at the risk of being greatly delayed, saying that he'd force his region to accept him willy-nilly. When I saw him so determined that he appeared on the point of flying into a rage with me, I made up my mind to travel with him, fearing he might commit some evil action before he had time to think it over, or might force Huriel to act badly and cause yet another calamity. We separated from each other only half a league down from here at the town of Sarzay,* and while he took the road for Nohant I took the path that led here, hoping to find Huriel in time, and reason with him. I told myself, too, that my legs could easily carry me on to Nohant this evening if it proved necessary.'

'Fortunately you'll be able to rest peacefully here tonight,' I told him. 'We can talk about it tomorrow. But are you really worried about these two suitors meeting each other? As far as I know, Joseph was never one to pick a quarrel, and I've always seen him fall silent as soon as you showed him your teeth.'

'Yes, yes, you saw that in the days when he was merely a sickly child, uncertain of his own strength, but still waters run deep, and it's not always a good idea to stir them up.'

'Won't you come into your new dwelling place and see your daughter?'

'You told me she was perfectly safe here, so I'm not worried about her. I'm more eager to find out the truth about Brulette. For, after all, however much my heart cries out against it, my reason tells me there must have been something in her behaviour that provoked criticism, and I must judge it before going any further.'

I was about to tell him what had taken place an hour ago before my very eyes, between Huriel and my aunt, when Huriel himself came towards us, sent ahead by Brulette, who feared Thérence would be in difficulties over putting Charley to sleep. Father and son then had a conversation in which Huriel, begging his father not to make him tell a secret he'd promised to keep, and that even Brulette thought he didn't know, swore to him most solemnly that Brulette was completely worthy of his blessing.

'Come and see her, father dear,' he added. 'That'll be very easy for you to do, for just now they're dancing out of doors, and you don't need an invitation to go and watch them. The way she embraces you will prove to you there's never been a sweeter, more lovable girl with such a clear conscience.'

'I don't doubt it, son, and I'll go, just to make you happy, and for the pleasure of seeing her. But let's wait just a moment, because I want to talk to you about Joseph.'

I thought I should leave them alone, and went off to tell my aunt the great woodcutter had arrived, knowing she'd welcome him warmly, and wouldn't let him stay out of doors. But the only person I found in the house was Brulette. The entire wedding party, with the minstrels at their head, had gone off to carry the wedding roast to the newly-weds, who'd withdrawn into a nearby house, since it was about eleven in the evening. This is an ancient custom that I've never found particularly pleasant, this going and disturbing a young bride's first shame with visits and joyous songs; and although the other girls had gone off with them, knowingly or not, Brulette had had the decency not to budge from the fireside where I saw her sitting, as if she were watching over a final bit of cooking, but at the same time taking some of the rest she needed. As she appeared to have dozed off, I didn't want to interrupt her or to spoil the wonderful surprise of being awakened by the great woodcutter.

I was very weary, too, and I sat down and leant against a table, with my arms outstretched and my head resting on them as one does when one wants a minute or two of sleep. But I thought of Thérence and didn't sleep. Just for a moment or two my thoughts were blurred. Then I heard a little noise and opened my eyes without raising my head, and saw that a man had come in and had gone over to the chimney.

Although they'd taken the candles away to visit the young couple, the fire from the logs was flaming sufficiently for me to recognize immediately the person who'd come in. It was Joseph, who, no doubt, had met some of the wedding guests on the way to Nohant, and, having learnt where we were, had decided to retrace his steps. He was covered with dust from his travels, and carried his pack on the end of a stick which he threw into a corner, while he stood stock still like a standing stone, watching Brulette sleep without paying any attention to me.

It was a year since I'd seen him, and in that time there had been as many changes in him as there had been in Thérence. He was in finer health than he'd ever been. You could say that he'd become a handsome man, and that his square face and his slender body were muscular rather than lean. His face was yellow, as much out of bile as through sun-tan, and that dark colouring was a good match for his great light eyes and his long straight hair. It was certainly still the same sad and thoughtful expression, but it now contained an element of determination and boldness that at last revealed the strong will he'd so long kept hidden within himself.

I didn't budge, for I wanted to know just how he'd approach Brulette, and what this might predict about his next meeting with Huriel. No doubt he was studying Brulette's face and trying to find the truth in it, and perhaps he realized that beneath her eyelids, which were closed by a light sleep, lay peace of heart, for she was a very pretty lass when seen like that in the firelight. Her face was still coloured with the pleasure of the dance, her mouth was smiling with contentment, and the fine silk of her lowered eyelids sent a very gentle shadow over her cheeks, which seemed to blink like those teasing, sideways glances young girls use in order to see more clearly. But she really was asleep, and doubtless dreaming of Huriel, without giving a thought either to attracting or repelling Joseph.

I saw he found her so beautiful that his chagrin clung on only by a hair, for he leant towards her, and with a determination I didn't think he possessed, he put his mouth very close to hers, and would have touched it, had I not been seized with a sudden fit of coughing that stopped his kiss halfway there.

Brulette woke up with a start, and I pretended the same thing had happened to me. Joseph felt a bit silly standing between the two of us, as we asked him how he was, without Brulette appearing embarrassed in the slightest or me looking crafty at all.

TWENTY-SIXTH EVENING

Joseph recovered very quickly, and, seizing his courage in both hands as if unwilling to fail, he said to Brulette: 'I'm very pleased to find you in here. It's been a year since we've seen each other: won't you give your old friend a kiss?' He went up to her again, but she drew back, astonished by his strange air, and replied: 'No, Joey, I'm not in the habit of kissing any boy, however old a friend he might be, and however pleased I might be to greet him.'

'You've become awfully touchy!' he answered, with an expression of mockery and anger.

'I don't think, Joey, that I've ever been touchy with you when you didn't deserve it. You've never put me in a situation where I would be touchy, and as you've never asked me to treat you in a familiar way I've never had any difficulty defending myself from your embraces. So what's changed in our friendship for you to demand that I give you something our relationship has never included?'

'That's an awful lot of fuss to make about a kiss,' said Joseph, gradually growing more and more wrathful. 'If I never asked you for something you gave others so readily, it's because as a child I was extremely stupid. I'd have thought you'd have given me a warmer welcome now I'm neither so foolish nor so fearful.'

'Whatever is the matter?' Brulette asked me, astonished and even frightened, as she drew nearer to me. 'Is it him, or is it someone who looks like him? I thought I recognized our Joey, but now he seems to have neither Joey's expressions nor his face nor his friendship.'

'What have I done wrong to you, Brulette?' asked Joseph, a little deflated and already repentant, as he thought of the past. 'Is it because I've got the courage I always lacked before, the courage to tell you that for me you're the loveliest girl in the world, and that I've always wanted to be in your good books? There's no offence in that! I may well be no less unworthy of you than many of the others you put up with.'

He said that with a return to his former bad temper, and looked directly at me, and I could see that he wanted to find a bone to pick with the first person who was willing to step into his trap. I was only too eager to draw his first fire.

'Joseph,' I said to him, 'Brulette's right when she finds you changed. There's nothing strange in that. We know what terms we're on when we leave someone, but we don't know what terms we'll be on when we meet again. So don't be surprised to find that I've changed a bit, too. I've always been gentle and patient, supporting you in all situations, and consoling you in all your misfortunes. But if you've become more unjust than you used to be, I've become more easily offended, and I think it's bad of you to say to my cousin in my presence that she's too free with her kisses, and that she puts up with too many people around her.'

Joseph looked at me with an expression of scorn, and a truly diabolic expression appeared on his face as he laughed at me. And then he crossed his arms and said, looking me up and down as if he wanted to take my measurements: 'Is that so, Tiennet? Is it really you? Well, I always suspected it from the kindness you used to show in pulling the wool over my eyes.'

'Whatever do you mean?' said Brulette, who was offended by this statement, and thought he must have lost his mind. 'What has given you the right to blame me, and however can you have taken it into your head to find something ridiculous or improper in my relationship with my cousin? Have you been drinking wine, or do you have a fever that makes you forget the respect you owe me, and the friendship I thought I deserved from you?'

That really stumped Joseph, who took Brulette's hand in his and said with eyes filled with tears: 'I'm in the wrong, Brulette. Yes, I was somewhat unnerved because I was weary and I'd been longing to get here. But as far as you're concerned, I feel only eagerness, and you shouldn't see it as something wrong. I know very well that you're reserved by nature, and that you want everyone to treat you submissively. Someone as lovely as you has the right to make such demands, and your beauty has merely increased, instead of fading away. But you've got to agree that you still love pleasure, and that, in dancing, partners kiss frequently. That's the way it is, and I'll find it's a good thing, provided I can profit from it in my turn. And profit I will, for I know how to dance now, just as well as anyone else, and for the first time in my life I'm going to dance with you. I can hear the pipes coming back. Come along, and you'll see that I'll no longer refuse the pleasure of being one of your beaux.'

'Joey,' Brulette answered, only half pleased with this speech, 'you're wrong if you think that I still have beaux. I may have been a flirt, that was in my nature, and I've no need to give an account of myself, but I also had the right to change, and that, too, was in my nature. So now I no longer dance with all and sundry, and this evening I'm not going to dance any more.'

'I'd have thought,' said Joseph, piqued by this reply, 'that I was not all and sundry for an old friend with whom I took my first communion, and who lived under the same roof as I did!'

The band and the guests who arrived with great noise and bustle interrupted them, and Huriel came in, full of animation, took Brulette in his arms, lifted her up as if she were made of straw, and carried her to his father. The great woodcutter was outside, and he kissed her joyously, to the great despair of Joseph, who followed them, and who, clenching his fists, saw her treat this old man as affectionately as a daughter treats her father.

Whispering in the woodcutter's ear, I pointed out to him that Joseph had come, and warned him that the boy was in a bad temper. I suggested he take Huriel away, while I could easily convince Brulette that she should leave too. In this way,

Joseph, who wasn't one of the wedding guests and whom my aunt wouldn't keep with her, would have nothing else to do but go and sleep at Nohant, or at some house in Le Chassin. The woodcutter agreed with me, and, pretending not to see Joseph, who was keeping away from us, he consulted with Huriel while Brulette went off to see if there was some corner in the house where she could spend the night.

But my aunt, who'd boasted of being able to put us up, hadn't imagined that Brulette would want to go to bed before three or four in the morning. The boys in a wedding party normally don't go to bed at all the first night, and do their best to keep the dance going for three nights and three days. If one of them feels too weary, he goes off to a haystack to take a nap. As for the girls and women, they all retire to the same room, but usually it's only the old and the ugly who abandon the company like that.

So, when Brulette went up to the bedroom where she thought she would find a place to sleep next to some relation or other, she found herself in the midst of a heap of snorers who wouldn't even yield her a spot bigger than her hand, and those she woke up told her to come back when it was day, and they'd be going off to wait on the tables again. She came back down to tell us about her difficulties, for she'd made up her mind too late to come to any arrangements with the neighbours, and there was not so much as a chair in a closed bedroom where she could spend the night.

'Well then,' said the woodcutter, 'you must go and sleep in Thérence's room. My lad and I will pass the time here. No one can say a word against that.'

I saw that we could easily remove any pretext for jealousy on Joseph's part if Brulette slipped away with me without saying anything to him, and the woodcutter went up to him to hold his attention by asking him questions, while I led my cousin to the old castle, by way of my aunt's garden.

When I returned, I found the woodcutter, Joseph, and Huriel sitting together at a table. They called me to them, and I began to sup with them, willing to eat, drink, prattle, and sing, anything to avoid the outburst of anger that could have been provoked by talk in which Brulette was the principal subject of conversation. Joseph saw that we were in cahoots to force him to behave properly, and at first he kept himself well in hand, and even revealed a degree of gaiety. But in spite of himself he soon started to bite even as he caressed, and one felt that under every joyful word there lurked a spur on the tip of his tongue which stopped him enjoying himself frankly.

The woodcutter would have liked to put his venom to sleep through a little wine, and I believe Joseph would willingly have allowed this to happen in order to forget himself, but wine had never held sway over him, and he felt its helping hand less than ever. He drank four times as much as anyone else, for we had no reason to bury our feelings, and yet his thoughts were all the more clear and his speech all the more distinct for it.

Finally, when he said something too unkind about the cleverness of women and the treachery of friends, Huriel thumped the table with his fist and grasped his father's arm. Père Bastien had long been pushing him with his elbow to remind him to be patient, but Huriel said: 'No, father. Forgive me, but I can't put up with any more, and it's better to bring things out into the open while we're about it. Whether it's tomorrow or in a week's time, or in a year's time, I know that Joseph's teeth will be just as sharp then as they are now, and even if I keep my ears shut until then, I'll still have to end up by opening them to hear his unjust reproaches. Look Joseph, I've known what you've been implying for at least an hour, and you've been too smart by half. Speak properly and I'll listen. Tell me what you have on your mind with all the whys and wherefores. I'll answer you just as frankly.'

'Very well!' said the woodcutter. 'Have it out, the two of you.' And he threw his cup over, making up his mind as he knew how to when it was necessary. 'We won't drink any more, unless it's to toast each other in frank friendship, for the devil's venom shouldn't be mixed with the good Lord's wine.'

'You really astonish me, the two of you,' said Joseph, who'd turned yellow to the whites of his eyes, but who went on laughing nastily. 'What the devil's up with you, and why are you scratching yourselves when there's nothing biting you? I don't have any bone to pick with anyone, it's just that I'm in a mood to mock everything, and I don't think you're going to change my humour.'

'We'll see about that!' retorted Huriel, irritated in turn.

'Just try then!' answered Joseph who was still sneering.

'That's enough!' said the woodcutter, striking the table with his heavy, knotted hand. 'Both of you be silent, and since you can't be open, Joseph, I'll talk frankly enough for two. You misjudged in your heart of hearts the woman you wanted to love. That's a wrong the good Lord can forgive you for, since it's not always given to a man to choose which friends he'll trust and which he'll distrust. But at the very least it's the sort of misfortune that's very hard to repair. You fell into that misfortune, and now you've just got to get used to it and put up with it.'

'Why should I, master?' said Joseph, arching himself up like a wild cat. 'Who took it on himself to speak of my mistake to a girl who knew nothing of it, and who never had cause to suffer from it?'

'No one!' said Huriel. 'I'm no sneak.'

'Well then, who will take it on himself?'

'You will,' answered the woodcutter.

'Who's going to make me?'

'Your own love for her will make you. Doubts never come singly, and if you're cured of the first doubt, a second will come and will burst from your lips with the first words you'll want to say to her.'

'It seems to me, Joseph,' I said in my turn, 'that you've already done so, and that this very evening you offended the person you want to fight about.'

'That may be,' he answered arrogantly, 'but that's between her and me alone. If I want her to get over it, who says she won't? I remember a song my master composed, a song with fine music and with words that went:

One gives to him who asks.

Very well then, Huriel! You ask in words and I'll ask in music, and we'll see if she's too involved with you to turn in my direction. Come on, let's try it openly, you who accuse me of going about things in an underhand fashion! There are two of us in the game and there's no need to disguise ourselves. A beautiful house has more than one door, and we'll each knock on our own.'

'I'm willing,' said Huriel. 'But just you pay attention to this: I don't want any more reproaches, either in earnest or in play. Even if I forget those reproaches I could make of you, I'm not so soft that I'll put up with criticisms I don't deserve.'

'I'd like to know what you can accuse me of!' said Joseph, whose anger made him forgetful.

'I forbid you to ask! You just think it out for yourself,' said the woodcutter. 'If you were to exchange some evil blows with my son you'd be washed none the whiter for it, and you'd have no reason to be proud if I withdrew the pardon that my heart, which doesn't need any words, has already given you!'

'My master,' exclaimed Joseph, heated with emotion, 'if you thought you had reason to pardon me, I thank you for it. But as far as I'm concerned I've given you no cause for offence. I never thought of deceiving you, and if your daughter had been willing to say yes, I wouldn't have withdrawn my offer. She's a girl who has no equal in terms of reason and propriety. I would have loved her, for better or for worse, but sincerely and without treachery. She may well have saved me from many wrongs and much suffering! But she didn't consider me worthy. Well, then, now I'm free to seek out whomsoever pleases me, and I find that the man who had my trust and who promised me his help has been very quick to profit from a moment of scorn on my part to try to supplant me.'

'That moment of scorn lasted an entire month, Joseph,' answered Huriel. 'Be just, will you! One month, during which you asked for my sister's hand on three occasions. I can't help feeling, therefore, that you thought pretty poorly of her, and that to justify yourself for treating me with such derision you ought to free me from all criticism. I took you at your word, that's my only fault. Don't make me think it's a mistake I'll end up repenting.'

Joseph remained silent for a while. Then he stood up, saying: 'Yes, you've worked it out quite perfectly. The two of you are stronger than I am, and I spoke and behaved like a man who doesn't really know his own mind. But you're more foolish than I am if you don't know that a man doesn't have to be a fool to want two contradictory things. You let me be what I am, and I'll let you be what you want to be. If you're a true heart, Huriel, I'll know it soon enough, and if you win the game by playing fair, I'll be just and withdraw without any animosity.'

'How will you know if my heart is true, if you haven't been able to judge it by now, and can't yet treat me as I deserve?'

'By what you tell Brulette about me,' said Joseph. 'It's easy for you to turn her against me and I can't repay you for it.'

'Wait!' I said to Joseph. 'Don't accuse anyone unjustly. Thérence has already told Brulette that you asked for her hand not two weeks ago.'

'But nothing else was said, and nothing else will be said,' added Huriel. 'Joseph, we're better than you think we are. We don't want to take Brulette's friendship from you.'

These words touched Joseph, and he put out his hand as if to take Huriel's, but this spontaneous movement stopped midway, and he went off without saying anything more to anyone.

'That's a really hard heart for you!' exclaimed Huriel, who was too kind not to suffer from such apparent ingratitude.

'No,' said his father, 'that's a very unhappy heart.'

Struck by this expression, I followed Joseph to chastise or console him, for it seemed to me that there was death in his eyes. I felt as annoyed with him as Huriel did, but I was drawn to him despite that, because I'd so long been in the habit of pitying and supporting him.

He walked along the Nohant path so quickly that he was soon lost from my sight; but he stopped beside the Lajon, which is a little pond on a deserted heath. It's a gloomy area, and the only shade there is provided by a handful of scrawny trees that have drawn little nourishment from the poor soil. But the marsh is rich in wild plants and, as it was the season when the white water-lily blooms, and thousands of other kinds of marsh grass as well, it smelt as good as if we were in a chapel filled with flowers.

Joseph had thrown himself into the reeds. He didn't know he'd been followed, and as he thought he was alone and hidden, he groaned and growled simultaneously, like a wounded wolf. I called out to him, just to let him know I was there, for I was certain he wouldn't want to reply, and I went right up to him.

'That's no way to deal with it,' I said to him. 'You've got to listen to yourself, and tears don't give any reasons.'

'I'm not crying, Tiennet,' he answered in a firm voice. 'I'm neither weak enough nor happy enough to find that kind of relief. Even in the worst moments the most that happens is that one poor tear escapes from my eyes, and the tear that's trying to escape just now is not of water but of fire, for it burns like a glowing coal. But don't ask me the reason why. I don't know how to put it into words, and I don't want to try. The time for confiding in others has passed. I'm strong now and no longer believe that others can help me. Their help was pity, and I don't need it any more. I want to rely on myself alone. Thank you for your good intentions. Farewell, leave me alone.'

'But where will you spend the night?'

'I'm going to see my mother.'

'But it's very late, and you've a long way to go from here to Saint Chartier.'

'It doesn't matter!' he said, standing up. 'I just can't keep still. We'll see each other tomorrow, Tiennet.'

'Yes, at home, since we're going back tomorrow.'

'It's all one to me. Wherever your Brulette goes, I'll be able to find her, and who knows, she may not have said her final word on the subject!'

He went away with an air of great determination, and when I saw how his pride gave him strength, I gave up trying to calm him. I figured that weariness, the pleasure of seeing his mother again, and a day or two to think things over would restore him to his senses. So my plan was to advise Brulette to stay at Le Chassin for a couple of days. Returning to the village, I found, in a corner of a meadow through which I was taking a short cut, the woodcutter and his son who, as they put it, were making their beds there. By that they meant they were preparing to sleep in the grass, since they'd no wish to disturb the two girls in the old castle, and they looked forward to resting under the stars in that mild spring weather.

It seemed a good idea to me, and fresh grass struck me as preferable to warm hay in some barn I'd have to share with thirty or so others. So I stretched out beside them, and looking at the small white clouds in the clear sky, breathing in the scent of the hawthorn and thinking of Thérence, I fell asleep, and slept more soundly than ever before.

I've always been a sound sleeper, and rarely in my youth did I wake up of my own accord. My two companions, who'd walked a long distance to reach Le Chassin, also let the sun rise, and woke up laughing at having been overtaken by it, something that rarely happened to them. They were even more amused to see me taking great care not to fall out of bed, and opening my eyes without the slightest idea of where I was.

'Come on!' said Huriel. 'Get up, lad, we're all late now. Do you know what? This is the last day of May, and in our region it's the custom to hang a bouquet on your sweetheart's door, if you weren't able to do so on the first day of the month. There's no chance we've been beaten to it, since, for one thing, no one knows where my sister and your cousin are staying, and for another, in your region you don't have this custom of a bouquet symbolizing affection. But perhaps our two beauties may already be awake, and if they leave their rooms before the May blossoms have been attached to the door they'll accuse us of being lazy.'

'As a cousin,' I answered with a laugh, 'I'll certainly allow you to hang your bouquet, and as a brother, you'll give me your permission. But the father here may well not see things that way.'

'Indeed I do!' said the woodcutter. 'Huriel has told me something about it. Trying isn't the hard part; it's succeeding that's another story! If you manage it, then we'll see, my boy. It's up to you!'

Encouraged by his friendly air, I ran to a nearby bush and joyously cut a large sprig of wild flowering cherry while Huriel, who'd acquired in advance one of those fine silk and gold ribbons that are sold in his country, and that the women place in their lace caps, intertwined white thorn with pink thorn, and tied them in a bouquet worthy of a queen.

It was only three strides from the meadow to the castle, and the silence assured us that our fair ones still slept, doubtless because they'd chatted together deep into the night, but we were amazed to see a superb May bouquet covered with silver and white ribbons hanging on the door we'd imagined would be completely bare.

'Well then!' said Huriel, preparing to rip off this suspect offering, and frowning at his dog who'd spent the night in the meadow. 'Is this the way you guard the house, Satan? Have you already made friends in the area? Was that what stopped you devouring the legs of whoever put this bouquet here?'

'Just a minute,' said the woodcutter, stopping his son as he was about to tear the bouquet from the door. 'There's only one person here Satan would be likely to respect, and who also knows the custom of the bouquet, since he's seen it practised in our district. Well, you promised that very person you wouldn't thwart him. So just be happy to give pleasure without at the same time displeasing a third person, and respect his offering, just as he would doubtless have respected yours.'

'Yes, father,' said Huriel. 'If only I were sure it was him! But who's to say it isn't someone else? Or that it's been left for Thérence?'

I pointed out to him that no one knew Thérence, and that in all likelihood no one had even seen her, and as I looked at the white water-lilies in the bouquet, water-lilies that had been freshly picked, I remembered that these plants were not common in this area and grew almost nowhere but in the Lajon marsh where I'd seen Joseph stop. No doubt instead of going to Saint Chartier he'd backtracked and had even gone deep into the water and the quicksands, which are dangerous in that marsh, in order to pick so many of them.

'Well,' said Huriel with a sigh, 'so we're at war with each other!' And he fixed his bouquet with a worried look that I considered very modest on his part, for it seemed to me he could be certain of his victory and had no need to fear anyone. I would certainly have liked to be as sure of my chances where his sister was concerned, and, as I attached my bouquet, my heart pounded as if I felt her presence behind the door all ready to hurl it in my face.

So I turned pale when the door opened, but it was Brulette who appeared first. She gave the woodcutter his morning kiss, shook hands with me, and blushed with pleasure on seeing Huriel, to whom, nevertheless, she didn't dare say a word.

'Oh, father!' said Thérence, who appeared too, and gave the woodcutter a smacking kiss. 'So you played at being a young man all night long, did you? Come on, come inside, and let me give you breakfast. But first, let me see these bouquets. Three, Brulette? Well, that's a bit much, my sweet! Is this procession going to continue all morning long?'

'Only two are for Brulette,' said Huriel. 'The third is for you, sister.' And he pointed out the cherry blossom, so weighed down with flowers that it had already left a white rain on the threshold.

'For me?' said Thérence in astonishment. 'Were you afraid I'd be jealous of Brulette, Huriel?'

'Brothers aren't as gallant as that,' said the woodcutter. 'Have you no inkling that there's a timid and discreet lover who says not a word and dares not declare his love?'

Thérence looked around her as if she were seeking someone other than me, and when she turned her dark eyes to my embarrassed and silly face, I thought she'd burst out laughing, which would have pierced my heart to its core. But she did nothing of the sort, and even blushed a little. Then she gave me her hand very frankly.

'Thank you, Tiennet. You wanted to remind me of you and I accept, without attaching any more to your gift than I should.'

'Well,' said the woodcutter, 'if you accept it, my daughter, you must follow the custom and attach a little of it to your cap.'

'Why no,' said Thérence, 'that might annoy some local girl, and I don't want poor Tiennet to have any reason to repent treating me so well.'

'Oh! no one will be angry with that!' I exclaimed. 'And if you aren't angry yourself, then I'll be extremely delighted.'

'So be it!' she said, and breaking a little branch of my flowers she attached them to her head-dress with a pin. 'We're only at Le Chassin here, Tiennet. If we were in your home town, I'd be more careful for fear of breaking your friendship with some local girl.'

'Break all my friendships, Thérence! I couldn't ask for anything better!'

'On account of this?' she said. 'That would be going too fast. When you rob your neighbour, you have to repay him, and I don't know you well enough yet, Tiennet, to say whether we'd both be winners.' Then, turning the subject away from herself with that self-effacement that was so much a part of her nature, she said to Brulette: 'Your turn, my dear. How are you going to give thanks for these two May bouquets, and which one will you choose for making your ornament?'

'Neither, if I don't know where they've come from,' answered my prudent cousin. 'Say something, Huriel, and stop me making a mistake.'

'I can't say anything,' said Huriel, 'except that this one is mine.'

'In that case, I'll take all of it,' she said, taking it down. 'And as for that bouquet from the river, it seems to me that it's not at all happy there on the door. It would be better in the ditch.'

So saying, she adorned her cap and her blouse with Huriel's flowers, and having put the rest in her room, she was on the point of throwing the other bouquet in the remains of a former ditch that separated the meadow from the little park, but as she reached out for it, since Huriel had refused to insult his rival in that way, the sound of bagpipes could be heard from the thicket that lay close to the little courtyard opposite us, and someone who, evidently, had been hidden close enough to hear and see everything we did and said, played the tune of the three woodcutters that père Bastien had composed.

At first he played it in the form we knew, and then rather differently, and finally he changed it completely, varying the modes and including his own inspiration which was certainly not of a lower standard, and even seemed to sigh and pray in so tender a manner that you couldn't help being moved to pity. Then he played it in a stronger and livelier way, as if it were a song of reproach or command, and Brulette, who'd gone forward and had stopped at the edge of the ditch ready to throw her bouquet into it, but unable to find the heart to do so, leaped back as if frightened by the anger the music revealed. Then Joseph, pushing aside the brush with his feet and shoulders, appeared on the bank of the ditch, his eyes blazing, playing still, and appearing through his playing and his expression to threaten Brulette with deep despair if she didn't abandon the affront she'd intended to inflict on him.

TWENTY-SEVENTH EVENING

'Now that's wonderful music and a fine musician!' exclaimed the woodcutter, clapping as soon as Joey stopped playing. 'That's beautiful work, and well played, Joseph. Someone who can seize the tiger by the tail like that has all the consolation they need! Come here and let me compliment you!'

'There is no consolation for an insult, my master!' answered Joseph, 'and our whole lives long there will be a ditch full of thorns between Brulette and me, if she throws the flowers I offered her into this ditch.'

'God forbid I should repay such a fine dawn serenade so poorly!' said Brulette. 'Come here, Joseph; there'll never be any thorns between you and me, except for those you yourself plant.'

Joseph, just like a wild boar, broke down the spiny thorns that held him on the edge of the ditch, and flying over the mud that gave a greenish tinge to the bottom of the ditch, leapt into the meadow. He seized the bouquet from Brulette's hands and tore out some flowers that he wanted to put on her head, next to the white and pink hawthorn Huriel had given her. He did this with an air of pride, like a man who has won the right to impose his own will, but Brulette stopped him and said: 'Just a moment, Joseph. I've my own plan and you must accept it. You'll soon be received as a master player, and since the good Lord has made me so sensitive to music, it must be true that

I understand something about it without ever having learnt it. I've a fancy to hold a competition and reward whoever plays best. Give your pipes to Huriel and let him show what he can do, just as you've shown what you can do.'

'Very well, I'll agree to that,' exclaimed Joseph, his face glowing with defiance. 'Your turn, Huriel. Make this goat's skin sing like a nightingale if you can!'

'Those aren't the conditions we accepted, Joseph,' Huriel answered. 'You said you'd leave words to me, and I've used them! I'll leave music to you. I concede you're a better player than I am. So take your bagpipes back, and speak to us again in your own language. No one here will grow tired of listening to you.'

'Since you confess you're defeated,' Joseph replied, 'I'll play again only if Brulette commands me to.'

'Play!' she said, and while he played wonderfully again, she braided a garland of white water-lily flowers together with the silver ribbons that bound the bouquet. When Joseph's performance was finished, she went to him and placed the garland around the drone of his bagpipes. Then she said: 'Joey, my fine musician, I receive you as a master piper and award you the prize. May this pledge bring happiness and glory, and serve to show how highly I value your fine talent.'

'Yes, yes, thank you!' said Joseph. 'Thank you, my Brulette. Now, take the final step in making me proud and happy by keeping for yourself one of these flowers you've given me. Pick the best one here and put it quickly against your heart, if you don't want to put it on your forehead.'

Brulette smiled, blushing, and looking as lovely as an angel, she glanced at Huriel, who grew pale at the thought that he'd lost.

'Joseph,' she answered, 'I gave you a fine prize there, the prize for music! You must be content with that and not ask for the prize of love as well, for love is won neither by force nor by knowledge but by the will of God.'

Huriel's features lit up and Joseph's darkened.

'Brulette,' he exclaimed, 'God's will must be my will!'

'Gently there!' she said. 'He alone is the master. Here we have one of his little angels who shouldn't hear anything contrary to our religion.' As she said that, she caught Charley up in her arms as he came bounding up behind her like a lamb gambolling up to its mother. Thérence, who'd returned to her room while Joseph played, had just woken him up, and without taking the time to allow himself to be dressed, he'd raced up to her, almost naked, to kiss his dearie with a masterful and jealous air that paid no heed to the pretensions of lovers.

Joseph, who'd forgotten all his suspicions and thought he'd been misled by the letter Carnat's son had written him, bounded back when Charley arrived, as if the child were a snake, and when he saw the boy caress Brulette so warmly and call her his darling mother, he was overcome with such giddiness he almost fainted. But immediately afterwards, transported with rage, he hurled himself at the child and, tearing him brutally from Brulette, he gasped out in a voice that sounded as if he were suffocating: 'So now we see the real truth! This is the trick you've been playing on me, and that's the love prize that has already been awarded.'

Frightened by Joseph's rage and Charley's screams, Brulette tried to wrench the child back from him, but Joseph could no longer control himself and dragged Charley towards him, laughing madly and saying he wanted to feast his eyes on him to see the likeness. In the struggle, unaware of what he was doing, he was squeezing the child so hard that he was suffocating him. Brulette was in despair, and dared not defend herself, terrified by the danger the child was incurring. She threw herself at Huriel crying: 'My baby! My baby! He's killing my poor little child.'

Huriel didn't wait to be asked twice. He seized hold of Joseph by the throat and squeezed so hard and with such strength that Joseph's tensed arms loosened, and I was able to catch Charley in mine and return him, almost unconscious, to Brulette. Joseph, too, almost fainted, as much from his outburst of rage as from the way in which Huriel had seized him. A battle would have ensued, and the woodcutter was already throwing himself between them, but Joseph had no inkling of what had happened. All he could think of was that Brulette was a mother, and that he'd been deceived by her and by us.

'So you're not hiding it any more?' he asked, his words broken by gasps.

'Whatever do you mean by that?' sobbed Brulette, sitting on the grass and stroking Charley's bruised arms. 'You're a wicked madman, that's all I know about it. Never come near me again and don't you ever attack this child again, unless you want the good Lord to curse you!'

'One word, Brulette!' said Joseph. 'If you're a mother, then say so. I'll pity and forgive you. I'll even support you if necessary, but if the only way to deny it is by lying, I'll despise you and cast you out of my memory!'

'His mother! You take me for his mother!' Brulette exclaimed, leaping up as if to push Charley away. 'Do you really believe I'm his mother?' she asked again, pressing the poor child, the cause of all this trouble, to her heart. Then she looked wildly around her, and seeking Huriel out with her eyes she asked: 'Can people really think such a thing of me?'

'The proof that they don't,' said Huriel, going up to her and caressing Charley, 'is that they love the child you love.'

'Brother, it would be better to say what you said to me yesterday,' Thérence exclaimed swiftly. '"Whether he's hers or not, he'll be mine, if she'll be mine."'

Brulette threw her arms around Huriel's neck and, clinging to him as a vine clings to an oak, she said: 'Be my master then, for I never have had, and never will have, any master but you.'

Joseph stared at the sudden agreement he'd precipitated, and there was so much grief and regret in his eyes that it was painful to see him. Brulette's cry of truth had struck home, and he believed he'd merely dreamed he'd just insulted her. He felt all was over between them, and without saying a word, he picked up his bagpipes and fled.

The woodcutter ran after him and brought him back, saying: 'No, no, that's no way to leave people, after you've been friends since childhood. Swallow your pride, Joseph, and beg this honest girl's pardon. Now she's my daughter, for she's made her promise, and I'm proud of it. But she must remain your sister. A brother can be forgiven for something one wouldn't forgive in a lover.'

'Let her forgive me if that's what she wants to do and she

finds she can do so!' said Joseph. 'But if I'm guilty then the only one who can absolve me is myself. Hate me, Brulette, that may well be better for me. I can see only too clearly that I've done exactly what I needed to do to lose your heart. There's no going back; but if you pity me, don't say so. I've nothing more to ask of you.'

'None of that would ever have happened,' Brulette replied, 'if you'd done your duty, which was to go and embrace your mother. Go to her, Joseph, and above all don't tell her what you accused me of. She'd die of grief.'

'My dear daughter,' said the woodcutter, still detaining Joseph, 'it's my belief you should scold children only when they're calm. Otherwise they mishear what you say to them and don't profit from your reproaches. As far as I'm concerned, Joseph has odd moments of madness, and if he doesn't make up for them as easily as other people do, it may be because he feels his wrongs very acutely and suffers more from his own disapproval than others do. Set him an example of reason and kindness. It's easy to forgive others when we're happy, and you must surely feel happy to be loved as deeply as you are here. It wouldn't be possible to be more truly loved, for I know things about you now that make me hold you in such high esteem that these two hands of mine would twist the neck of any man or woman who insulted you deliberately. But when Joseph insulted you, he didn't do so deliberately. That insult arose from his fever and not from any reflection, and it was so swiftly followed by shame that his heart has already made you full amends for it. Come on, Joseph, add something of your own to my speech, I won't ask any more of you, and Brulette will be satisfied with that, won't you, daughter?'

'You don't know him at all, if you think he'll say anything, dear father,' said Brulette. 'But I won't insist on it, because what I most want to do is please you. And so, Joseph, I forgive you, even though you don't care whether I do or don't. Stay and have breakfast with us, and let's talk of something different. What was said has been forgotten.'

Joseph didn't say a word, but he took off his hat and set down his stick, as if he'd decided to stay. The two girls went back into the house to prepare the meal, and Huriel, who took great care of his horse, began to curry-comb it and groom it. I looked after Charley whom Brulette had entrusted to me, and the woodcutter, wanting to give Joseph something else to think about, talked to him about music and heaped praise on his arrangement of the song.

'Never speak to me of that song again! It can only remind me of grief and I want to forget it.'

'Well then,' said the woodcutter, 'play me something else of your own, straight away, just as the notes come to you.'

Joseph went off with him into the park, and we heard him playing tunes that were so sad and melancholy that the bagpipes seemed to be a soul abasing itself in repentance and contrition.

'Do you hear him?' I asked Brulette. 'That's his way of confessing, no doubt, and if sorrow is a way of making amends, he's making amends to you now in full measure.'

'I find it hard to believe that a tender heart beats under such wild pride,' said Brulette. 'I'm like Thérence now. A little tenderness attracts me more than a lot of knowledge. But I have forgiven him, and if my pity isn't as great as Joseph demands in his own language, that's because I know he has a consolation he won't be deprived of if he forgets me. I mean, the value that others and he himself will place on his talents. If Joseph didn't place such judgements above friendship, then his tongue wouldn't be silent, and his eyes wouldn't be dry when friendship reproaches him. You only know how to beg well for something you really want.'

'Well,' said the woodcutter, returning from the park alone, 'did you hear him, my dears? He said all he could say and all he wanted to say, and pleased at having made me shed tears with the music he composed, he's leaving in a calmer frame of mind.'

'You weren't able to make him stay for a meal, all the same,' said Thérence with a smile.

'No,' answered her father, 'he played too well not to be three quarters consoled and he preferred to leave it at that, rather than risk saying something stupid at table.'

TWENTY-EIGHTH EVENING

When we gathered for the meal, we were all relieved to set
aside the fears we'd felt the previous day when Huriel and
Joseph had fallen out. Moreover, as Thérence made it perfectly clear, both when he was absent and when he was
present, that she neither harboured any resentment towards
him, nor yearned for him, I shared the calm and humorous
mood of Huriel and the woodcutter. Charley, seeing everyone
make much of him and caress him, began to forget *the man*
who'd terrified and bruised him. From time to time, he'd still
swing around at the slightest noise, and Thérence soothed him
with a laugh, telling him that the man had gone away and
wouldn't come back again. We were like one family, and as I
served Thérence with the highest respect, I told myself that I
would be less domineering in will and more patient in love
than Joseph had been.

Brulette alone remained careworn and downcast, as if her
feelings had been dealt a cruel blow. Huriel was troubled by it;
the woodcutter, who knew the human heart in all its hidden
corners, and whose face and words were so kindly that they
put balm on all her wounds, took her little hands in his, and
drawing her pretty head against his chest, told her, at the end
of the meal: 'Brulette, there's a request we'd like to make of
you, and if you look sad and troubled, my son and I won't
dare to make it. Won't you give us a little smile of encouragement?'

'Go ahead, father, tell me what you want.'

'Well, daughter, you must agree to introduce us to your
grandfather tomorrow, so he can accept Huriel as his
grandson.'

'It's too soon, father,' Brulette replied, shedding yet more
tears. 'Or rather, it's too late. If you'd asked me an hour ago,
before Joseph let fall certain words in my hearing, I'd have
consented with all my heart. But now, I confess, I'd be
ashamed to accept an honest man's faith so freely when I see
I no longer pass for an honest girl. I knew people accused me
of being frivolous and coquettish. Your son himself scolded

me about that, gently, last year. Thérence accused me of it, but gave me her friendship all the same. So when I saw that Huriel had the heart to leave me without asking anything of me, I spent some time in serious thought. The good Lord came to my aid in putting me in charge of this little child, who didn't please me at first, and whom I may perhaps have refused, had it not been for my sense of duty, and the thought that a little suffering and virtue would make me more worthy of being loved than did my chatter and my clothes. So I thought I'd made up for my years of thoughtlessness, and that I'd trampled underfoot the excessive love I'd felt for my own little self. I saw, of course, that people in the village criticized and abandoned me, but I consoled myself by saying: "If he comes back, he'll see I don't deserve any criticism for having become reasonable and serious." But now I discover something quite different, as much by what Joseph did as by what Thérence said. It wasn't just Joseph who thought I'd long since gone off the rails, it was Huriel, too, since his love was strong enough and his heart great enough to say to his sister yesterday: "Guilty or not, I love and take her as she is." Oh! Huriel! I thank you for that! But I don't want you to marry me without knowing me. I'd suffer too much if I saw you were being criticized as you will be, no doubt, because of me. I respect you too much to let anyone say you're having to accept the paternity of a foundling. Come! Let's agree I must have behaved in a very brazen way in the past, to give such accusations any credence. Well, I want you to judge me by the way I behave every day, and I want you to know I'm not just a fine dancer at a wedding, but a good housekeeper as well. We'll come and live here, as you've asked. And, in a year, if I am not able to prove to you that I have no reason to blush for looking after Charley, at least I'll have given you, in every thing I do, the proof that my mind is as rational as my conscience is clear.'

Huriel snatched Brulette from his father's arms, devotedly kissed the tears that streamed from her fine eyes, and putting her back where he had found her, said: 'Bless her well, father, for you can judge for yourself whether I lied to you when I said she was worthy of your blessing. She's spoken very well,

my dear golden-tongued girl, and there's nothing left to say,
except that we don't need a year, or even a day, of trial, and
that this very evening we'll go and ask her grandfather for her
hand. To spend even one more night waiting for his consent is
more than I have courage for, now that's the only thing I need,
if I'm to feel I'm king of all the world.'

'Now do you see,' père Bastien asked Brulette, 'what you
get when you ask for a reprieve? Instead of asking tomorrow,
we'll ask for your hand today. Come, child, you must submit,
and that's how your bad behaviour in the past is to be punished.'

At last joy spread all over Brulette's face, and the evil Joseph
had done was forgotten. Yet when we left the table, she still
suffered a little from it. Charley had heard Huriel call the
woodcutter 'father', and called him by the same name, which
earned him even more kisses. But Brulette was still a little
upset.

'Hasn't the time come,' she said, 'to take the trouble to
invent a family for this child? Every time he calls me mother
now, I'll feel as if he hurts those who love me.'

We were about to reassure her on that score when Thérence
said: 'Lower your voices, someone's listening.' We all turned
our eyes in the direction of the gate, and saw the end of a stick
lying on the ground, and the bulge of a full begging-sack,
which indicated only too clearly that there was a beggar there,
waiting for someone to pay attention to him, and capable of
overhearing things that were no concern of his.

I went over to him and recognized Brother Nicholas, who
immediately came up to us, and confessed to us without the
slightest embarrassment that he'd been listening to us for a
quarter of an hour, and what's more had taken a great deal of
pleasure in hearing it.

'I felt certain that was Huriel's voice,' he said, 'but as I made
my rounds I so little expected to find him in here, dear friends,
that I wouldn't have been sure except for various other things
that were said in this place, where Brulette knows I'm not
unwanted.'

'But we know that, too,' said Huriel.

'You do? Yes, that must be so.'

'That's because your aunt told me everything last night,' Huriel said to Brulette. 'You see, my darling, that I'm not as worthy as you think me.'

'Yes,' said Brulette, much relieved, 'but yesterday morning! . . . Well, since you know all about my business,' she said, talking to the monk, 'what's your advice, Brother Nicholas? You, who were used as a go-between in Charley's affairs, can't you find some story to spread abroad to protect his parents' secret and repair the damage done to my honour?'

'A story?' said the friar. 'You're asking me to advise and abet in lying? I'm not one of those who can damn themselves for the love of a girl, my sweet! I'd get nothing from it. I'll have to help you in other ways. I've already put in more work on that than you think. Be patient, and everything will fall into place as easily as it did in another matter in which master Huriel knows I was no poor friend to him.'

'I know perfectly well that I owe you my life's peace and calm,' answered Huriel, 'so people can say what they like about monks, but I know at least one for whom I'd allow myself to be cut into pieces. Sit down, Brother, and spend the day with us. What is ours is yours, and the house we're in is also your house.'

Thérence and the woodcutter were about to add their invitation to Huriel's when my aunt Marghitonne arrived and wouldn't allow us to spend another moment away from her. It was time for the cabbage ceremony, which is the great and ancient farce traditionally associated with the day after the wedding, and already the guests were beginning to walk in our direction. There was singing and dancing and drinking at each stopping point. There was no longer any way in which Thérence could keep out of it all, and she accepted my arm to go and meet the procession while Huriel led Brulette. My aunt took charge of the child, and the woodcutter, leading the monk off with him, was soon able to convince him that he too should join in.

The lad on the bier who played the role of the gardener, or, as we say here, the pagan, was adorned in a way that amazed everyone. Near the little park he'd picked up a beautiful garland of water-lilies bound with silver ribbons, and he'd

made them into a belt that went over the hunch back he'd
fashioned out of hemp. It didn't take us long to recognize the
garland. Joseph must have lost it or hurled it aside when he
left us. The ribbons were the envy of the bridesmaids, who
made plans to prevent them being spoiled, and they all threw
themselves on the pagan, and even though, as he defended
himself, he kissed more than one with his muzzle smeared
with wine lees, they stripped him of it, and divided this rich
wedding booty among themselves. So Joseph's scattered ribbons glittered all day long on the heads of the loveliest young
girls of the region, and were put to even better use than he'd
imagined when he abandoned them.

The play was performed from door to door in the village,
and was as mad as it usually is. It ended with a great meal and
dancing that went on until nightfall. After that, Brulette and
I took our leave, and, accompanied by the woodcutter,
Thérence and Huriel, we set out for Nohant with the monk
going ahead, leading the clairin by the bridle, and on the
clairin sat fat Charley, a little intoxicated by all he'd seen,
laughing like a madman, and trying to sing just like he'd heard
people singing all day long.

Although today's youth has really gone downhill since then,
you'd often see fifteen-year-old girls walk five leagues in a
morning, and the same in the evening, on their own legs, in
order to spend the day dancing, even on the hottest days, and
so you won't imagine we reached home in a state of exhaus-
tion. On the contrary, along the way, the four of us danced
some more, indeed several times, as the woodcutter played the
bagpipes, and Charley slept on the horse, while the monk told
us we were all crazy, scolded us, and couldn't refrain from
laughing and clapping his hands to egg us on.

At last we reached Brulette's door, at nearly ten o'clock that
evening, and père Brulet was asleep in his bed when the joyful
company came into his room. As he was fairly deaf, and slept
soundly, Brulette put the child to bed, served us a meal, and
discussed with us how we would wake him up, while he slept
his first sleep.

At last he turned over in our direction, recognized his
granddaughter and me, was astonished to see the others, and

sitting on his bed, looking as serious as a judge, he listened to what the woodcutter said to him loudly and succinctly, but most frankly. The friar, in whom père Brulet had the highest confidence, added his words of praise for the Huriel family, and Huriel declared his feelings and all his fine sentiments for the present and the future.

Père Brulet listened to it all without saying a word, and I was afraid he hadn't understood a thing; but, although he looked as if he were dreaming, he'd lost none of his faculties, and answered as befits a wise man, saying that he recognized in the woodcutter the son of an old friend of his, that he valued the whole family highly, that he considered Brother Nicholas to be trustworthy, and that above all else, he trusted the mind and fine judgement of his granddaughter. According to him, she hadn't delayed her choice for so long and refused so many good suitors just to end up by committing a folly, and since she wanted to marry Huriel, Huriel must, therefore, be a good husband.

The way he spoke showed he was perfectly aware of everything, but there was one point on which his memory failed him. He remembered just at the moment we were leaving, that Huriel was a mule-driver: 'And,' he said, 'that's the one thing that troubles me. Is my granddaughter to be left alone for three quarters of the year?'

He was reassured to learn that Huriel had abandoned his profession as a mule-driver and had become a woodcutter, and he accepted the idea of going to work at Le Chassin during the summer.

So we separated, each very happy with the others. Thérence stayed with Brulette, and I took the others off to my home.

The next evening we learned through the friar, who'd strolled around the whole day, that Joseph had not set foot in Nohant town, but had gone to spend an hour with his mother, after which he'd set out to wander through the neighbourhood, saying that he planned to assemble the region's pipers for a gathering, during which he'd demand the right to play as a master piper. Mariton was deeply upset by this decision, for she believed the Carnats and all the local minstrels, of whom there were already too many for our needs, would object, and cause trouble and difficulties. But Joseph wouldn't listen to her, he just went on saying he wanted to allow her to retire from servitude and take her away with him, even though she didn't seem as willing to go as he would have liked.

The following day, all our preparations were ready, and the first banns for Huriel and Brulette had already been read during the parish sermon, so we all returned to Le Chassin. You'd have thought we were embarking on a pilgrimage to the end of the world. As we had to take our furniture with us, and as Brulette wanted to be sure her grandfather would lack none of his usual comforts, we'd hired a cart, and all the village gaped to see us carry off everything including the kitchen sink. She forgot neither goats nor chickens, and Thérence was delighted at the thought of caring for them, for she knew nothing about looking after animals, and said she wanted to seize the opportunity to learn.

That suggested to me that I could jokingly offer myself as an animal for her to care for, as I was the most obedient and faithful animal in the whole flock. She wasn't angry, but she gave me no encouragement to move from banter to serious talk. Yet it struck me that she wasn't displeased to see me so happily leave my country and my family to follow her, and if she didn't actively draw me to her, neither did she push me away.

Brulette was proud to depart with such a handsome lover, in the teeth of all the lovers who'd misjudged her. But at the moment when père Brulet and the women climbed onto the cart, together with Charley, the monk came to bid us farewell, and added, for the benefit of any curious onlooker: 'In fact, I'm heading in your direction, and will go with you for a fair section of the journey.'

He got in beside père Brulet, and after a league or so, along a covered path, he made us stop. Huriel was leading the clairin, who was as good a carriage horse as he was a beast of burden, and we were walking a little ahead of them, the woodcutter and I. Realizing the cart had been delayed, we turned round, thinking there'd been an accident, and saw Brulette in tears, hugging Charley, who clung to her, bellowing, because the friar wanted to take him away. Huriel was pleading for another course of action, and was so distressed by Brulette's unhappiness that he was close to tears himself.

'What's going on then?' asked the woodcutter. 'Goodness me, daughter, do you want to part from the poor child? Is this the result of the thoughts you had the other day?'

'No, father,' answered Brulette, 'his true parents have asked to have him back, and it's for his own good. The poor little fellow doesn't understand, and although I, for my part, do understand it, my heart fails me. But there are good reasons for this to be done without delay, so give me strength instead of taking it away from me.'

While she spoke of strength, she herself had none, faced with Charley's tears and caresses, for she'd grown to love him very tenderly, and Thérence was obliged to help her. The maid of the woods had in her expression, and in the slightest thing she said, such proof of goodness that she would have persuaded the very stones, and the child felt this, even though he didn't know how. She succeeded in making him understand that he had to calm down, and that he was being left only for a very short while, so that Brother Nicholas was able to take him without any resistance, and we set off again to the sound of a kind of round that he sang to amuse Charley, a song that was more like a church psalm than a normal song; but Charley enjoyed it, and when their voices faded away, that of the friar covered the last sobs of the poor little love.

'Come, Brulette, on our way,' said the woodcutter. 'We all love you so much we'll cheer you up.'

Huriel climbed on to the cart in order to be with her, and throughout the journey he talked to her so gently that when we arrived she said: 'Don't think I'm inconsolable, my true friend! My heart failed me for a moment, but I know perfectly well where I can place the affection I felt for that child, and where I'll rediscover the joy he used to give me.'

It didn't take us long to install ourselves in the castle, and even to make ourselves at home. There were several habitable rooms, even though they weren't particularly smart, and you'd have thought them about to collapse on us, but the wind had been blowing around the ruins so long without toppling them, that they were quite capable of lasting as long as we would.

Aunt Marghitonne, delighted to have us near her, provided us with everything we needed in the way of the few luxuries to which we were accustomed, luxuries that the Huriel family let themselves be persuaded into sharing with us, although they were unused to them, and didn't set much store by such things. The Bourbonnais workers the woodcutter had hired arrived, and he hired others from the area. The result was that we formed a kind of colony there, camped partly in the town and partly in the ruins, all working with a will under the leadership of a just man who knew how to reduce hardship and recompense courage. We would gather together every evening to eat with one another on the meadow, to listen to stories, and tell them ourselves, to sing and frolic in the cool evening air, and on Sundays to dance with all the local youth who were so grateful to us for our Bourbonnais music that they brought us all manner of little presents and held us in the highest esteem.

The work was strenuous, because the copse sloped down almost perpendicular to the river, and felling was very dangerous. In the woods of Alleu, I had come to know the woodcutter's hasty nature. As he had only the best workers under his command, and as the loggers worked hard, he had no cause to be impatient. But it was my ambition to please him by becoming a first-class woodcutter, and I feared my apprenticeship might earn me accusations of clumsiness and recklessness, which would have mortified me in Thérence's presence. So I begged Huriel to teach me in private how to do things, and to watch me closely when I was working. He did his best, and I was so eager that in a very short time I astonished my master with my skill. He complimented me on it, and even asked me in his daughter's presence why I worked so valiantly at a job I had no need to perform in my own country. 'That's because I'd be more than glad to be able to earn my living in any country I happened to be in. One never knows what may happen, and if I loved a woman who wanted to take me into the woods, I'd follow her, and I'd support her as well as the next man could.'

And to show Thérence that I wasn't as soft as she might think, I practised sleeping hard, living soberly, and tried to become as solid a forester as those who surrounded her. I didn't feel any the worse for it, indeed I even felt my mind grow sharper and my ideas clearer. Many things that at first I'd understood only after detailed explanations gradually clarified themselves before my eyes, and she no longer laughed at my clumsy questions. She chatted with me without growing bored, and showed she trusted my judgement.

Nevertheless, two weeks passed before I began to feel a little hope, and, as I complained to Huriel that I didn't have the courage to say a word to a girl who seemed too far above me ever to want to look at me, he answered: 'Rest assured, Tiennet, that my sister's heart is the most just that ever beat, and if, like all girls, she has moments of day-dreaming, there's no dream in her imagination that won't make way before her love of a beautiful truth and amends frankly made.'

Huriel's words, which were just what his father had said to me, gave me plenty of courage, and Thérence recognized in me such a good servant, I was so careful that she should have no cause for complaint, weariness, or impatience about anything it was in my power to alter, I was so mindful not to look at any other girl, and, moreover, I had so little desire to do so, in a word, I behaved towards her with such marked respect and showed her so clearly how highly I regarded her, that she opened her eyes to my feelings, and several times I saw her watch me anticipate her wishes before she'd expressed them, with a very gentle air of reflection, and she repaid me with thanks that filled me with pride. She wasn't accustomed, as Brulette had been, to finding herself pampered, and wouldn't have known, as Brulette knew, how to suggest gently that she would like to be pampered. She always seemed amazed that anyone should think of it; but when it happened she showed herself to be very grateful, and my cup flowed over when she would say to me, in her serious voice, and without false modesty: 'Really, Tiennet, you're too kind-hearted,' or: 'Tiennet, you take such pains over me that I would like to have the chance to do the same for you.'

One day when she was speaking to me in this way, in front

of the other woodcutters, one of them, a handsome
Bourbonnais boy, remarked, only half under his breath, that
she seemed to find me very interesting.

'I certainly do, Léonard,' she replied, looking at him with a
steady gaze. 'I feel for him all the interest he deserves, given
the care he takes of me, and his friendship for my family.'

'Don't you think,' asked Léonard, 'that anyone would do
the same if he thought he'd be as well paid?'

'I'd treat everyone fairly,' she replied, 'if I wanted or needed
everyone's goodwill. But that's not the case, and given my
nature, the friendship of a single person is all I need.'

I was sitting on the grass beside her while she said this, and
I seized her hand in mine, without daring to do any more than
to retain it for a short while. She withdrew it from me, but not
without touching my shoulder as she passed, with a sign of
trust and partnership.

Nevertheless, matters went no further than that, and I was
beginning to suffer greatly from my restraint with her, all the
more so in that the love between Huriel and Brulette was so
tender and so happy, that it disturbed my heart and my spirits.
Their great day drew nearer, and I couldn't see mine coming
at all.

TWENTY-NINTH EVENING

One Sunday, that of Brulette's last banns, the woodcutter and
his son who, from early morning, had seemed to me to be
consulting in secret, went off together saying that an urgent
affair concerning the marriage demanded their presence at
Nohant. Brulette, who knew perfectly well where things stood
as far as her wedding was concerned, was astonished that they
should needlessly expend so much energy, and equally surprised not to be told what was going on. She was even
tempted to be sulky with Huriel, who announced that he'd be
away for twenty-four hours, but Huriel wouldn't be dissuaded
and was able to calm her down, letting her believe that he was
leaving her only in order to work for her, and to prepare a fine
surprise for her.

Meanwhile Thérence, whom my eyes never left, seemed to me to be doing her best to hide her disquiet, and as soon as Huriel and her father had left, she led me off into the little garden where she spoke to me in the following terms: 'Tiennet, I'm really worried, and I don't know what to do. I'll tell you what's happened, and you tell me what we can do to prevent any mishaps. Last night, when I lay awake, I heard my brother and my father resolving to go to Joseph's aid. This is what I was able to gather from their conversation. Although Joseph was very poorly welcomed by all the local minstrels he visited to demand an examination, he persisted in wanting to receive his credentials from them, which is something they can't, after all, openly refuse him, without having put this talents to the test.

'It turned out that Carnat's son was to be received by the brotherhood in his father's place, for the elder Carnat is retiring, and that's to take place this very day, so Joseph is going to turn up and disturb something which had been taken as a mere formality, something promised and decided in advance.

'Well, our lumberjacks, when they were trying out the local inns, overheard the evil plots hatched by your local minstrels' band, and surprised them planning to throw Joseph out, if they can, by rejecting all his knowledge. If it were merely a question of suffering injustice and disappointment, it wouldn't be enough to disturb me as much as you can see I am disturbed, but my father and brother, who are master pipers, and who have a voice in all chapters of the musical fraternity, no matter where they are, believed it their duty to go and demand their place at the examination merely in order to come to Joseph's aid. And then, in all this, there's something I don't know about, because the pipers have a brotherhood secret about which my brother and father speak only between themselves, and using words that make no sense to me. In any event, either in their claim to judge the examination, or in some other ceremony for which the tests are said to be very harsh, there is certainly danger for them, because under their cloaks they took short sticks of hazel wood, and that's a weapon whose bite you have witnessed; and they also sharpened their sickles and hid those about their bodies as well, saying to each other around daybreak: "Devil take this lad, who brings happiness neither to himself nor to others. But all the same, we better help him, since he's throwing himself into the lions' den, without any thought for his own skin or that of his friends." And my brother complained, saying that, on the eve of his wedding, he wasn't particularly pleased at the thought of either breaking someone else's head or not bringing his own back in perfect condition. To which my father replied that he shouldn't speak forebodingly of the future, but simply go forward where human kindness demanded that he should succour his neighbour.

'As they quoted our friend Léonard among those who'd brought back evil stories, I questioned Léonard myself, very quickly and briefly. He told me that Joseph, and therefore those who want to support him, had been the object of serious threats for a week, and the pipers had spoken not merely of refusing him his credentials at the examination but even of making sure he neither would want, or be able, to present himself at a future examination. I know, from having heard people say so when I was small, at the time when my brother was received as a master piper, that you have to show great bravery and submit to goodness knows what tests of strength and courage. But in Bourbonnais, because the pipers lead a wandering life and don't all live from their minstrelsy, they don't annoy each other, and hardly torment the aspiring pipers at all. It seems, from the precautions my father took, and from what Léonard said, that it's different here, and that there have at times been battles from which not all the participants have returned. Help me, Tiennet. I feel half dead from fear and sorrow. I dare not arouse our woodcutters, for if my father thought I'd overheard and betrayed some secret of the brotherhood, he'd no longer value and trust me. He's used to seeing me as courageous as a woman can be in danger, but since that unfortunate affair with Malzac, I confess to you, I haven't an ounce of courage left, and I'm tempted to throw myself into the battle, so greatly do I fear its consequences for those I love.'

'And that, my brave girl, is what you call having no courage?' I replied to Thérence. 'Come, keep calm and let me do what needs to be done. The devil will have to be very cunning if he's to prevent me from discovering and surprising the pipers' secret all by myself, without anyone suspecting you; and if your father blames me, and drives me away from him, destroying all the happiness I'd hoped to win . . . it makes no odds, Thérence! Provided I bring him back to you, or at least send him back safe and sound, together with Huriel, I'll be amply rewarded, even if I never see you again. Farewell, don't be scared, say nothing to Brulette, she'd lose her head. I'll soon know what I must do. Don't look as if you know anything about it. I'll take everything on my own shoulders.'

Thérence flung her arms around me and kissed me on both cheeks with all a good girl's innocence. I set to work full of confidence and good cheer.

I began by going in search of Léonard, for I knew he was a good lad, very strong and bold, and greatly attached to père Bastien. Although he was a little jealous of me because of Thérence, he accepted my plan, and I asked him if he knew how many pipers had been summoned to the examination, and where we might go to watch them. He could tell me nothing about the first matter, but as for the second, he informed me that the examination wasn't held in secret, and was fixed for the hour after vespers in Benoît's inn at Saint Chartier. The deliberations that would follow were the only part when the pipers would retire to be alone together, but that always took place in the same house as the examination, and their judgement was given in public.

This led me to believe that half a dozen very determined lads would be enough to restore the peace if, as Thérence predicted, quarrels broke out. As justice was on our side, we'd certainly find a few good souls there who'd lend us a hand. I chose my companions therefore, together with Léonard, and we found four who were ready and willing to go with us, which, with the two of us, made up the desired number. The only thing that made them hesitate was the fear of displeasing their master in helping him against his will, but I swore to them that the woodcutter would never know their good intentions if that was what they wanted; we'd arrive as if by chance, and if any one of us was to be reprimanded, they could place all the blame on me, saying I'd led them all to the inn for a drink, telling them nothing more.

We were all agreed, therefore, and I went to tell Thérence we were ready to confront any danger at all. Each of us chose a good stick and we reached Saint Chartier at the hour chosen for the examination.

Benoît's inn was so crowded you couldn't turn round in it, and we were obliged to accept a table outside. All things considered, I wasn't unhappy to install my reserves there, and, advising them strongly not to get drunk, I slipped into the house where I counted sixteen professional pipers, not including Huriel and his father, who were sitting in the darkest corner of the room, hats over their eyes and all the more difficult to recognize in that few of those who were there had seen or met them in the region. I pretended not to see them, and speaking loudly enough for them to hear, I asked Benoît about this band of pipers all gathered together in his inn, as if it was something I hadn't even heard mentioned, and whose cause was a complete mystery to me.

'What?' exclaimed the host, who was just recovering from his illness, and looked very pale and thin from it. 'Don't you know that Joseph, your old friend, my barmaid's boy, is to enter an examination, together with Carnat's lad? I won't hide from you the fact that it's utter folly,' he added in a whisper. 'His mother's in despair. She's afraid of the malicious acts that take place in this kind of examination. And she's so upset, she's lost her head, and people are complaining of being badly served in here for the first time ever.'

'Can I do anything to help?' I asked him, hoping to have an excuse for remaining inside and wandering around the tables.

'Well, boy, if you're willing, you can indeed help me out. I won't pretend I've got all my strength back, and I can't bend down to draw the wine without feeling giddy; but I trust you. Here's the cellar key. You can be in charge of serving the jugs of wine and keeping them filled up. I hope Mariton and the kitchen hands will be enough for the other tasks.'

I didn't need to be told twice. I went to let my companions

know what I'd be doing for the good of the cause, and I took on the role of wine waiter, which let me see and hear everything.

Joseph and young Carnat were seated at opposite ends of a large table, sharing the bill for the gathering of pipers. There was more noise there than pleasure. People were shouting and singing, to avoid the need for conversation, for everyone was on the defensive, and you could feel the presence of personal interests, and sense the envy that had been aroused.

I soon realized that not all the pipers were on the Carnats' side against Joseph, as I'd feared, since, however well run a brotherhood may be, there's always some old quarrel to sow discord. But, little by little, I also saw that Joseph could draw small comfort from that discord, because those who didn't want his rival didn't want him either, but would have preferred to see the number of pipers reduced by the retirement of the elder Carnat. It even seemed to me that this was the majority view, and I predicted that both would be refused their credentials.

After the merriment had been going on for about two hours, the examination began. Silence wasn't demanded, since when bagpipes are played in a room, they're not an instrument that can be drowned out by other noises, and the singers didn't go on for much longer. A crowd came in from outside. My five friends climbed in through the open window, and I positioned myself not far from them. Huriel and his father didn't budge from their corner. Carnat, who'd drawn the straw to begin, climbed up on the bread arch,* and, urged on by his father, who couldn't refrain from marking the beat for him with his clogs, began to play for about half an hour on the traditional local bagpipes, with their small drone.

He played very badly, being very nervous, and I saw that most of the pipers were pleased that he played so poorly. They remained silent, as was their wont, since that made them look important but the other members of the audience also kept quiet, much to the poor lad's annoyance, because he'd hoped for a little encouragement, and his father began to mutter in rage, revealing his usual vindictive bad temper.

When Joseph's turn came, he broke away from his mother,

who hadn't stopped begging him in a whisper not to take part in the examination. He climbed up on the arch, carrying in an easy manner the great Bourbonnais bagpipes which dazzled the eyes of all present with their silver ornaments, their mirrors, and their long drones. Joseph looked proud as he cast an apparently pitying glance at his audience. You couldn't help noticing how handsome he'd become, and the local girls wondered if this were really Joseph the dreamer who'd been considered so simple-minded, and whom they'd last seen looking so thin and spindly. Nevertheless, his haughty air wasn't agreeable, and as soon as he'd filled the room with the sound of his bagpipes, he caused the little girls almost more fear than pleasure.

As there were, however, plenty of people there who knew their piping, particularly local pipers, hemp workers, who are great experts in songs, and old women, who are famous guardians of the best things from the past, Joseph was quickly appreciated, not only for the way in which he played the instrument without wearying himself, and for the purity of the sound he produced, but also for the taste he revealed in offering new tunes of unequalled beauty. As the Carnats pointed out that he had the advantage because his pipes gave a better sound, he dismantled them and kept only the high drone, which he used so well that he still produced agreeable sounds that gave the impression that it was quite a different instrument from the one we'd heard first.

The judges revealed nothing of what they were thinking, but the rest of the audience, stamping with joy and clapping loudly, decided that nothing so beautiful had been heard in our lands, and mère Bline of La Breuille,* who was eighty-seven years old, and who wasn't yet deaf or stupid, went up to the pipers' table, and striking her stick in their midst, told them with the frankness permitted to the old: 'It's all very well for you to curl up your lips and shake your heads, none of you could beat this lad; people will be talking of him in two hundred years from now, and all your names will be forgotten before your carcasses have rotted in the earth.'

Then she went out, saying (and everyone agreed with her) that if the pipers refused to accept Joseph in their brotherhood, they'd be committing the worst possible injustice and revealing the most contemptible envy.

The time for judgement had come, and the pipers went up to the upper room whose door I opened for them in the sole aim of trying to discover something when I listened to them talking on the staircase. The last who came to the door were the woodcutter and Huriel, but then the elder Carnat, who recognized the younger of the two from having seen him at the midsummer dance, asked them what they wanted and what right they had to come to the council.

'The right our credentials give us,' answered père Bastien, 'and if you doubt it, ask us the usual questions and test us in whatever kind of music you choose.'

They were allowed to go in and the door was closed. I tried my best to hear, but they spoke so softly I couldn't be certain of anything except that they accepted the strangers' rights, and that they discussed the examination without making any uproar and without arguing.

Through the slit in the door I saw they were gathering in groups of four or five, and exchanging views softly before taking the vote. But when the moment came for voting, one of the pipers came to see if anyone was eavesdropping, and I was obliged to hide and go downstairs immediately, through fear of being caught out in a transgression that it would be difficult for me to justify without shame, for nothing could have given me the impression that my friends needed my assistance in so calm a meeting.

Downstairs I found my young men and many others I knew sitting at the tables, feasting, and complimenting Joseph. The younger Carnat was sad and alone in a corner, as forgotten and humiliated as possible. The friar was there, too, in the fireplace, asking Mariton and Benoît what was going on in their inn. When he knew what it was all about, he went up to the largest table, where everyone wanted to drink with Joseph and ask him about the land in which he'd learnt his skills.

'Friend Joseph,' said Nicholas, 'we know each other, you and I. I want to compliment you on the applause you've just received in here, and well deserved it was. But let me point out to you that it's as generous as it's wise to console the defeated,

and that if I were in your place I'd go and offer my friendship
to Carnat's son, whom I see over there, looking very sad and
lonely.'

The friar spoke in a whisper that could be heard only by
Joseph and a few others nearby, and I thought he did so as
much because his heart told him to as because Joseph's
mother had asked him to, for she'd have liked to see the
Carnats forget their dislike of Joseph.

Joseph was flattered by the way the friar appealed to his
generosity.

'You're right, Brother Nicholas,' he said, and added in a
louder voice: 'Come, François, why be sulky with your
friends? You didn't play as well as you can, I'm sure of
that, but you'll get your revenge another time, and, what's
more, the judgement hasn't yet been handed down. So
instead of turning your back on us, come and have a drink
with us, and let's be as calm as two oxen yoked to the same
plough.'

Everyone approved of what Joseph had said, and Carnat,
afraid of appearing too envious, accepted his invitation and
came to sit near him. Up until then all was well, but Joseph
couldn't refrain from showing how much more he valued his
own knowledge than that of others, and in behaving politely
towards his rival he assumed protective airs that hurt him all
the more.

'You talk as if you already had your credentials,' said
Carnat, looking pale and haughty, 'but you don't have anything yet. It's not always the one who has the subtlest fingers
and the cleverest inventions that the connoisseurs most acclaim. It's sometimes the person who's best known and most
highly valued in the region, and who therefore promises to be
a good comrade for the other minstrels.'

'Oh, that's just what I expect will happen,' said Joseph. 'I've
been absent a long time, and even if I pride myself that my
behaviour deserves as much admiration as anyone else's, I
know quite well that they'll have recourse to the bad reason
that people don't know me here. Well, that's all one to me,
François! I didn't expect to find a gathering of true musicians here, men capable of judging me, and sufficiently in love
with fine skills to prefer my talent to their interests and those

of their acquaintances. All I hoped for was to get a hearing and be judged in my mother's presence and that of my friends, by healthy ears and reasonable people. Now that's over, I don't give a damn for your moaners of noisy bagpipes! I believe, and God will forgive me for this, that I'd be prouder if they rejected me than if they accepted me.'

The friar remarked gently to Joseph that this was no sensible way to talk. 'You mustn't take exception to judges you've requested of your own free will,' he told him. 'Haughtiness always mars the highest merit.'

'Let him keep his pride,' said young Carnat. 'I'm not envious of the talent he's displayed. He needs a little talent to console himself for his other flaws, because if ever there's a case for saying it, he's the person about whom you can say: "Fine player, finely duped."'

'Whatever do you mean by that?' said Joseph, putting down his glass and looking him straight in the eyes.

'I hardly need tell you,' the other answered. 'Moreover everyone here catches my drift.'

'But I don't catch it, and as I'm the one you're talking to, I'll call you a coward if you're too afraid to explain what you mean.'

'Oh! I can say it to your face, for it isn't anything that's meant to offend you. Perhaps it's no more of a flaw in you to be unlucky in love, than it's a flaw in my character to have been unlucky in music this evening.'

'Oh, come on then!' said one of the girls who happened to be there. 'Leave Josephine alone. She found someone to marry her and it's nobody's business any more.'

'It seems to me,' said another, 'that it wasn't Joseph who was the dupe in that story, so much as the man who's going to accept his handiwork.'

'Who are you talking about?' exclaimed Joseph, as if struck by vertigo. 'Who are you calling Josephine? And what evil chatter are you inflicting on me?'

'Be quiet!' shouted Mariton, red and shaking with fury and grief, as she always was when anyone accused Brulette. 'I wish all your evil tongues could be torn out and nailed to the church door!'

'Lower your voices,' said one of the boys. 'You know quite

well that Mariton won't let anyone say anything against Joey's girl. Beautiful women back each other up, and Mariton isn't yet so old she can't belong to that sisterhood.'

Joseph tried to understand just what he was being accused of and mocked about.

'Tell me what it's all about,' he said to me, dragging at my arm. 'Don't leave me without anything to say or any way of defending myself.'

I was about to get involved in it, although I'd sworn not to get into any argument which didn't affect the woodcutter and Huriel, when François Carnat interrupted me.

'Good lord,' he said to Joseph with a snigger, 'Tiennet can't say anything more than what I wrote to you.'

'Is that what you're talking about?' said Joseph. 'Well, I can swear that you're a liar, and that you wrote and spoke false witness. Never . . .'

'Oh, very well,' said Carnat. 'You could have profited from my letter, and if, as people here generally believe, you are the kid's father, you weren't too stupid to push the ownership on to your friend. He's a very faithful friend, since he's upstairs supporting you in the council. But if, as I think, you came to demand what's yours by right, and were refused, as seems clear from a very funny scene that took place at the castle of Le Chassin and was seen from afar . . .'

'What scene?' asked the friar. 'You better explain yourself, young man, for I may well have been a witness too, and I want to know just how you tell these stories.'

'Have it your own way,' answered Carnat. 'I'll describe the scene as I saw it with my own eyes, without hearing the words that were spoken, but you can give whatever explanation of it you please. Well then, you others, let me tell you that on the last day of the month that's just passed, Joseph, who had got up early to carry a May bouquet to Brulette's door, and having seen there a stout little chap of about two years of age which can only be his own child, no doubt wanted to reclaim him, since he seized him to carry him away, and there ensued a dispute in which his friend, the Bourbonnais woodcutter, the very one who's now upstairs with his father, and who's marrying Brulette this coming Sunday, struck him some fine blows, and then kissed the mother and child; after which

Joseph star-gazer was gently expelled and has never returned. Now that's the finest story I've ever come across. You can arrange it as you like. It still has a child who finds himself fought over by two fathers, and a girl who, instead of giving herself to the first seducer, kicks him away, as someone unworthy or unable to raise the child he has produced.'

Instead of answering this accusation as he had boasted of doing, Brother Nicholas turned towards the chimney, and said something softly, but sharply, to Benoît. Joseph was so stunned to hear such an interpretation of an adventure that, when all was said and done, he couldn't completely explain, that he looked around for someone to help him. As Mariton had gone running out of the room like a madwoman, there was only me left to overturn Carnat. His speech had caused a lot of amazement, and no one thought of standing up for Brulette, against whom most of them still bore a real grudge. I tried to take her part, but Carnat interrupted me at the first words I said.

'Well, as for you, her cousin, no one's accusing you. No one doubts your good faith in all this, even if it's well known that you tried to pull the wool over people's eyes by bringing home a child who'd already been raised in Bourbonnais. But you're so simple you probably didn't see the wood for the trees. Devil take me,' he added, talking to those present, 'if this lad isn't as thick as a plank. He could quite well have acted as godfather to the child, thinking he was baptizing a bell. He'll have gone to Bourbonnais to see his godson, and they'll have convinced him that the child was found among the cabbages. He probably brought him here in his sack, thinking that that evening he could spit-roast a young goat. And he's such a good servant and cousin to the girl that if she wanted to make him believe that fat Charley looks like him, he'd have been delighted to learn it.'

THIRTIETH EVENING

It was in vain that I tried to answer and protest, growing more and more angry; people were more eager to laugh than to listen, and it's always been a great source of amusement for ill-behaved boys to slander a poor girl. They rush in to sully her, knowing they can always go back on their word later if they discover she didn't deserve such treatment.

But in the midst of the uproar caused by all these evil words, a loud voice could suddenly be heard, diminished a little by illness, but still able to drown all the other voices in a noisy inn. It was the tavern-keeper's voice, long used to governing the storms aroused by wine, and the din of people making merry.

'Hold your tongues and listen to me, or, even if it means closing the inn forever, I'll make all of you leave on the spot. Try to keep quiet about a good lass whom you decry only because you found her too well behaved. As for the true parents of the child who's provoked so many tales, you can now tell them at last to their faces the criticisms you have of their behaviour, for they stand before you. Yes,' he said, embracing the weeping Mariton, who held Charley in her arms, 'this is the mother of my son and heir, and here is my son, whom I have recognized through my marriage to this fine woman. If you ask me the exact date, I'll tell you to keep your nose out of other people's business, but if anyone has a good reason for asking the question, I could show documents that demonstrate I've always accepted paternity of this child, and that, before he was born, his mother was already my legal wife, even though we kept the matter secret.'

There was a long, astonished silence, and Joseph, who'd leapt to his feet at the first words, stood stock-still as if turned to stone. The monk, seeing doubt, shame, and anger in his eyes, thought it proper to give a few additional explanations. He told us that Benoît had been prevented from making his marriage public by the opposition of a relative, from whom he was to inherit and who had lent him money for his business, a man who could have ruined him by demanding that the money be repaid. And as Mariton feared her good name would be smirched, and had been especially concerned for her son Joseph's sake, she'd hidden Charley's birth, and put him in the care of a wet-nurse at Sainte Sévère. After a year, however, she found him so badly trained that she'd begged Brulette to take charge of him, knowing that no one else would look after him so well. She hadn't foreseen that any harm could come to the reputation of that beautiful lass, and when she learnt of it, she'd wanted to take the child back, but Benoît's illness had prevented her from doing so, and Brulette, too, had grown so fond of Charley that she'd been unwilling to give him up.

'Yes, yes,' said Mariton firmly, 'the poor soul! She really showed how courageous her friendship could be! "You have enough to worry about as it is," she said to me, "for if you lose your husband, your marriage may then be attacked by his family. He is too ill for you to want him to become embroiled in all the arguments that would ensue if you were to declare your marriage now. Everything will work out perfectly, if God allows you the grace of restoring him to health."'

'And if I did recover,' said Benoît, 'it's thanks to the care of this worthy woman, who is my wife, and to the kindness of the young girl in question, who patiently exposed herself to criticism and insults, rather than push me into ruin by revealing our secrets. But here's another faithful friend,' he added, pointing to the friar, 'a man of thought, of action, and of frank speech, who was my schoolmate, in the days when I was brought up at Montluçon. He's the one who went in search of my old devil of an uncle, and who eventually, no later than this very morning, got him to agree to my marriage with my fine barmaid. And when he promised to leave me his money and the inheritance, he learnt that the priest had already passed this way, and he was shown plump Charley, whom he found to be a fine lad and very like his sire.'

Benoît's pleasure made everyone gay again, and all present were struck by a resemblance that no one had noticed up until then, I no more than anyone else.

'And so, Joseph,' added the innkeeper, 'you can and should love and respect your mother as I love and respect her. I take my oath here that she's the bravest and most helpful Christian woman you could wish to have at your side when you're ill. And I swear I never hesitated for a moment in my desire to declare sooner or later what I've declared today. We're in good shape where the business is concerned, praise be to God, and as I've sworn to her and before God that I'll replace the father you lost. If you're willing to stay with us, I'll make you a partner in the business and give you a good share of the profits. So, you don't need to throw yourself into bagpipe-playing, since your mother sees problems in it for you and worries for herself. Your plan was to protect her. That's my affair now, and I'm willing to protect you too. Will you listen to us, now, and give up that damned music? Won't you stay in your own land and live with your family? Will you blush to have an honest innkeeper as stepfather?'

'You are my stepfather, there's no doubt about that,' said Joseph, without showing either joy or sorrow, but staying rather coldly on the defensive. 'You're an honest man, I know, and I can see you're rich: if my mother is happy with you . . .'

'Indeed I am, Joseph! The happiest woman in the world, especially today!' exclaimed Mariton, kissing him, 'for I hope you'll never leave me again.'

'You're mistaken there, mother,' said Joseph. 'You don't need me any more, and you're happy. All's well. You were the only duty that bound me to this region, you were the only person left that I could love, since Brulette, and I want every-one to hear this from my own mouth, never felt anything for me but the affection of a sister for her brother. Now I'm free to follow my destiny, which is not a kindly one, but which is too clearly set out for me not to prefer it to all the money the business can bring in, and all the comfort a family can pro-vide. Farewell then, mother! God repay those who succour you; as for me, I no longer need anything, neither a position in this region, nor credentials granted me by ignorant people who have nothing but bad intentions where I'm concerned. I have intentions of my own. My bagpipes will go everywhere with me, and any way of earning a living will suit me, since I know that, wherever I go, I'll be easily recognized merely by playing my music.'

As he was saying this, the door to the stairs opened and the whole assemblage of pipers returned in silence. Père Carnat called for the attention of those present, and in a joyous and resolute tone that astonished everyone said: 'My son François Carnat, after examination of your talents and discussion of your rights, you have been declared too much of a novice to receive your credentials. You are therefore enjoined to study a little more without losing heart, merely in order to present yourself later at an examination that may be more favourable for you. And you, Joseph Picot, from the town of Nohant, the council of local master pipers informs you that, as a result of your unparalleled talent, you are received unanimously as a master piper of the highest class.'

'Well,' Joseph replied, apparently indifferent to this fine victory and the approval that was given to it by all present, 'since that's the way things have worked out, I accept, even though, as I'd hardly expected it, I attached little importance to it.'

No one approved of Joseph's arrogance, and père Carnat was quick to say, in a manner in which I detected a great deal of hidden malice: 'It would seem, Joseph, that you want to have the honour and the rank, but that your intention is not to take your place among the local minstrels?'

'I've no idea at this stage,' said Joseph, out of sheer bravado, assuredly, and so as not to please his judges too quickly. 'I'll give it some thought.'

'It's my belief,' the younger Carnat said to his father, 'that he already has thought about it and that he won't have the courage to take it further.'

'The courage?' asked Joseph swiftly. 'And what courage do I need, may I ask?'

Then the senior piper, old Paillous from Verneuil,* said to Joseph: 'You're not unaware, young man, that it's not merely a question of playing an instrument if you want to be received in our brotherhood. There's a musical catechism you must know and on which you'll be questioned, if, that is, you feel knowledgeable enough and bold enough to answer. And there are further tasks to be performed. If you're not unwilling, you must decide within the hour and the whole matter must be over by tomorrow morning.'

'I understand,' said Joseph. 'There are the trade secrets, the conditions, and the trials. These are really stupid, as far as I can see, and music plays no part in them, for I defy you to answer any musical question I might put to you. So the questions you claim to ask me can hardly touch on a subject with which you are as familiar as frogs in a pond. They'll merely be old wives' riddles.'

'If that's how you're going to take it,' said Renet, the piper from Mers,* 'we're willing to let you believe you're a great sage and we're a herd of donkeys. Fine! Keep your secrets, we'll keep ours. We're in no hurry to tell them to someone who holds them in such contempt. But in that case, just you remember this: here are your master piper's credentials, delivered to you by our hands, and they're full and complete, according to these Bourbonnais pipers, who are your friends and who wrote them and signed them with us. You're free to exercise your talents where they're needed or where you can; but you're forbidden to try to use them within the parishes we service, numbering some one hundred and fifty according to the way in which they've been divided among us. The list of these will be given to you. If you break that command, we're obliged to warn you that you won't be suffered to remain, regardless of your own wishes, and that it'll be at your own risk.'

Here Mariton spoke up: 'You've no need to threaten him,' she said. 'You can leave him to his own devices, for all he wants to do is play the pipes without trying to make any money from it. He has no need to, thank the Lord, and, moreover, his lungs aren't strong enough for him to assume the profession of a minstrel. Come on Joseph, thank them for the honour they've paid you and don't elbow in on their financial interests. Let's make it a convention that's quickly concluded, and my good husband here will pay the costs with a good hogshead of either Issoudon wine or Sancerre wine, as the company wishes.'

'That's all very well and good,' said Carnat. 'We're willing to let the matter stop there. That would be the best solution for your lad, for you must be neither stupid nor cowardly if you're to get involved in the trials, and it's my opinion that the poor boy isn't up to attempting them.'

'That's what we'll find out!' said Joseph, falling into the trap, despite the warnings the woodcutter was whispering to him. 'I demand the trials, and as you have no right to refuse me, after you've given me my credentials, I claim that I'll be a minstrel if I so choose, or, at the very least, prove to you that I won't be prevented by any one of you.'

'Granted!' said the senior piper, revealing, like Carnat and several others, the evil joy they took in it. 'We'll go and prepare the feast for your reception, friend Joseph; but remember, there's no going back on your word, now, and that you'll be considered a paper tiger and a braggart if you change your mind.'

'Go on then!' said Joseph, with much aplomb.

'We'll expect you,' Carnat murmured in his ear, 'at the first stroke of midnight.'

'Where?' said Joseph, still with aplomb.

'At the cemetery gate,' replied the senior piper very softly. Without accepting Benoît's wine or listening to his wife's protests, they all went off together, warning that anyone who followed or spied on their mysteries would rue the day.

The woodcutter and Huriel went with them, without saying another word to Joseph. I could see from their behaviour that, if they opposed the evil the other pipers wished to perpetrate against him, they nevertheless considered it their sacred duty not to give him any warnings nor to betray in any regard the secret of the brotherhood.

Despite the threats that had been made, I wasn't in the least put off following them at a distance without taking any precautions other than going along the same path, my hands in my pockets and a tune on my lips, as if I didn't have the slightest interest in their affairs. I knew perfectly well they wouldn't let me come close enough to hear what plots they were hatching, but I wanted to see where they planned to set their ambush, so later on I could find a means of coming closer without being spotted.

With that in mind, I'd signalled to Léonard to keep the others at the inn, until I came back to tell them what to do; but my pursuit didn't take long. The inn was on the road that goes down to the river, the one that today is the post road to Issoudun. In those days, it was a little, twisty street with poor paving, lined with old houses with pointed gables and stone braces. The last of these houses was demolished last year. From the river, which ran beside the wall of the Crowned Ox,

the road shot uphill, steep as an arrow, to the square which
was, then as now, that long bumpy street bordered with trees,
on the left-hand side of which are very old houses, and on the
right a great ditch, which at that time was full of water, and
the large wall of the castle, which in those days was still intact.
At the end of the square stands the church, and two little paths
head off, one to the curate's house, the other alongside the
cemetery. It was this path the pipers chose. They were a good
stone's throw ahead of me, which gave them time to follow
the path along the cemetery and head out into the countryside,
by the gateway in the English Tower, unless they decided to
stop there, which would hardly have been comfortable, for the
path, bordered on the right by the castle's ditch, and on the
left by the cemetery mound, had room for only one person at
a time.

I waited long enough for them to reach the gateway, then I
turned the corner by the castle, following an arcade which in
those days afforded passage to pedestrians beneath a gallery
that had allowed the castle lords to reach the parish church.

I was alone on the path where, after sunset, no Christian
ever ventured, both because it bordered the cemetery and
because the north side of the castle had a bad reputation.
There was talk of goodness knows how many people drowned
in the ditch in the time of the war against the English, and
people even swore they'd heard the cockatrice crow there in
times of epidemics.

You know that the cockatrice is a kind of lizard which
sometimes seems as small as your little finger, and sometimes
as large as an ox some five or six yards long. This animal,
which I've never seen and whose existence I wouldn't swear
to, is reputed to vomit a venom that poisons the air and brings
the plague.

Even though I didn't really believe in it, I wasn't particularly
happy in that passage where almost all the light was blocked
out by the great wall of the castle and the large trees in the
cemetery. I walked quickly, looking neither right nor left, and
came out at the English gateway, of which today not a stone
remains.

But there, although it was a fine night and the moon had
risen, I could see neither close at hand nor in the distance any

trace of the eighteen people I'd been following. I searched in all the neighbourhood and even in père Bégneux's house, which was the only dwelling they could possibly have entered. Everyone there was sound asleep, and neither along the paths nor in the open country was there any sound or trace or glimpse of a living soul.

I therefore guessed that the miscreant band had gone into the cemetery to weave some evil spell, and although I hadn't the slightest desire to do so, but was resolved to risk everything for Thérence's kith and kin, I went back through the gateway and returned to that accursed little English street, walking softly, moving close to the mound, whose tombs I all but touched, and straining my ears for the slightest sound I could surprise.

I could hear the screech owl complaining in the keep, and the snakes hissing in the black water of the ditch, but that was all. The dead were sleeping under the earth as calmly as the living in their beds. I took courage, and climbed up on to the mound so that I could look into the burial plot. Everything was in order, and of my pipers I found no more trace than if they'd never passed that way.

I walked around the castle. It was completely shut, and as it was close to ten o'clock, masters and servants were dead to the world.

Then I went back to the Crowned Ox, unable to imagine what had happened to the pipers, but wanting to hide my friends along the English path, since from there we would see quite well whatever happened to Joseph, when the time came for his meeting at the cemetery gate.

I found them on the bridge, wondering whether to return home, and saying they no longer saw any danger for the Huriels, since they'd come to such a good agreement with the others in the council. As far as Joseph was concerned, they couldn't care less, and tried to dissuade me from getting involved. I pointed out to them that as far as I was concerned it would be in the upcoming trials that the danger lay for all three of them, since the ill will of the pipers was so obvious, and since the Huriels would go to Joseph's aid exactly as they'd planned to that morning.

'Are you already fed up with what we decided?' I asked

them. 'Is it because there are only eight of us against sixteen? Don't you feel there's heart enough in every one of you for two of them?'

'Who exactly are you including?' Léonard asked me. 'Do you think the woodcutter and his son will join us to fight their colleagues?'

'I got my sums wrong,' I answered. 'There are nine of us. Joseph won't put up with too much rough treatment, and given that the two Huriels have taken up arms, it seems to me perfectly certain that they've done so in order to defend themselves, should it turn out that they're unable to make the others listen to them.'

'It's not that,' said Léonard. 'Even if there were only six of us, and twenty against us, we'd still go in without counting them. But there's something else that gives us less pleasure than the battle. We've just been talking about it in the tavern, with everyone telling their own story. The friar accused those practices of being impious and abominable; Mariton was filled with a terror that everyone there felt too, and even though Joseph laughed at it all, we can't be certain there isn't some element of truth in it. There was talk of candidates nailed into a coffin, of them being thrown into burning fireplaces, and crosses of red-hot iron they were made to embrace. Those things seem to me a bit hard to believe, but if I were sure that was all there was to it, I'd be quite happy to go and punish people wicked enough to force a poor fellow to do them. Unfortunately . . .'

'Come now,' I said to him, 'I can see you let yourselves be frightened. What else is there? Tell me everything, so we can laugh it off and protect ourselves.'

'The thing is,' said one of the boys, seeing that Léonard was too ashamed to confess, 'that we saw the devil in person and none of us wants to make his acquaintance.'

'Oh! Really!' I answered, realizing they were all relieved the confession had been made, and were all about to tell the same tale. 'So it's all about Lucifer himself is it? Well and good! I'm too stout a Christian to fear him, I'll put my soul in God's hands, and I promise you that all on my own I'll seize this enemy of humankind by the hair, every bit as resolutely as I'd seize a he-goat by the beard. He's been harming those who fear him for long enough by now, and it strikes me that if a good lad polled his head for him he'd lose half his power for evil, and that would at least be something we'd gained.'

'Heavens above!' said Léonard, ashamed of his fear. 'If that's the way you take it, I won't back out, and if you break his horns for him, I want at the very least to try and tear off his tail. They say it's a good one, and we'll see if it's made of gold or hemp.'

There's no better remedy for fear than laughter, but I won't hide from you the fact that when I talked about the matter in that way I wasn't the slightest bit eager to measure myself with the *Georgeon*, as he's called in our region. To tell the truth, I was probably every bit as scared as the others, but for Thérence's sake, I'd have thrown myself into the devil's very throat. I'd given her my word, and the good Lord himself wouldn't have turned me aside from my plan.

But that's not well put. The good Lord, on the contrary, gave me strength and faith, and the more worried I felt that night, the more I thought of Him and sought His aid.

When our other friends saw us so resolute they decided to follow us. Just to make matters even more sure, I returned to the inn, counting on finding other friends there who, without knowing what it was all about, would follow us as if it were a party and would help us if necessary; but it was late, and at the Crowned Ox there was only Benoît supping with the friar, Mariton praying, and Joseph, who'd thrown himself on a bed and was sleeping, I must say, with a tranquillity that made us ashamed of our misgivings.

'I've only one hope,' said Mariton as she rose from her prayers, 'and that's that he'll let the hour go past and won't wake up until tomorrow morning.'

'That's women for you!' said Benoît with a laugh. 'They think you can live comfortably with your shame. But as for me, I've promised the boy I'll wake him before midnight and I won't fail him.'

'Ah, you don't love him!' exclaimed his mother. 'We'll see if you'll push our Charley into danger when his turn comes.'

'You don't know what you're talking about, wife,' said the

innkeeper. 'Go and sleep with the child. As for me, I tell you I won't let your boy oversleep. I don't want him to reproach me for having led to his dishonour.'

'Moreover,' said the monk, 'what danger are you imagining there is in the follies they're going to commit? I tell you, you're dreaming, my good woman. The devil doesn't eat people, God wouldn't allow it, and you haven't brought your son up so badly that you're afraid he'll damn himself for the sake of music, have you? I'll say again that the pipers' evil practices are, after all, nothing more than clear water, impious jokes, things intelligent people can easily protect themselves against, and all Joseph needs to do is mock the demons they tell him about, and that will put them all to flight. There's no need for any other kind of exorcism, and I can assure you that I wouldn't want to waste one drop of holy water over the devil they'll put on show tonight.'

The friar's words put fresh heart into my friends.

'If it's all a farce,' they said, 'we'll throw ourselves into it and beat the evil spirit into a pulp. But why don't you tell Benoît what you plan to do? He might well help us.'

'To tell you the truth,' I answered, 'I'm not at all sure about that. He has the reputation of being a very brave man, but you never know what the truth is about couples, especially when there are children from an earlier marriage. Stepfathers don't always look on them with a kindly eye, and Joseph wasn't particularly friendly with him tonight. Let's go without breathing a word, that'd be the best solution, since it's not long before we have to be ready.'

Taking the path to the church, silently and in single file, we went and posted ourselves in English street. The moon was so low that when we lay down on the mound we could remain hidden even if someone passed very close to us. My friends, who were strangers to this country, didn't feel the same repugnance for this spot that I'd felt at first, and I could leave them there in order to go forward and hide myself in the cemetery, close enough to the door to see who came in, and close enough to them to warn them if it should prove necessary.

I waited for a fairly long time, and it seemed all the longer, as time never passes swiftly in the cheerless company of the dead. At last the church clock struck midnight, and I saw a man's head appear round the little wall that bounded the cemetery, right next to the gate. A good quarter of an hour dragged past without my seeing anyone or hearing anything apart from that man who, bored with waiting, began to whistle a Bourbonnais tune, which revealed to me that it was Joseph, who was no doubt disappointing his enemies' hopes in feeling no fear in the proximity of the dead.

Finally, another man, who was clinging to the inside of the doorway, and whom I hadn't seen because my view was blocked by a big box tree, stuck his head swiftly over the little wall as if to catch Joseph by surprise, but Joseph didn't move at all and merely said to him with a laugh: 'Well, père Carnat, you're late, and had you delayed much longer I'd have fallen asleep waiting for you. Will you open the door for me, or do I have to enter through the gap in the nettle garden?'

'No,' said old Carnat, 'that would annoy the priest, and men of the church must not be openly flouted. I'll come to you.'

He stepped over the wall and told Joseph he must let his head and arms be covered with a very thick sack, and follow without resisting in any way.

'Go ahead,' said Joseph, in a tone of mockery and almost of scorn.

I followed him with my eyes as he went over the wall, and I saw them go into the little path known as the English way. I cut straight across to the mound where my young friends were hiding, but could find only four of them. The youngest one had softly taken to his heels without a word, and I wasn't entirely sure the others wouldn't follow his lead, for they'd all found the time slow in passing, and they told me they'd heard strange noises that seemed to them to come from under the earth.

We soon saw Joseph approaching, walking blindfolded and

led by Carnat. They came towards us, but left the path twenty yards or so before reaching us. Carnat made Joseph go down to the edge of the ditch, and we thought he intended to drown him. We, therefore, had just leapt to our feet ready to prevent such treachery, when we saw both of them go into the water, which was not deep at that point, and reach a low arcade at the foot of the great wall of the castle against which the ditch water lapped. They went in, thus showing me where the others had disappeared to, when I'd so painstakingly sought them out.

It was important for us to do the same as them, and that struck me as no easy matter, for I had a great deal of difficulty persuading my companions. They'd heard tell that the castle foundations stretched out under the countryside as far as Déols, some nine leagues off, and that anyone who didn't know the route could be lost forever.

I was forced to tell them that I knew the way perfectly well, even though I'd never set foot there, and hadn't the slightest idea whether or not I'd find an entire underground town, as some claimed was the case.

I went first, unable even to see where I was putting my feet, feeling the walls, which created a very narrow passage, and where you hardly needed to raise your head to reach the ceiling.

We'd been proceeding in this way for some time when there came from below us such a din that you'd have thought forty thunderbolts were rolling through the devil's caves. It was so strange and terrifying a noise that I stopped dead to try and understand what it was all about, and then walked forward quickly, unwilling to allow my ardour to be damped by imagining some devilry, and telling my friends to follow me. But the noise was too loud for them to hear my words. Thinking they were on my heels, I went even further in until, not hearing anything any more, I turned around to ask if they were there, and received no reply.

As I didn't want to shout, I took four or five more steps back than I'd taken forward. I stretched out my hands, calling softly; but it was a case of farewell friends, they'd left me completely alone.

I thought that as I wasn't far from the entrance I'd catch up with them either inside or outside, so I walked along quickly and surely, and went back through the arcade by which I'd entered. I looked and searched up and down the English way, but what had happened to the pipers seemed to have happened to my friends: the earth seemed to have swallowed them up.

For a moment I had a kind of fever during which I thought I'd have to abandon everything or go back into those accursed cellars all alone at the risk of falling into the ambushes and terrors that had been laid for Joseph. But then I asked myself whether, if he alone had been involved, I would have withdrawn tranquilly from the dangers that faced him. My Christian soul told me that I would not, and I asked my heart if my love for Thérence was not as strong within it as the love of my neighbour was firm in my conscience, and the answer I received sent me back resolutely through the black and muddy arcade, and running through the cellars, not as gaily, but certainly as swiftly, as if I'd been going to my own wedding.

As I kept feeling my way along I found on my right the entrance to another gallery that I hadn't found the first time, when I'd been feeling along the left-hand side, and I told myself that my friends, on their way out, must have come across it and lost their way there, thinking they were going towards the exit. I went in too, for there was no proof that my first track was the one that would bring me to where the pipers had gone.

I didn't find my friends there, but as for the pipers, I hadn't taken twenty-five steps when I heard their din much nearer at hand than I had the first time, and soon a wavering light showed me that I was heading for a great round cavern which had three or four black exits, each looking like the throat of hell.

I was amazed to find I could see almost clearly in a vaulted place where there was no source of light, and, bending over, I discovered that this light came up from below, through the floor on which I was walking. I also observed that this floor swelled into a vault under my feet, and, fearing that it might not be solid, I didn't venture in the middle but followed by the wall. There I saw several crevices I could easily gaze through by lying flat on the floor. In this way I could see everything that was going on in another round cavern situated immediately below the one in which I happened to be.

It was, as I learnt later, a former hiding place, situated next to that of the great dungeon, whose mouth could still be seen not thirty years ago from the high rooms within the castle. I guessed this must be the case from the remains of bones that had been arranged into a kind of scarecrow at the back of the wall, with resin candles planted in the skulls. Joseph was there on his own, eyes free of their blindfold, arms crossed, as calm as I was anxious. He seemed to be listening scornfully to the pandemonium of eighteen bagpipes all brawling together and prolonging the same note in a kind of roar. This madmen's music came from the next-door cavern where the pipers were hiding and where, no doubt, they knew that a strange echo increased the resonance thirty-fold. As for me, who knew nothing about it, and who only worked it all out on reflection, I first thought that the pipers of Berry, Auvergne, and Bourbonnais must all be gathered together there.

When they were tired of making their instruments growl, they began to howl and miaow in sounds that, repeated by the echoes, appeared to be those of a great crowd of men and wild animals of every kind. But to all that, Joseph, who was truly a man whose like I've rarely seen among our peasants, went on shrugging his shoulders and yawning as if bored by a game played out by idiots.

His courage was infectious and I began to feel like laughing at the comedy when a little noise made me turn my head. Just behind me, at the entrance to the gallery by which I'd entered, my eyes fell on a figure that turned my blood to ice.

He was like a lord of by-gone days, with an iron breast-plate, a well-sharpened pike, and leather garments of a kind no longer seen. But the most terrifying thing about him was his face, which offered the true image of a skull.

I recovered a little, telling myself that it must be a disguise assumed by one of the band to test Joseph, but the more I thought about it, the more I realized my own danger, since if he was one of them, then, when he found me eavesdropping he would surely punish me.

But although he could see me just as well as I could see him, he didn't move but stayed stock-still like a ghost, half in the shadow, half in the light which came from below, and because the light came and went according to whether it was moved or not, there were moments when I could no longer make him out, and thought I'd merely imagined him, but suddenly, he reappeared perfectly clearly except for his legs, which still remained in the shadow behind a kind of stairway, so it seemed to me that he was floating like a figure in the clouds.

I don't know how many minutes I spent tormenting myself with this vision, having completely forgotten to watch Joseph, and afraid that I was going mad as a result of taking on more than I was able to do. I remembered that in one of the castle rooms, I'd seen an old painting that seemed to be the portrait of an unaccommodating old warrior whom the local lord, his very own brother, had ordered to be thrown into the prison. The iron and leather gear I had before my eyes, worn as it was by a dried-up skeleton, was so like the painted image, that the idea came to me quite naturally that this was a soul in fury and pain, who'd come to look at the desecration of his tomb, and who might well find a way of showing his displeasure.

What made this calculation seem reasonable was that this soul said nothing to me, and seemed to take no note of me, knowing, perhaps, that in being there I had no ill intentions as far as his poor carcass was concerned.

However, a noise which was different from the others tore my eyes away from this spell that had been binding them. I looked into the cellar Joseph was in, and there I saw something very strange and very ugly.

Joseph was still standing on his feet looking self-assured, facing an abominable creature, clad in a dog's skin and wearing horns on his hairy head, with a red face, claws, and a tail. He was leaping about and grimacing like one possessed. This was a horrible sight, and yet I wasn't duped by it for long, because, however much he changed his voice, it seemed to me that I could recognize in it that of Doré-Fratin, the Pouligny piper,* one of the strongest men of the area, and a man who loved a fight.

'It's all very well for you to say,' he was remarking to Joseph, 'that you laugh at me and have no fear of hell, I'm still the king of the musicians, and without my permission you won't play your pipes until you've sold me your soul.'

Joseph answered him: 'Whatever would a devil as stupid as you are do with a musician's soul? He'd have no way of using it.'

'Watch your tongue!' the other answered. 'Don't you know that here you've either got to give yourself to the devil or prove yourself stronger than him?'

'Yes, of course,' answered Joseph, 'I know the saying: you must kill the devil or he'll kill you.'

On that word, I saw Huriel and his father come out from a side vault and approach the devil as if to talk to him, but they were held back by other pipers, who suddenly appeared all around him; and père Carnat addressed Joseph, saying: 'It's obvious you've no fear of magic spells and we'll judge you to have passed that test, if you're willing to accept the normal practice of fighting the devil as proof of your refusal to submit to him.'

'If the devil is willing to accept a drubbing, give me permission straight away. We'll see if his hide is harder than mine. What weapons are used?'

'Nothing but your fists,' said Carnat.

'You'll play fair, I hope?' asked the woodcutter.

Joseph didn't take time to make sure of that point, but, enraged by the way he was being held up to ridicule, he leapt at the devil, tore off his headgear, and seized him so resolutely around the body that he threw him to the ground and fell upon him.

Yet he stood up again immediately, and it seemed to me that he cried out in surprise and pain, but all the pipes began to play, except those of Huriel and his father, who pretended to play, and watched the struggle with looks of doubt and disquiet.

Meanwhile Joseph rolled the devil over and seemed to be the stronger of the two, but it struck me he was in a fury that didn't seem at all natural. That made me fear he might put himself in the wrong by using too much violence. The pipers seemed to be helping him in this, for instead of going to their comrade's aid, when he'd been thrown down three times, they ran around the contest, playing continuously and stamping to encourage him to keep at it.

Suddenly the woodcutter separated the combatants, by striking the devil's hands with a stick and threatening to do better the second time if he wasn't obeyed. Huriel ran to his side, raising his stick as well, and all the others stopped playing and turning, so that all was motionless and quiet.

It was then that I saw that Joseph, overcome by pain, was wiping his torn hands and his face, which were covered with blood. If Huriel hadn't caught him in his arms he would have fallen unconscious, whereas Doré-Fratin threw down his costume, puffing with the heat of battle, and merely wiped away with a sneer the sweat of a little weariness.

'What does this mean?' asked Carnat coming up to the woodcutter with a threatening gesture. 'With what right do you impede the trial?'

'I impede it at my own risk and to your shame,' answered the woodcutter. 'I'm no false brother and you are evil masters, as treacherous as you are immoral. I greatly suspected that you were deceiving us to cause suffering and perhaps serious injury to this young man! You hate him because you feel he'll be preferred to you, and that wherever he's heard, no one will want to listen to you again. You didn't dare refuse him his credentials, because everyone would have condemned you for such a flagrant injustice, but, to put him off practising in parishes that you've usurped, you're making the trials so dangerous and so difficult that none of you could have supported them for any length of time.'

'I haven't the slightest idea what you mean!' answered the senior piper, old Pailloux of Verneuil, 'and the accusations you're making in front of the candidate are unparalleled in their insolence. We don't know how candidates are received in your region, but here, we're following our normal practices, and we'll permit no one to criticize them.'

'I for my part will criticize them,' said Huriel, who was still stanching Joseph's blood with his handkerchief, and, having leant him against his knee, was helping him recover. 'Unable and unwilling to accuse you outside these walls because of the oath we've taken, I'll at least tell you, to your faces, that you're torturers. In our region, we fight the devil purely for fun, and take care no one is harmed. Here you choose the strongest among you, and you place on him hidden weapons with which he tries to gouge out eyes and pierce veins. Look! This young man is exhausted and, in the rage that your evil deeds threw him into, he'd have let himself be killed if we hadn't stopped him. What would you have done then? Would you have thrown him into that pit of oblivion, where so many other poor wretches have perished, wretches whose bones should stand up to accuse you of being as evil as your former lords?'

Huriel's words reminded me of the apparition I'd forgotten, and I turned around to see if this invocation would summon it to Huriel's side. I couldn't see it any more and decided to find the way to the lower cellar, where I felt more and more strongly that I could be useful to my friends.

I found the stairway immediately and went down to the entrance, where I didn't even bother to hide, for the quarrelling and confusion there were so great they didn't leave anyone free to pay the slightest attention to me.

The woodcutter had picked up the animal-skin headgear, and showed how it was full of sharp points like the instrument used to skin oxen, and the mittens this false devil wore had in their palms stout nails firmly fixed with their points uppermost. The others were furious to find themselves criticized in Joseph's presence. 'What a lot of fuss for a few scratches!' Carnat remarked. 'Isn't it fitting for the devil to have claws? And that innocent who attacked him with so little prudence, doesn't he know that you can't play with him without getting your nose scratched a little? Come now, don't pity him so much, it's nothing. And since he's had enough, let him withdraw and confess he lacks the strength to amuse himself with us. Let him admit there's no way he can be a member of our company.'

'I will be a member!' said Joseph, who tore himself from Huriel's arms, revealing his blood-stained chest and his torn shirt. 'I shall be a member despite you all! I demand that the battle recommence. One or other of us must remain behind here.'

'I oppose it,' said the woodcutter. 'I command that this young man be declared the winner, or I swear that I will bring into this land a band of pipers who will teach you how to behave, and will establish justice once again.'

'You?' asked Fratin, drawing a kind of pike from his belt. 'You can do so, but not without bearing our marks, just so people will believe your report.'

The woodcutter and Huriel took up defensive positions. Joseph flung himself on Fratin to tear his pike from his hands, and with a bound I'd joined them; but before we could exchange any blows the figure that had so disturbed me appeared on the threshold of the prison, held out his pike, and approached us with a step that was quite enough to terrify all those with evil intentions. As we stopped, frozen with dread and astonishment, a plaintive voice could be heard in the depths of the prison reciting the mass for the dead.

That was all enough to terrify the brotherhood, and when one of the pipers had cried out, 'The dead! The dead have risen!', all took to their heels, pell-mell, shouting, and shoving their way through all the exits, except for the one that led to the prison, in which there appeared another figure covered with a shroud, chanting in the most lamentable way you could possibly imagine. The result was that in a minute we were abandoned by our enemies. Then the warrior threw off his helmet, and showed us the delighted face of Benoît, while the friar, unwinding his shroud, held his sides with laughter.

'Lord forgive this mascarade!' he said. 'But I did it with the best of intentions and it seemed to me that those rascals deserved a good lesson to teach them not to mock the devil, who scares them more than the people in front of whom they themselves act the devil.'

'I was sure,' said Benoît, 'that once they'd set eyes on our little play they'd start trembling right in the middle of their own.' But then he spotted Joseph's injuries, and showed so much concern and worry about him that this, together with the aid he'd given him, proved to me quite clearly the friendship he felt for Joseph, and the kindness of his heart, about which I'd had my doubts.

While we were making sure that Joseph wasn't too gravely

wounded, the friar told us how the castle wine-servant had told him he was in the habit of allowing the pipers and other joyful bands to carry out their ceremonies in the dungeons. Those in which we found ourselves were sufficiently remote from the buildings inhabited by the dowager lady of Saint Chartier for her not to hear the noise, and in any case, she would only have laughed at it, for no one imagined that any evil could be mixed up in it. But Benoît, who suspected there were some evil intentions, had asked the same servant to provide him with a disguise and the keys to the dungeons, and that was how he came to be there in time to avert danger.

'Well,' said the woodcutter, 'thanks for your help. But I'm sorry the idea came to you, for those men are quite capable of accusing me of having requested your presence and thus of having betrayed the secrets of my trade. Take my advice, and let's all leave silently, and let them believe they really did see ghosts.'

'All the more so,' said Benoît, 'in that their hostility could take their trade away from me, and that's no small matter. I just hope they didn't recognize Tiennet. By the way, how the devil does Tiennet come to be here?'

'Didn't you bring him?' asked Huriel.

'No indeed!' I replied. 'I came on my own account because of all the tales I heard about this devilish behaviour. I was curious to see it, but I can swear to you that their minds were too disturbed and their eyes too alarmed to let them recognize me.'

We were about to leave when we heard the sound of angry voices and muffled din, as if a quarrel had broken out.

'Great heavens!' said the friar. 'Now what's up? It looks as if they're returning and we haven't yet finished with them. Quickly, back into our disguises!'

'Don't worry,' said Benoît, listening. 'I see what's happened. On my way in here through the castle cellars, I came across four or five bold lads, one of whom I knew. It was Léonard, your Bourbonnais workman, Bastien. Those boys probably also came through curiosity, but they'd wandered astray in the cellars and weren't in the best of moods. I gave them my lantern and told them to wait for me. They must have been discovered by the pipers as they fled, and they're no doubt amusing themselves by chasing them.'

'They might well be the hares in that chase,' said Huriel, 'if there aren't enough of them. Let's go and see!'

We were about to go when the footsteps and the noise came closer, and we saw Carnat, Doré-Fratin, and a group of eight others who, indeed, had exchanged a few good blows with my friends, and had recovered from their cowardice when they realized they'd been dealing with men who really were alive. They'd come back to attack us, heaping accusations of betrayal on Huriel, and saying he'd led them into an ambush. The woodcutter defended himself against these attacks, and the friar attempted to bring peace by accepting responsibility for everything, and reprimanding them for their evil behaviour, but they felt they had the upper hand because at every moment others arrived to support them, and when they saw they were more or less at full strength, they raised the tone and began to exchange threats for mere insults, and then to move from threats to blows. Feeling there was no way of avoiding an encounter—all the more so in that they'd drunk a great deal of brandy during the trials and were no longer in their right minds—we took up defensive positions, standing close to one another and facing the enemy in all directions, as cattle stand when a pack of wolves attacks them in their pasture. The friar had lost his high moral tone and his Latin, and he also lost his patience, for he seized hold of a bagpipe drone that had fallen in the mêlée, and used it as well as a man could to protect his skin.

Unfortunately, Joseph had been weakened by the loss of blood, and Huriel, who'd never recovered from the death of Malzac, was afraid of causing more harm than he received. Concentrating on protecting his father, who went at it like a lion, he placed himself in great danger. Benoît fought very well for a man who'd just recovered from illness, but when all was said and done, we were only six against fifteen or sixteen, and when blood began to flow, anger swelled, and I could see that men were unsheathing their knives. I only had time to throw myself in front of the woodcutter, who, refusing to draw any sharp weapon, was the target of the greatest anger.

I received a blow to the arm which I hardly felt but which nevertheless made it hard for me to continue. I felt we were losing the battle, when, by a stroke of luck, my four friends, who'd decided to come and see what was causing all the pandemonium, brought us sufficient aid to put to flight for the second and final time that night our exhausted enemies, who were attacked from behind and had no idea whether more fighters might not arrive.

I saw that victory was ours and that none of our friends was gravely injured. Suddenly realizing that I myself had been too seriously wounded for any one man, I fell like a sack of potatoes and neither knew nor felt anything else.

THIRTY-SECOND EVENING

When I regained consciousness, I found myself lying in the same bed as Joseph, and it took me not a little trouble to gather my wits again. At last I realized I was in Benoît's own room, that the bed was good, the sheets very white, and that my arm was bound in a way that suggested I'd been bled. The sun shone on the yellow bed-curtains and, apart from feeling very weak, I could find no other injury. I turned towards Joseph, who had many marks on him but none that would disfigure him permanently, and who said to me as he hugged me: 'Well, Tiennet old friend, here we are as we used to be in the past, when we came back from catechism, and used to rest in the ditch after fighting with the Verneuil lads. It's just as it was in those days, you defended me and suffered for it, and just as it was in those days, I don't know how to thank you properly. But you've always guessed, or so it seems to me, that my heart wasn't as barren as my tongue.'

'That's what I've always thought, old friend,' I answered, hugging him back, 'and if I've helped you once again, I'm pleased that it should be so. Nevertheless, you shouldn't take too much of the blame. I had another idea in mind as well . . .' I stopped, for I didn't want to give into a mental weakness that had come very close to making me let slip the name of

Thérence; but a white hand gently drew the curtains aside, and I saw before me the very image of Thérence, who bent towards me, while Mariton, walking around to the other side of the bed, caressed and questioned her son.

Thérence lent over me, as I said, and in my astonishment, I thought I must be dreaming. I was sitting up to thank her for visiting me, and to tell her I was in no danger, when, as stupid as someone who is ill and blushing as much as a young girl, I received from her the finest kiss that has ever brought a dead man back to life.

'What are you doing, Thérence?' I asked, seizing her hands that I would have loved to eat with kisses. 'Do you want to drive me mad?'

'I want to thank you and love you my whole life long, for you kept your word to me; you restored my father and brother to me whole and hearty, this very morning, and I know all you did, everything that happened to you for the love you bore them and me. So I'm here, and I'm determined never to leave you again while you're ill.'

'Well, that's very good, Thérence,' I said with a sigh. 'It's more than I deserve. I hope the good Lord never lets me get better, because I don't know what would happen to me afterwards.'

'Afterwards?' said the woodcutter, who'd just come in with Huriel and Brulette. 'Come, daughter, what will we do with him afterwards?'

'Afterwards?' said Thérence, blushing deeply for the first time.

'Come, come! Thérence the sincere,' said the woodcutter, 'say what the girl who has never told a lie ought to say.'

'Well, father, *afterwards*, I shall never leave him either.'

'Off you go!' I exclaimed. 'Close the curtains, for I want to get dressed, I want to get up, and then leap and dance and sing, for I'm not ill. I'm in heaven . . .' But with those words I collapsed again and through a kind of haze I could just see Thérence holding me in her arms and caring for me.

That evening I felt better. Joseph was already on his feet, and I could have been too, but I wasn't allowed to get up. Instead, I was obliged to spend the evening in bed, while my friends chattered in the room, and my Thérence, sitting by the bed, listened to me gently and let me pour forth in words all the balm I felt in my heart.

The friar talked with Benoît, both of them washing down their conversation with several jugs of white wine that they swallowed as a kind of cooling health tea. Huriel chatted with Brulette in a corner; Joseph was talking with his mother and the woodcutter.

Then Huriel said to Brulette: 'I did indeed say to you, the first day I saw you, when I showed you your pledge hanging on my ear-ring: "It will always stay there, unless the ear is no longer there." Well, the ear was slit in the battle but it's still there, and the ring may be broken, but here it is with the pledge a little misshapen. The ear will heal and the ring can be reforged and everything will be back in place, the good Lord be thanked.'

Mariton was saying to the woodcutter: 'Well, what will come of this battle? They're capable of killing my poor boy for me, if he tries to play in this part of the country.'

'No,' replied the woodcutter. 'Everything has turned out for the best, for they received a good lesson, and there were enough witnesses from outside the brotherhood to stop them daring to attempt anything else against Joseph and against us. They're quite capable of doing evil when things happen within their own circle and when, through brute force or through friendship, they've exacted from a candidate the promise to keep silent. Joseph swore nothing of the sort, but he will keep quiet because he's generous, and so will Tiennet, just as my young woodcutters will on my advice and at my command. But your pipers know very well that if they were now to touch a hair of our heads, tongues would wag, and the matter would be brought before the courts of justice.'

The friar was saying to Benoît: 'I can't laugh over the adventure I had with you, because I had an explosion of rage for which I must confess and do penance. I willingly pardon them for the blows they tried to aim at me, but not for those they forced me to aim at them. Oh! The prior of my monastery was quite right to scold me from time to time, and tell me I must fight within myself not only the former man but also the former peasant, the one who loves wine and war. Wine,' went on the friar with a sigh and filling his glass to the very brim, 'is no longer a sin of mine, thank the Lord, but I realized last night that my blood still loves a quarrel, and that one blow drives me crazy.'

'But weren't you in a situation where self-defence was necessary and legal?' asked Benoît. 'Come then! You spoke as well as you ought to have, and you raised your fist only when you were forced to do so.'

'True, true. But my cunning devil of a prior will ask me questions. He'll worm my secrets out of me, and I'll be obliged to confess that instead of going into it regretfully and with reservations, I let myself be carried away by the delight of pounding away like a madman, forgetting the monk's robe I wear, and imagining I was back in the days when I used to guard the cattle with you in the Bourbonnais fields, and would go in search of quarrels to the other pastures all around, just for the worldly pleasure of showing I was the strongest and the stubbornest.'

Joseph said nothing, and no doubt he suffered from seeing the two happy couples he no longer had any right to sulk over, having received so much help from Huriel and from me.

The woodcutter, who felt a particular affection for him as a musician, encouraged his dreams of glory. So he made great efforts to watch the joy of others without jealousy, and we were obliged to recognize that there was in this cold, proud, young man a strength of mind and a desire to win that were truly rare.

He remained hidden, as did I, inside his mother's house until the marks of battle had faded; for my comrades had kept the affair secret, although through Léonard, who behaved very wisely and boldly, they'd threatened the pipers that they would tell everything to the local judges if they didn't keep the peace once and for all.

When they were all back on their feet again, for more than one had been injured, especially père Carnat, whose wrist I had apparently torn out of its joint, promises were exchanged and agreements reached. It was decided that Joseph would be given several parishes and he accepted them, even though he had no intention of exploiting them.

I was a little more ill than I'd thought, not so much because of my wound, which wasn't very serious, nor because of the blows my body had received, but from the overzealous bleeding the friar, with the best of intentions, had given me. Huriel and Brulette were charming enough to postpone their wedding merely in order to await my own; and, one month afterwards, the two weddings took place together. Indeed, there were even three, for Benoît wanted to make his wedding public and celebrate it at the same time as ours. This good man, happy to have an heir so well brought up by Brulette, tried to get her to accept a generous gift, but she obstinately refused it, throwing herself into Mariton's arms and saying: 'Does this mean you've forgotten this woman treated me as a mother treats her child for a good dozen years? Do you think I could take money, when I haven't yet paid off my debts to her?'

'Yes,' said Mariton, 'but bringing you up was nothing but honour for you and pleasure for me, whereas my little Charley caused you suffering and insults.'

'My dear,' said Brulette, 'that's the only thing that makes the two cases more or less equal. I'd have liked to bring happiness to your Joseph in exchange for your goodness to me. But that didn't depend on my poor heart, and so, to make up for the pain I caused him, it was my duty to expose myself to suffering for the love of your other child.'

'There's a girl for you!' exclaimed Benoît, wiping his big round eyes which weren't accustomed to weeping. 'Yes, yes, what a girl . . .' And he could say nothing more.

To avenge himself for Brulette's refusal, he wanted to take on the expenses of her wedding and those of mine into the bargain. And as he spared no expense and invited at least two hundred people, he was up for a fat sum, over which he showed not the slightest regret.

The friar had made us too firm a promise to break it, all the more so in that his prior had put him on water for a month as a penance, and on our wedding day the interdiction was at last lifted. He didn't abuse this privilege, and behaved in such a friendly way that we all formed the same kind of friendship with him that already existed among him, Huriel, and Benoît.

Joseph behaved most courageously up until the day of the wedding. That morning he was pale and seemed weighed down with thought; but when we came out of the church, he took the pipes from my father-in-law's hands and played a wedding march he himself had composed the night before for this very purpose. It was so fine a piece of music, and everyone praised it so highly, that his sadness disappeared, and he triumphantly played his finest dance tunes and lost himself in the delight of music throughout the entire feast.

Then he followed us to Le Chassin, and there the woodcutter, having sorted everything out for us, said: 'My children, now you're happy enough and rich enough for country folk. I'll leave you to deal with this copse, which is a good piece of business. Moreover, all I possess is yours. You'll spend more or less the whole of the year here, and during that time you can decide what you'll do in the future. You come from different lands and you have different tastes and habits. You should each try to find out what sort of life you want to give your wife to make her completely happy, so she won't have cause to regret a union that began so well. I'll return in a year's time. Do your best to see that by then I have two fine little grandchildren to caress. You can tell me then what you've decided. Take your time, something that seems good today may seem worse or better the following day.'

'And where are you going, father?' asked Thérence, putting her arms around him in fear.

'I'm going to play a little music along the ways with Joseph,' he answered, 'for he needs to do that, and as for me, I've been longing to do it for thirty years.'

Since neither tears nor pleas could retain him, we went with them half-way to Sainte Sévère. There, while we were tearfully embracing the woodcutter, Joseph said to us: 'Don't be sad. I know he's denying himself, for my sake, the sight of your happiness, since he loves me, too, with a father's heart, and he knows I'm the child who most needs his pity. But it may well be that I won't need him for long. It seems to me you'll see him again sooner than he thinks himself.'

At that he went down on his knees before my wife and Huriel's, and said: 'My dear sisters, I've offended both of you and I've been punished enough for my thoughts. Won't you forgive me so I can go my way more tranquilly?'

Both of them embraced him most affectionately, and then he came over to us, and, with surprising warmth, he said the best and gentlest things to us that he'd ever said in his life, and begged us, too, to forgive him for his faults and to keep his memory fresh.

We climbed a little eminence to watch them for as long as we could. The woodcutter was playing his pipes generously, and from time to time he would turn round to wave his bonnet and send us kisses with his hand.

Joseph didn't turn round. He walked in silence, head bowed, as if shattered or lost in thought. I couldn't help saying to Huriel that I'd found in his face at the moment he left something I'd often noticed in his youth, something that in our land is connected with a person over whom hangs an evil destiny.

Little by little our tears dried in happiness and hope. My dear and lovely wife put more effort into it than did the others, for since she'd never left her father, she felt she was losing half her soul, and I could easily see that despite her courage, her love for me, and the happiness she soon felt in the hope of becoming a mother, she still missed something for which she sighed in secret.

I therefore gave all my thought to arranging my life in such a way that we could be reunited with the woodcutter, even if it meant selling my land, leaving my family, and following my wife wherever she wanted to go.

It was the same with Brulette, who was resolved to consult only the wishes of her husband, especially when her grandfather, after a brief illness, passed away most tranquilly, just as he'd lived, surrounded by the care and love of his dear child.

'Tiennet,' she would often say to me, 'I can see that the Berry in us must be conquered by the Bourbonnais. Huriel loves this hard life and these frequent changes too deeply for our sleepy plains to please him. He makes me too happy for me to want to give him any hidden sorrow. I no longer have any family in our old home; all my friends, apart from you, have caused me such pain that now I live only in Huriel. Wherever he's happy, that's where I'll feel most contented.'

Winter found us still in the Le Chassin woods. We'd caused a great deal of damage to this lovely area, whose oak copse had been its finest adornment. The snow covered the corpses of those splendid trees, which we'd stripped and thrown down head first in the stream which held them in the ice, even colder and more dead than ever. Huriel and I were eating our supper near a fire of faggots that our wives had just lit to warm up our soup, and we were happily watching them, for each of them was in the process of fulfilling the promise we'd made the woodcutter to give him some heirs.

Suddenly they both exclaimed, and Thérence, forgetting that she was no longer as light as she'd been in the spring, flung herself almost right across the fire to embrace a man who'd been hidden from us by the thick smoke from the wet leaves. It was her good father, who soon had too few arms and mouths to reply to all our caresses. After our first joy had subsided, we asked him about Joseph and saw his face darken and his eyes fill with tears.

'He said you'd see me again sooner than I thought! He felt a kind of warning of his fate, and God, who softened his heart at that moment, no doubt warned him to reflect about himself.'

We didn't dare ask any more questions. The woodcutter sat down, opened his bag, and drew out the pieces of a broken bagpipe.

'This is all that's left of that poor child. He couldn't escape his star. I thought I'd softened his pride, but where music was concerned he became prouder and wilder every day. Perhaps it's my fault! I wanted to console him for his suffering in love by showing him the happiness he could find in his talent. At least he tasted the sweetness of praise, but the more he fed on it, the more violent his thirst for it became. We were far away from here. We'd gone as far as the mountains of the Morvan where there are many pipers, even more envious than those who live here, but not so much through financial interest as through vanity. Joseph wasn't careful enough, he offended them by things he said at a meal they'd most honestly offered him, where they'd initially had only the best of intentions.

'Unfortunately I hadn't gone with him, for I was slightly unwell and hadn't been suspicious of the good humour that reigned among them when they set out.

'He spent the night away from home as he often did; and as I'd noticed that he was sometimes a little envious of the applause people gave my old songs, I didn't want to annoy him. In the morning I set out, although I was still shaking a bit with fever, and learnt in the town that a set of broken bagpipes had been found beside a ditch. I ran to see it and recognized it immediately. I went to the place where it had been found and broke the ice on the ditch. There I discovered his ill-starred corpse completely frozen. There were no marks of violence on him, and the other pipers swore they'd left him a league away from there, without any quarrelling and drunkenness. It was in vain that I sought his murderers. It's a wild area, where men of justice fear the peasant, and where the peasant fears only the devil. I had to accept their sad and silly remarks, and leave them. In that land they firmly believe something that's more or less believed here too, which is that you can become a musician only by selling your soul to the devil, and that one day or another, Satan tears the pipes from the piper's hands and breaks them on his back, which drives him mad, makes him lose his way, and brings him to destroy himself. That's how they explain the revenge the pipers extract from each other, and the pipers don't contradict it, for it's their way of making themselves feared and of escaping the consequences. That's why they're held in such low esteem and such great fear, that I could get no one to listen to my complaints. And that's why, if I'd remained there, I myself would have been accused of calling on the devil to free myself of my companion.'

'Alas!' exclaimed Brulette in tears. 'Poor Joseph, my poor friend. What ever will we say to his mother?'

'We shall tell her,' said the woodcutter sorrowfully, 'not to let Charley fall in love with music. She's too harsh a mistress for people such as us. Our heads aren't hard enough for us not to grow giddy on the heights to which she carries us!'

'Oh father!' cried Thérence. 'If only you could give it up. Goodness knows what misfortune it will lead you into as well!'

'Don't worry, my love,' the woodcutter replied. 'Here I am back again. I want to live with my family, bring up my grandchildren, whom I already dream of bouncing on my knees. Where are we going to live, dear children?'

'Wherever you want!' exclaimed Thérence.

'Wherever our husbands want!' exclaimed Brulette.

'Wherever my wife wants!' I exclaimed too.

'Wherever all of you want to live!' exclaimed Huriel in his turn.

'Well,' said the woodcutter, 'as I know your moods and your means, and as I'm bringing you back a little money, I calculated along the road that it would be very easy to make everyone happy. When you want the peach to ripen, you mustn't tear out the stone. The stone is Tiennet's land. We'll extend it and on it we'll build a good house for all of us. I'll be happy to grow some wheat, to stop cutting down the fine shade trees the good Lord has given us, and to compose my old-fashioned little songs, each evening, in the doorway, surrounded by my family, without going off to drink wine and without making anyone jealous. Huriel loves to rove the countryside and now his wife is just like him. They'll undertake tasks like the cutting of this copse, where I see you've worked very well, and they'll spend the summer in the woods. If their family gives them problems when they're very young, Thérence is strong enough and courageous enough to control a double brood, and we'll all gather together again at the end of each autumn with redoubled pleasure, until the day when my son, having long since closed my eyes, will feel the need for rest the year through, just as I feel it now.'

Everything my father-in-law said came to pass just as he had counselled and foreseen. The Lord blessed our obedience, and, as life is a mixture of happiness and sorrow, poor Mariton often came to weep with us, and the good friar often came to laugh.

EXPLANATORY NOTES

3 *Lambert*: Eugène Lambert, born in Paris on 25 September 1825, had been a friend of George Sand's son Maurice at Delacroix's studio. He came to visit Nohant in June 1844 and stayed twelve years. A lively and entertaining young man, he made a rich marriage and became a popular painter, well known for his paintings of cats and dogs. His son Georges was George Sand's godson. He died in Paris on 17 May 1900.

7 *Saint Chartier*: Saint Chartier is some 2 or 3 kilometres north of Nohant, George Sand's estate and the village that was home to Tiennet, Joey, and Brulette.

9 *Unable to read, even less able to write*: traditionally, in France, children were taught first to read, then to write, and finally to do arithmetic. Many country children never progressed beyond the first stage.

16 *the Crowned Ox in Saint Chartier, a tavern owned by M. Benoît*: Benoît, and the inn called the Crowned Ox really did exist at Saint Chartier. In a letter to Pierre Bocage in April 1851, George Sand tells her correspondent how Benoît came to ask her to put him in a work of hers, 'so that in 3 or 4 thousand years from now people will talk of me' (*Correspondance*, x. 183).

My mother: a slip on George Sand's part, as a few pages later she asserts that Tiennet's father had long been a widower.

19 *the area around Boussac, or between Châteauroux and Vatan*: Boussac is an ancient fortified city on the borders of Berry and La Marche, some 60 kilometres south of Nohant. Châteauroux, now the capital of lower Berry, is some 25 kilometres from Nohant, while Vatan, in Cher, is about 40 kilometres north of Nohant.

30 *bourrée*: peasant dance. See introduction, p. xviii.

33 *Verneuil*: a small town on the Igneraie river about 3½ kilometres from Saint Chartier.

Englishmen's track: a former military road which saw the invasion and retreat of the English army, driven by du Guesclin from its stronghold at Sainte Sévère in the fourteenth century.

34 *the oak*: an ancient oak, very well known in George Sand's area.

34 *Saint Aoust*: Saint Août, as the town is now known, is 7 kilometres north of Saint Chartier.

37 *Igneraie ford*: the river Igneraie runs through Saint Chartier, joining the Indre a few kilometres further west.

38 *Lourouer*: about 4 kilometres east of Nohant.

  the Rake Elm: mentioned by George Sand in her study of local superstitions, *Les Visions de la nuit dans les campagnes*. According to her, the tree and its associated myths go back to the time of Charles VII in the fifteenth century. A man some 20 feet tall, carrying a rake, was supposed to drive away all those who attempted to come within the elm tree's shade.

39 *the Spring of Springs*: discussed in George Sand's *Rustic Legends*; it has associations with souls in torment, and is situated about 2 kilometres from Saint Chartier.

40 *Berthenoux*: the town of Berthenoux, with its vast twelfth-century church, is about 8 kilometres north-east of Nohant.

51 *Midsummer's Day*: Midsummer's Day, or Saint John's Day, is widely celebrated in France with dancing and bonfires.

59 *the Bourbonnais woods through those of Meillant and L'Epinasse to reach the woods of Cheurre*: the woods of Meillant are due south of Bourges, while the forest of L'Epinasse is about 15 kilometres to the west, and the forest of Cheurre, or Choeurs, is south of Issoudun and about 30 kilometres north-east of Nohant.

  Huriel: Huriel is named for a town just west of Montluçon, in Bourbonnais.

  Ardentes: Ardentes is 11 kilometres south of Châteauroux, and about 13 kilometres from Nohant.

84 *Marche*: Marche was a province of France on the borders of Berry, a region now known as Cher.

86 *hurdy-gurdy*: like bagpipes, still a traditional and popular instrument in this area.

  Chambérat: Chambérat is a few kilometres south-east of Mesples, where Joseph was working, about 15 kilometres north-west of Montluçon, and some 50 kilometres from Nohant.

92 *Sioule river*: this stream flows to the south of the village called Huriel.

92 *Dôme mountains*: these mountains are a chain of extinct volcanoes in the Auvergne; their high point is the Puy de Dôme.

forest of Alleu: this is the wood around Mesples; its former name was the forest of the 'Loeuf', or 'fief'.

96 *Saint Amand*: the nearest town to the forest of Meillant, approximately midway between Bourges and Montluçon, and some 50 kilometres north-east of Nohant.

97 *the Maritet woods*: about a kilometre north-west of Saint Saturnin and about 22 kilometres south-east of Nohant.

101 *Joyeuse*: this stream flows into the Arnon near Sidiailles. Several tributaries feed into it, and it would therefore be subject to rapid flooding after storms coming in from the west.

Sidiailles: about 6 kilometres east of Saint Saturnin.

113 *Mesples*: some 20 kilometres north-west of Montluçon between the Arnon and the Dionne rivers. Chambérat is about 5 kilometres south-east.

126 *Chambérat*: about 5 kilometres south-east of Mesples.

148 *Malzac*: word used for a kind of snake.

166 *I was so gentle and patient that I didn't have the courage of a hare*: hares in French tradition are considered cowardly.

168 *Forez mountains*: a complex chain of granitic mountains beginning some 50 kilometres south of Mesples.

172 *Sainte Sévère*: on the Indre river, some 25 kilometres north-west of Mesples and 25 kilometres south-east of Nohant.

173 *Saint Palais in Bourbonnais, and Préveranges . . . Saint Prejet and Pérassay*: all these towns are on the route from Mesples to Sainte Sévère. The name Saint Prejet has been changed to Saint Priest la Marche. See map.

206 *Le Chassin*: about 9 kilometres west of Nohant.

217 *Montaigu*: this forest is about 25 kilometres south of Montluçon.

248 *Ausances*: now spelt Auzances, some 40 kilometres south-west of Montluçon. A small town, it is known for its beautiful Romanesque church.

Sarzay: about 6 kilometres north-west of La Châtre and 6 kilometres south-west of Nohant.

285 *bread arch*: bread oven.

286 *La Breuille*: a hamlet attached to Saint Chartier.

295 *Verneuil*: about 3 kilometres east of Saint Chartier.

296 *Mers*: 7 kilometres west of Saint Chartier.

307 *Pouligny*: there are two villages with this name in the area near Sainte Sévère: Pouligny-Notre-Dame and Pouligny-Saint-Martin.

THE WORLD'S CLASSICS

A Select List

HANS ANDERSEN: Fairy Tales
Translated by L. W. Kingsland
Introduction by Naomi Lewis
Illustrated by Vilhelm Pedersen and Lorenz Frølich

ARTHUR J. ARBERRY (Transl.): The Koran

LUDOVICO ARIOSTO: Orlando Furioso
Translated by Guido Waldman

ARISTOTLE: The Nicomachean Ethics
Translated by David Ross

JANE AUSTEN: Emma
Edited by James Kinsley and David Lodge

Mansfield Park
Edited by James Kinsley and John Lucas

Persuasion
Edited by John Davie

HONORÉ DE BALZAC: Père Goriot
Translated and Edited by A. J. Krailsheimer

CHARLES BAUDELAIRE: The Flowers of Evil
Translated by James McGowan
Introduction by Jonathan Culler

WILLIAM BECKFORD: Vathek
Edited by Roger Lonsdale

R. D. BLACKMORE: Lorna Doone
Edited by Sally Shuttleworth

KEITH BOSLEY (Transl.): The Kalevala

JAMES BOSWELL: Life of Johnson
The Hill/Powell edition, revised by David Fleeman
Introduction by Pat Rogers

MARY ELIZABETH BRADDON: Lady Audley's Secret
Edited by David Skilton

GIORGIO VASARI: The Lives of the Artists
Translated and Edited by Julia Conaway Bondanella and Peter Bondanella

JULES VERNE: Journey to the Centre of the Earth
Translated and Edited by William Butcher

IZAAK WALTON and CHARLES COTTON:
The Compleat Angler
Edited by John Buxton
Introduction by John Buchan

OSCAR WILDE: Complete Shorter Fiction
Edited by Isobel Murray

A complete list of Oxford Paperbacks, including The World's Classics, OPUS, Past Masters, Oxford Authors, Oxford Shakespeare, and Oxford Paperback Reference, is available in the UK from the Arts and Reference Publicity Department (BH), Oxford University Press, Walton Street, Oxford OX2 6DP.

In the USA, complete lists are available from the Paperbacks Marketing Manager, Oxford University Press, 200 Madison Avenue, New York, NY 10016.

Oxford Paperbacks are available from all good bookshops. In case of difficulty, customers in the UK can order direct from Oxford University Press Bookshop, Freepost, 116 High Street, Oxford, OX1 4BR, enclosing full payment. Please add 10 per cent of published price for postage and packing.